BIG FAT Little Lit

Harry Bliss

Ian Falconer

Patrick McDonnell

Joost Swarte

Barbara McClintock

Walt Kelly

Neil Gaiman

Kim Deitch

Art Spiegelman

Kaz

David Sedaris

Richard McGuire

Martin Handford

Charles Burns

Lorenzo Mattotti

Jules Feiffer

Claude Ponti

Gahan Wilson

Lewis Trondheim

David Macaulay

J. Otto Seibold

Daniel Clowes

Vivian Walsh

Richard Sala

Crockett Johnson

William Joyce

David Mazzucchelli

Tony Millionaire

Marc Rosenthal

Lemony Snicket

Basil Wolverton

François Roca

Maurice Sendak

edited by Art Spiegelman & Françoise Mouly

BIG FAT Little Lit

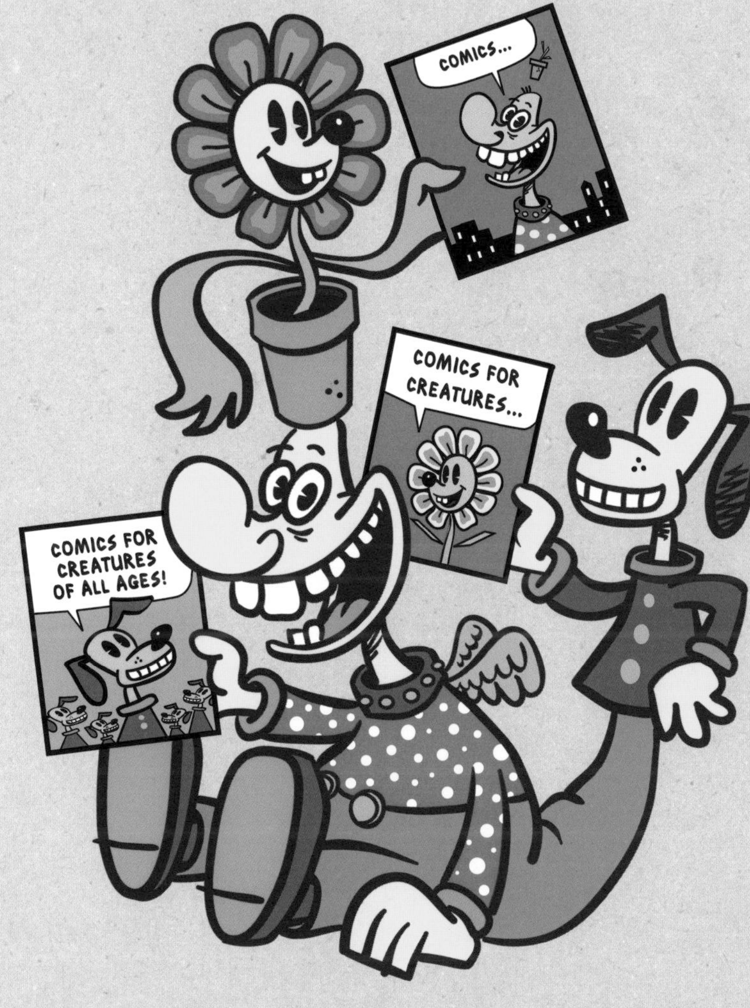

COMICS...
COMICS FOR CREATURES...
COMICS FOR CREATURES OF ALL AGES!

edited by Art Spiegelman & Françoise Mouly

PUFFIN BOOKS

Comics...

COMICS FOR
CREATURES
OF ALL AGES!

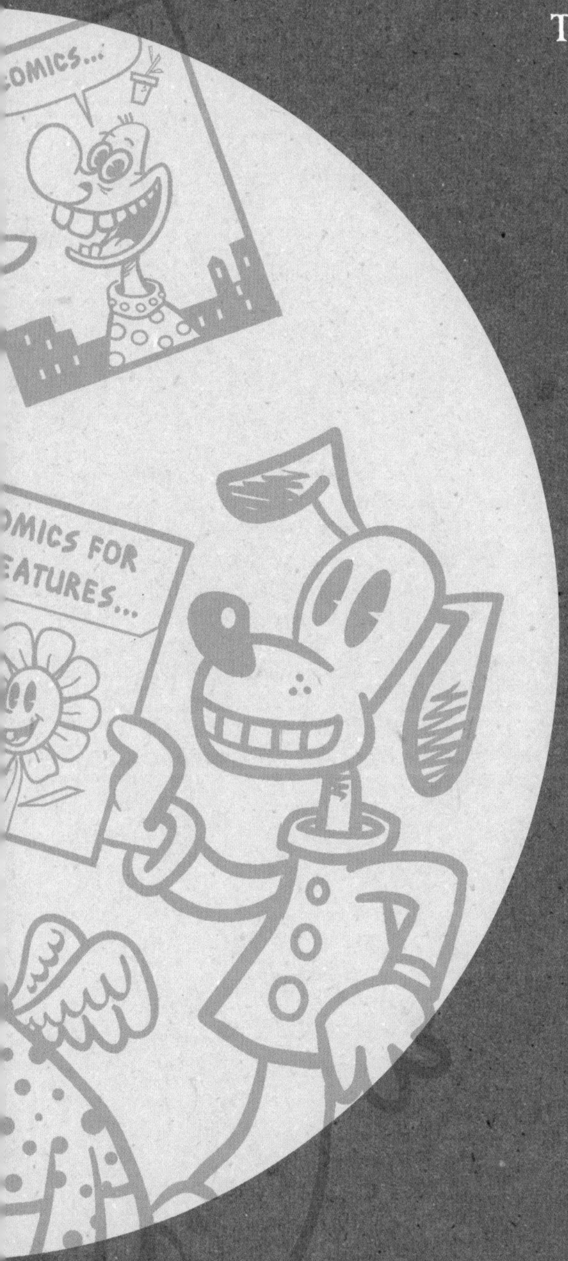

...and games!

designed by FRANÇOISE MOULY

dedicated to DASHIELL and NADJA
who are the inspiration

with special thanks to JOANNA COTLER
whose faith in Little Lit made it possible

editorial associates:
ELIZABETH GERY
LISA KIM

associate designer:
CHARLES ORR

production:
BARBARA KOPELOFF
FRANÇOISE MOULY

with grateful thanks to the PUFFIN team
for their hard work and enduring support:
EILEEN KREIT
JENNIFER BONNELL
GERARD MANCINI
JEANINE HENDERSON

PUFFIN BOOKS
Published by the Penguin Group.
Penguin Young Readers Group, 345 Hudson Street, New York, New York 10014, U.S.A.
Penguin Group (Canada), 90 Eglinton Avenue East, Suite 700, Toronto, Ontario, Canada M4P 2Y3 (a division of Pearson Penguin Canada Inc.)
Registered Offices: Penguin Books Ltd, 80 Strand, London WC2R 0RL, England
First published in the United States of America by PUFFIN BOOKS, a division of Penguin Young Readers Group, 2006

 These stories were selected from Little Lit: Folklore & Fairy Tale Funnies, Little Lit: Strange Stories for Strange Kids, and Little Lit: "It Was a Dark and Silly Night...," published by HarperCollins Children's Books, a division of HarperCollins Publishers Inc. Library of Congress Cataloging-in-Publication Data available on demand.
PUFFIN BOOKS ISBN 0-14-240706-2.
Printed in China. 10 9 8 7 6 5 4 3 2 1

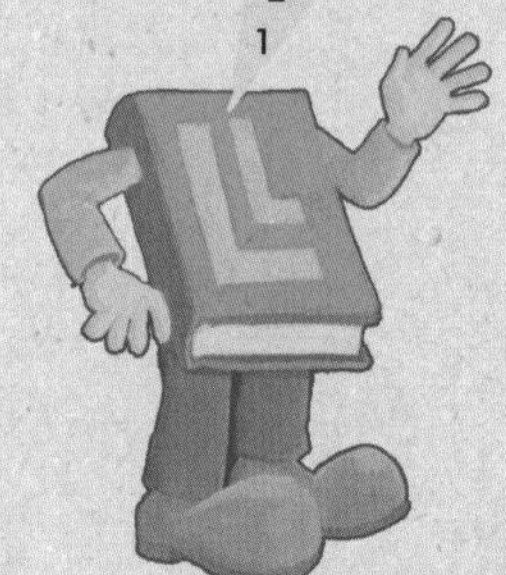

visit us at www.little-lit.com

THE HUNGRY HORSE

ONE DAY IN THE VILLAGE MARKETPLACE...

POTS FOR SALE.

RUGS FOR SALE.

HORSE FOR SALE.

WRITTEN AND DRAWN BY **Kaz**

THAT HORSE LOOKS PRETTY SKINNY, WITCH.

DON'T BE FOOLED BY HIS LOOKS, FARMER.

HE'S AN ENCHANTED HORSE.

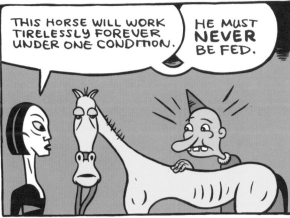

THIS HORSE WILL WORK TIRELESSLY FOREVER UNDER ONE CONDITION.

HE MUST **NEVER** BE FED.

NOT **ONCE**, NOT **EVER**. NOT EVEN A SCRAP!

I'LL SELL HIM FOR SIX GOLD COINS.

SORRY. I'M TOO POOR TO BUY HIM.

BUT THAT NIGHT, AS THE WITCH SLEPT, THE POOR FARMER STOLE THE HORSE.

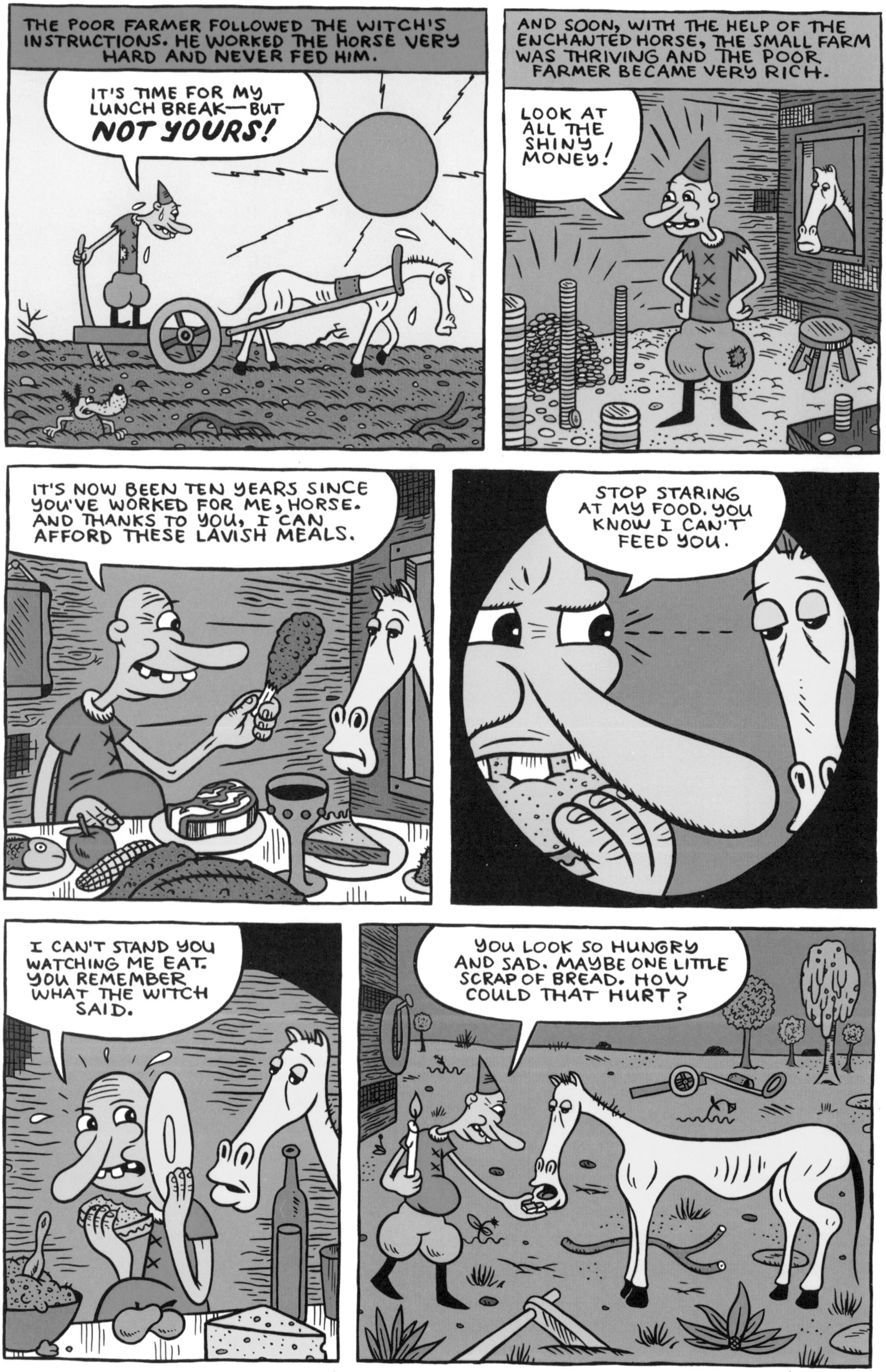
THE POOR FARMER FOLLOWED THE WITCH'S INSTRUCTIONS. HE WORKED THE HORSE VERY HARD AND NEVER FED HIM.
IT'S TIME FOR MY LUNCH BREAK—BUT NOT YOURS!
AND SOON, WITH THE HELP OF THE ENCHANTED HORSE, THE SMALL FARM WAS THRIVING AND THE POOR FARMER BECAME VERY RICH.
LOOK AT ALL THE SHINY MONEY!
IT'S NOW BEEN TEN YEARS SINCE YOU'VE WORKED FOR ME, HORSE. AND THANKS TO YOU, I CAN AFFORD THESE LAVISH MEALS.
STOP STARING AT MY FOOD. YOU KNOW I CAN'T FEED YOU.
I CAN'T STAND YOU WATCHING ME EAT. YOU REMEMBER WHAT THE WITCH SAID.
YOU LOOK SO HUNGRY AND SAD. MAYBE ONE LITTLE SCRAP OF BREAD. HOW COULD THAT HURT?

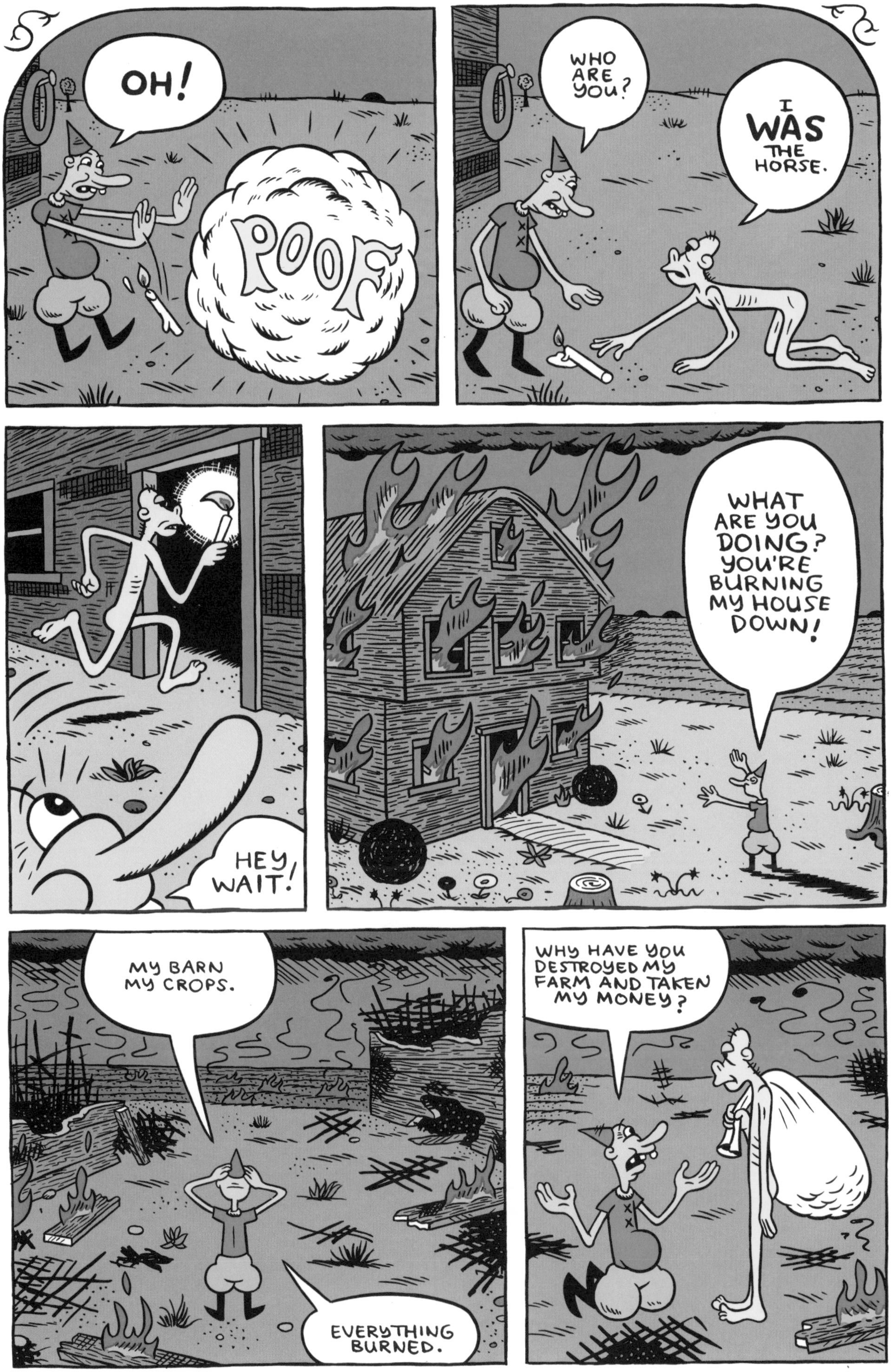
OH!
POOF
WHO ARE YOU?
I WAS THE HORSE.
HEY, WAIT!
WHAT ARE YOU DOING? YOU'RE BURNING MY HOUSE DOWN!
MY BARN MY CROPS.
EVERYTHING BURNED.
WHY HAVE YOU DESTROYED MY FARM AND TAKEN MY MONEY?

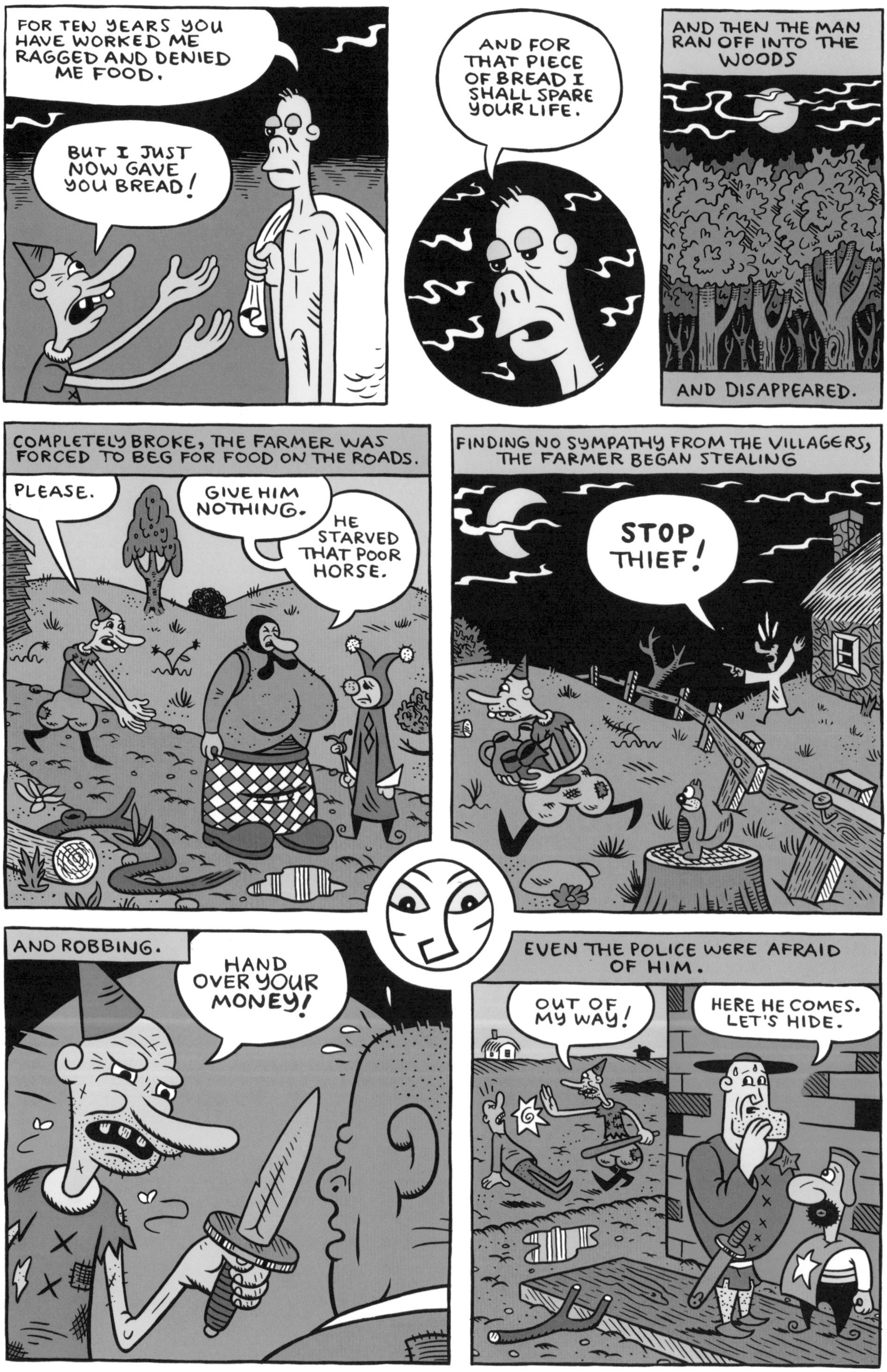
FOR TEN YEARS YOU HAVE WORKED ME RAGGED AND DENIED ME FOOD.
BUT I JUST NOW GAVE YOU BREAD!
AND FOR THAT PIECE OF BREAD I SHALL SPARE YOUR LIFE.
AND THEN THE MAN RAN OFF INTO THE WOODS
AND DISAPPEARED.
COMPLETELY BROKE, THE FARMER WAS FORCED TO BEG FOR FOOD ON THE ROADS.
PLEASE.
GIVE HIM NOTHING.
HE STARVED THAT POOR HORSE.
FINDING NO SYMPATHY FROM THE VILLAGERS, THE FARMER BEGAN STEALING
STOP, THIEF!
AND ROBBING.
HAND OVER YOUR MONEY!
EVEN THE POLICE WERE AFRAID OF HIM.
OUT OF MY WAY!
HERE HE COMES. LET'S HIDE.

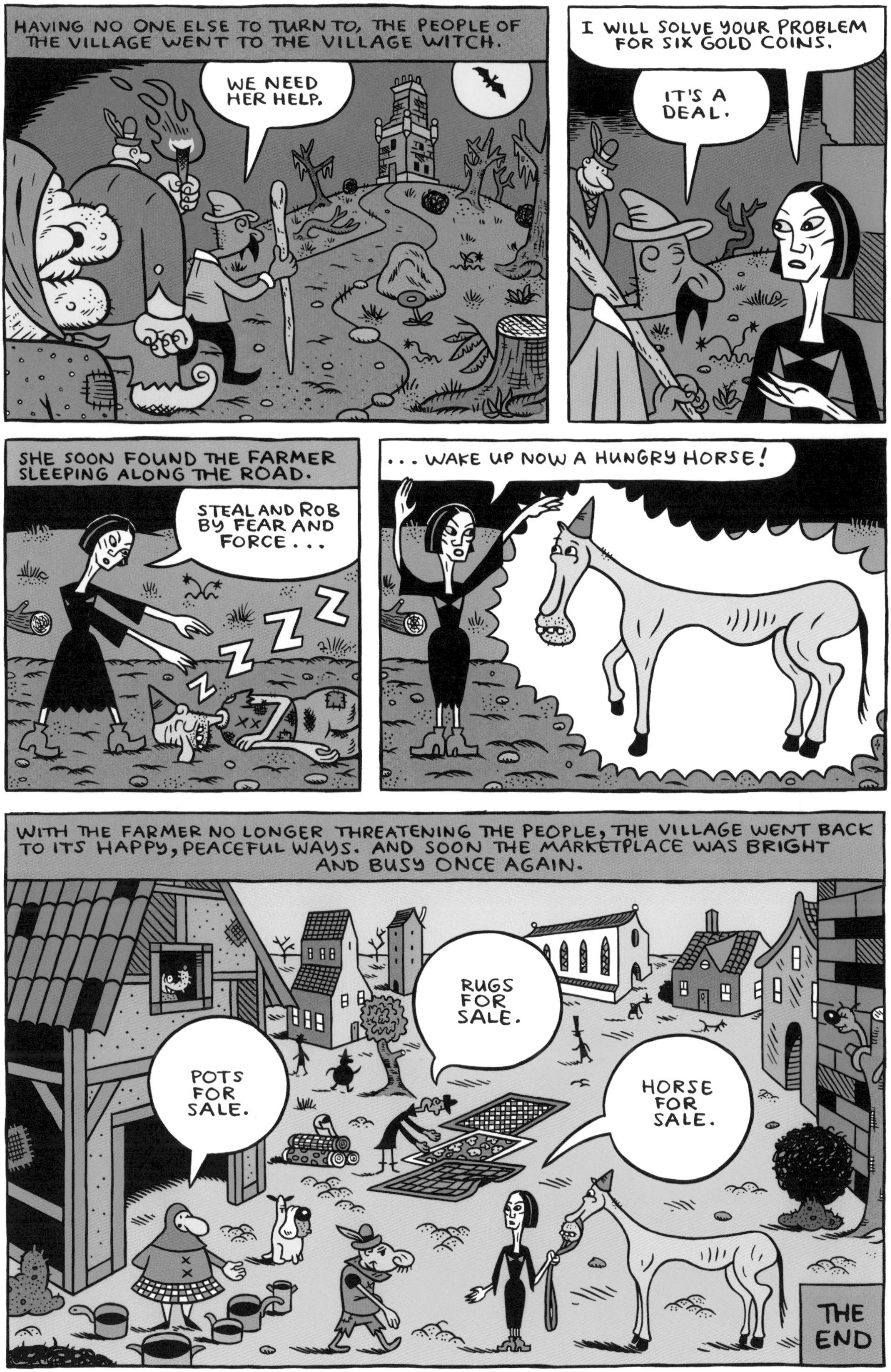
HAVING NO ONE ELSE TO TURN TO, THE PEOPLE OF THE VILLAGE WENT TO THE VILLAGE WITCH.
WE NEED HER HELP.
I WILL SOLVE YOUR PROBLEM FOR SIX GOLD COINS.
IT'S A DEAL.
SHE SOON FOUND THE FARMER SLEEPING ALONG THE ROAD.
STEAL AND ROB BY FEAR AND FORCE...
ZZZZ
...WAKE UP NOW A HUNGRY HORSE!
WITH THE FARMER NO LONGER THREATENING THE PEOPLE, THE VILLAGE WENT BACK TO ITS HAPPY, PEACEFUL WAYS. AND SOON THE MARKETPLACE WAS BRIGHT AND BUSY ONCE AGAIN.
RUGS FOR SALE.
POTS FOR SALE.
HORSE FOR SALE.
THE END

ian falconer & david sedaris

PRETTY UGLY

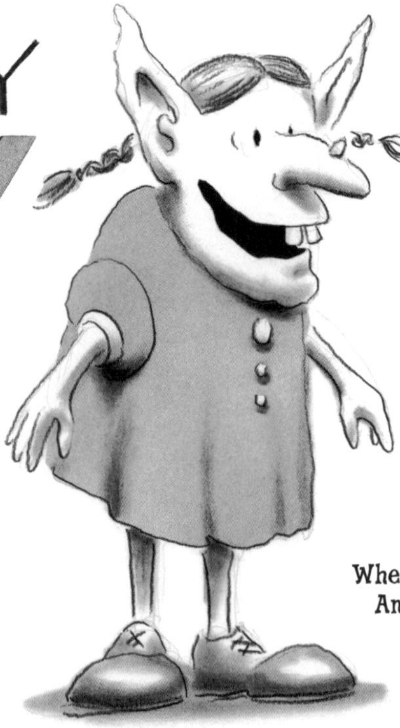

When she was good,
Anna Van Ogre...

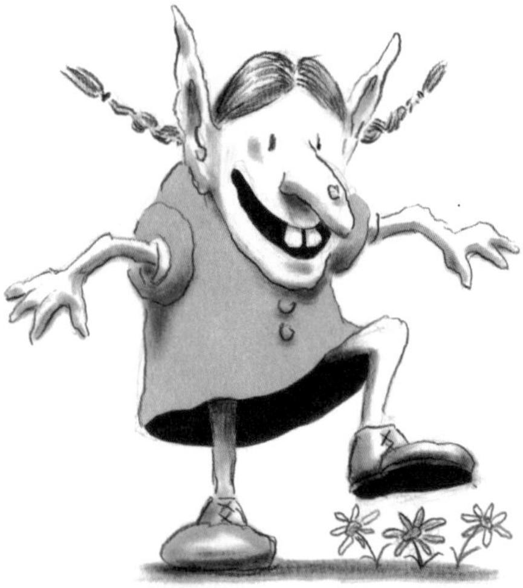

stomped on the flowers...

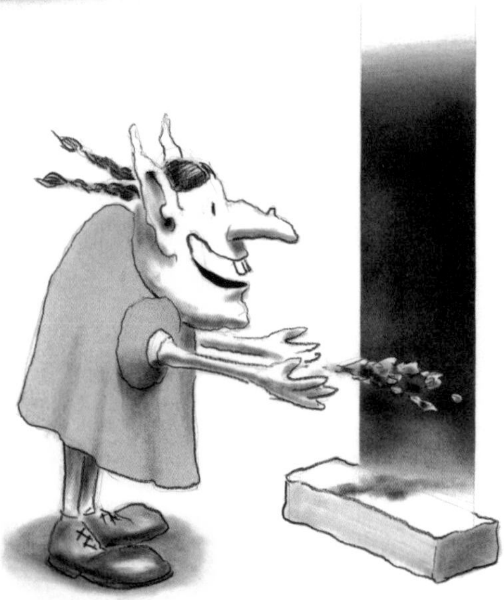

threw dirt into the house...

and talked with her mouth full.

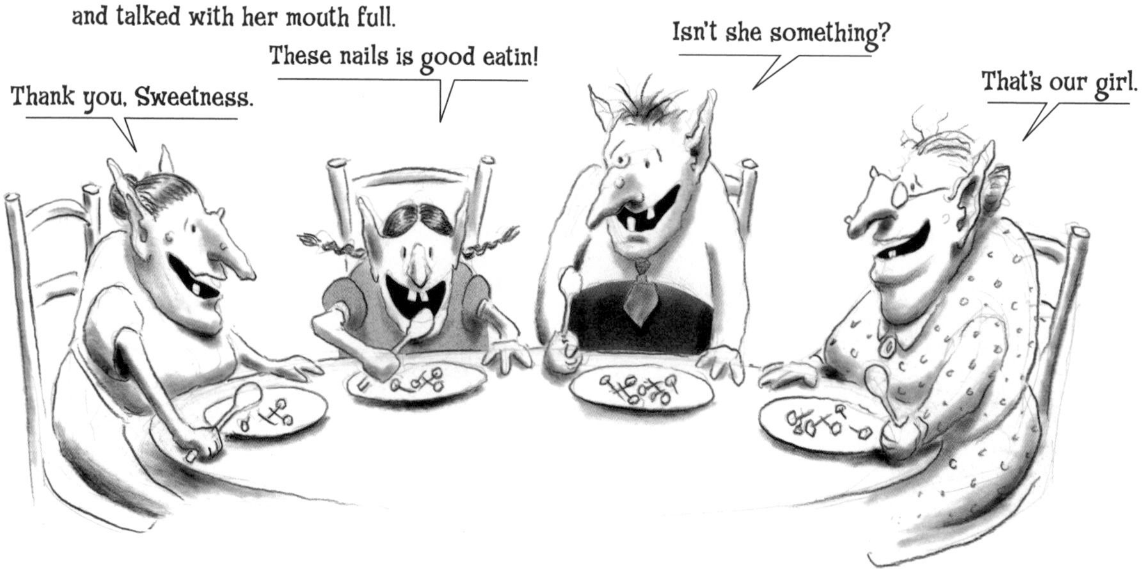
Thank you, Sweetness.
These nails is good eatin!
Isn't she something?
That's our girl.

And when she was bad, Anna made faces, terrible faces...

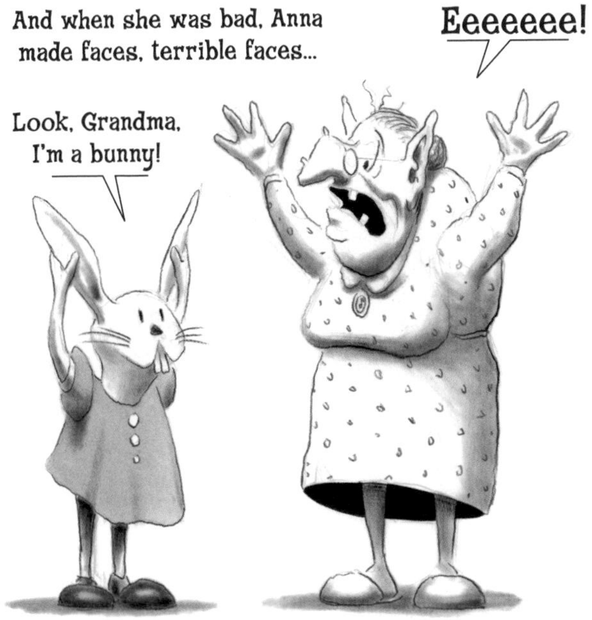
Eeeeeee!
Look, Grandma, I'm a bunny!

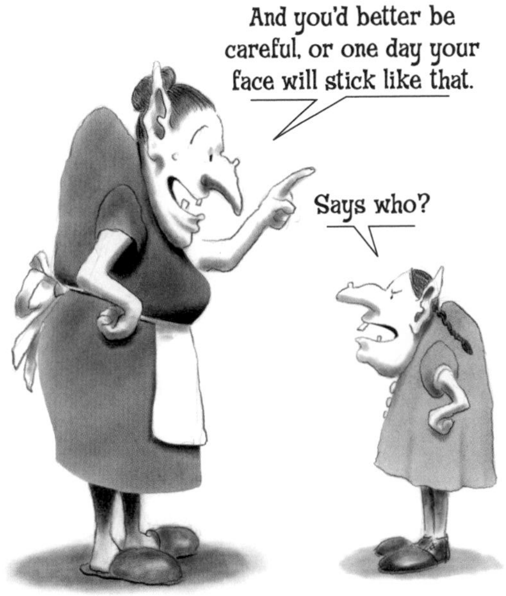
And you'd better be careful, or one day your face will stick like that.
Says who?

Then one day she made the scariest face of all... and it stuck!

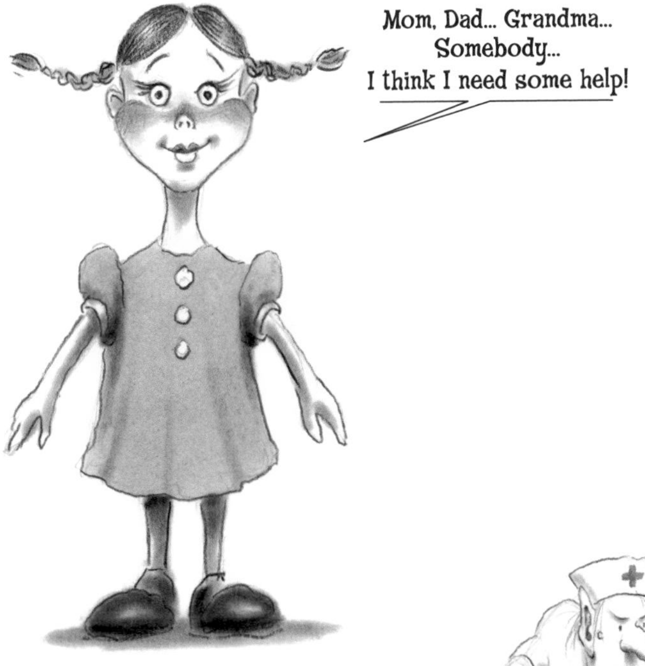
Mom, Dad... Grandma... Somebody... I think I need some help!

Her family tried everything... Then they sent her to a doctor who tried everything else...

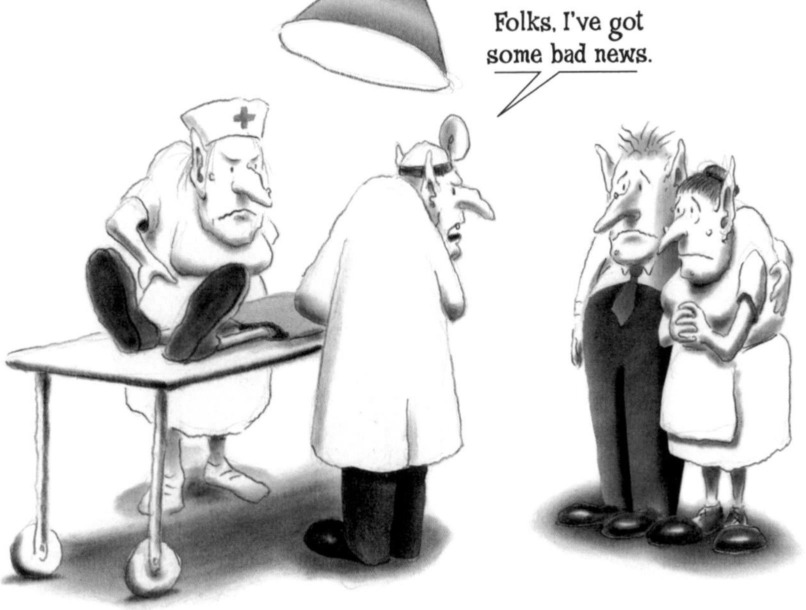
Folks, I've got some bad news.

Her family was good about it...

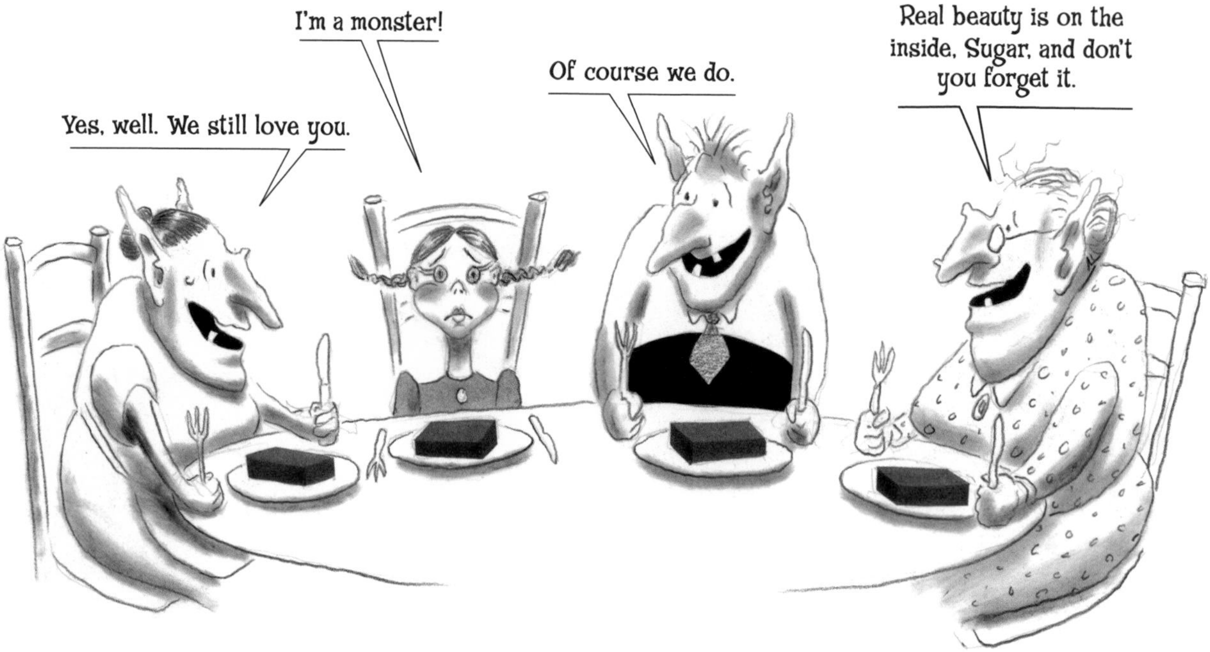
Yes, well. We still love you.
I'm a monster!
Of course we do.
Real beauty is on the inside, Sugar, and don't you forget it.

But outside of the house her life was unbearable...

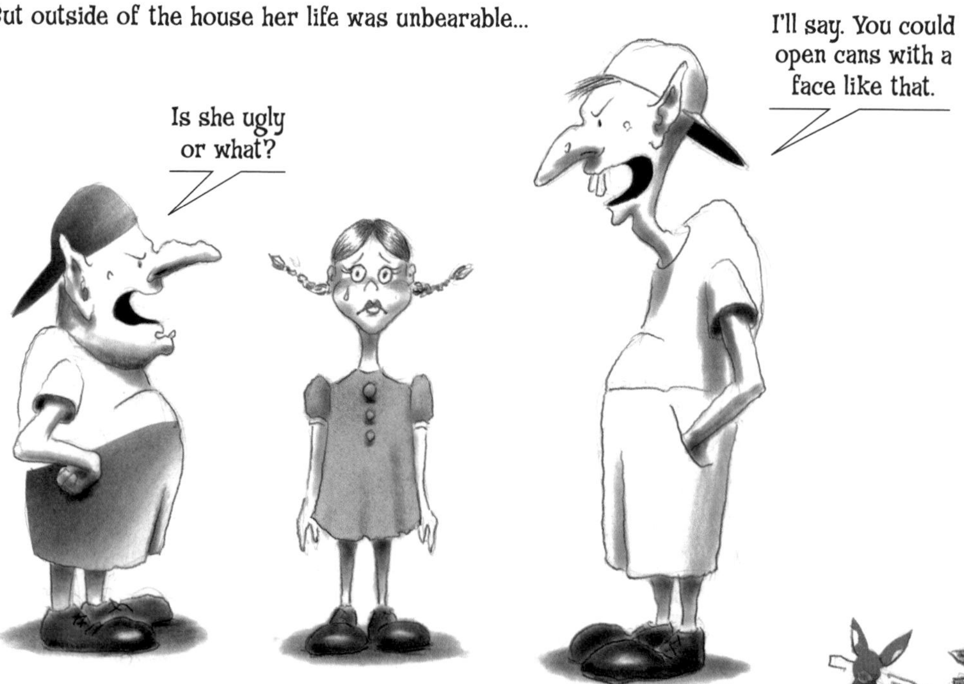
Is she ugly or what?
I'll say. You could open cans with a face like that.

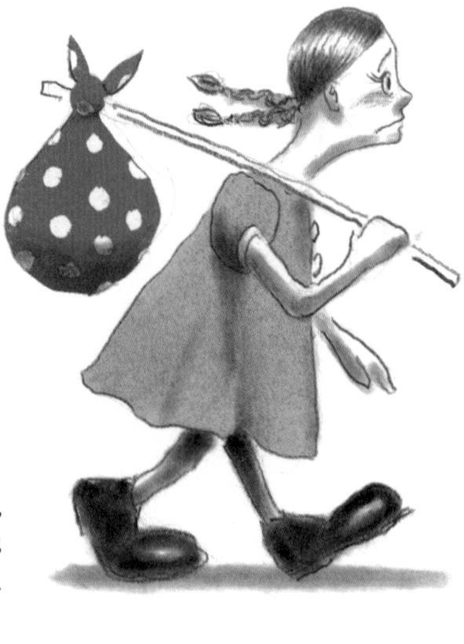

When she could stand it no longer,
Anna packed a few thumbtack sandwiches
and locked herself in the woodshed.

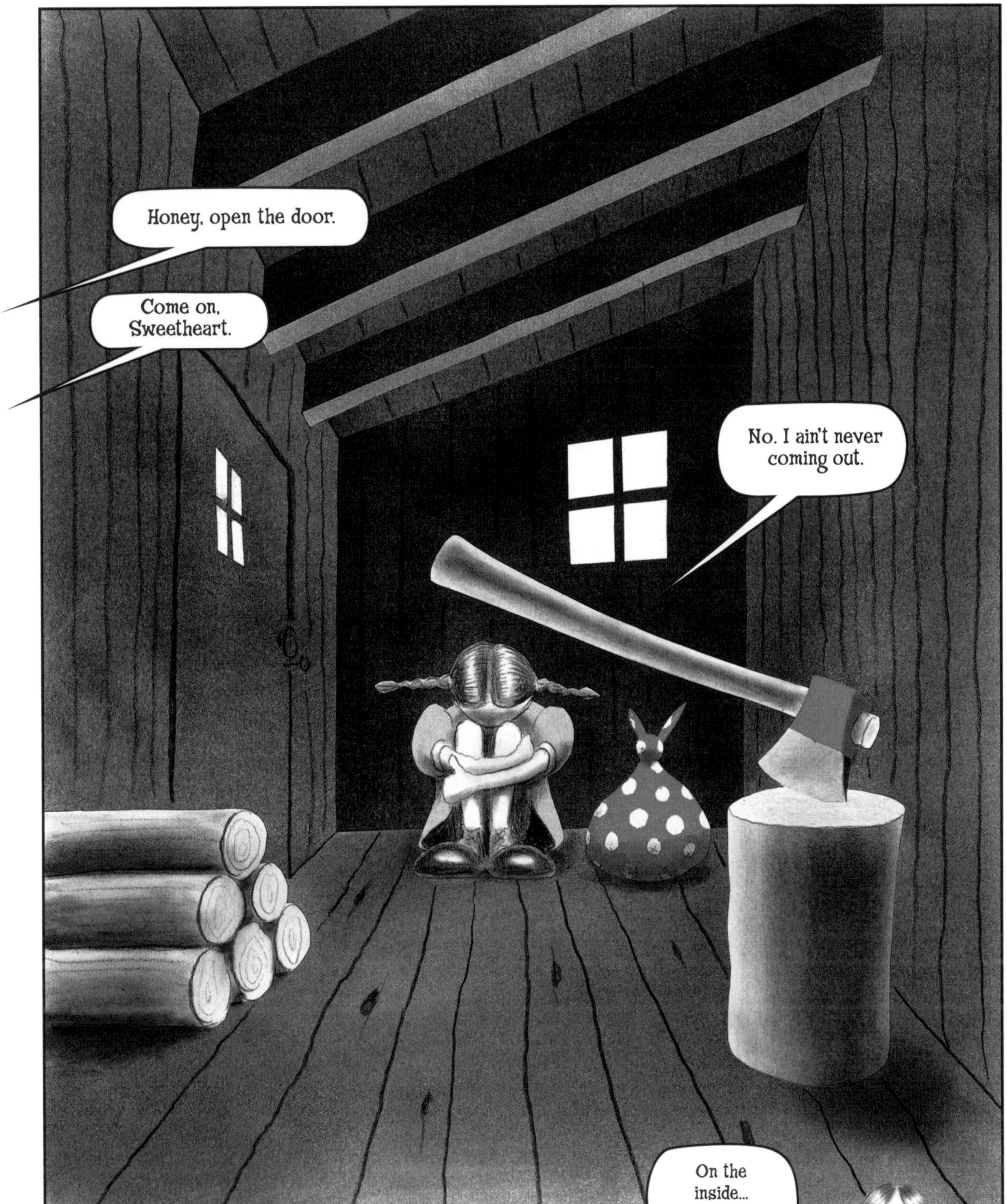
Honey, open the door.
Come on, Sweetheart.
No. I ain't never coming out.

She stayed for three days and three nights, thinking all the while of what her grandmother had said.

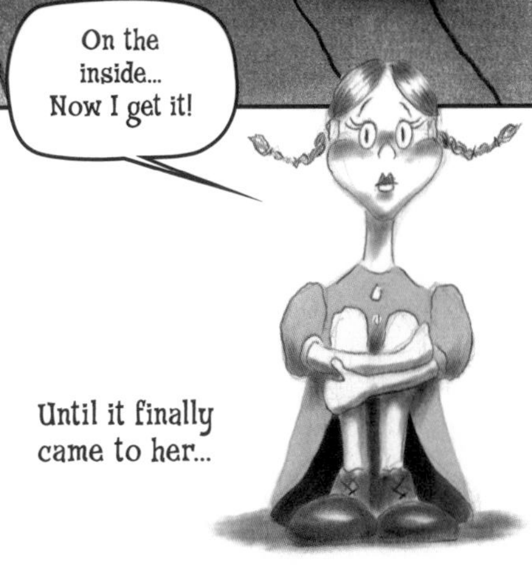
On the inside... Now I get it!

Until it finally came to her...

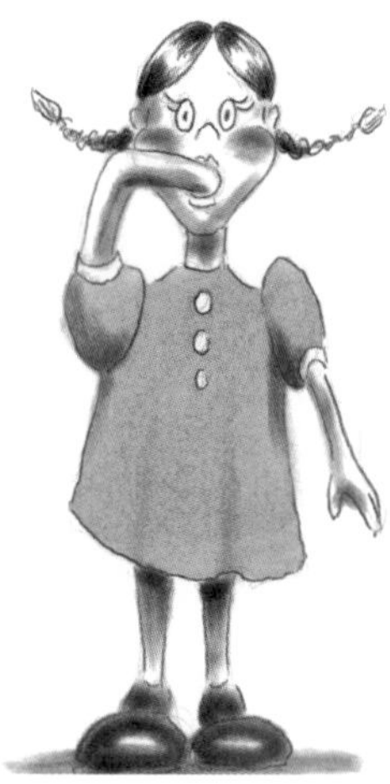

She stuck her hand down her throat...

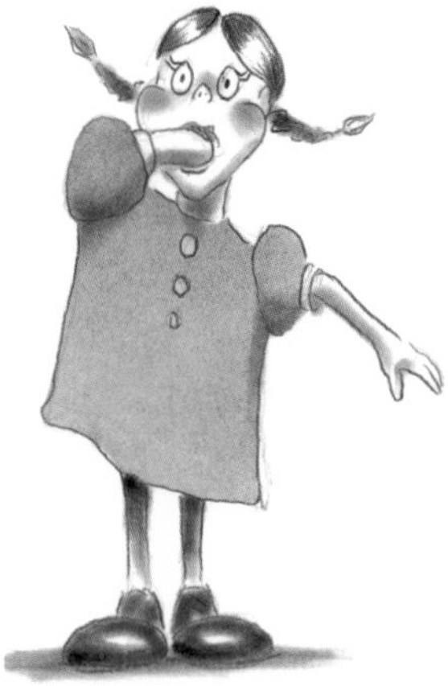

as far as it could go...

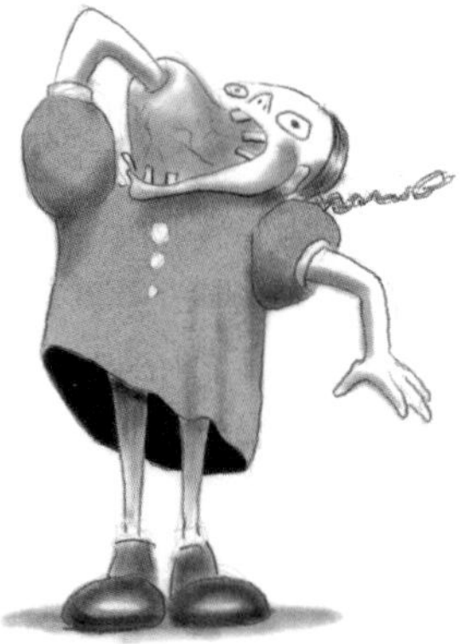

and she yanked...

until she'd turned herself inside out... and was beautiful again.

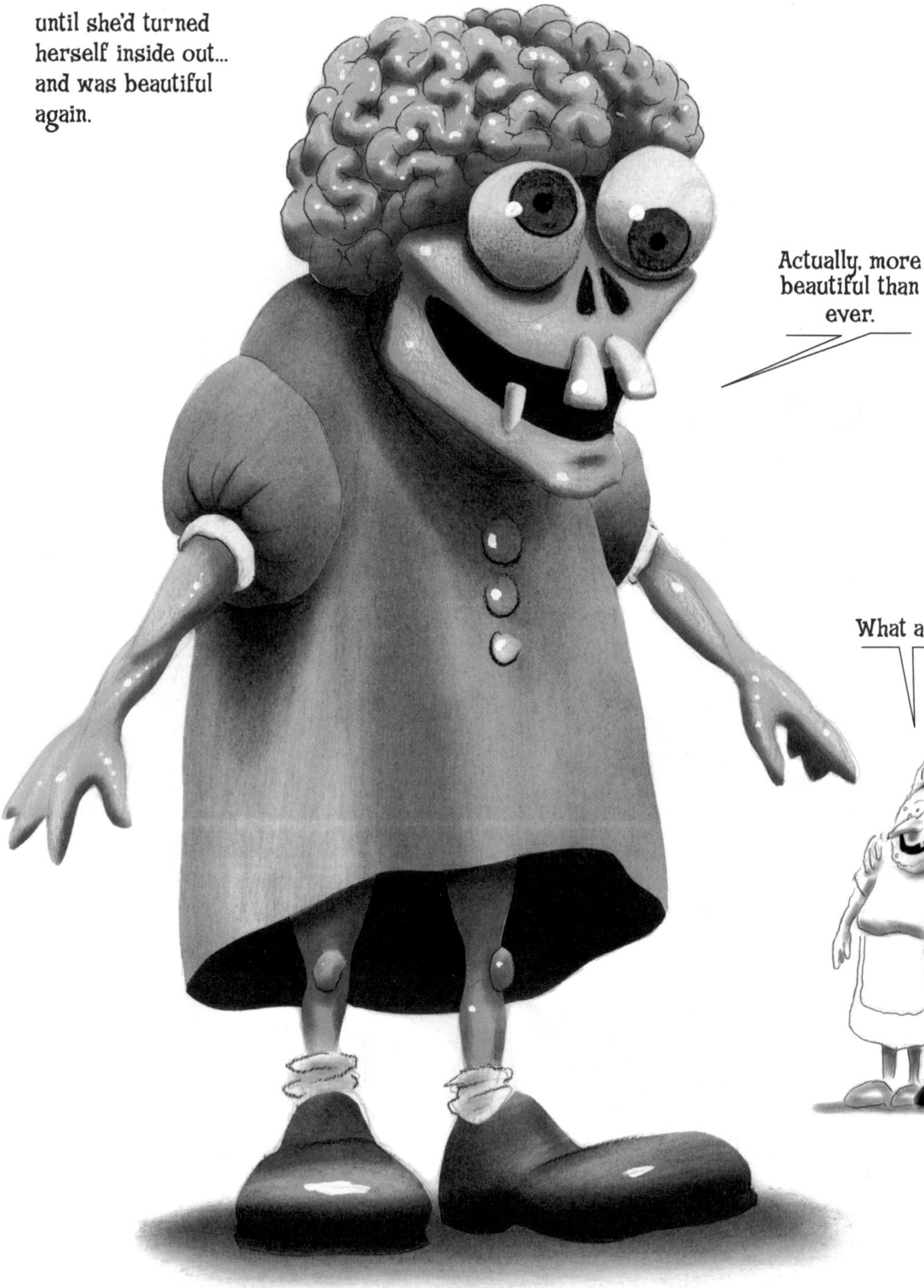
Actually, more beautiful than ever.

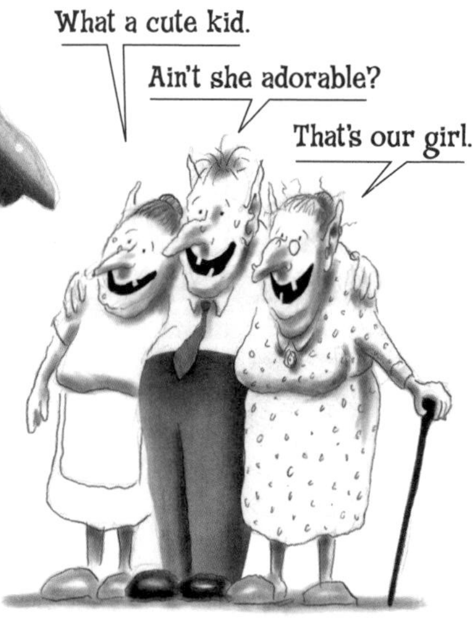
What a cute kid.
Ain't she adorable?
That's our girl.

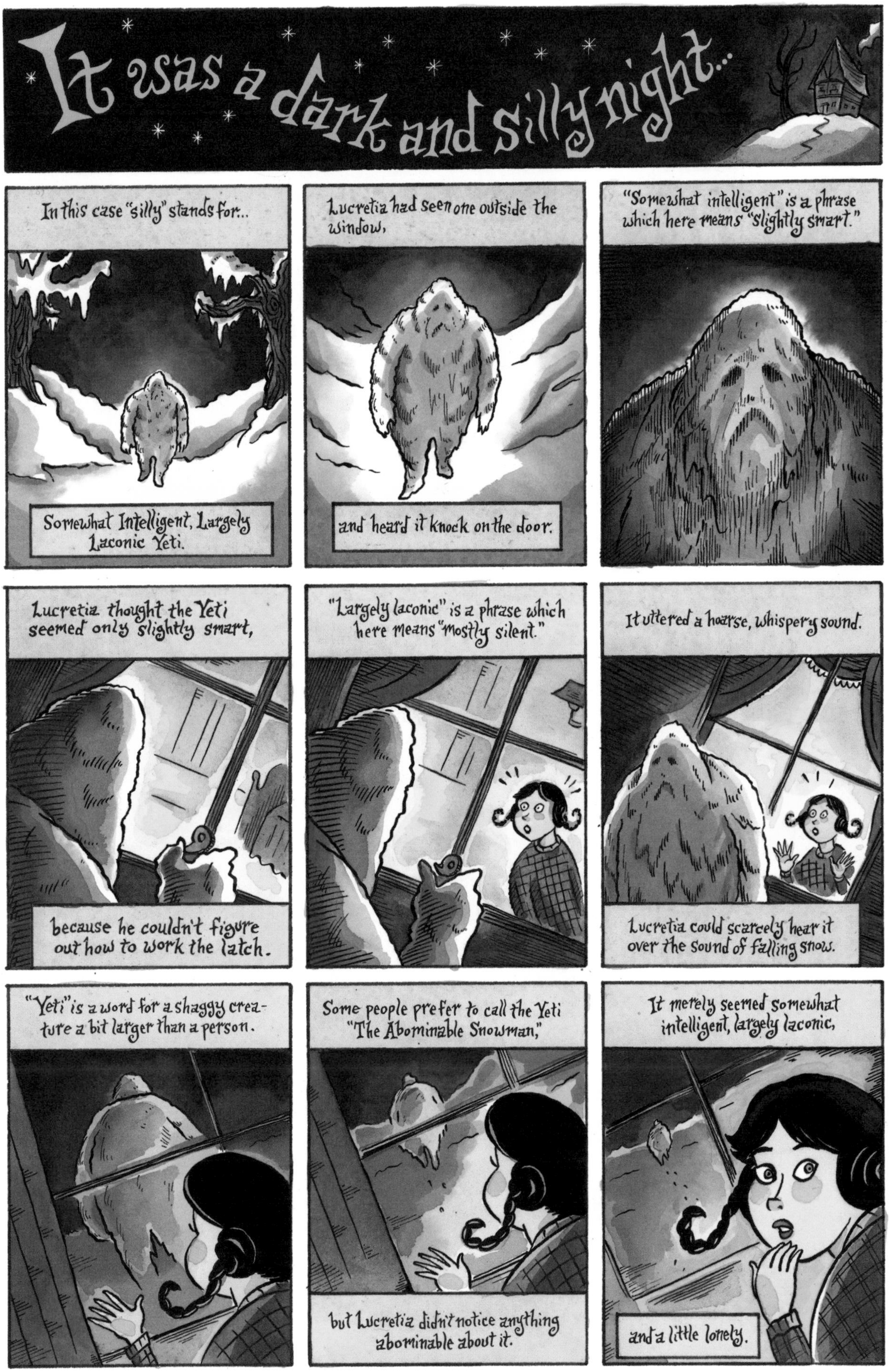
It was a dark and silly night...
In this case "silly" stands for...
Somewhat Intelligent, Largely Laconic Yeti.
Lucretia had seen one outside the window,
and heard it knock on the door.
"Somewhat intelligent" is a phrase which here means "slightly smart."
Lucretia thought the Yeti seemed only slightly smart,
because he couldn't figure out how to work the latch.
"Largely laconic" is a phrase which here means "mostly silent."
It uttered a hoarse, whispery sound.
Lucretia could scarcely hear it over the sound of falling snow.
"Yeti" is a word for a shaggy creature a bit larger than a person.
Some people prefer to call the Yeti "The Abominable Snowman,"
but Lucretia didn't notice anything abominable about it.
It merely seemed somewhat intelligent, largely laconic,
and a little lonely.

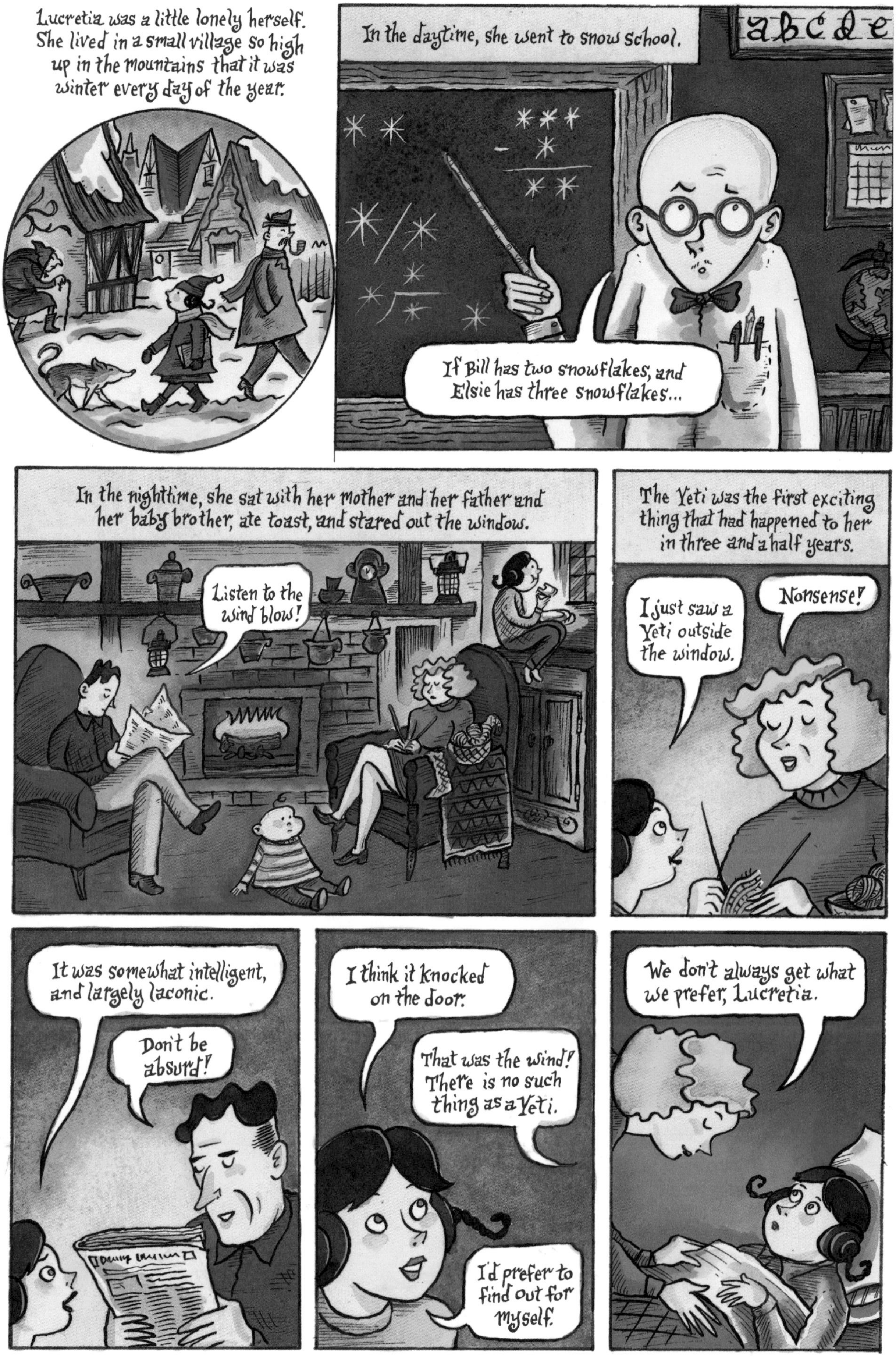
Lucretia was a little lonely herself. She lived in a small village so high up in the mountains that it was winter every day of the year.
In the daytime, she went to snow school.
abcde
If Bill has two snowflakes, and Elsie has three snowflakes...
In the nighttime, she sat with her mother and her father and her baby brother, ate toast, and stared out the window.
Listen to the wind blow!
The Yeti was the first exciting thing that had happened to her in three and a half years.
I just saw a Yeti outside the window.
Nonsense!
It was somewhat intelligent, and largely laconic.
Don't be absurd!
I think it knocked on the door.
That was the wind! There is no such thing as a Yeti.
I'd prefer to find out for myself.
We don't always get what we prefer, Lucretia.

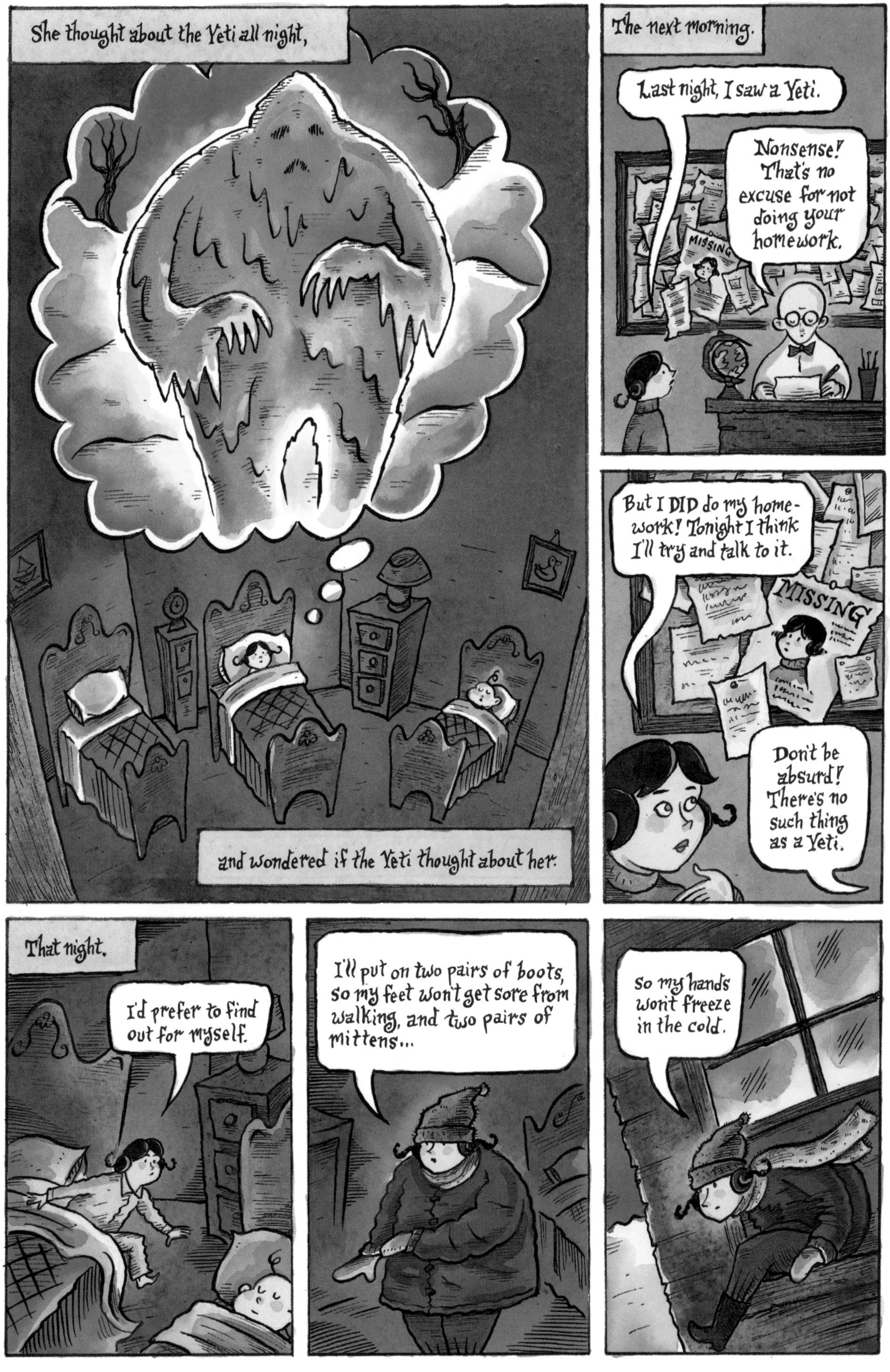
She thought about the Yeti all night,
and wondered if the Yeti thought about her.
The next morning.
Last night, I saw a Yeti.
Nonsense! That's no excuse for not doing your homework.
MISSING
But I DID do my home-work! Tonight I think I'll try and talk to it.
MISSING
Don't be absurd! There's no such thing as a Yeti.
That night.
I'd prefer to find out for myself.
I'll put on two pairs of boots, so my feet won't get sore from walking, and two pairs of mittens...
So my hands won't freeze in the cold.

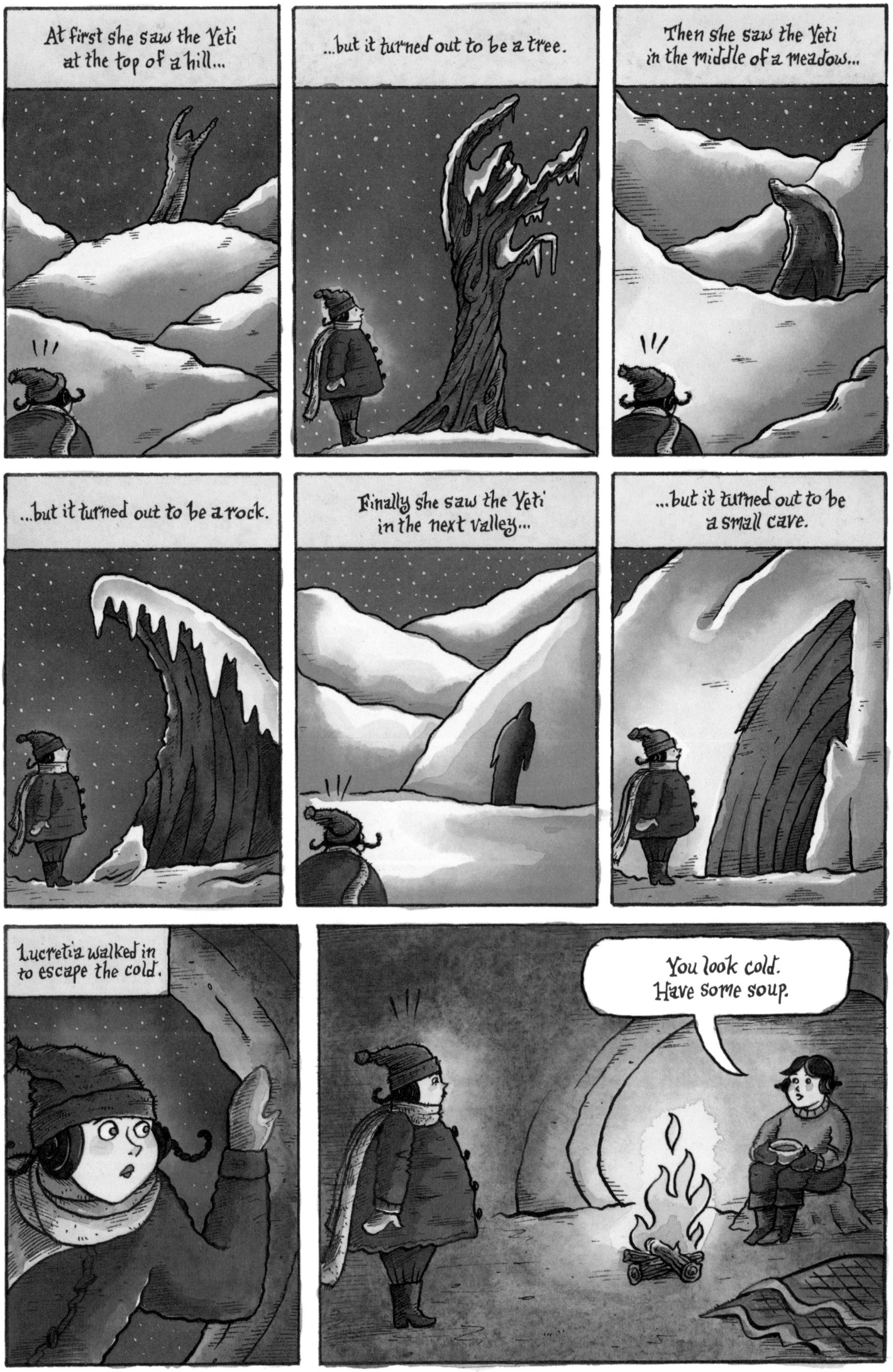
At first she saw the Yeti at the top of a hill...
...but it turned out to be a tree.
Then she saw the Yeti in the middle of a meadow...
...but it turned out to be a rock.
Finally she saw the Yeti in the next valley...
...but it turned out to be a small cave.
Lucretia walked in to escape the cold.
You look cold. Have some soup.

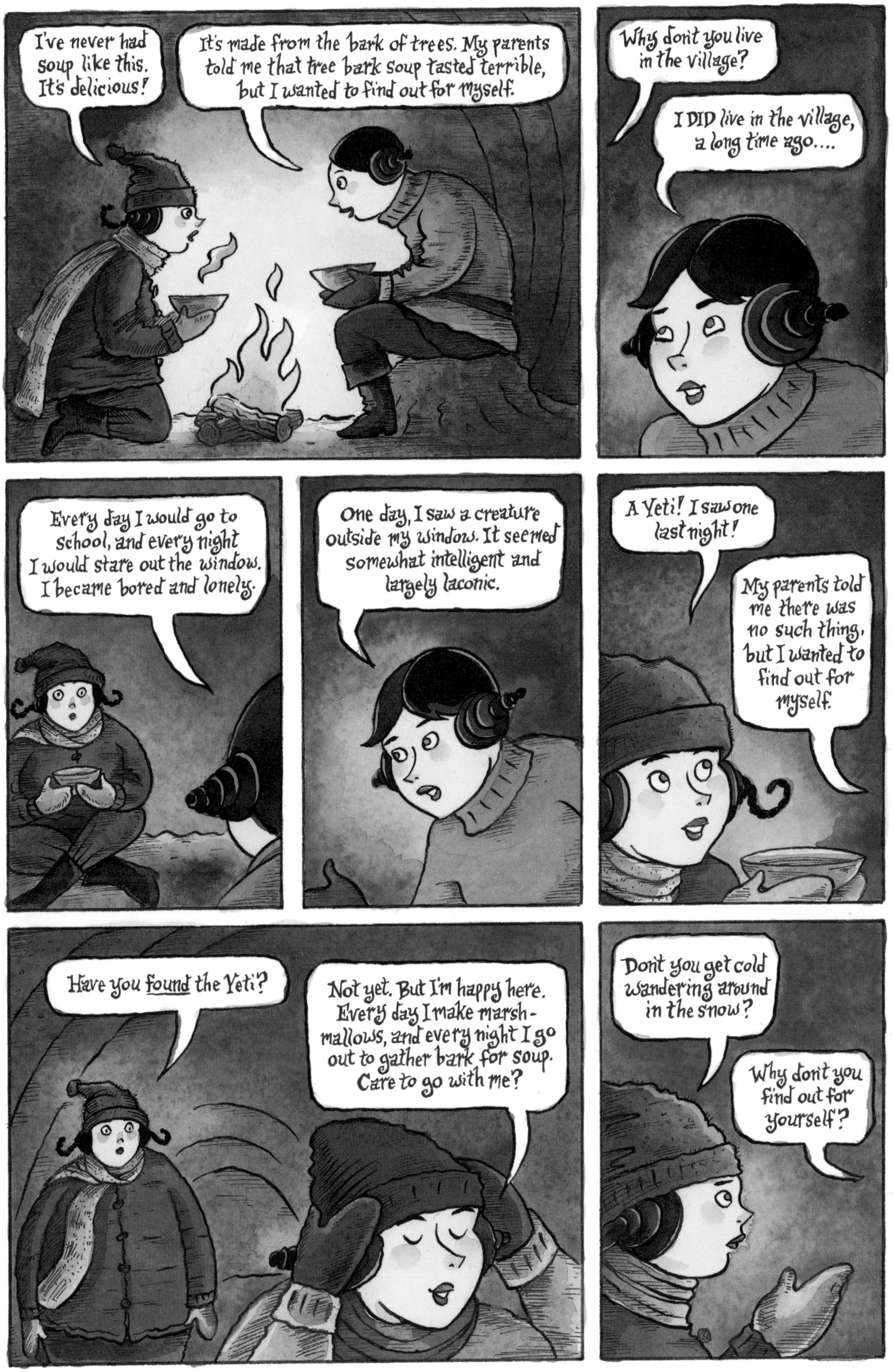
I've never had soup like this. It's delicious!
It's made from the bark of trees. My parents told me that tree bark soup tasted terrible, but I wanted to find out for myself.
Why don't you live in the village?
I DID live in the village, a long time ago....
Every day I would go to school, and every night I would stare out the window. I became bored and lonely.
One day, I saw a creature outside my window. It seemed somewhat intelligent and largely laconic.
A Yeti! I saw one last night!
My parents told me there was no such thing, but I wanted to find out for myself.
Have you found the Yeti?
Not yet. But I'm happy here. Every day I make marsh-mallows, and every night I go out to gather bark for soup. Care to go with me?
Don't you get cold wandering around in the snow?
Why don't you find out for yourself?

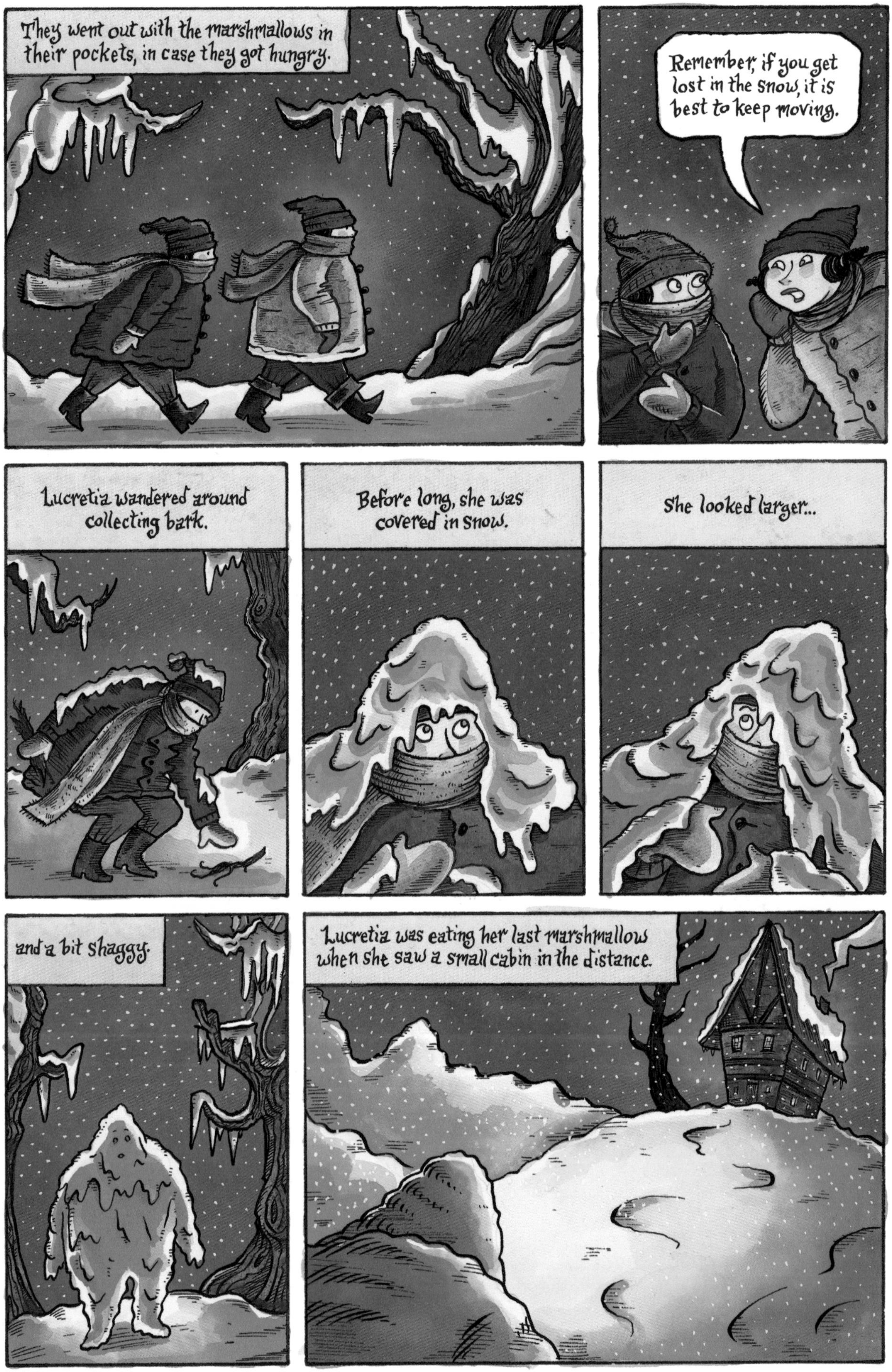
They went out with the marshmallows in their pockets, in case they got hungry.
Remember, if you get lost in the snow, it is best to keep moving.
Lucretia wandered around collecting bark.
Before long, she was covered in snow.
She looked larger...
and a bit shaggy.
Lucretia was eating her last marshmallow when she saw a small cabin in the distance.

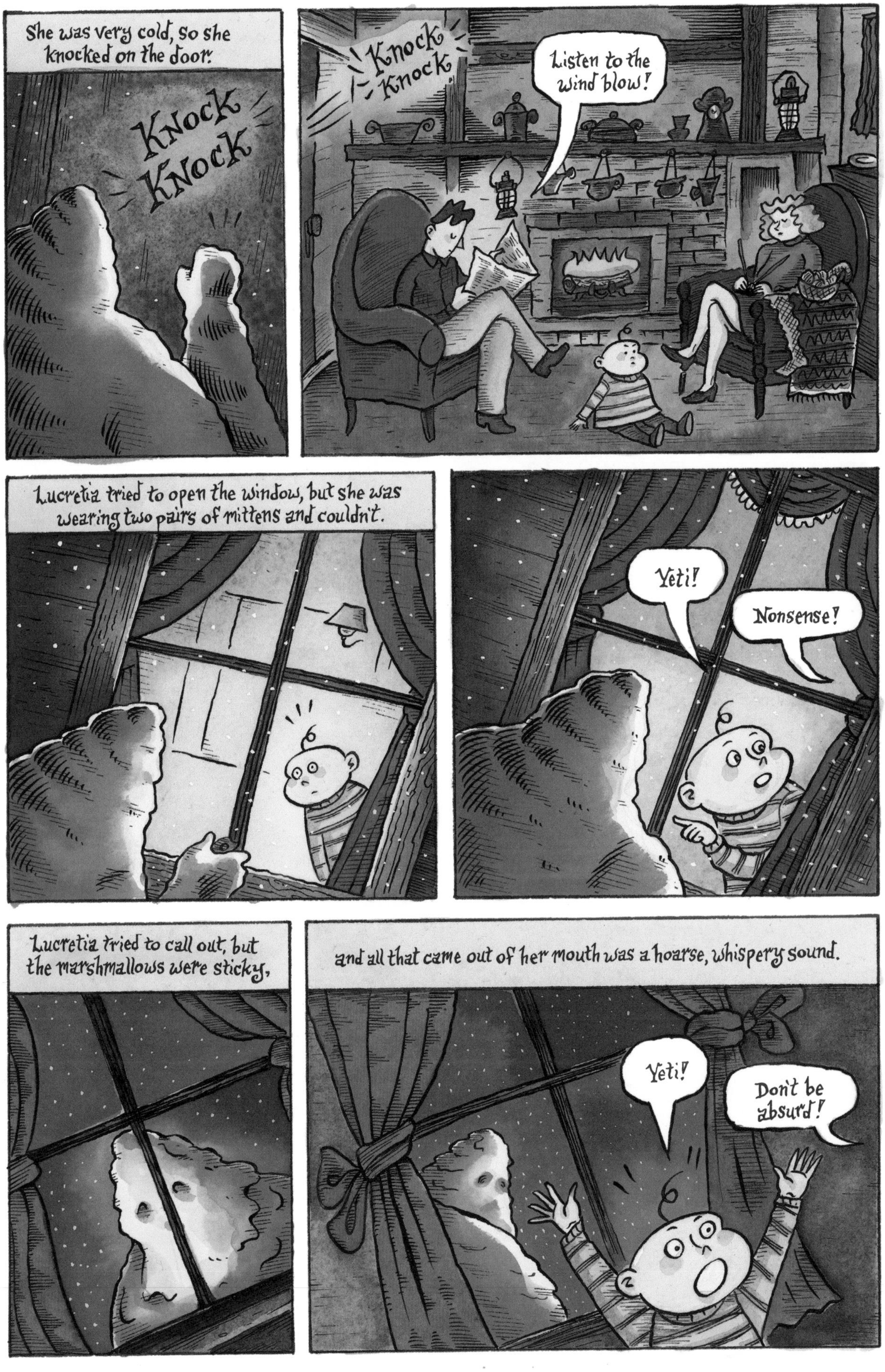
She was very cold, so she knocked on the door.
KNOCK KNOCK
Knock Knock
Listen to the wind blow!
Lucretia tried to open the window, but she was wearing two pairs of mittens and couldn't.
Yeti!
Nonsense!
Lucretia tried to call out, but the marshmallows were sticky,
and all that came out of her mouth was a hoarse, whispery sound.
Yeti!
Don't be absurd!

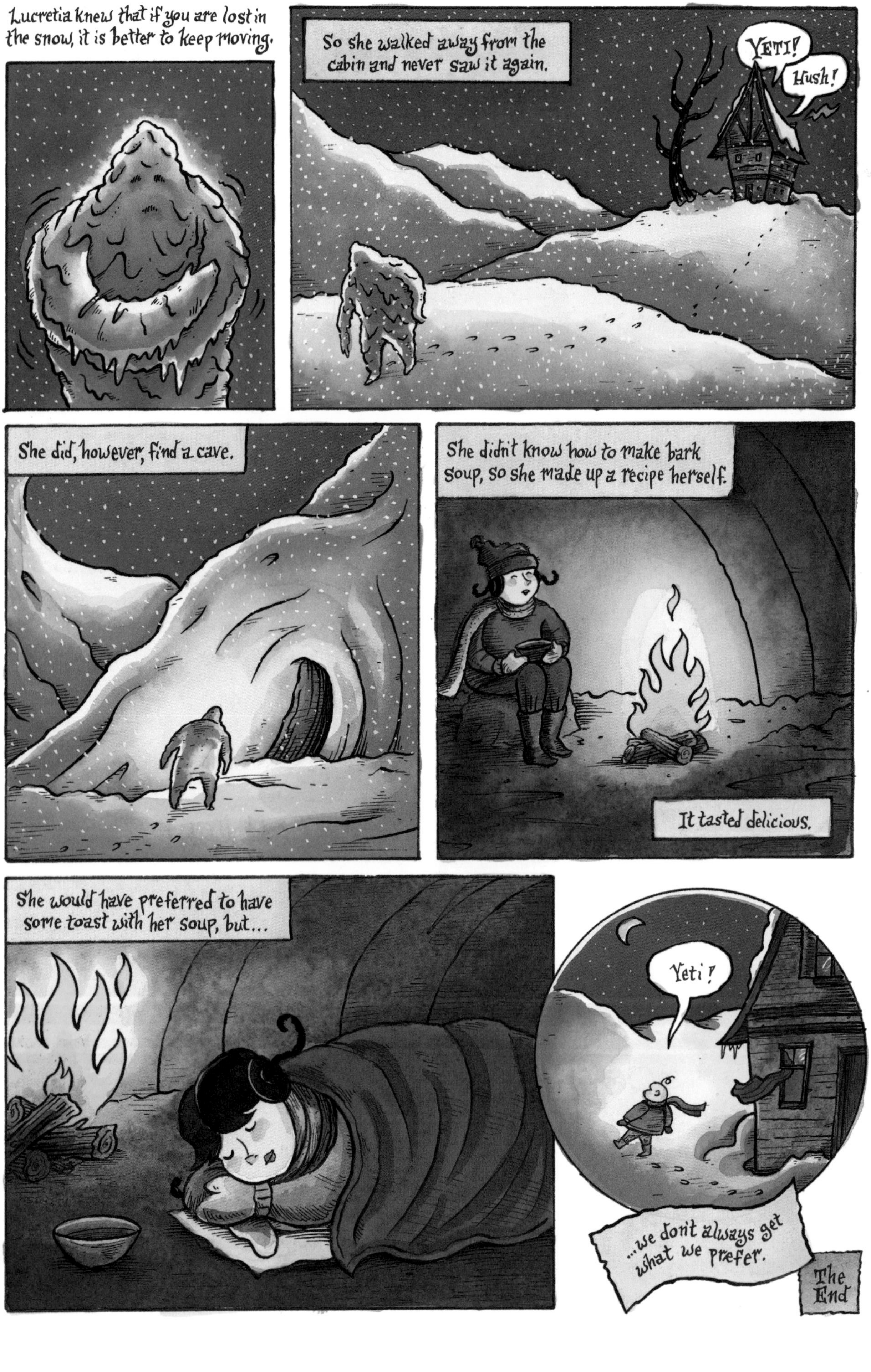
Lucretia knew that if you are lost in the snow, it is better to keep moving.
So she walked away from the cabin and never saw it again.
YETI!
Hush!
She did, however, find a cave.
She didn't know how to make bark soup, so she made up a recipe herself.
It tasted delicious.
She would have preferred to have some toast with her soup, but...
Yeti!
...we don't always get what we prefer.
The End

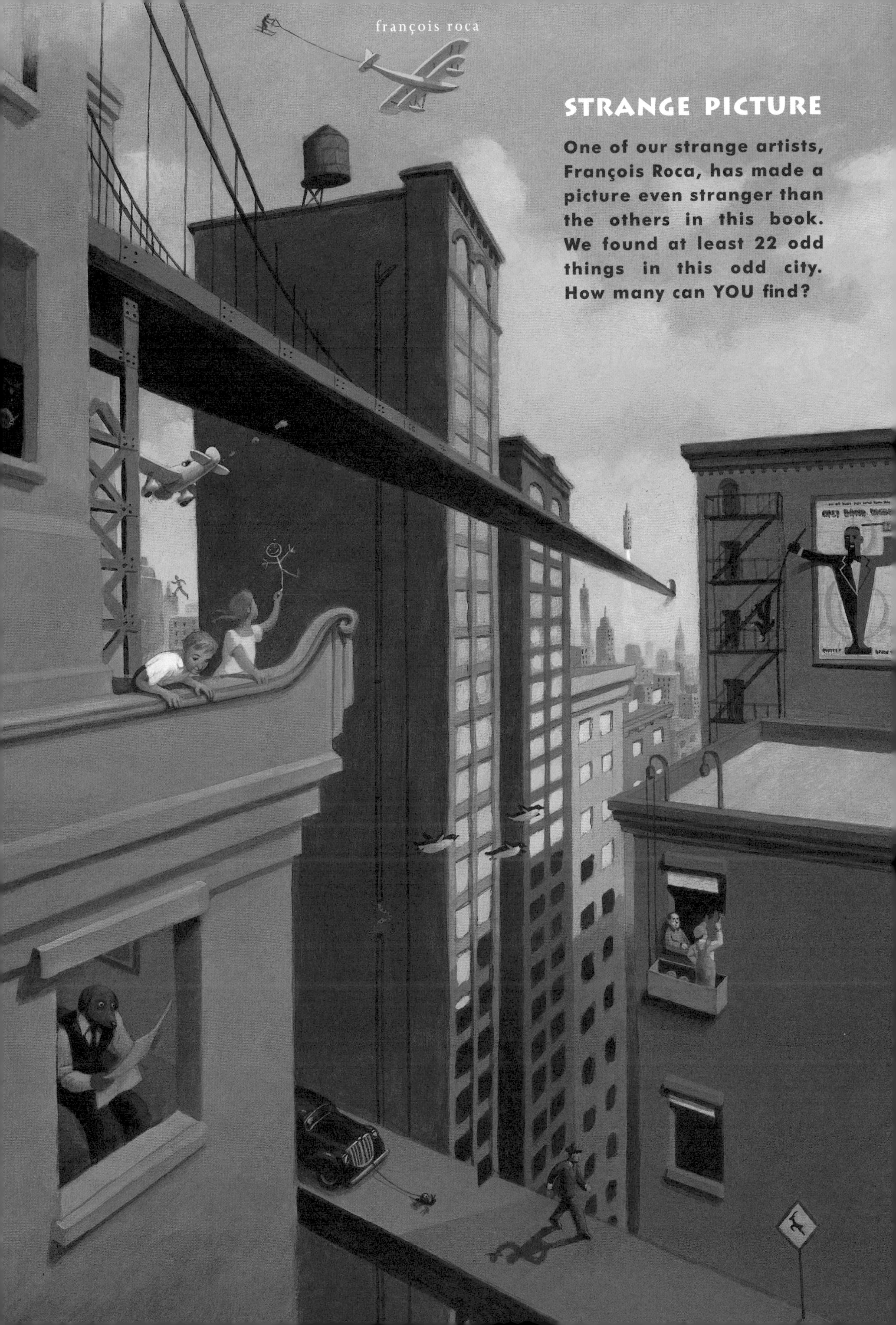

STRANGE PICTURE

One of our strange artists, François Roca, has made a picture even stranger than the others in this book. We found at least 22 odd things in this odd city. How many can YOU find?

j. otto seibold

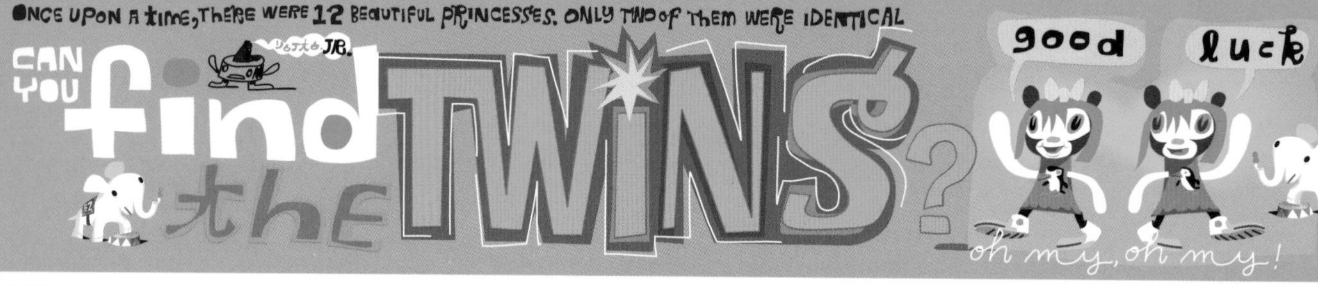
ONCE UPON A TIME, THERE WERE 12 BEAUTIFUL PRINCESSES. ONLY TWO OF THEM WERE IDENTICAL
CAN YOU find THE TWINS?
JOTTO JR.
good
luck
oh my, oh my!

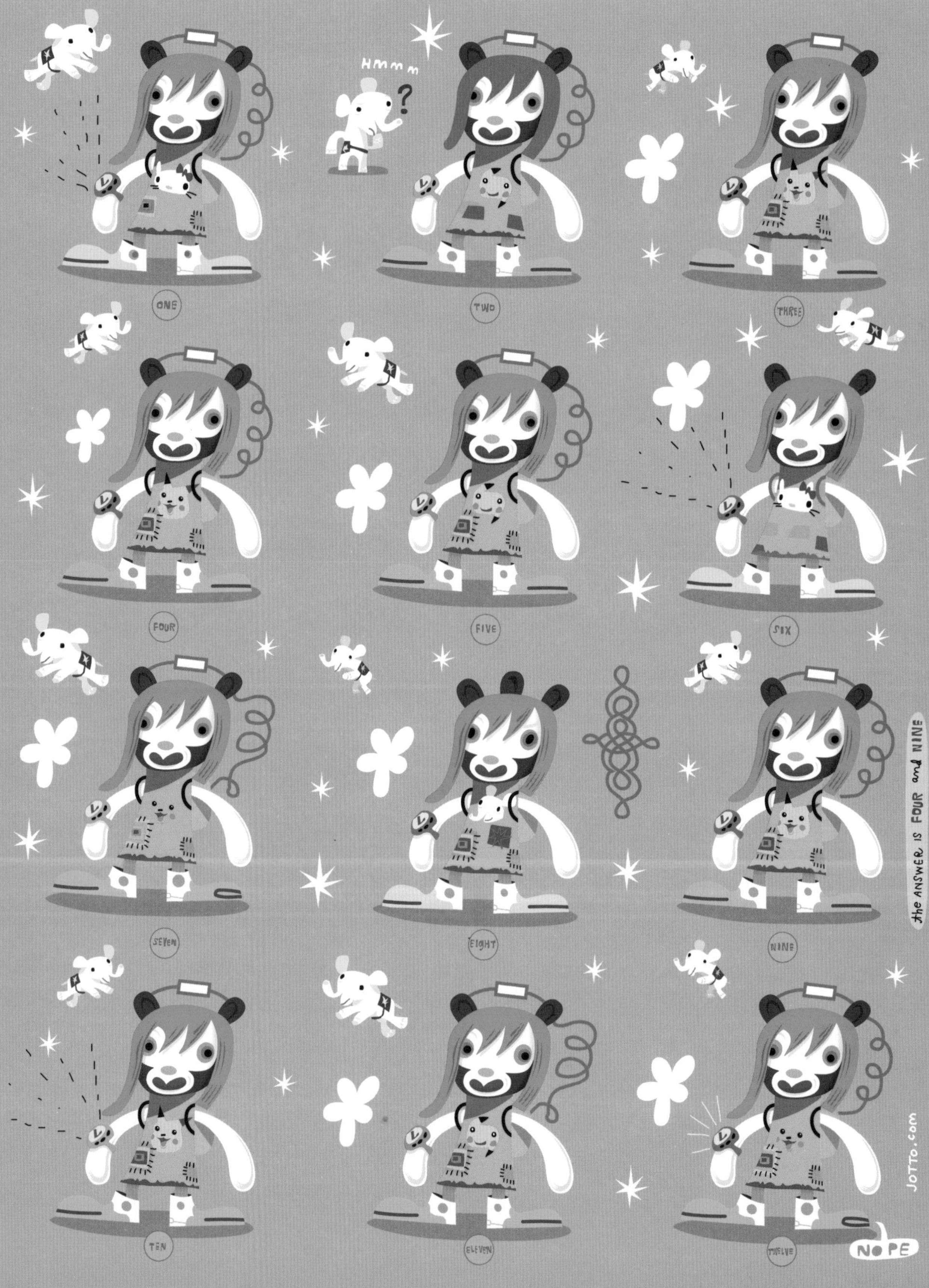
HMMM
ONE
TWO
THREE
FOUR
FIVE
SIX
SEVEN
EIGHT
NINE
THE ANSWER IS FOUR and NINE
TEN
ELEVEN
TWELVE
JOTTO.com
NOPE

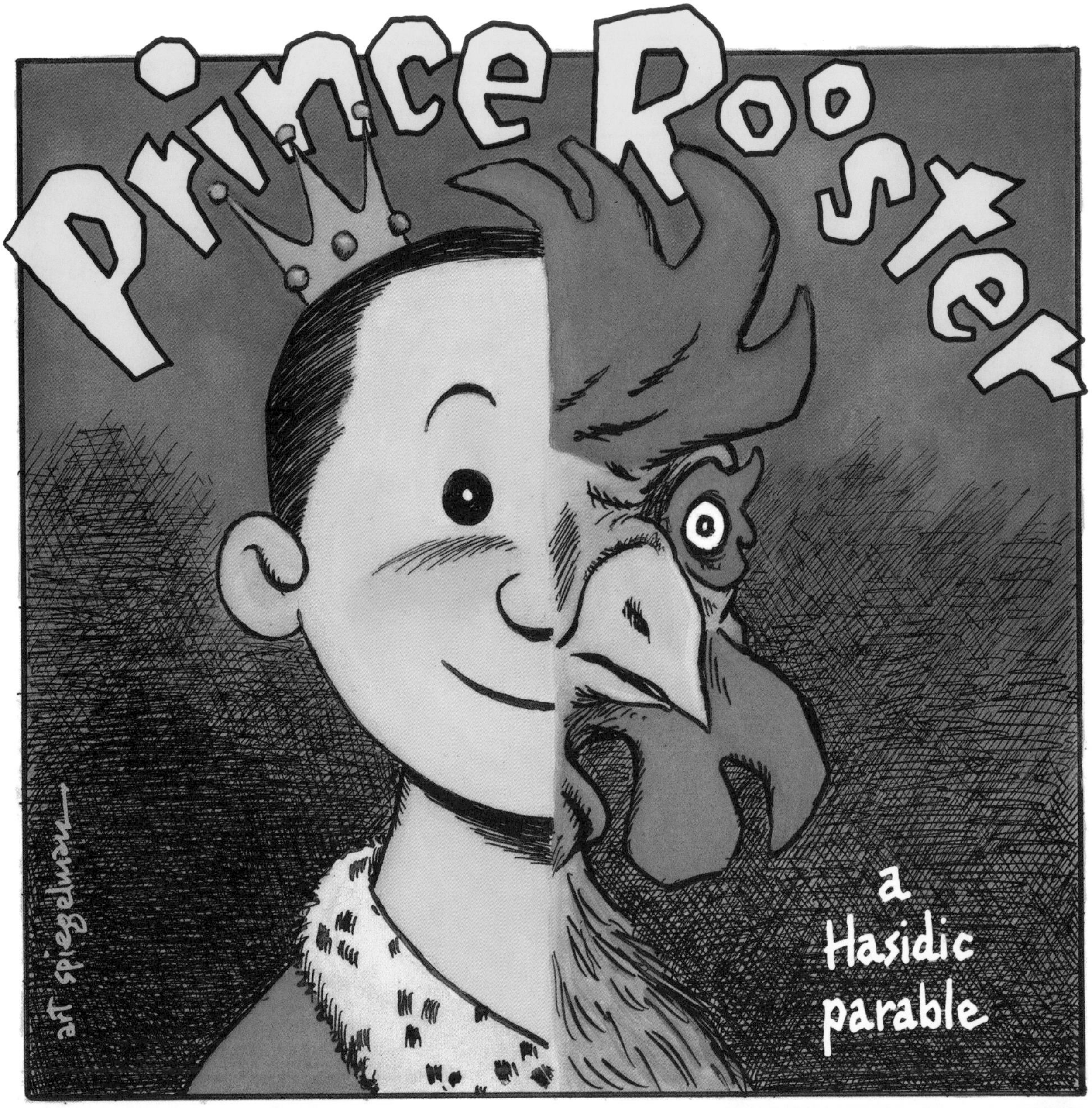
Prince Rooster
art spiegelman
a Hasidic parable

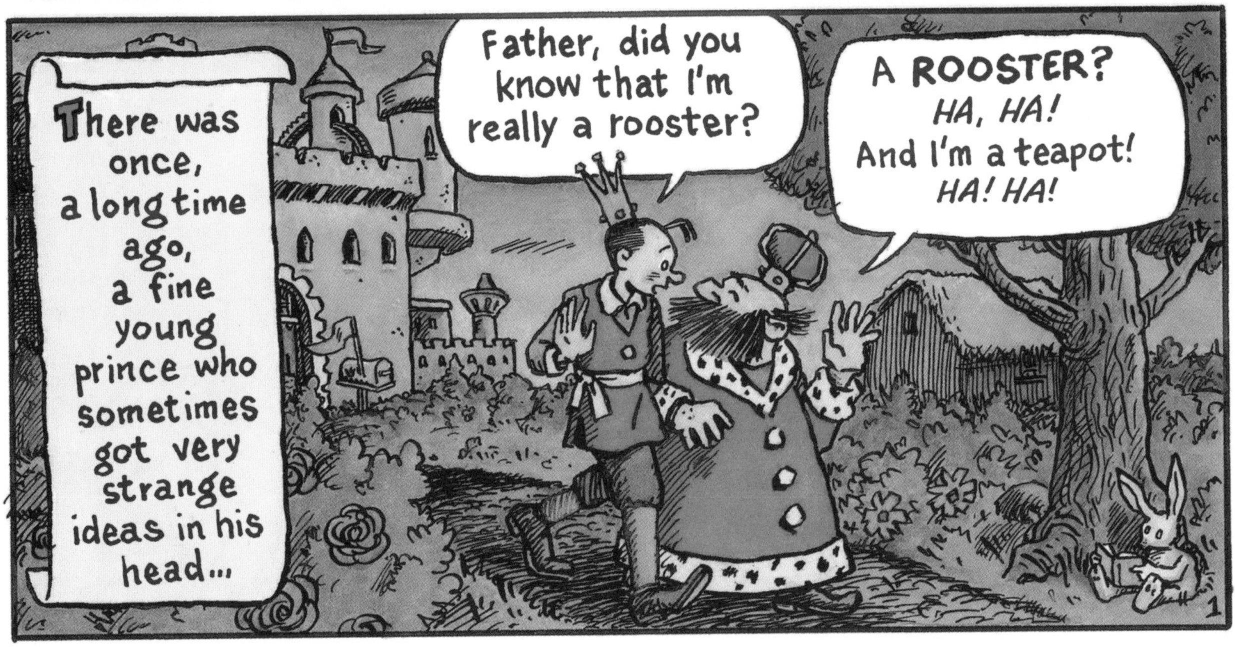
There was once, a long time ago, a fine young prince who sometimes got very strange ideas in his head...
Father, did you know that I'm really a rooster?
A ROOSTER? HA, HA! And I'm a teapot! HA! HA!
1

A teapot? Really?!

Sigh. I was just joking.

But I'm not joking— I AM a rooster!

COCK-A-DOODLE DOO!

The prince stripped off his clothes and flapped all around the castle...

COCK-A-DOODLE-OODLE DOO!

C-come on, junior. Let's eat lunch!

Sit down and eat your roast beef!

NO! Roosters don't sit in chairs and never eat roast beef!

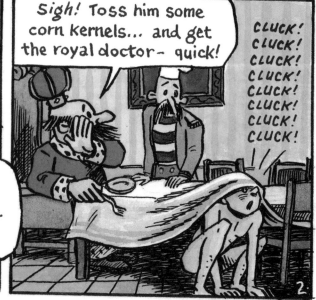

Sigh! Toss him some corn kernels... and get the royal doctor— quick!

CLUCK!
CLUCK!
CLUCK!
CLUCK!
CLUCK!
CLUCK!
CLUCK!
CLUCK!

2

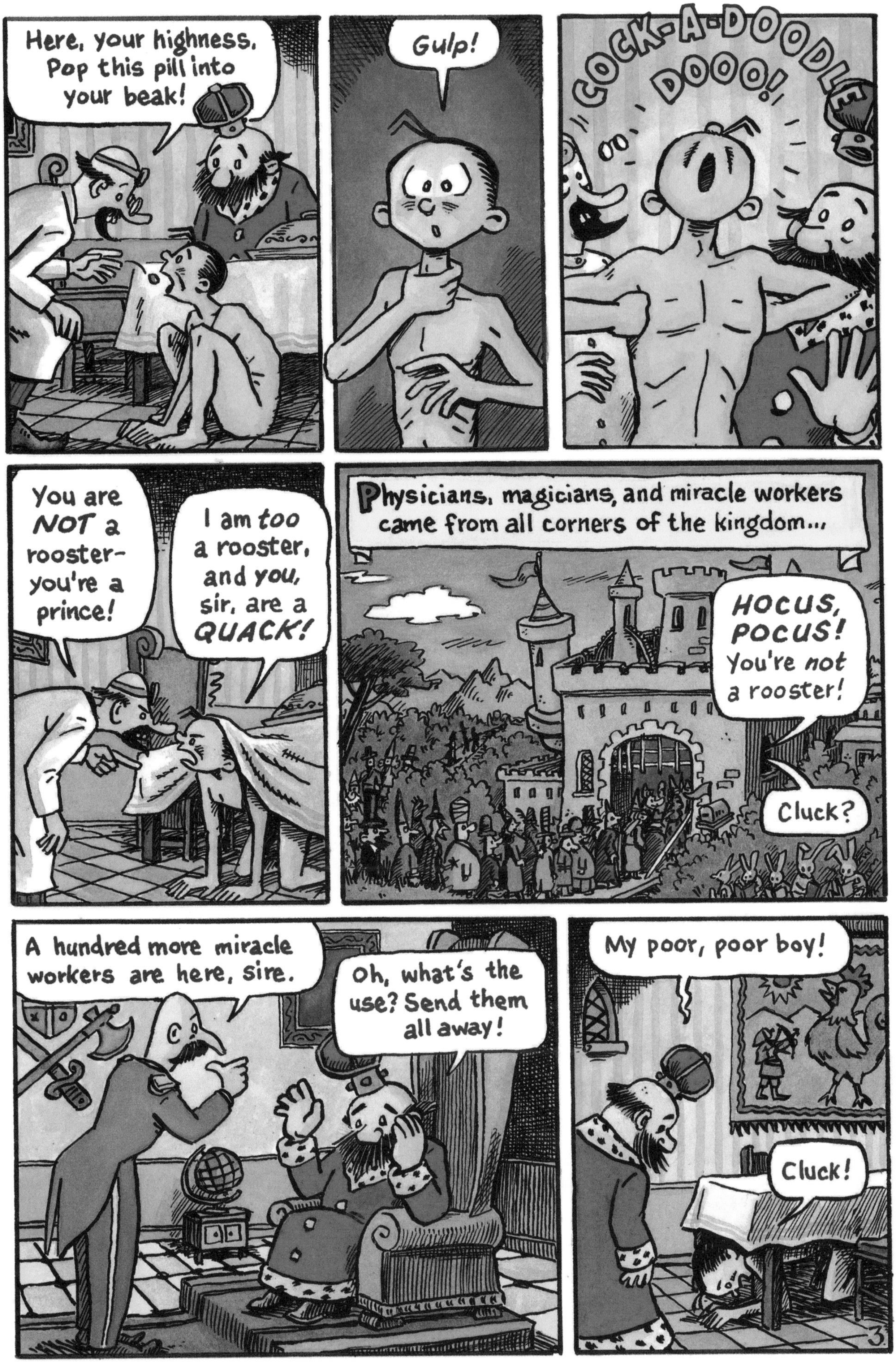

Here, your highness. Pop this pill into your beak!
Gulp!
COCK-A-DOODLE DOOO!
You are NOT a rooster- you're a prince!
I am too a rooster, and you, sir, are a QUACK!
Physicians, magicians, and miracle workers came from all corners of the kingdom...
HOCUS, POCUS! You're not a rooster!
Cluck?
A hundred more miracle workers are here, sire.
Oh, what's the use? Send them all away!
My poor, poor boy!
Cluck!

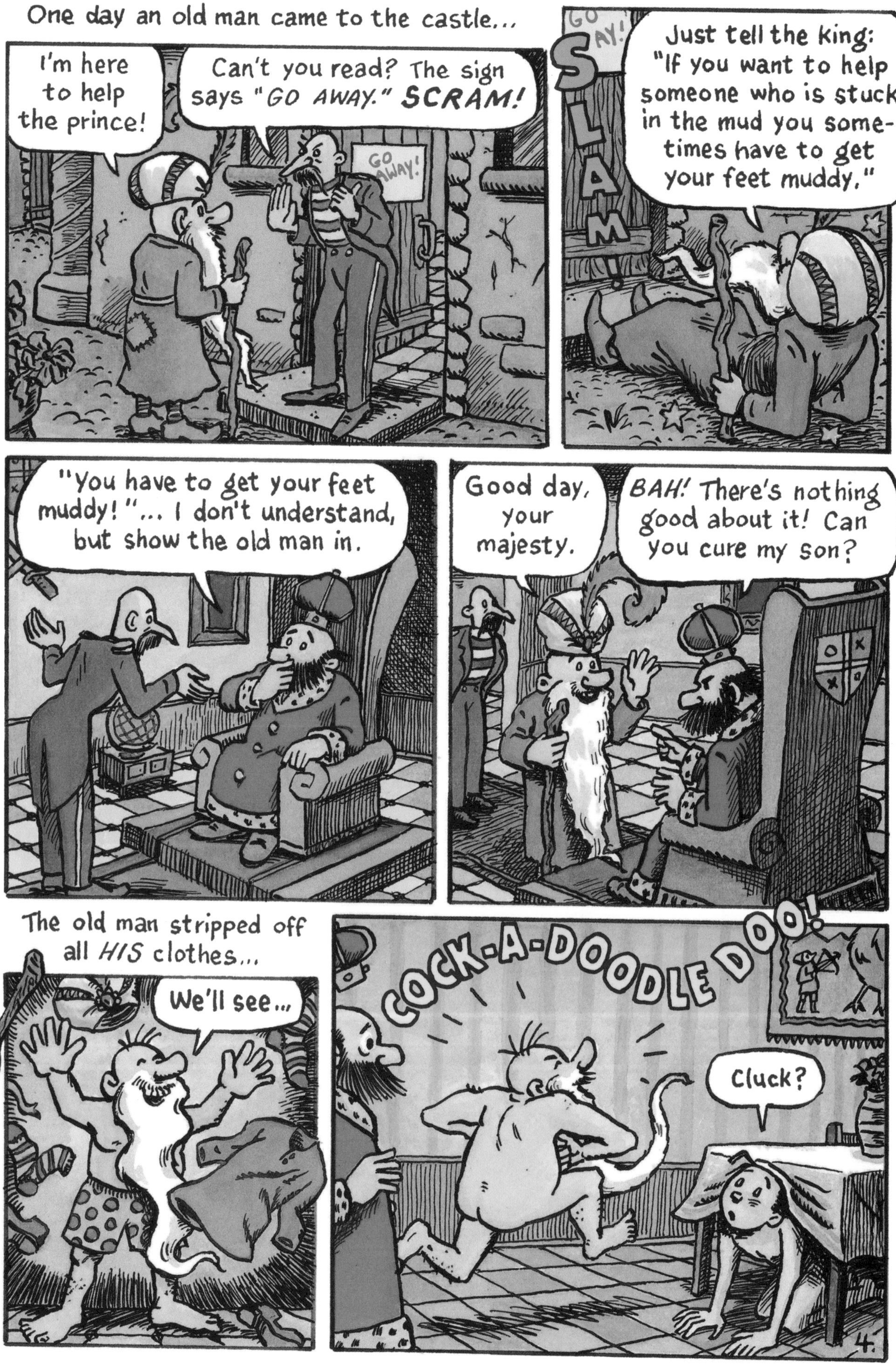
One day an old man came to the castle...
I'm here to help the prince!
Can't you read? The sign says "GO AWAY." SCRAM!
GO AWAY!
SLAM
Just tell the king: "If you want to help someone who is stuck in the mud you sometimes have to get your feet muddy."
"You have to get your feet muddy!"... I don't understand, but show the old man in.
Good day, your majesty.
BAH! There's nothing good about it! Can you cure my son?
The old man stripped off all HIS clothes...
We'll see...
COCK-A-DOODLE DOO!
Cluck?
4.

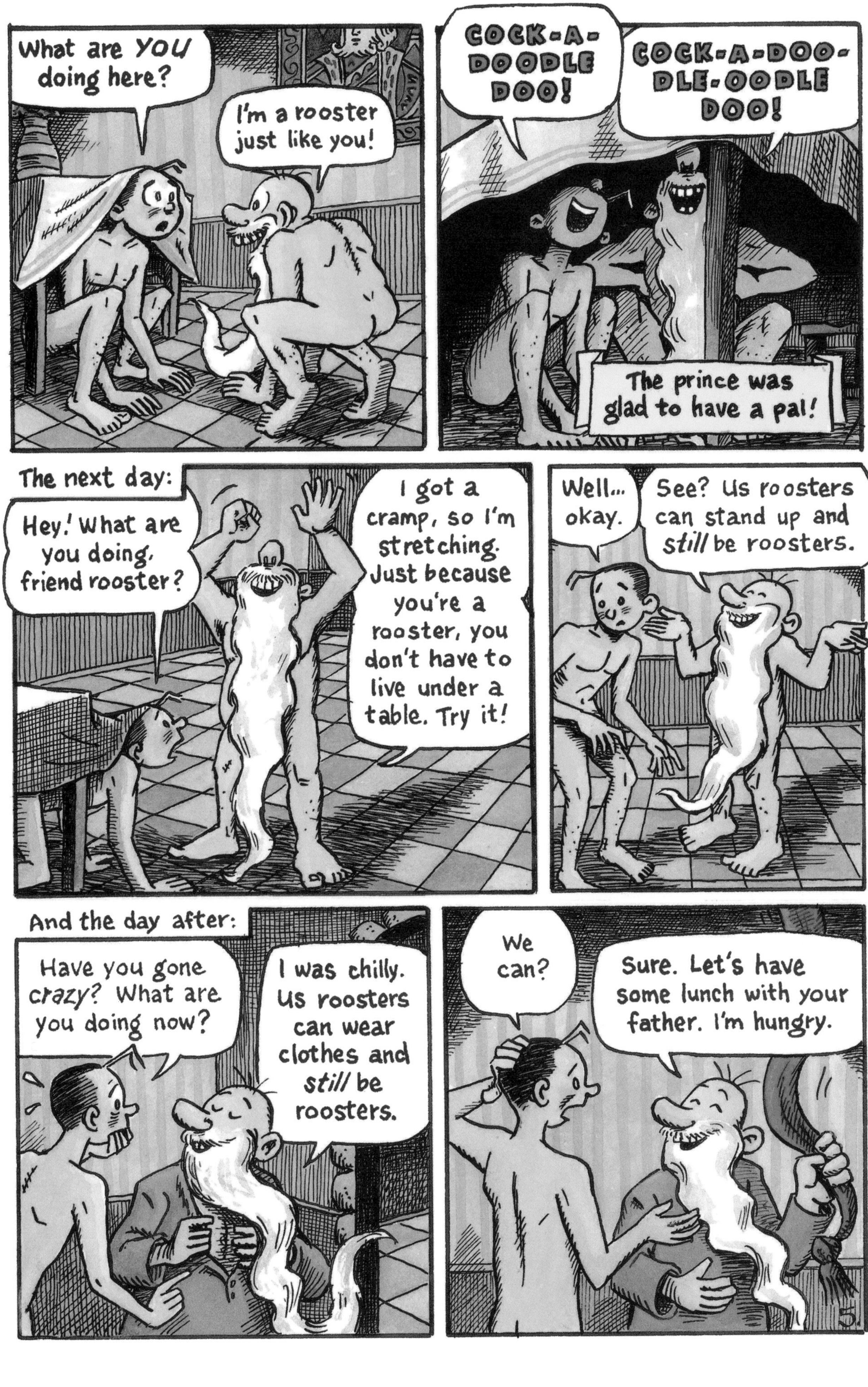

What are YOU doing here?
I'm a rooster just like you!
COCK-A-DOODLE DOO!
COCK-A-DOO-DLE-OODLE DOO!
The prince was glad to have a pal!
The next day:
Hey! What are you doing, friend rooster?
I got a cramp, so I'm stretching. Just because you're a rooster, you don't have to live under a table. Try it!
Well... okay.
See? Us roosters can stand up and *still* be roosters.
And the day after:
Have you gone *crazy*? What are you doing now?
I was chilly. Us roosters can wear clothes and *still* be roosters.
We can?
Sure. Let's have some lunch with your father. I'm hungry.
5.

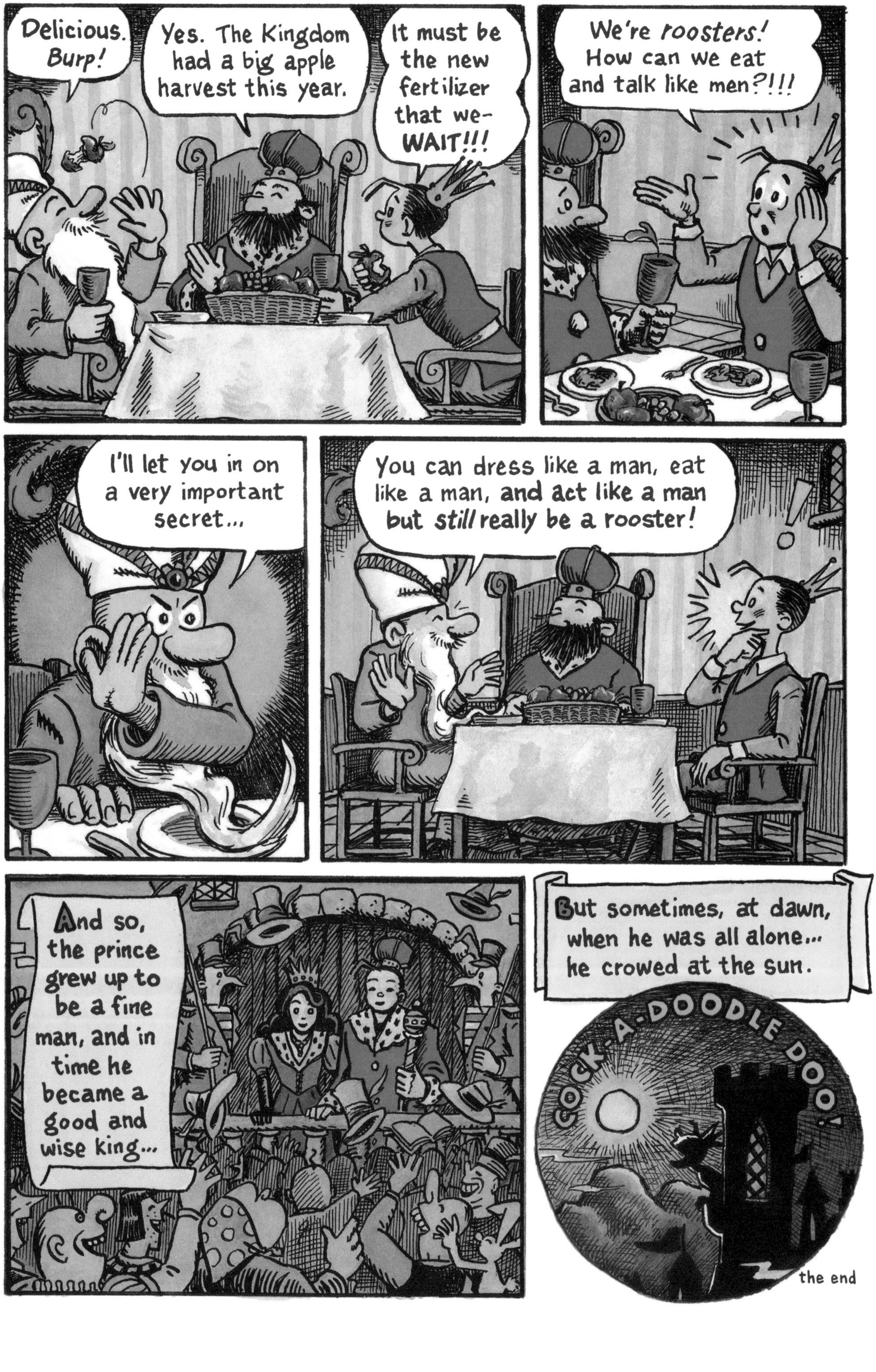
Delicious. Burp!
Yes. The Kingdom had a big apple harvest this year.
It must be the new fertilizer that we- WAIT!!!
We're roosters! How can we eat and talk like men?!!!
I'll let you in on a very important secret...
You can dress like a man, eat like a man, and act like a man but still really be a rooster!
!
And so, the prince grew up to be a fine man, and in time he became a good and wise king...
But sometimes, at dawn, when he was all alone... he crowed at the sun.
COCK-A-DOODLE DOO!
the end

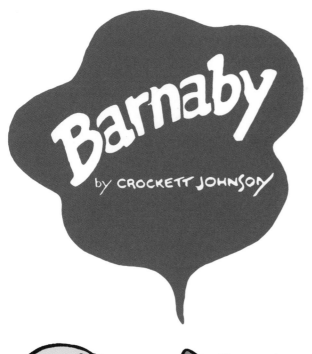

Barnaby
by CROCKETT JOHNSON

"A bright star shone outside the castle window and the Prince's Fairy Godmother appeared..."

Fairy Godmother, eh?

"She waved her magic wand and said, 'Your wish is granted.'"

Very neat!... I don't suppose I've got a Fairy Godmother, by any chance?

No, I'm sure there aren't any Fairy Godparents taking care of you, Barnaby... Sometimes I wish there were.

What this house needs is a couple of good Fairy Godmothers... Anyway, I wish...

Hey!

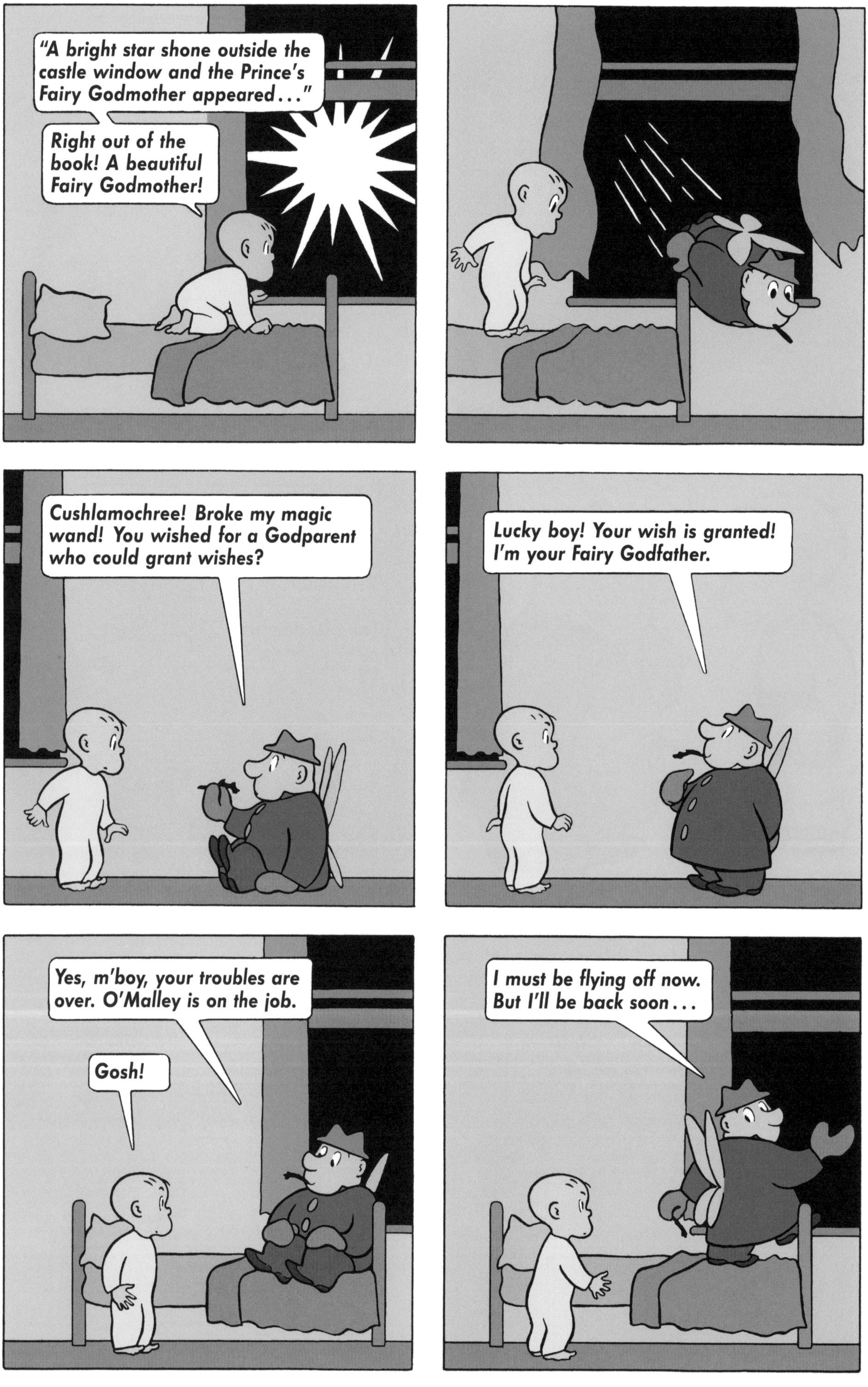
"A bright star shone outside the castle window and the Prince's Fairy Godmother appeared..."
Right out of the book! A beautiful Fairy Godmother!
Cushlamochree! Broke my magic wand! You wished for a Godparent who could grant wishes?
Lucky boy! Your wish is granted! I'm your Fairy Godfather.
Yes, m'boy, your troubles are over. O'Malley is on the job.
Gosh!
I must be flying off now. But I'll be back soon...

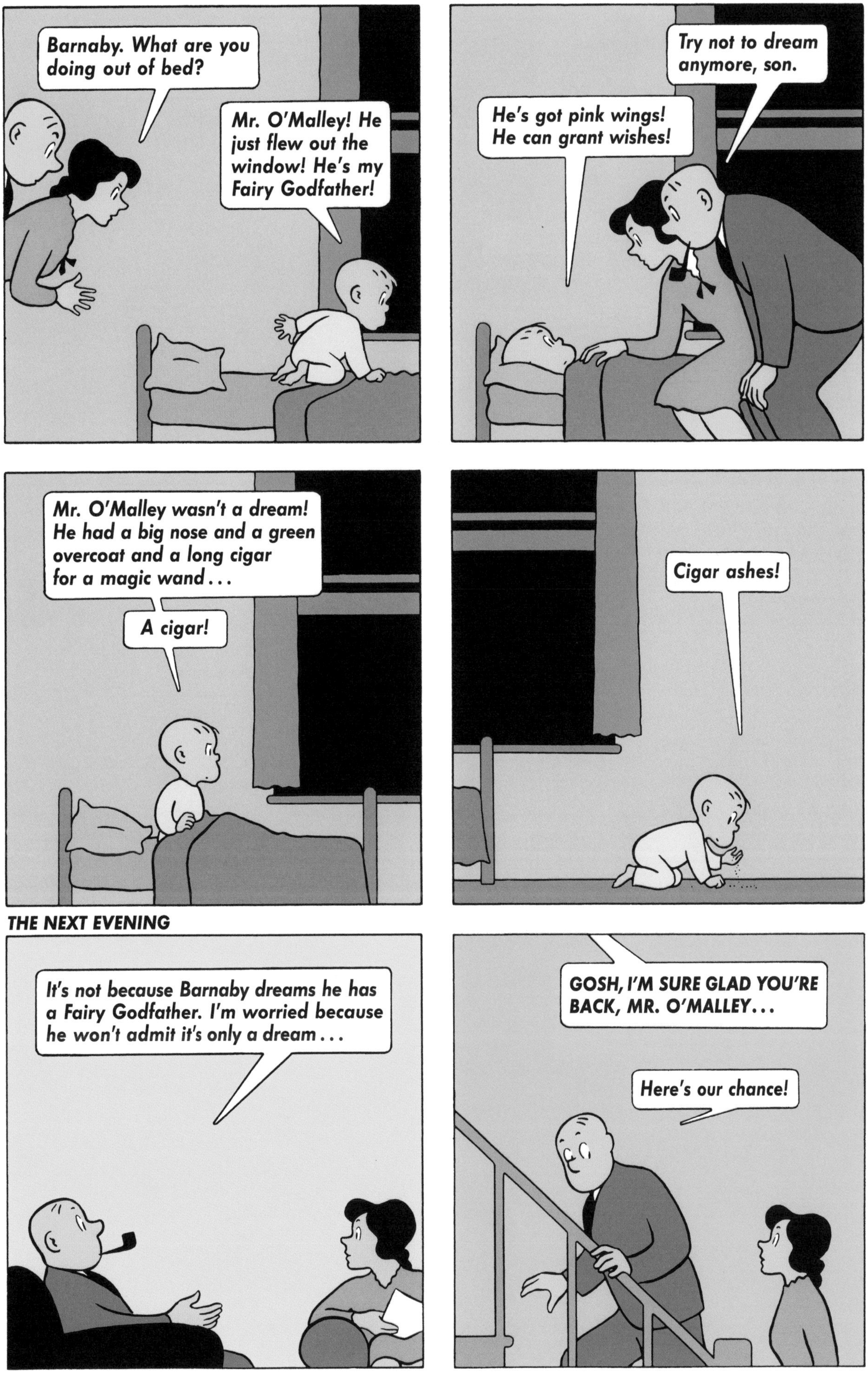
Barnaby. What are you doing out of bed?
Mr. O'Malley! He just flew out the window! He's my Fairy Godfather!
Try not to dream anymore, son.
He's got pink wings! He can grant wishes!
Mr. O'Malley wasn't a dream! He had a big nose and a green overcoat and a long cigar for a magic wand...
A cigar!
Cigar ashes!
THE NEXT EVENING
It's not because Barnaby dreams he has a Fairy Godfather. I'm worried because he won't admit it's only a dream...
GOSH, I'M SURE GLAD YOU'RE BACK, MR. O'MALLEY...
Here's our chance!

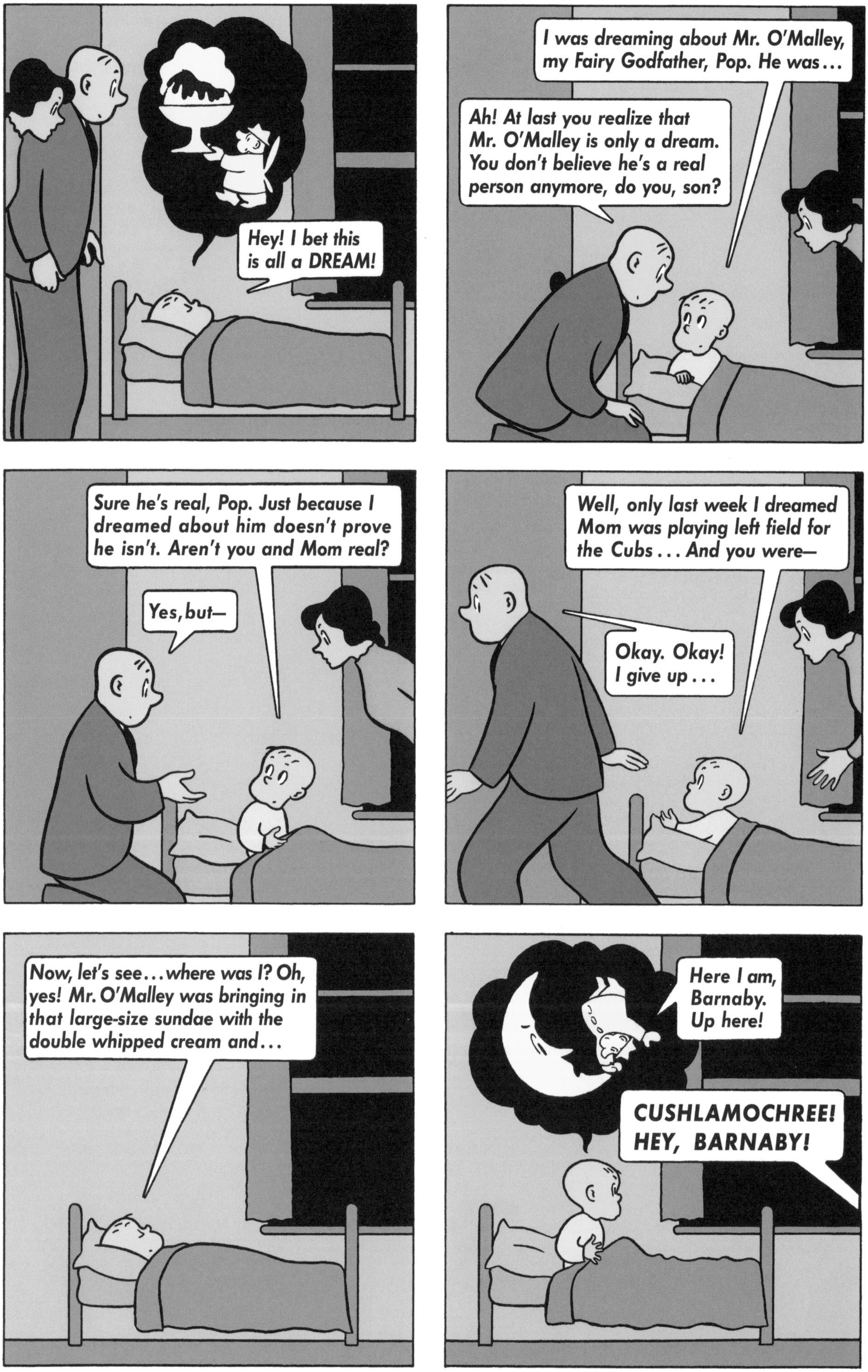

Hey! I bet this is all a DREAM!
I was dreaming about Mr. O'Malley, my Fairy Godfather, Pop. He was...
Ah! At last you realize that Mr. O'Malley is only a dream. You don't believe he's a real person anymore, do you, son?
Sure he's real, Pop. Just because I dreamed about him doesn't prove he isn't. Aren't you and Mom real?
Yes, but—
Well, only last week I dreamed Mom was playing left field for the Cubs... And you were—
Okay. Okay! I give up...
Now, let's see...where was I? Oh, yes! Mr. O'Malley was bringing in that large-size sundae with the double whipped cream and...
Here I am, Barnaby. Up here!
CUSHLAMOCHREE! HEY, BARNABY!

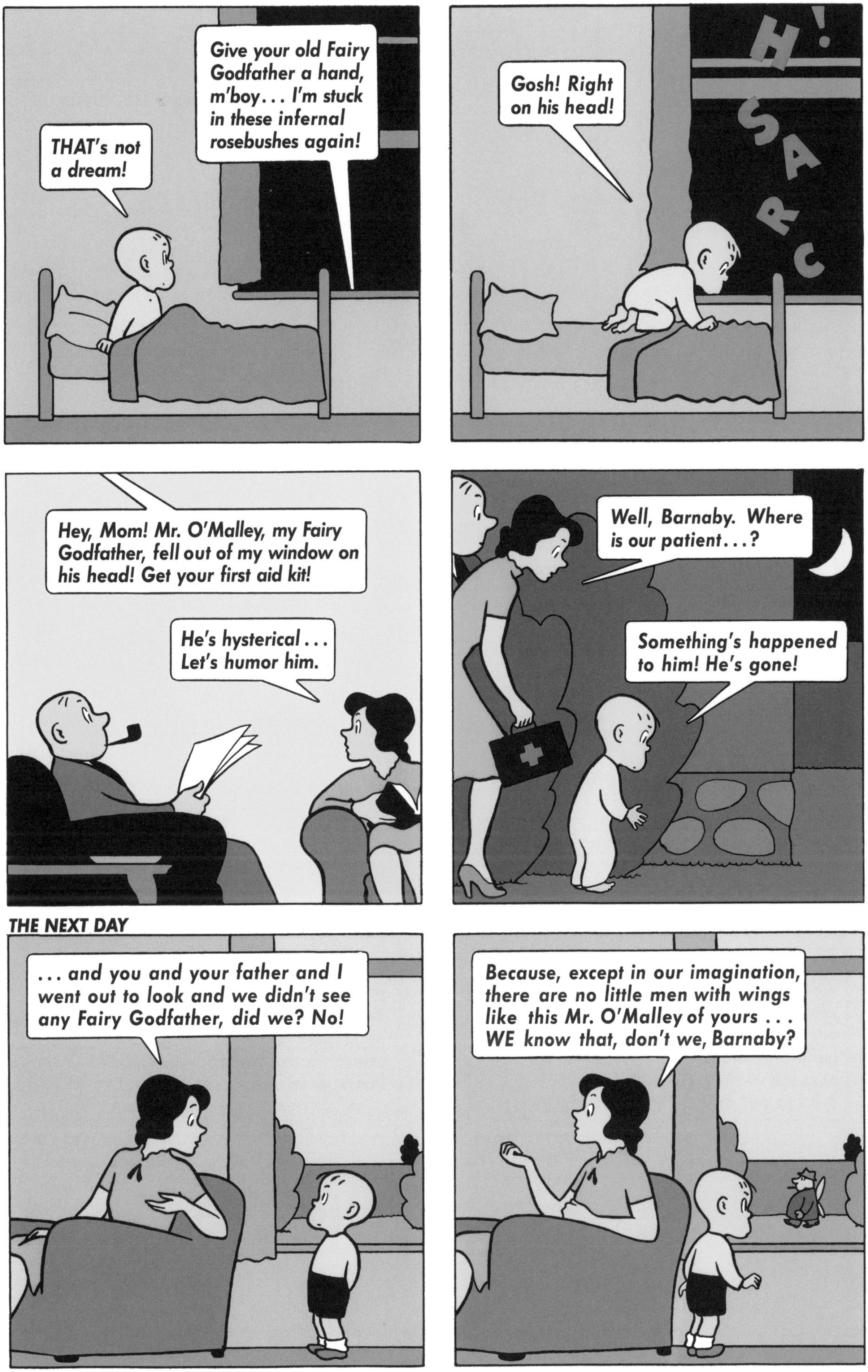
THAT's not a dream!
Give your old Fairy Godfather a hand, m'boy... I'm stuck in these infernal rosebushes again!
Gosh! Right on his head!
CRASH!
Hey, Mom! Mr. O'Malley, my Fairy Godfather, fell out of my window on his head! Get your first aid kit!
He's hysterical... Let's humor him.
Well, Barnaby. Where is our patient...?
Something's happened to him! He's gone!
THE NEXT DAY
... and you and your father and I went out to look and we didn't see any Fairy Godfather, did we? No!
Because, except in our imagination, there are no little men with wings like this Mr. O'Malley of yours... WE know that, don't we, Barnaby?

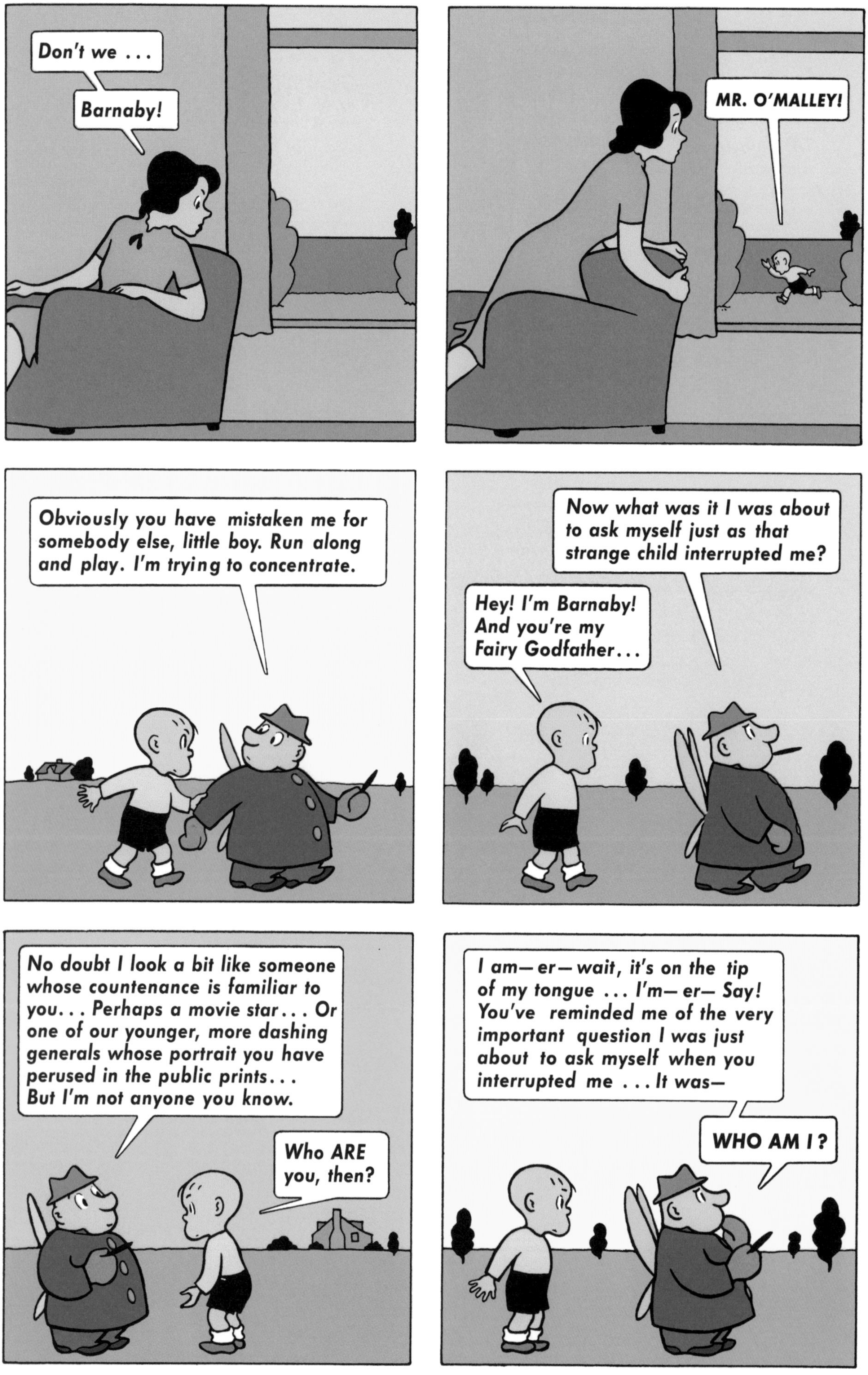
Don't we . . .
Barnaby!
MR. O'MALLEY!
Obviously you have mistaken me for somebody else, little boy. Run along and play. I'm trying to concentrate.
Now what was it I was about to ask myself just as that strange child interrupted me?
Hey! I'm Barnaby! And you're my Fairy Godfather . . .
No doubt I look a bit like someone whose countenance is familiar to you . . . Perhaps a movie star . . . Or one of our younger, more dashing generals whose portrait you have perused in the public prints . . . But I'm not anyone you know.
Who ARE you, then?
I am— er— wait, it's on the tip of my tongue . . . I'm— er— Say! You've reminded me of the very important question I was just about to ask myself when you interrupted me . . . It was—
WHO AM I?

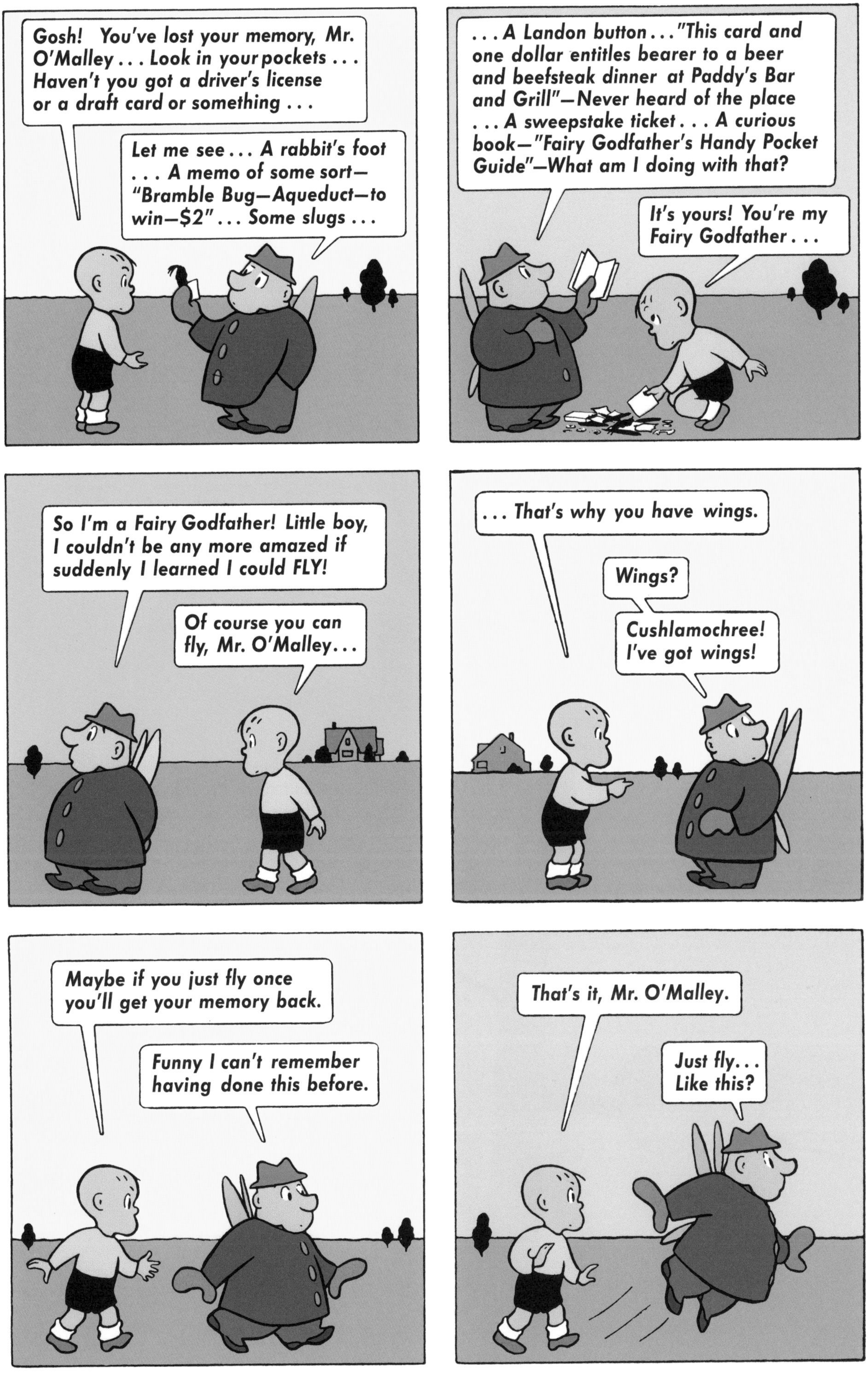
Gosh! You've lost your memory, Mr. O'Malley . . . Look in your pockets . . . Haven't you got a driver's license or a draft card or something . . .
Let me see . . . A rabbit's foot . . . A memo of some sort—"Bramble Bug—Aqueduct—to win—$2" . . . Some slugs . . .
. . . A Landon button . . . "This card and one dollar entitles bearer to a beer and beefsteak dinner at Paddy's Bar and Grill"—Never heard of the place . . . A sweepstake ticket . . . A curious book—"Fairy Godfather's Handy Pocket Guide"—What am I doing with that?
It's yours! You're my Fairy Godfather . . .
So I'm a Fairy Godfather! Little boy, I couldn't be any more amazed if suddenly I learned I could FLY!
Of course you can fly, Mr. O'Malley . . .
. . . That's why you have wings.
Wings?
Cushlamochree! I've got wings!
Maybe if you just fly once you'll get your memory back.
Funny I can't remember having done this before.
That's it, Mr. O'Malley.
Just fly . . . Like this?

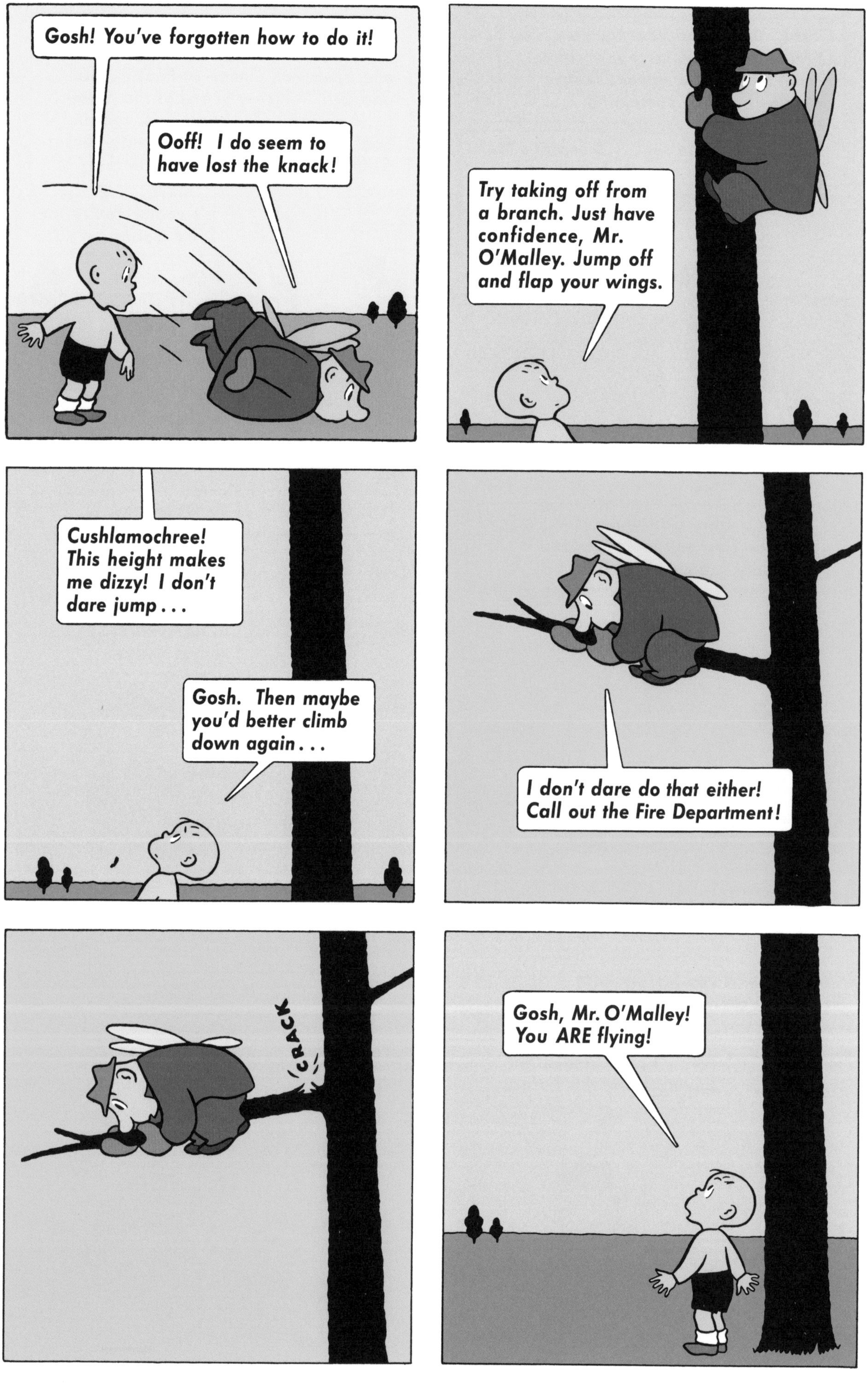

Gosh! You've forgotten how to do it!
Ooff! I do seem to have lost the knack!
Try taking off from a branch. Just have confidence, Mr. O'Malley. Jump off and flap your wings.
Cushlamochree! This height makes me dizzy! I don't dare jump . . .
Gosh. Then maybe you'd better climb down again . . .
I don't dare do that either! Call out the Fire Department!
CRACK
Gosh, Mr. O'Malley! You ARE flying!

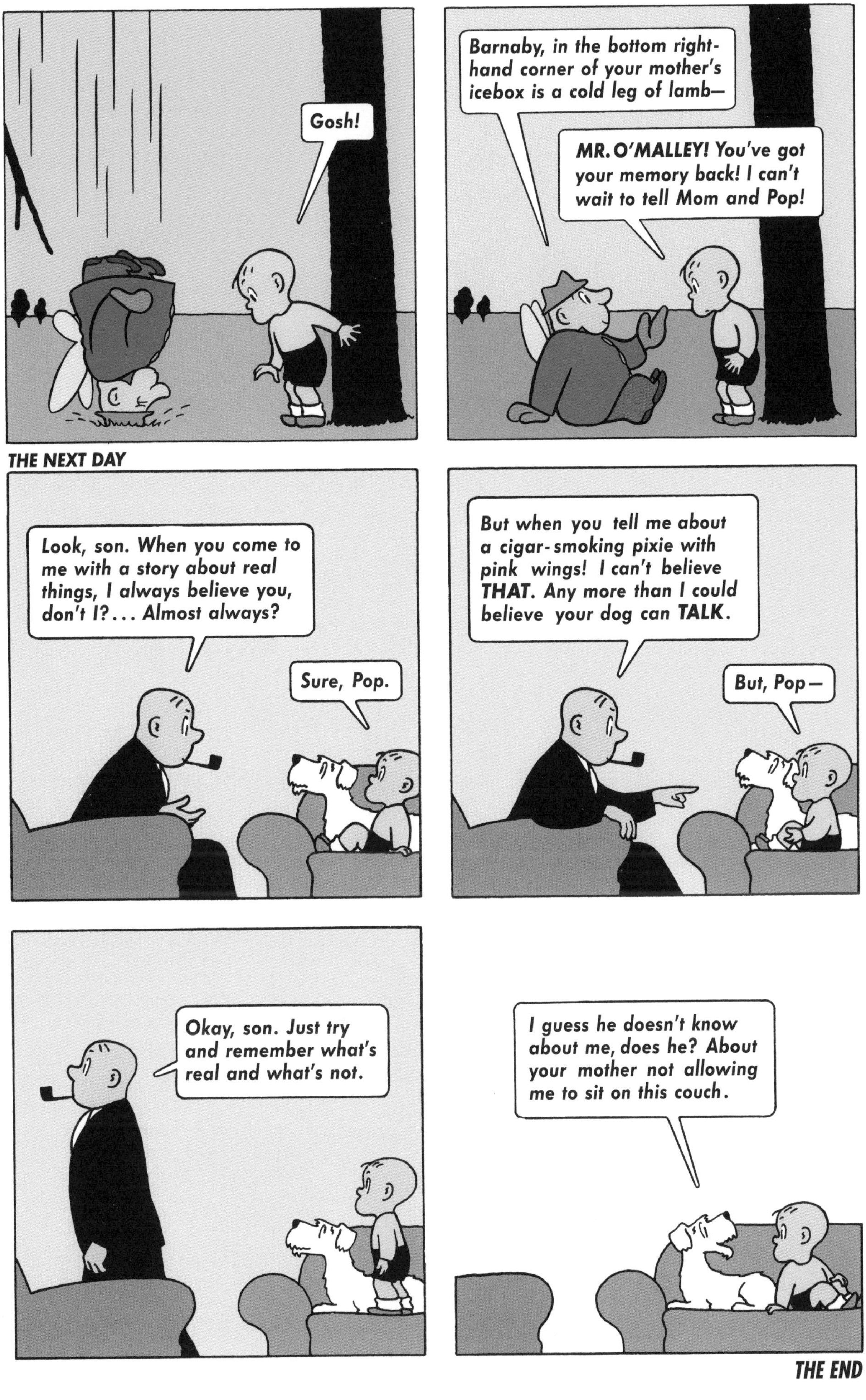
Gosh!
Barnaby, in the bottom right-hand corner of your mother's icebox is a cold leg of lamb—
MR. O'MALLEY! You've got your memory back! I can't wait to tell Mom and Pop!
THE NEXT DAY
Look, son. When you come to me with a story about real things, I always believe you, don't I?... Almost always?
Sure, Pop.
But when you tell me about a cigar-smoking pixie with pink wings! I can't believe THAT. Any more than I could believe your dog can TALK.
But, Pop—
Okay, son. Just try and remember what's real and what's not.
I guess he doesn't know about me, does he? About your mother not allowing me to sit on this couch.
THE END

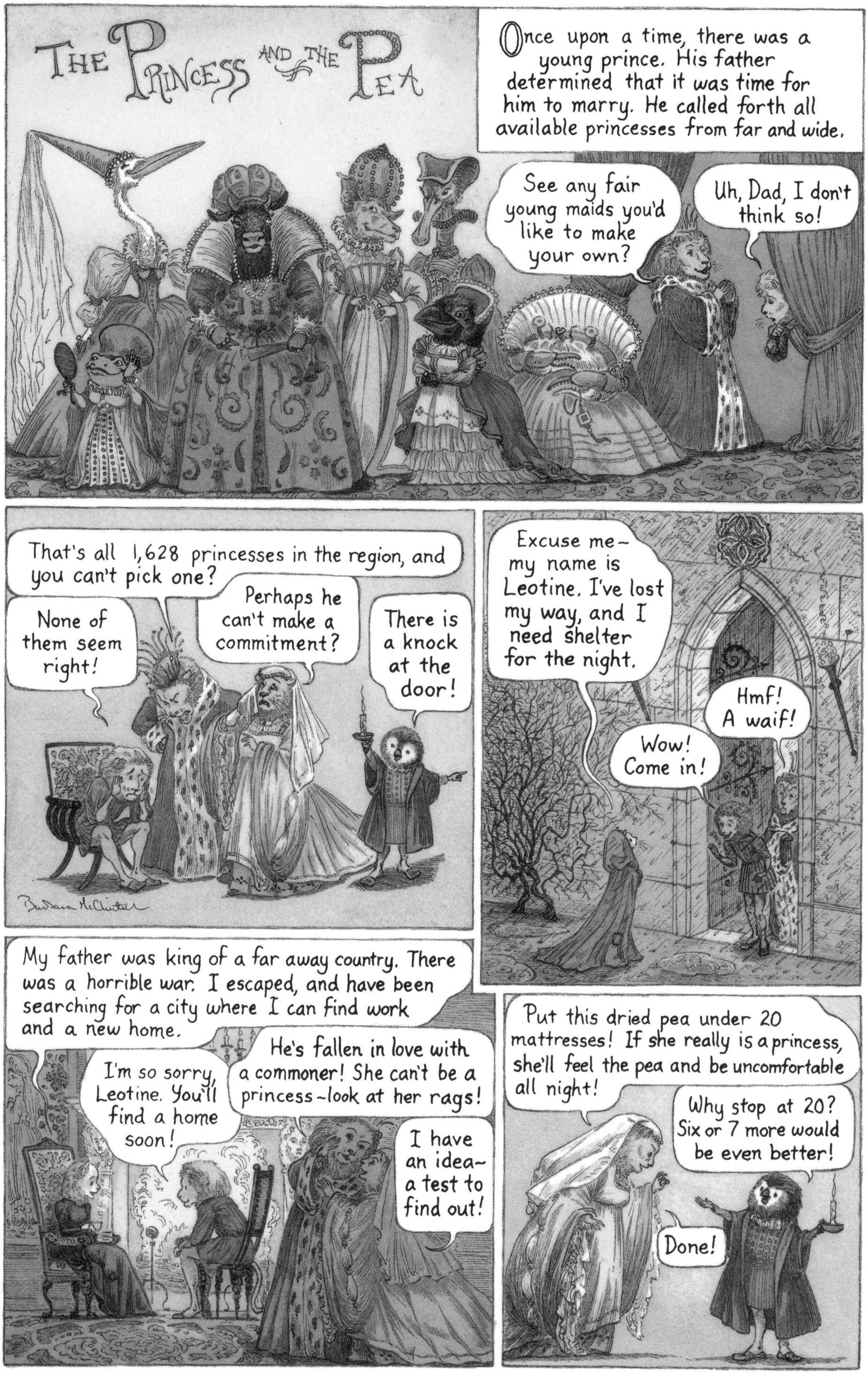
THE PRINCESS AND THE PEA
Once upon a time, there was a young prince. His father determined that it was time for him to marry. He called forth all available princesses from far and wide.
See any fair young maids you'd like to make your own?
Uh, Dad, I don't think so!
That's all 1,628 princesses in the region, and you can't pick one?
None of them seem right!
Perhaps he can't make a commitment?
There is a knock at the door!
Excuse me– my name is Leotine. I've lost my way, and I need shelter for the night.
Hmf! A waif!
Wow! Come in!
My father was king of a far away country. There was a horrible war. I escaped, and have been searching for a city where I can find work and a new home.
I'm so sorry, Leotine. You'll find a home soon!
He's fallen in love with a commoner! She can't be a princess–look at her rags!
I have an idea– a test to find out!
Put this dried pea under 20 mattresses! If she really is a princess, she'll feel the pea and be uncomfortable all night!
Why stop at 20? Six or 7 more would be even better!
Done!

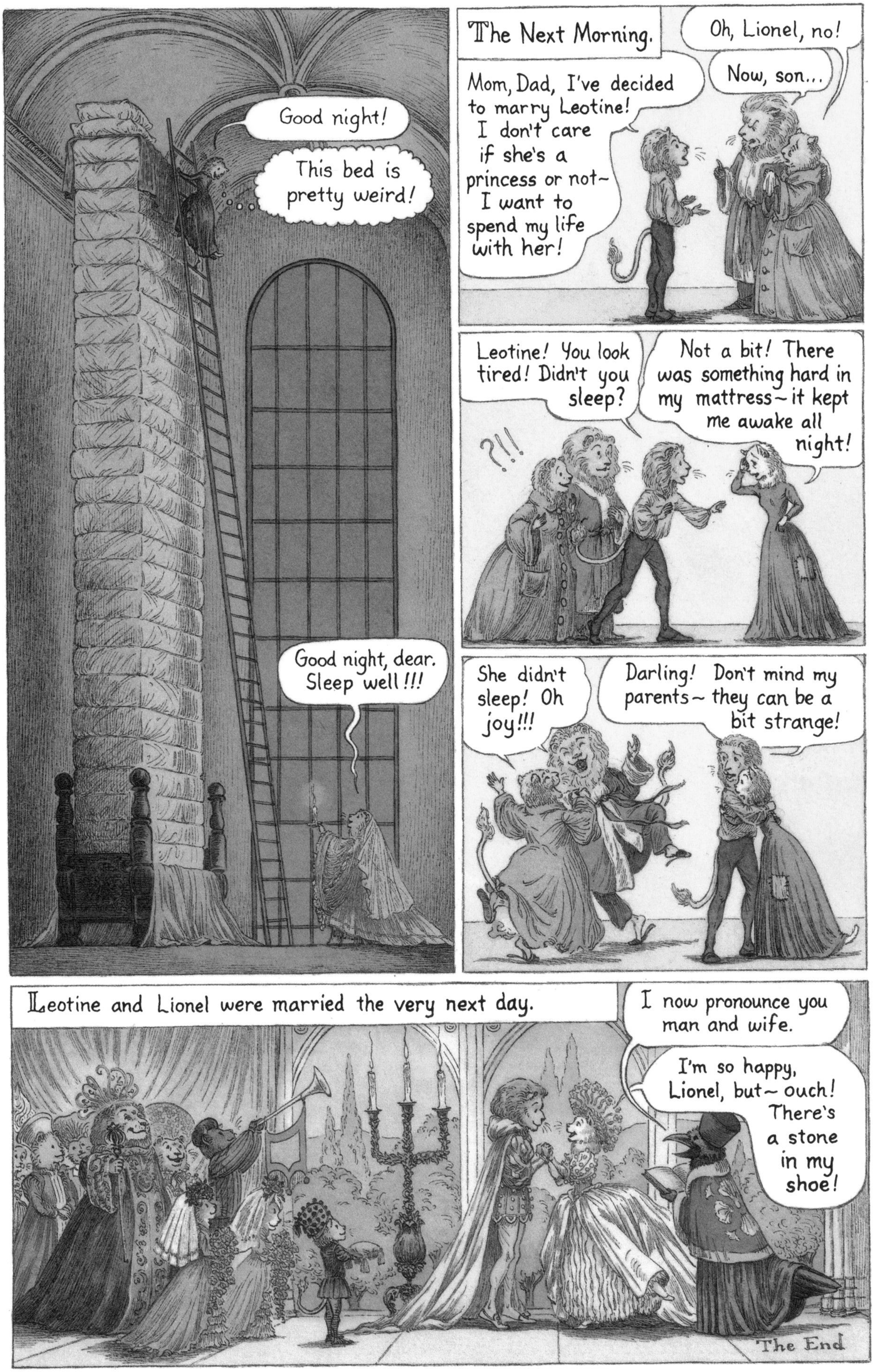
Good night!
This bed is pretty weird!
Good night, dear. Sleep well!!!
The Next Morning.
Mom, Dad, I've decided to marry Leotine! I don't care if she's a princess or not~ I want to spend my life with her!
Oh, Lionel, no!
Now, son...
Leotine! You look tired! Didn't you sleep?
Not a bit! There was something hard in my mattress~ it kept me awake all night!
?!!
She didn't sleep! Oh joy!!!
Darling! Don't mind my parents~ they can be a bit strange!
Leotine and Lionel were married the very next day.
I now pronounce you man and wife.
I'm so happy, Lionel, but~ ouch! There's a stone in my shoe!
The End

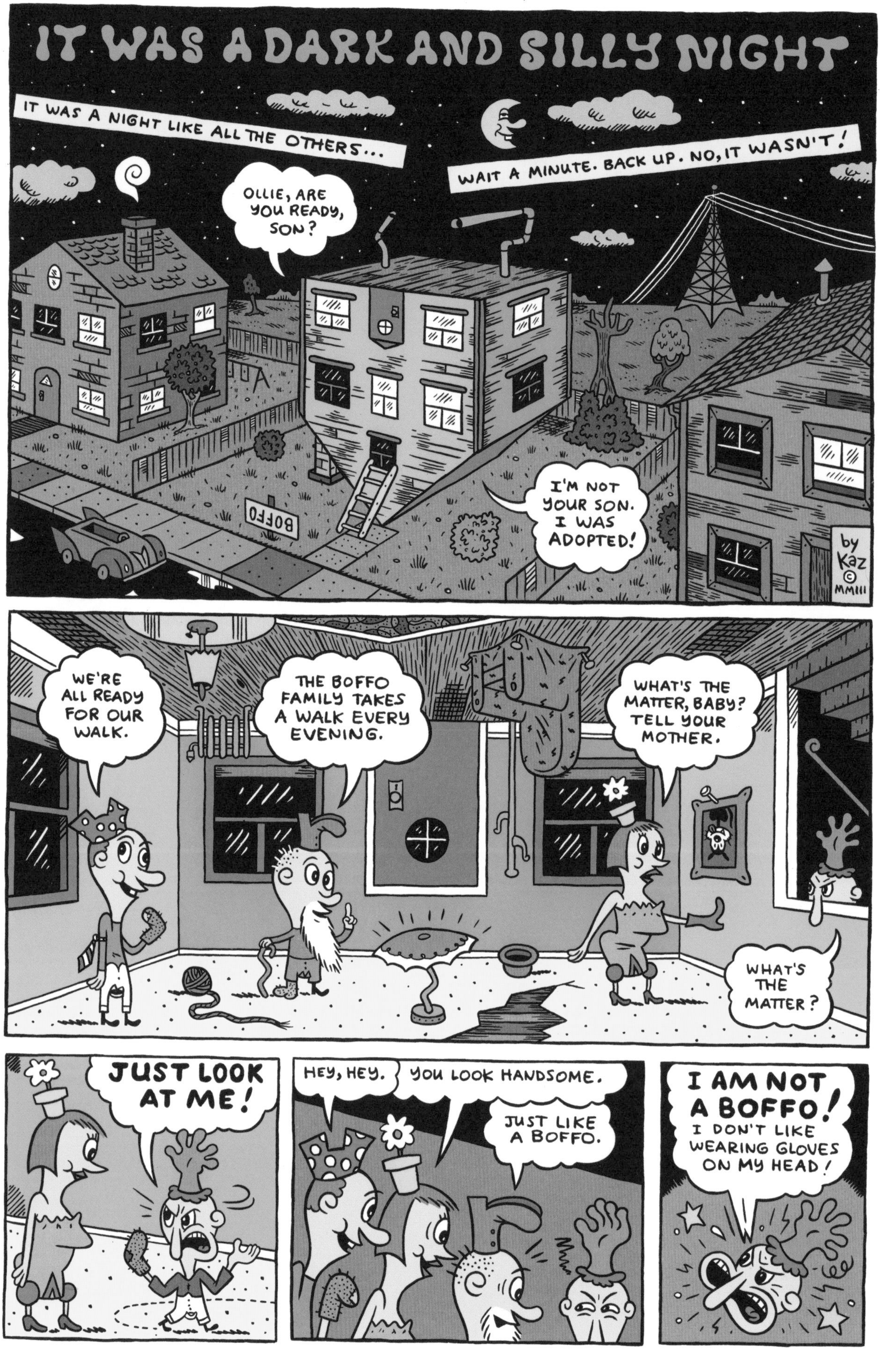
IT WAS A DARK AND SILLY NIGHT
IT WAS A NIGHT LIKE ALL THE OTHERS...
WAIT A MINUTE. BACK UP. NO, IT WASN'T!
OLLIE, ARE YOU READY, SON?
I'M NOT YOUR SON. I WAS ADOPTED!
by Kaz © MMIII
WE'RE ALL READY FOR OUR WALK.
THE BOFFO FAMILY TAKES A WALK EVERY EVENING.
WHAT'S THE MATTER, BABY? TELL YOUR MOTHER.
WHAT'S THE MATTER?
JUST LOOK AT ME!
HEY, HEY.
YOU LOOK HANDSOME.
JUST LIKE A BOFFO.
I AM NOT A BOFFO! I DON'T LIKE WEARING GLOVES ON MY HEAD!

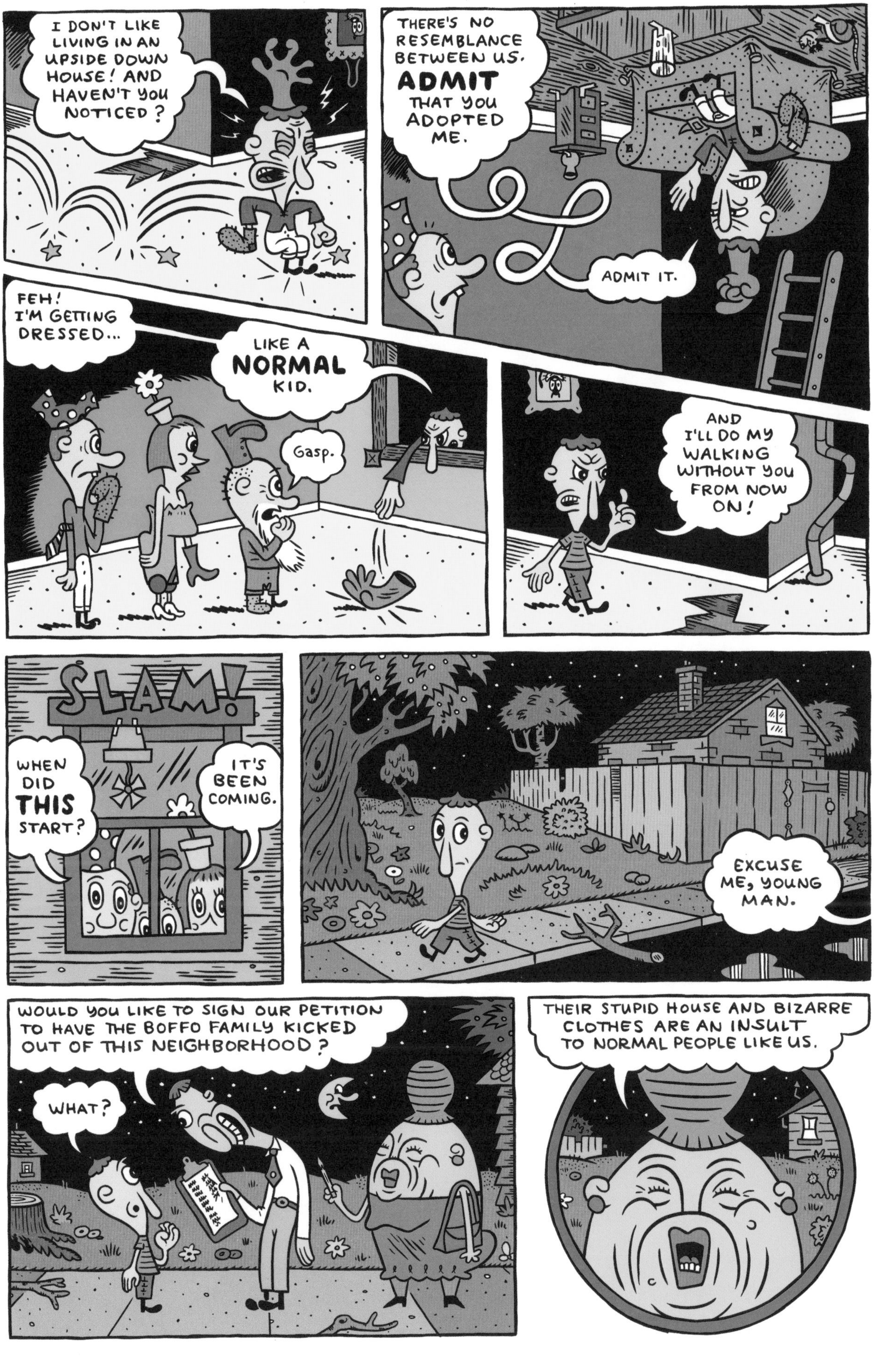
I DON'T LIKE LIVING IN AN UPSIDE DOWN HOUSE! AND HAVEN'T YOU NOTICED?
THERE'S NO RESEMBLANCE BETWEEN US. ADMIT THAT YOU ADOPTED ME.
ADMIT IT.
FEH! I'M GETTING DRESSED...
LIKE A NORMAL KID.
Gasp.
AND I'LL DO MY WALKING WITHOUT YOU FROM NOW ON!
SLAM!
WHEN DID THIS START?
IT'S BEEN COMING.
EXCUSE ME, YOUNG MAN.
WOULD YOU LIKE TO SIGN OUR PETITION TO HAVE THE BOFFO FAMILY KICKED OUT OF THIS NEIGHBORHOOD?
WHAT?
THEIR STUPID HOUSE AND BIZARRE CLOTHES ARE AN INSULT TO NORMAL PEOPLE LIKE US.

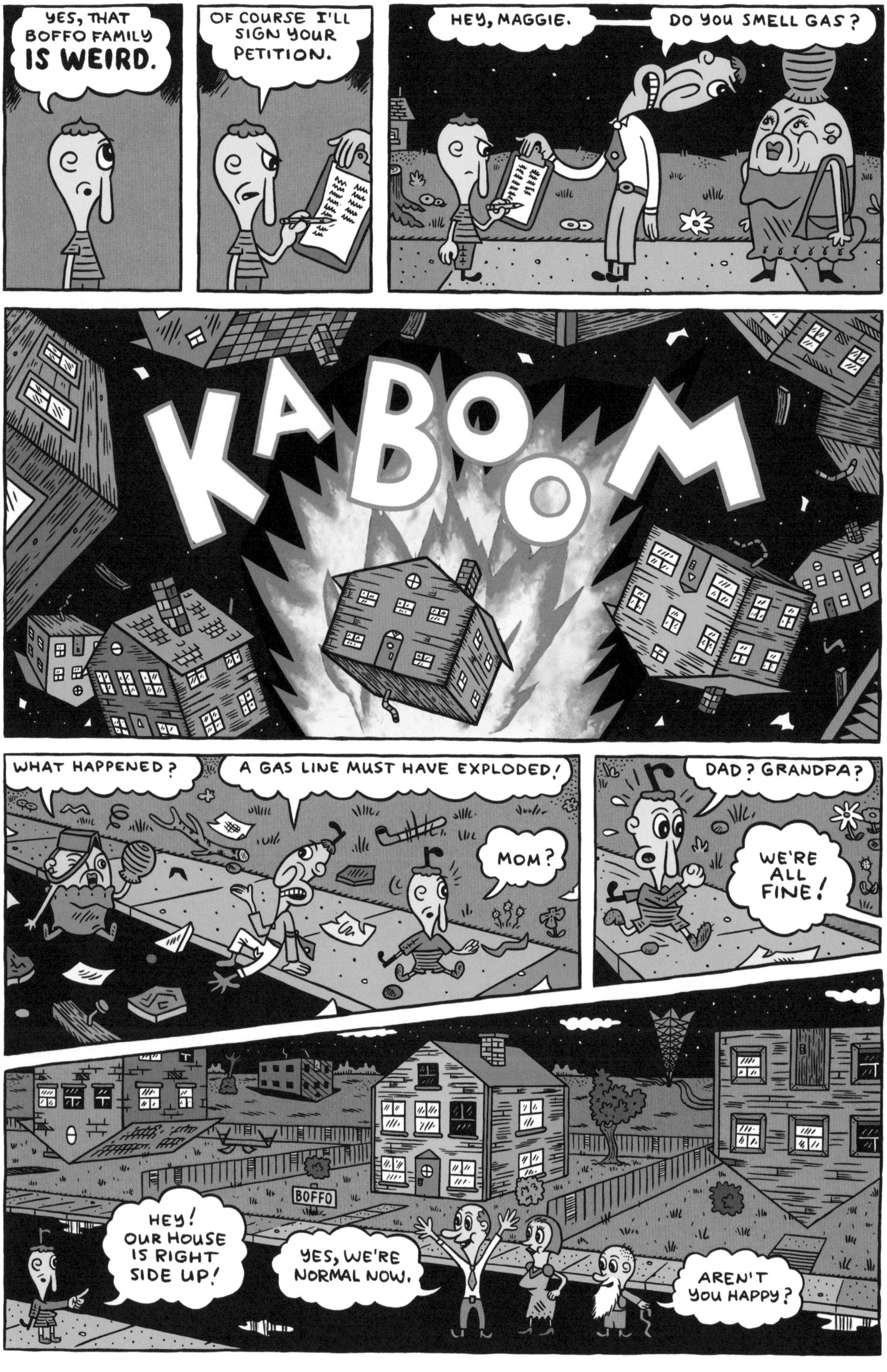
YES, THAT BOFFO FAMILY IS WEIRD.
OF COURSE I'LL SIGN YOUR PETITION.
HEY, MAGGIE.
DO YOU SMELL GAS?
KABOOM
WHAT HAPPENED?
A GAS LINE MUST HAVE EXPLODED!
MOM?
DAD? GRANDPA?
WE'RE ALL FINE!
BOFFO
HEY! OUR HOUSE IS RIGHT SIDE UP!
YES, WE'RE NORMAL NOW.
AREN'T YOU HAPPY?

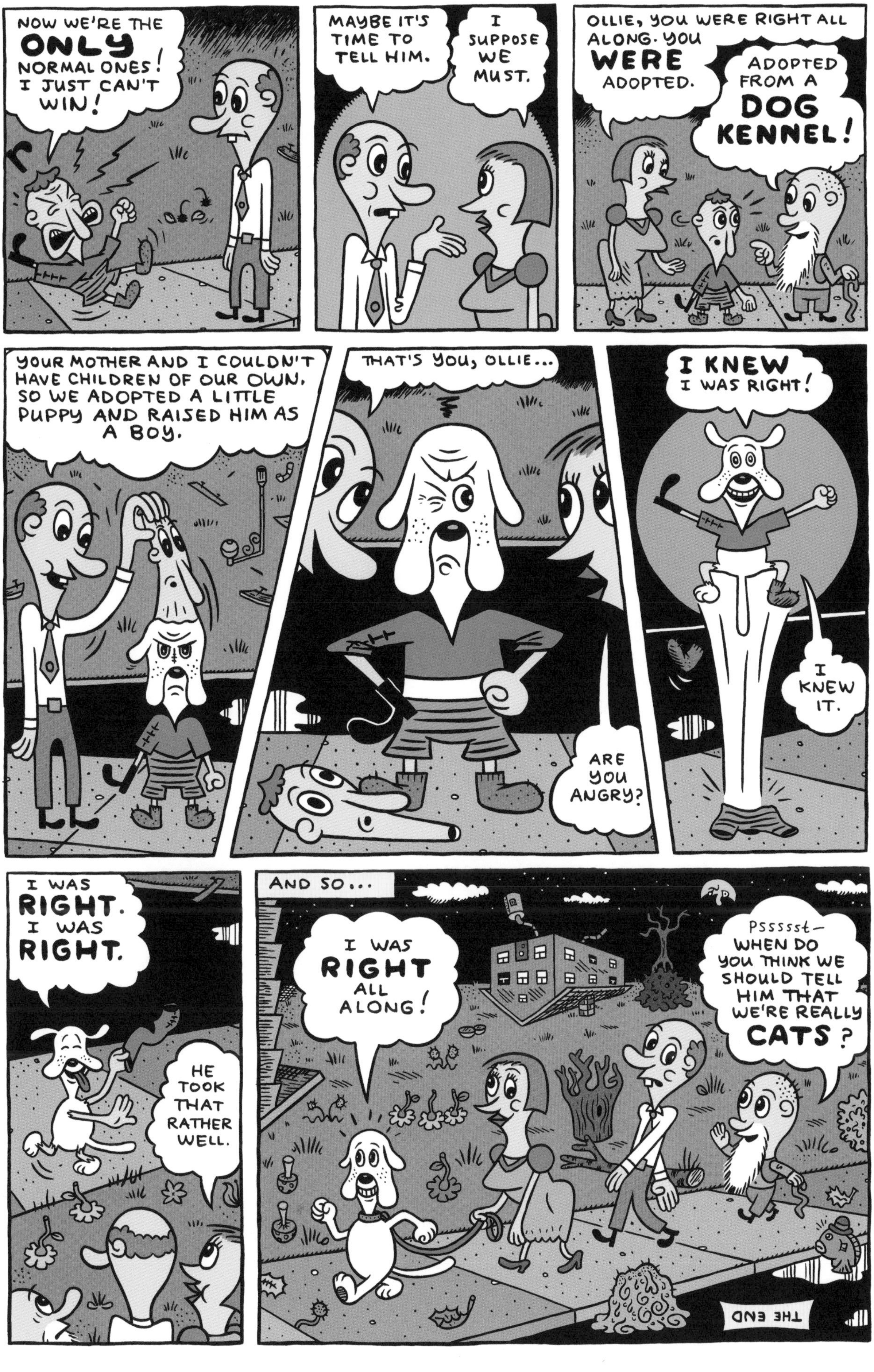
NOW WE'RE THE ONLY NORMAL ONES! I JUST CAN'T WIN!
MAYBE IT'S TIME TO TELL HIM.
I SUPPOSE WE MUST.
OLLIE, YOU WERE RIGHT ALL ALONG. YOU WERE ADOPTED.
ADOPTED FROM A DOG KENNEL!
YOUR MOTHER AND I COULDN'T HAVE CHILDREN OF OUR OWN, SO WE ADOPTED A LITTLE PUPPY AND RAISED HIM AS A BOY.
THAT'S YOU, OLLIE...
ARE YOU ANGRY?
I KNEW I WAS RIGHT!
I KNEW IT.
I WAS RIGHT. I WAS RIGHT.
HE TOOK THAT RATHER WELL.
AND SO...
I WAS RIGHT ALL ALONG!
Psssst— WHEN DO YOU THINK WE SHOULD TELL HIM THAT WE'RE REALLY CATS?
THE END

barbara mcclintock

TEDDY BEARS' PICNIC

These Teddy bears picnic at midnight. "What's the difference?" they ask. Well, there are twelve. Can you find them?

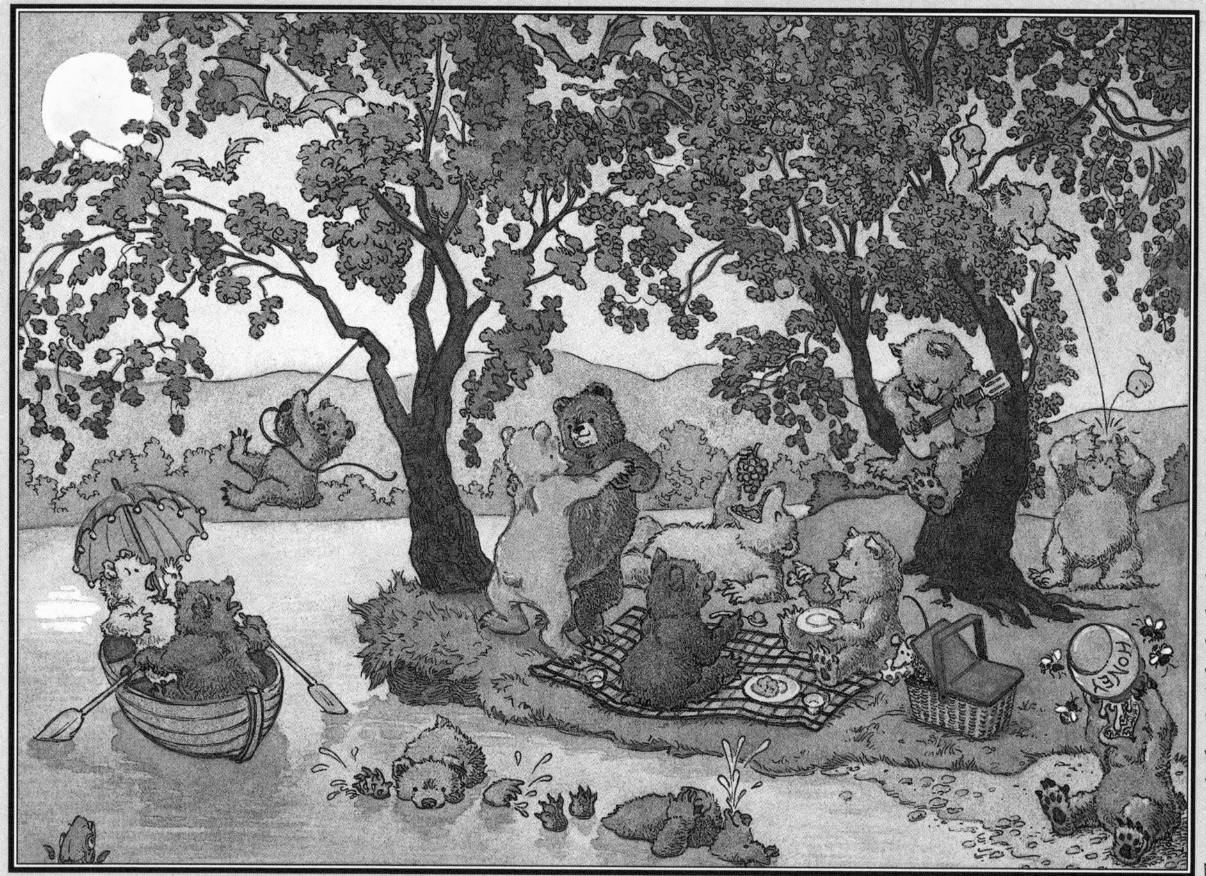
HONEY

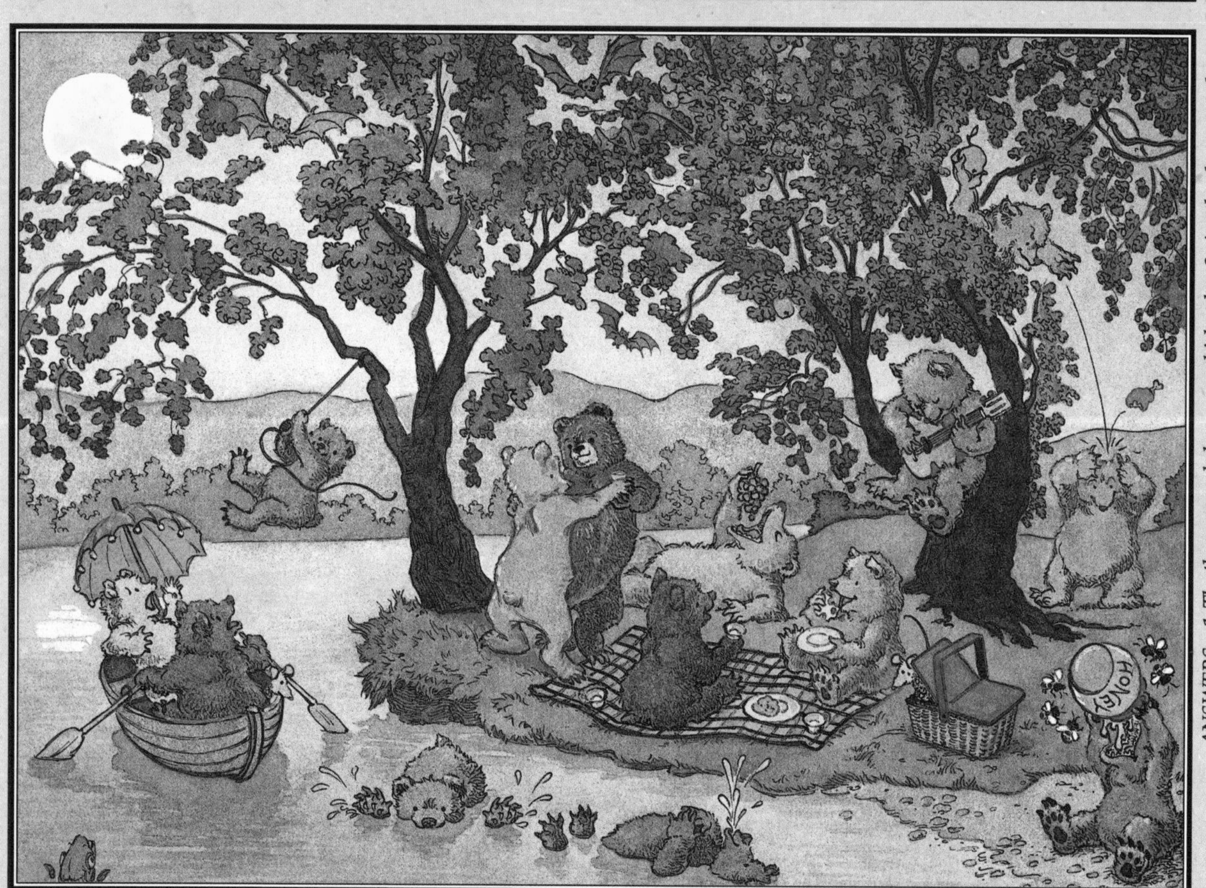
HONEY

ANSWERS: 1. The thrown apple became a chicken leg. 2. Another bee wants honey. 3. The mouse in the picnic basket lost her cheese. 4. A brown bear is eating her cheese. 5. A bear sitting on the blanket has a cup of water. 6. The dancing bears are sharing a drink. 7. The rowboat has a stowaway mouse. 8. A bat near the sun has disappeared. 9. The umbrella lost some tassels. 10. The swimming gray bear's left paw was changed. 11. A bat has appeared above the dancing bears. 12. One more apple has grown in the tree.

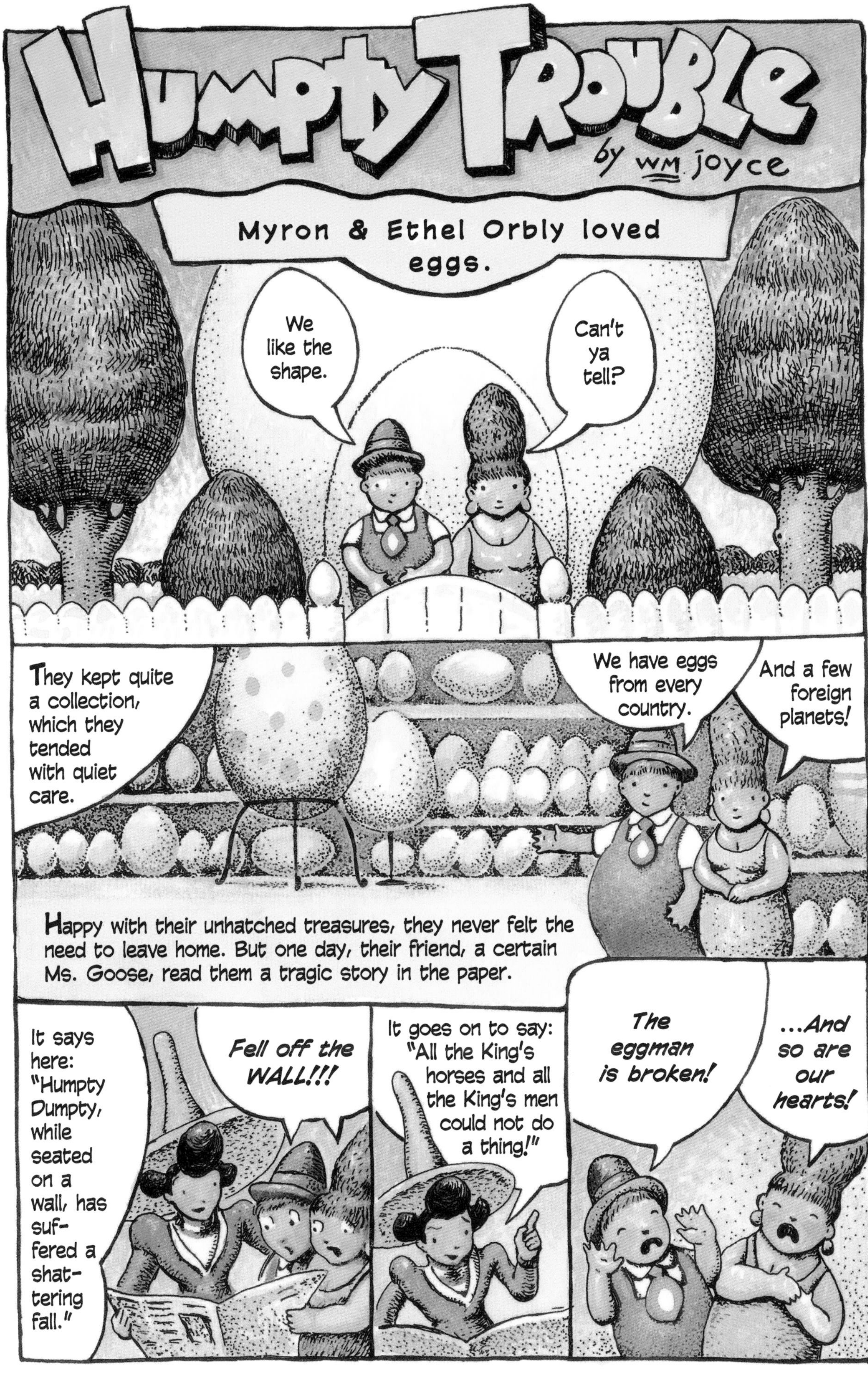
HUMPTY TROUBLE
by WM. joyce
Myron & Ethel Orbly loved eggs.
We like the shape.
Can't ya tell?
They kept quite a collection, which they tended with quiet care.
We have eggs from every country.
And a few foreign planets!
Happy with their unhatched treasures, they never felt the need to leave home. But one day, their friend, a certain Ms. Goose, read them a tragic story in the paper.
It says here: "Humpty Dumpty, while seated on a wall, has suffered a shattering fall."
Fell off the WALL!!!
It goes on to say: "All the King's horses and all the King's men could not do a thing!"
The eggman is broken!
...And so are our hearts!

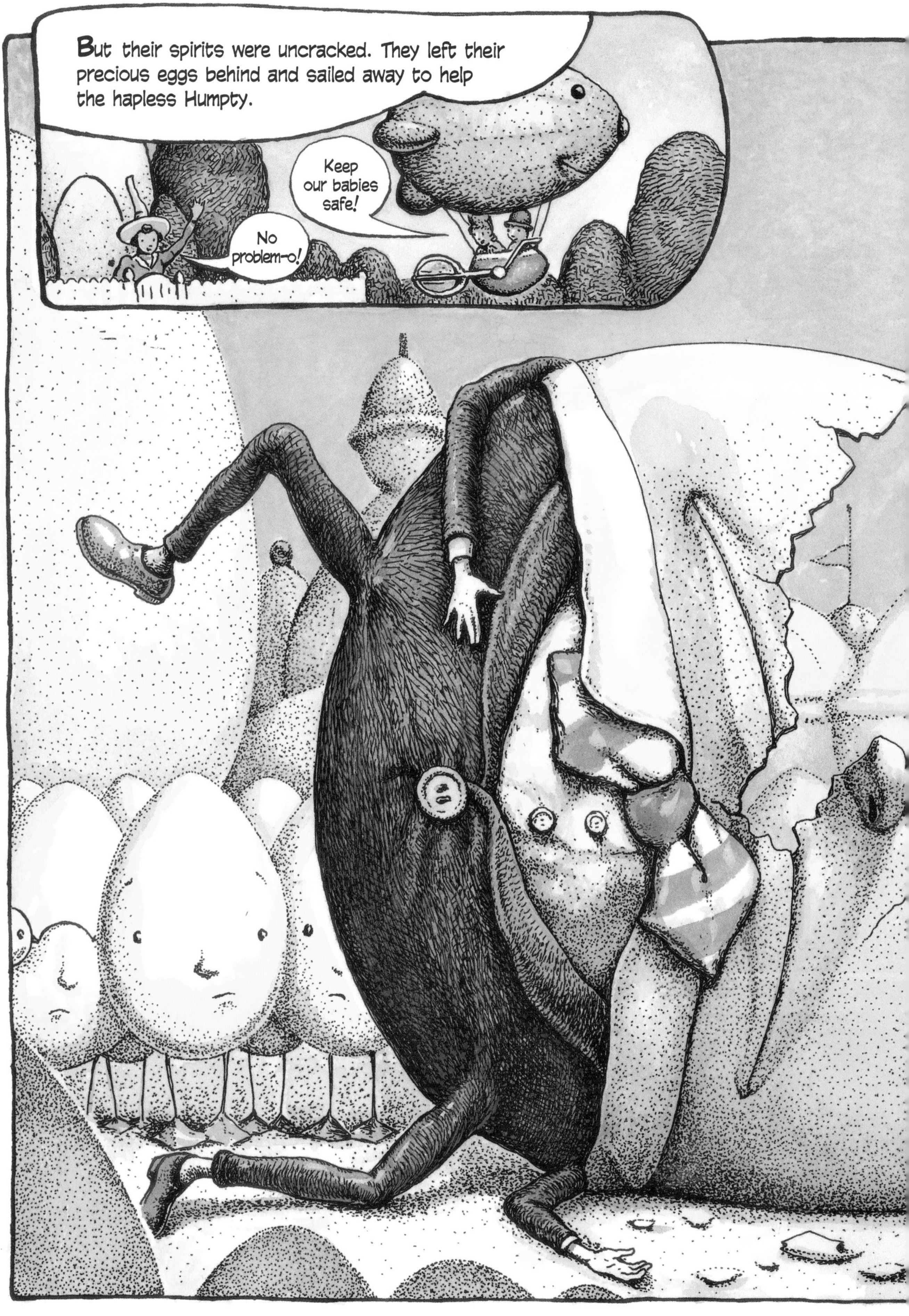
But their spirits were uncracked. They left their precious eggs behind and sailed away to help the hapless Humpty.
Keep our babies safe!
No problem-o!

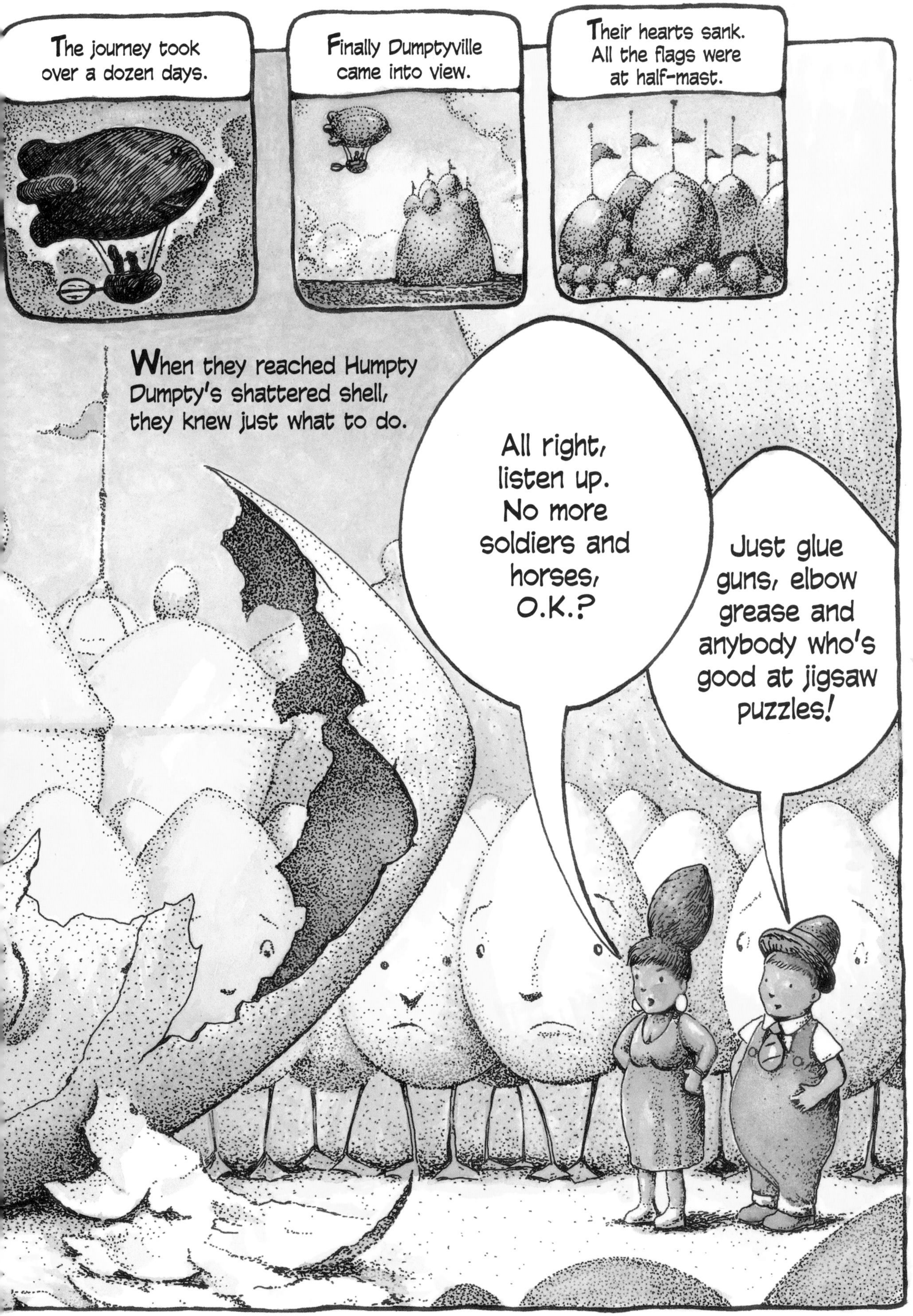
The journey took over a dozen days.
Finally Dumptyville came into view.
Their hearts sank. All the flags were at half-mast.
When they reached Humpty Dumpty's shattered shell, they knew just what to do.
All right, listen up. No more soldiers and horses, O.K.?
Just glue guns, elbow grease and anybody who's good at jigsaw puzzles!

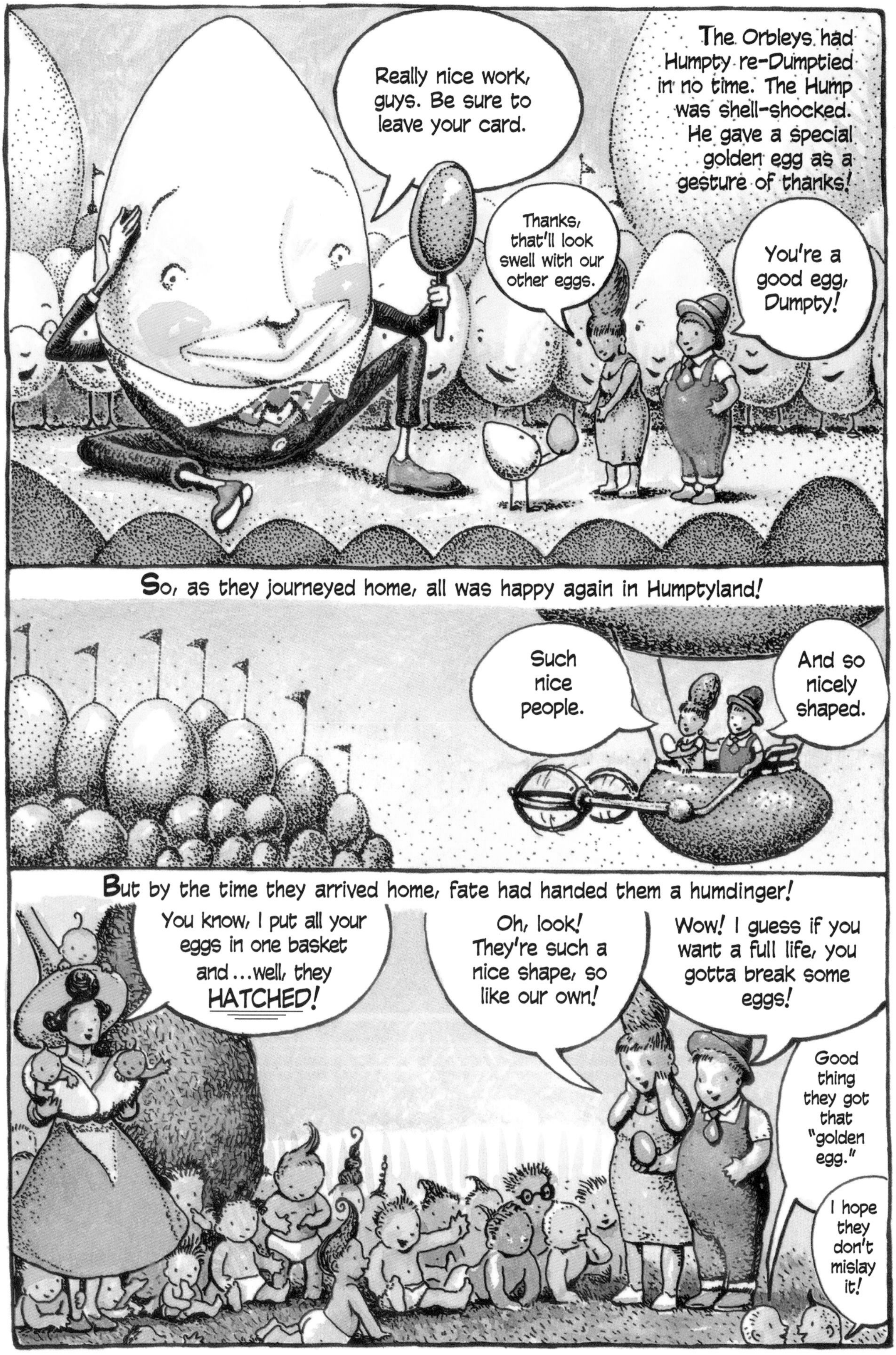
Really nice work, guys. Be sure to leave your card.
The Orbleys had Humpty re-Dumptied in no time. The Hump was shell-shocked. He gave a special golden egg as a gesture of thanks!
Thanks, that'll look swell with our other eggs.
You're a good egg, Dumpty!
So, as they journeyed home, all was happy again in Humptyland!
Such nice people.
And so nicely shaped.
But by the time they arrived home, fate had handed them a humdinger!
You know, I put all your eggs in one basket and ...well, they HATCHED!
Oh, look! They're such a nice shape, so like our own!
Wow! I guess if you want a full life, you gotta break some eggs!
Good thing they got that "golden egg."
I hope they don't mislay it!

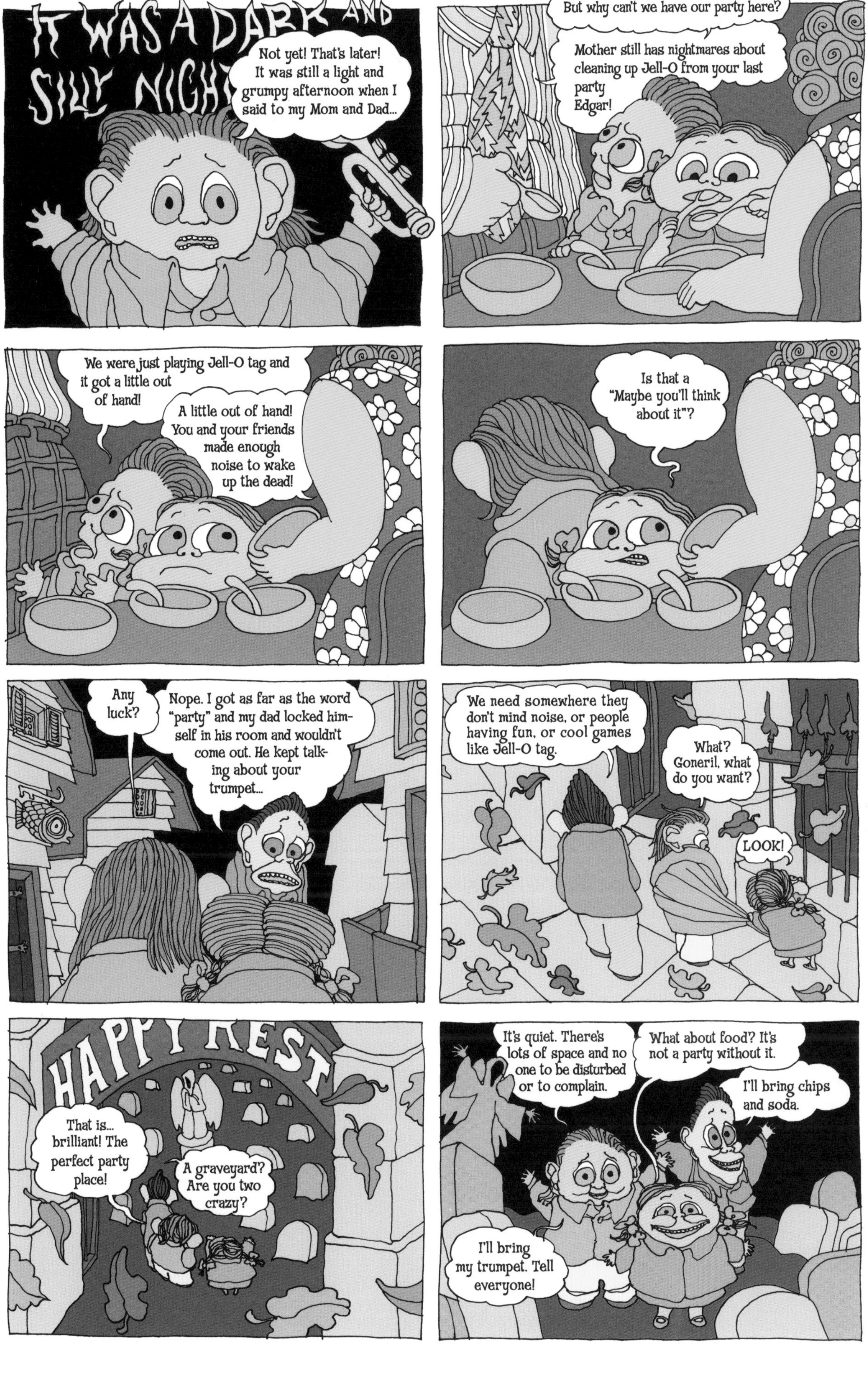
IT WAS A DARK AND SILLY NIGHT
Not yet! That's later! It was still a light and grumpy afternoon when I said to my Mom and Dad...
But why can't we have our party here?
Mother still has nightmares about cleaning up Jell-O from your last party Edgar!
We were just playing Jell-O tag and it got a little out of hand!
A little out of hand! You and your friends made enough noise to wake up the dead!
Is that a "Maybe you'll think about it"?
Any luck?
Nope. I got as far as the word "party" and my dad locked himself in his room and wouldn't come out. He kept talking about your trumpet...
We need somewhere they don't mind noise, or people having fun, or cool games like Jell-O tag.
What? Goneril, what do you want?
LOOK!
HAPPY REST
That is... brilliant! The perfect party place!
A graveyard? Are you two crazy?
It's quiet. There's lots of space and no one to be disturbed or to complain.
What about food? It's not a party without it.
I'll bring chips and soda.
I'll bring my trumpet. Tell everyone!

And so...

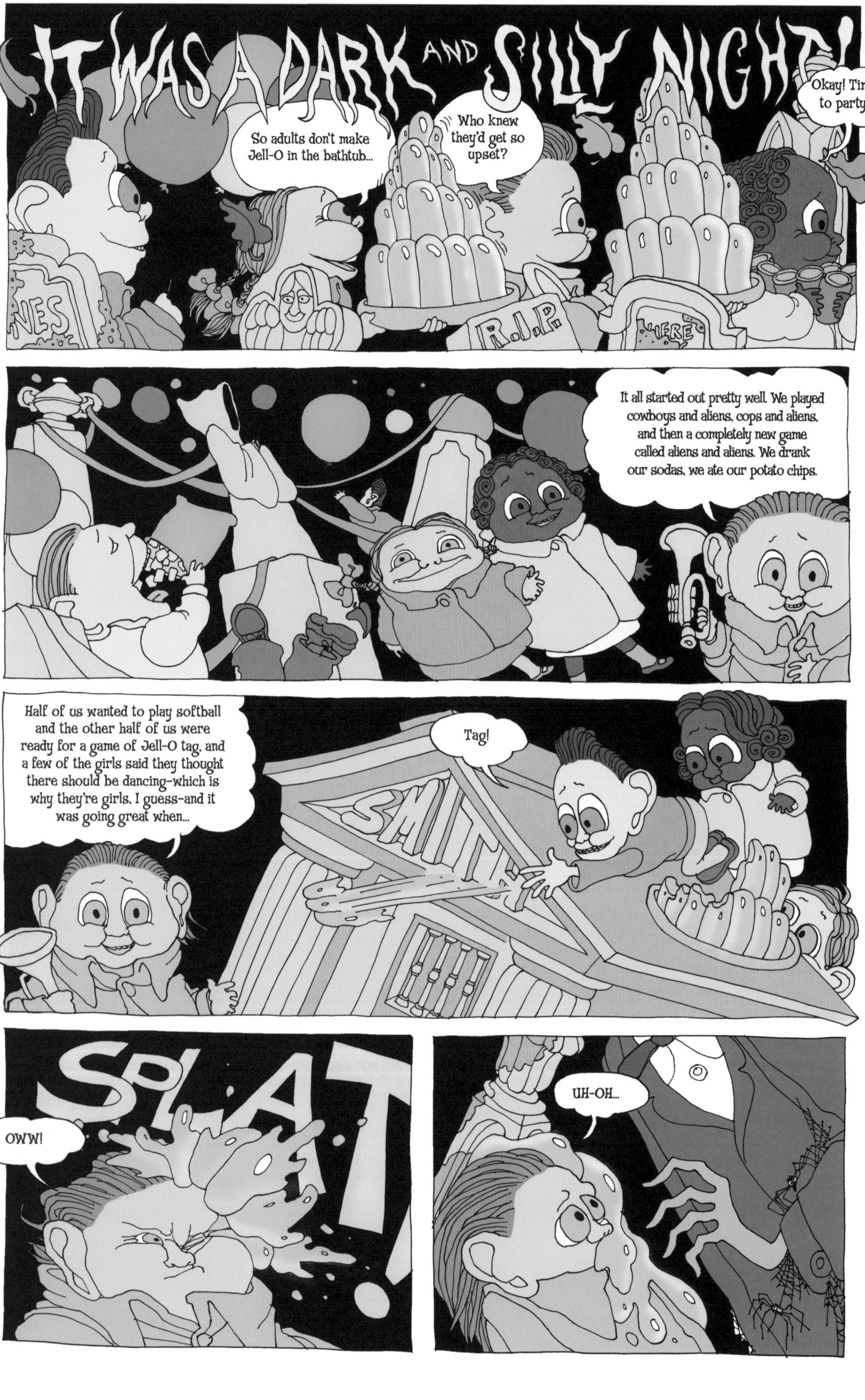
IT WAS A DARK AND SILLY NIGHT!
So adults don't make Jell-O in the bathtub...
Who knew they'd get so upset?
Okay! Time to party!
R.I.P.
It all started out pretty well. We played cowboys and aliens, cops and aliens, and then a completely new game called aliens and aliens. We drank our sodas, we ate our potato chips.
Half of us wanted to play softball and the other half of us were ready for a game of Jell-O tag, and a few of the girls said they thought there should be dancing–which is why they're girls, I guess–and it was going great when...
Tag!
SPLAT!
OWW!
UH-OH...

Then, in a scratchy voice that sounded like no one had used it in a hundred years, one corpse said:

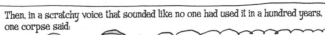

Who...has...the...trumpet?

M-me.

Do... you... know...

ALEXANDER'S RAGTIME BAND?

N-no.

We can hum it!

Well, at this point I'm still pretty scared, but the dead people started humming and I began to play along with my trumpet.

URK! URK! URK!

NNNG!

GNARG!

Pretty soon they were teaching us a lot of cool games like blind corpse's bluff...

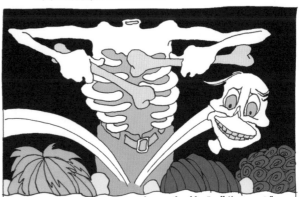

and some games only dead people can play, like "roll the noggin" and "musical ribs"!

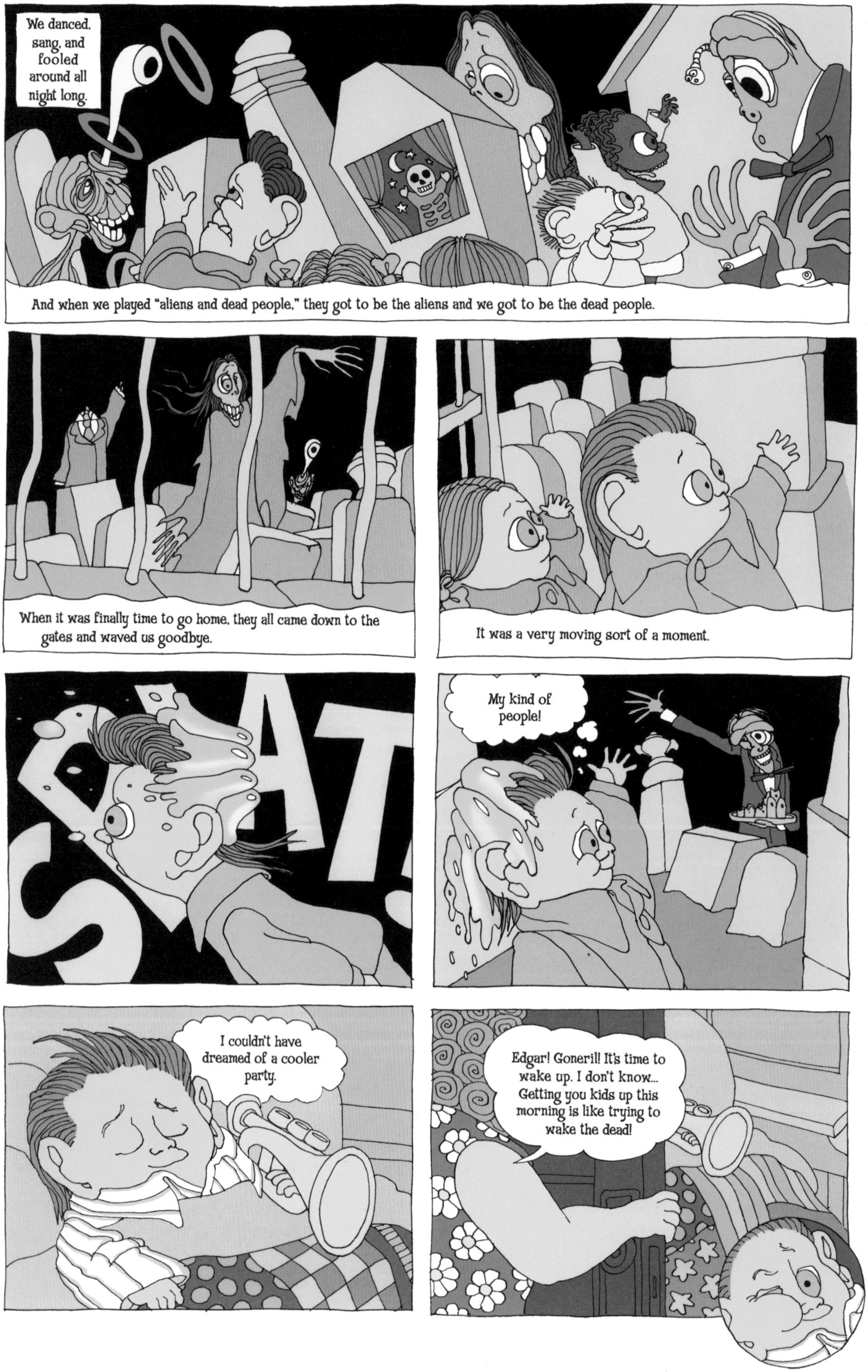
We danced, sang, and fooled around all night long.
And when we played "aliens and dead people," they got to be the aliens and we got to be the dead people.
When it was finally time to go home, they all came down to the gates and waved us goodbye.
It was a very moving sort of a moment.
My kind of people!
I couldn't have dreamed of a cooler party.
Edgar! Goneril! It's time to wake up. I don't know... Getting you kids up this morning is like trying to wake the dead!

THE BAKER'S DAUGHTER

The baker's daughter was a mean soul. She never gave so much as a crumb away.

That will be eight dollars, ladies. How lovely you both look.

Shoo! Clear away from my window! There's nothing for you two here!

?

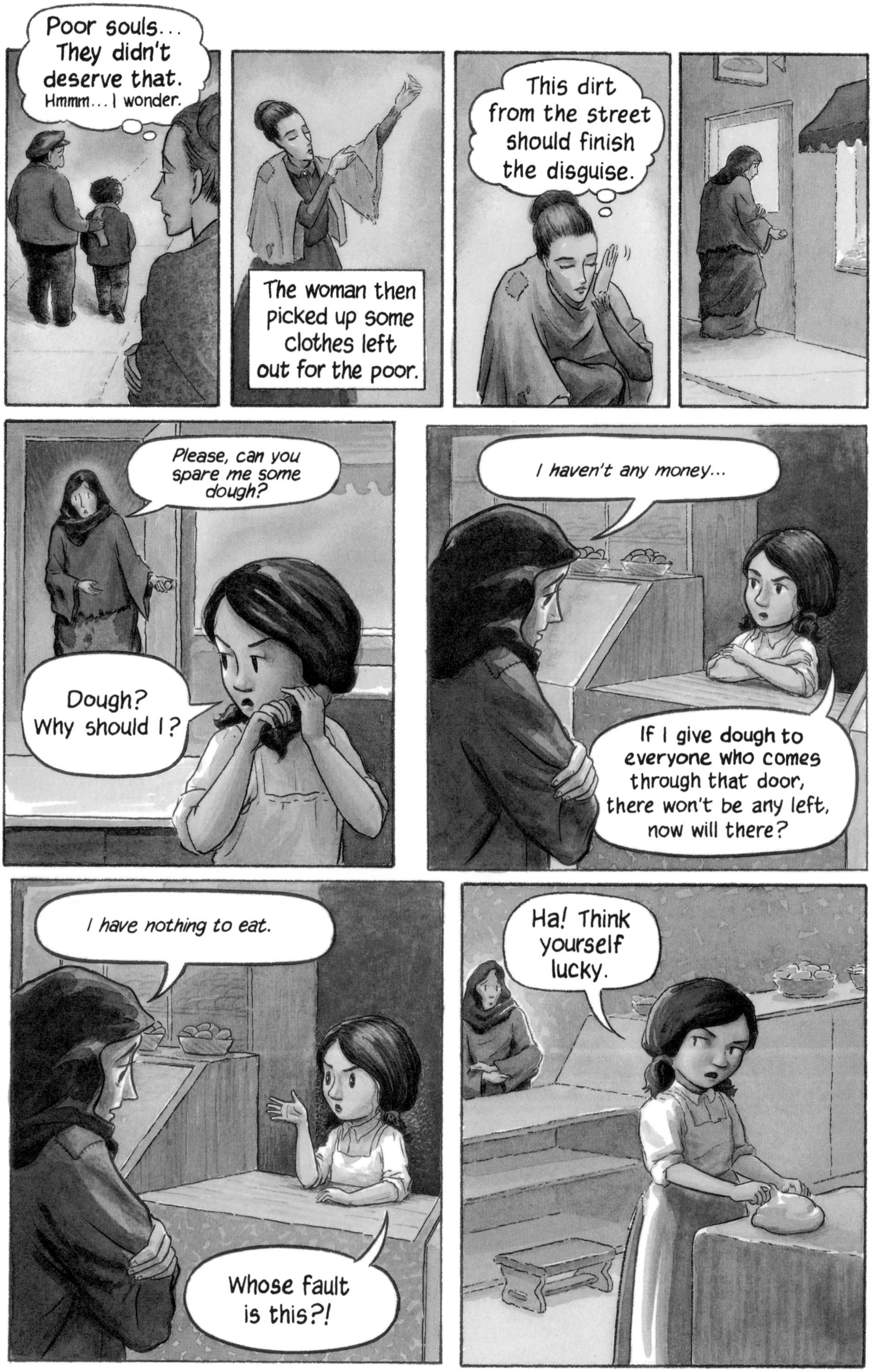
Poor souls... They didn't deserve that. Hmmm... I wonder.
The woman then picked up some clothes left out for the poor.
This dirt from the street should finish the disguise.
Please, can you spare me some dough?
Dough? Why should I?
I haven't any money...
If I give dough to everyone who comes through that door, there won't be any left, now will there?
I have nothing to eat.
Whose fault is this?!
Ha! Think yourself lucky.

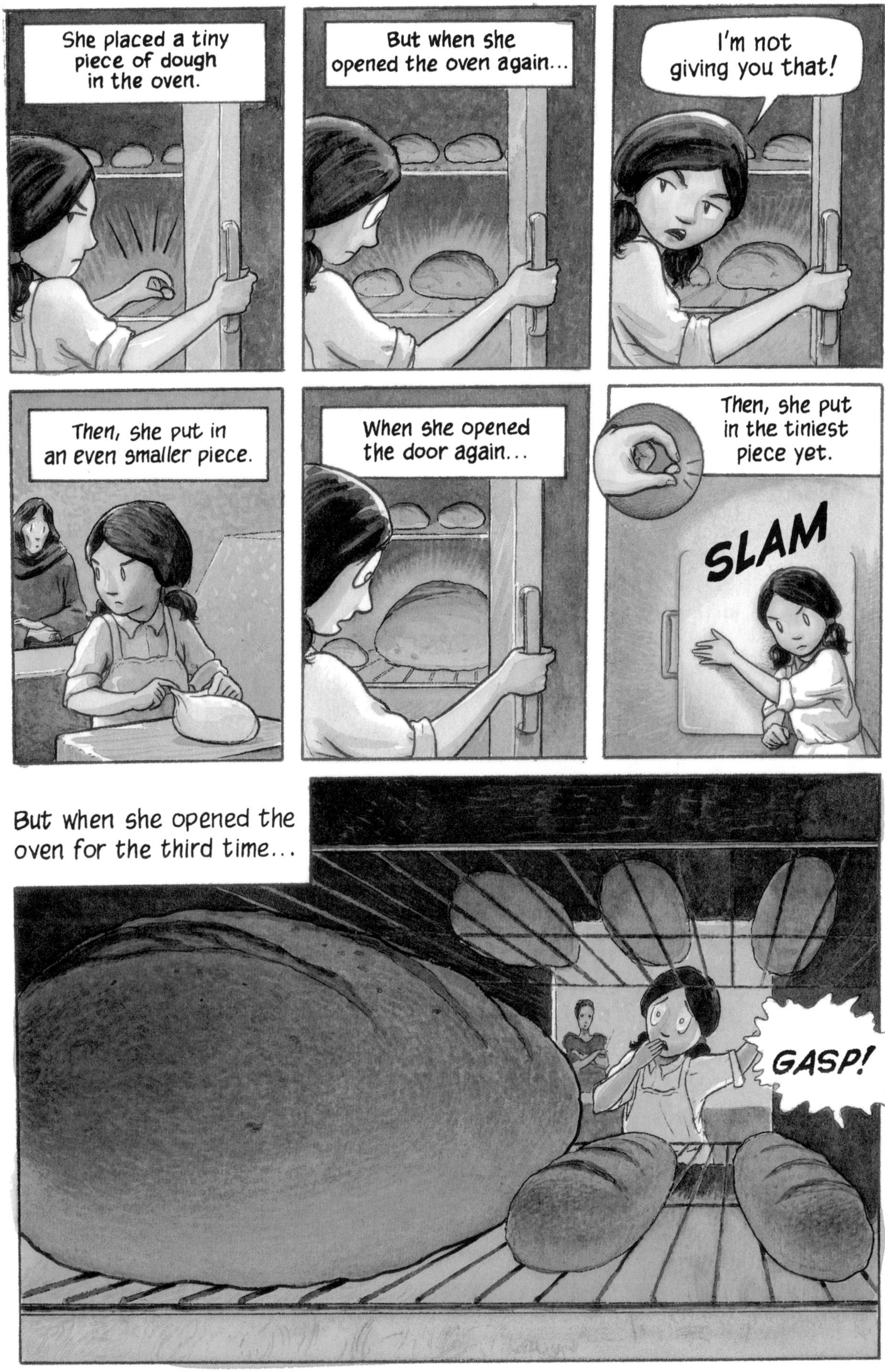
She placed a tiny piece of dough in the oven.
But when she opened the oven again...
I'm not giving you that!
Then, she put in an even smaller piece.
When she opened the door again...
Then, she put in the tiniest piece yet.
SLAM
But when she opened the oven for the third time...
GASP!

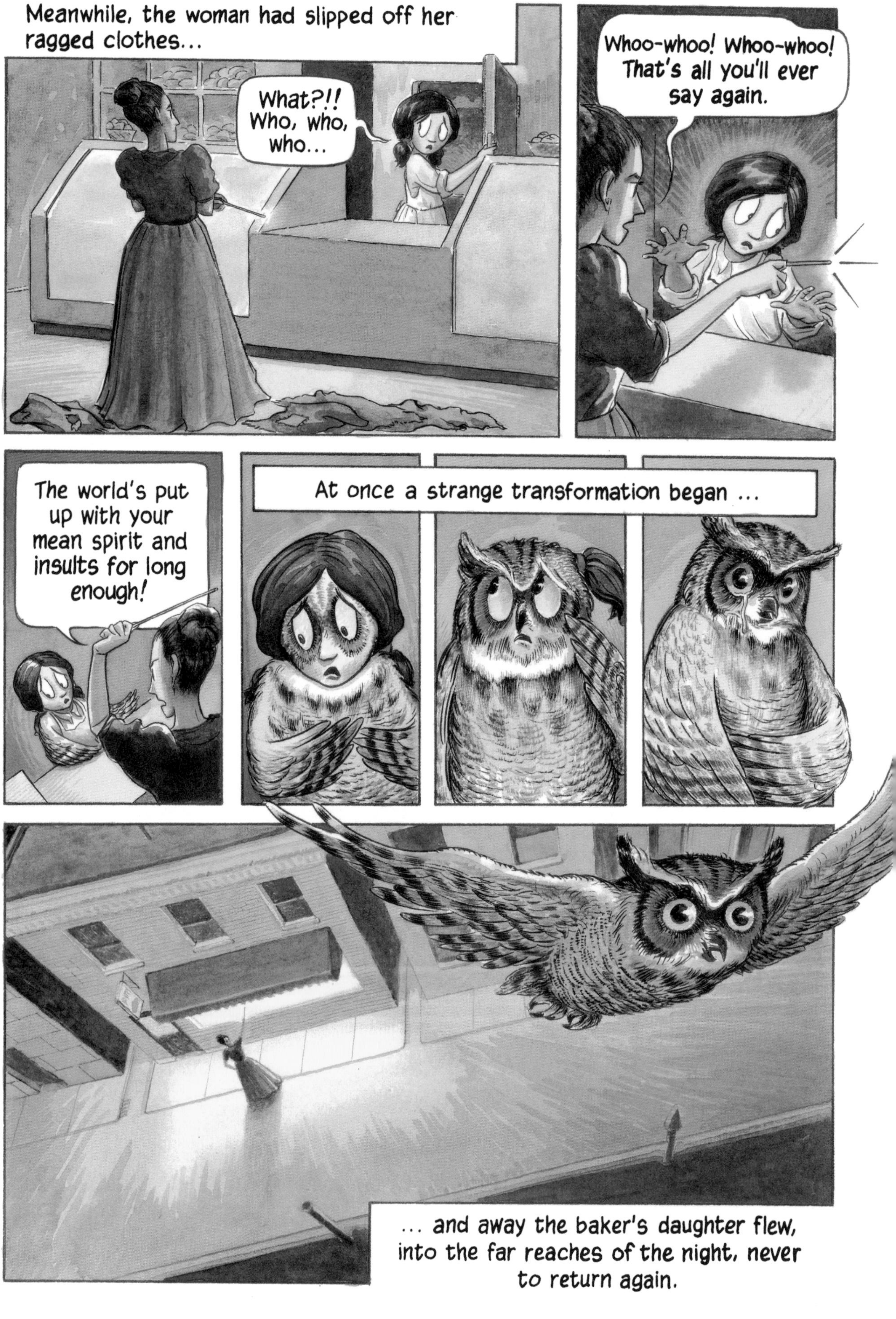
Meanwhile, the woman had slipped off her ragged clothes...
What?!! Who, who, who...
Whoo-whoo! Whoo-whoo! That's all you'll ever say again.
The world's put up with your mean spirit and insults for long enough!
At once a strange transformation began ...
... and away the baker's daughter flew, into the far reaches of the night, never to return again.

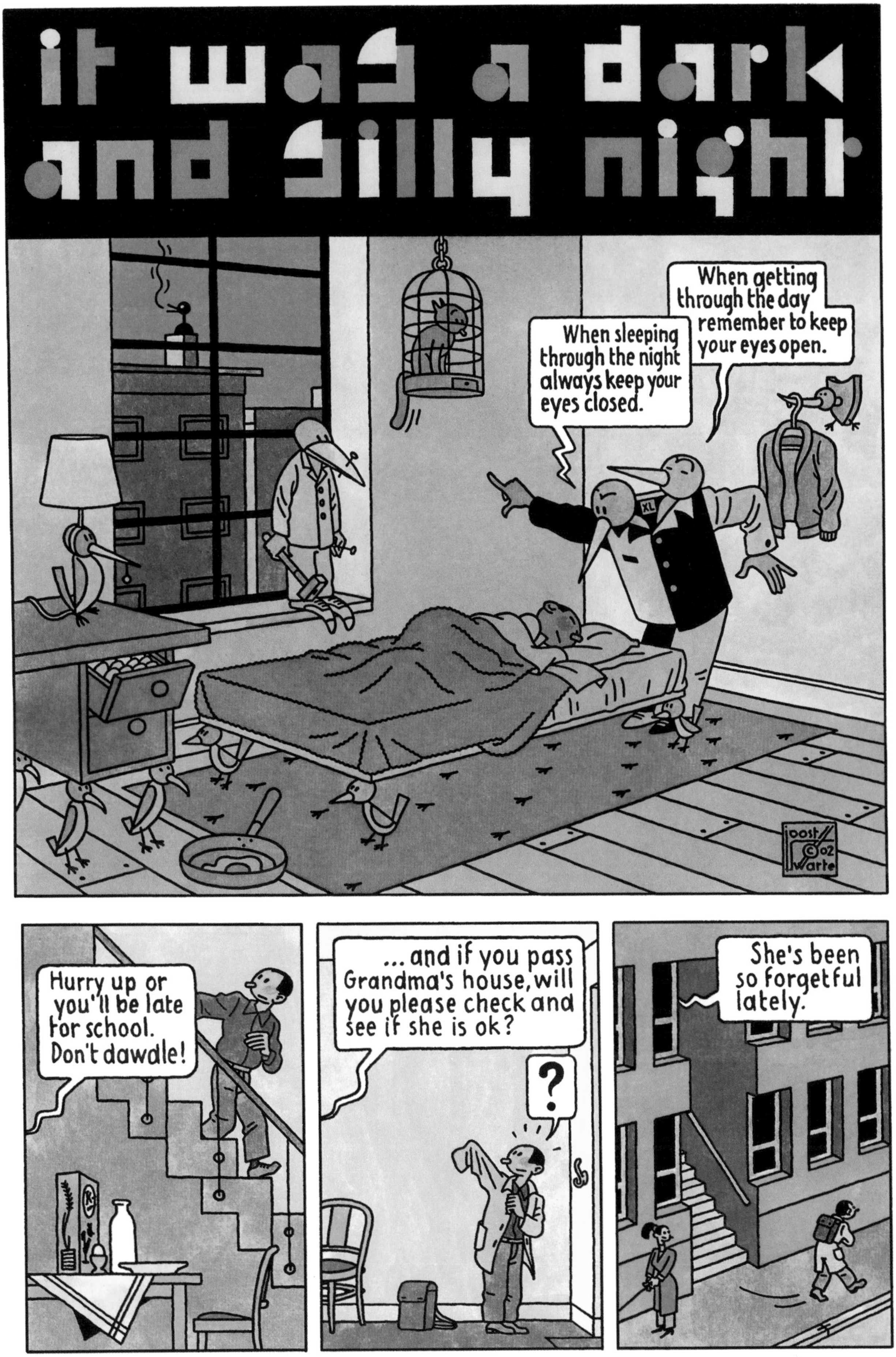
it was a dark and silly night
When sleeping through the night always keep your eyes closed.
When getting through the day remember to keep your eyes open.
joost ©02 swarte
Hurry up or you'll be late for school. Don't dawdle!
... and if you pass Grandma's house, will you please check and see if she is ok?
?
She's been so forgetful lately.

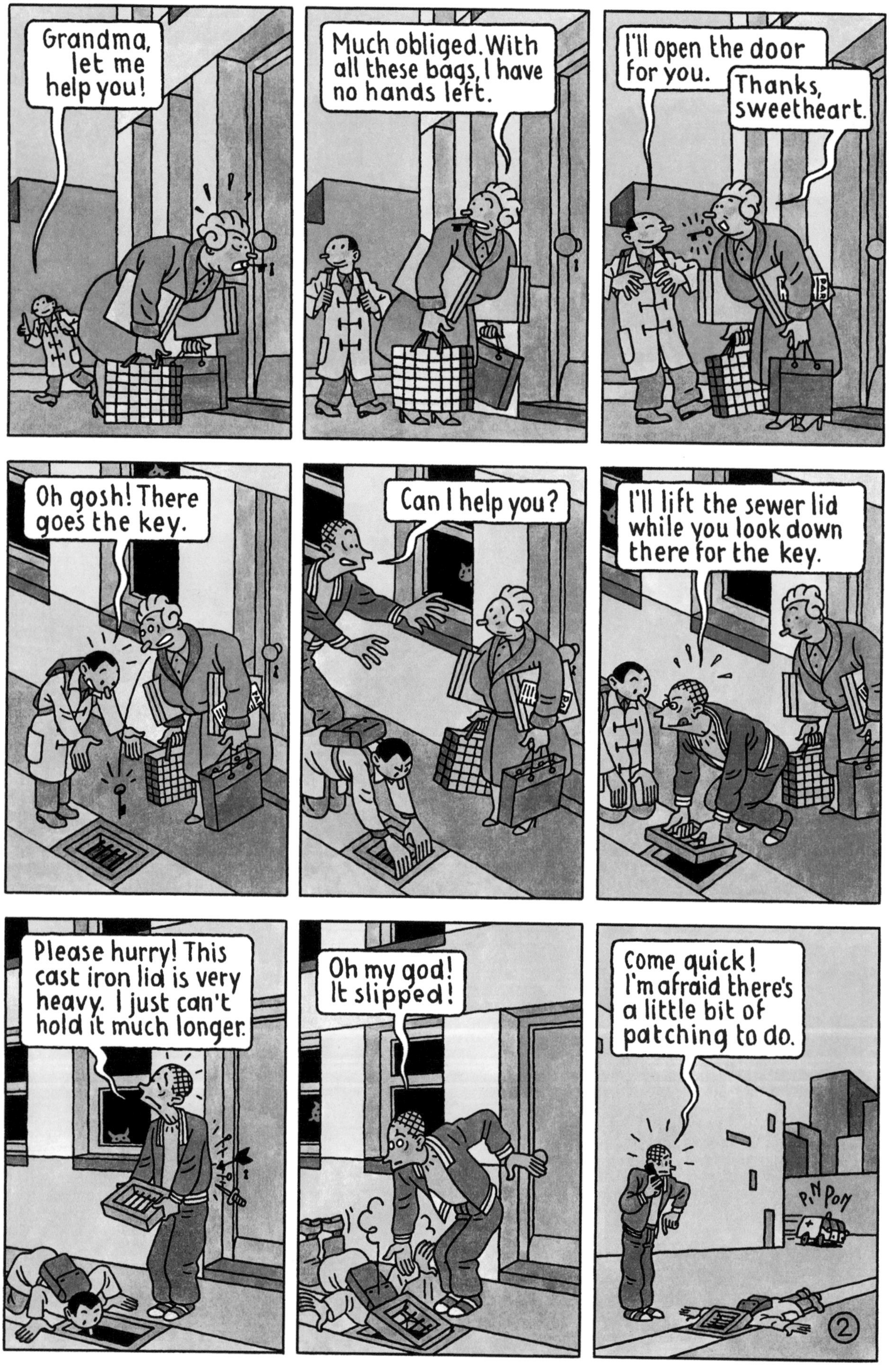
Grandma, let me help you!
Much obliged. With all these bags, I have no hands left.
I'll open the door for you.
Thanks, sweetheart.
Oh gosh! There goes the key.
Can I help you?
I'll lift the sewer lid while you look down there for the key.
Please hurry! This cast iron lid is very heavy. I just can't hold it much longer.
Oh my god! It slipped!
Come quick! I'm afraid there's a little bit of patching to do.
PiN PoN
2

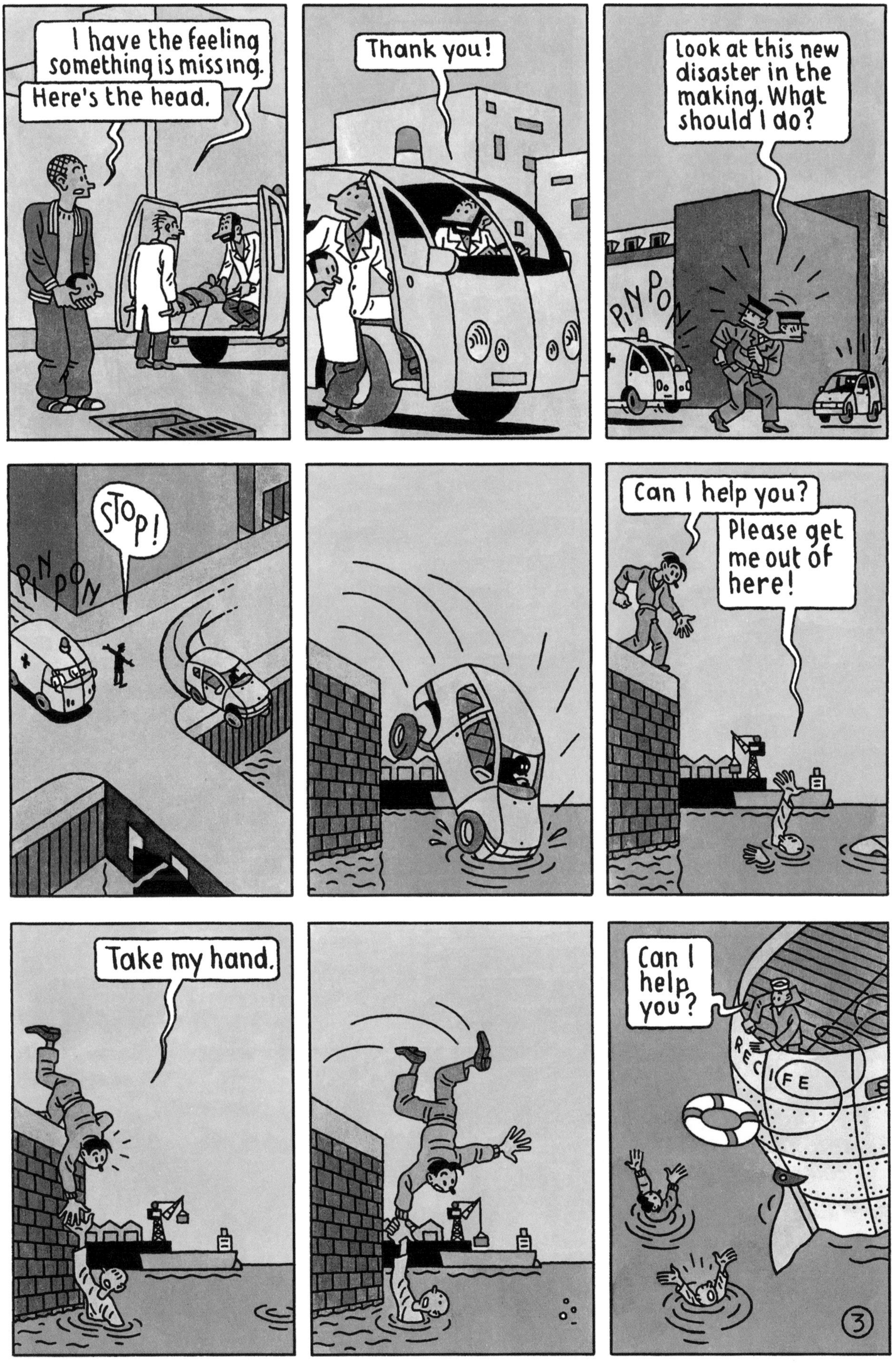
I have the feeling something is missing.
Here's the head.
Thank you!
Look at this new disaster in the making. What should I do?
PIN PON
PIN PON
STOP!
Can I help you?
Please get me out of here!
Take my hand.
Can I help you?
RECIFE
3

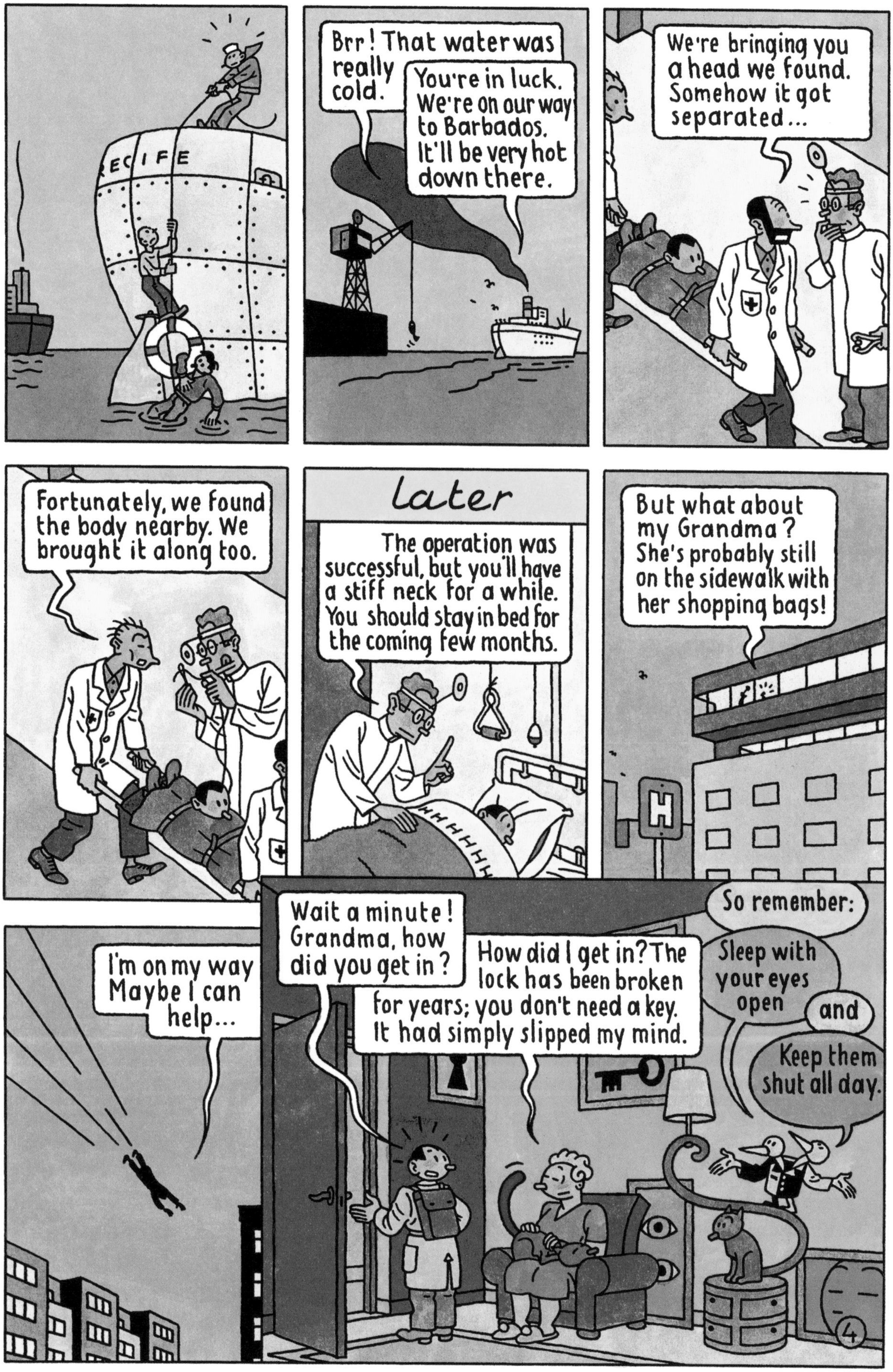
ECIFE
Brr! That water was really cold.
You're in luck. We're on our way to Barbados. It'll be very hot down there.
We're bringing you a head we found. Somehow it got separated...
Fortunately, we found the body nearby. We brought it along too.
later
The operation was successful, but you'll have a stiff neck for a while. You should stay in bed for the coming few months.
But what about my Grandma? She's probably still on the sidewalk with her shopping bags!
H
I'm on my way Maybe I can help...
Wait a minute! Grandma, how did you get in?
How did I get in? The lock has been broken for years; you don't need a key. It had simply slipped my mind.
So remember:
Sleep with your eyes open
and
Keep them shut all day.
4

The Enchanted Pumpkin

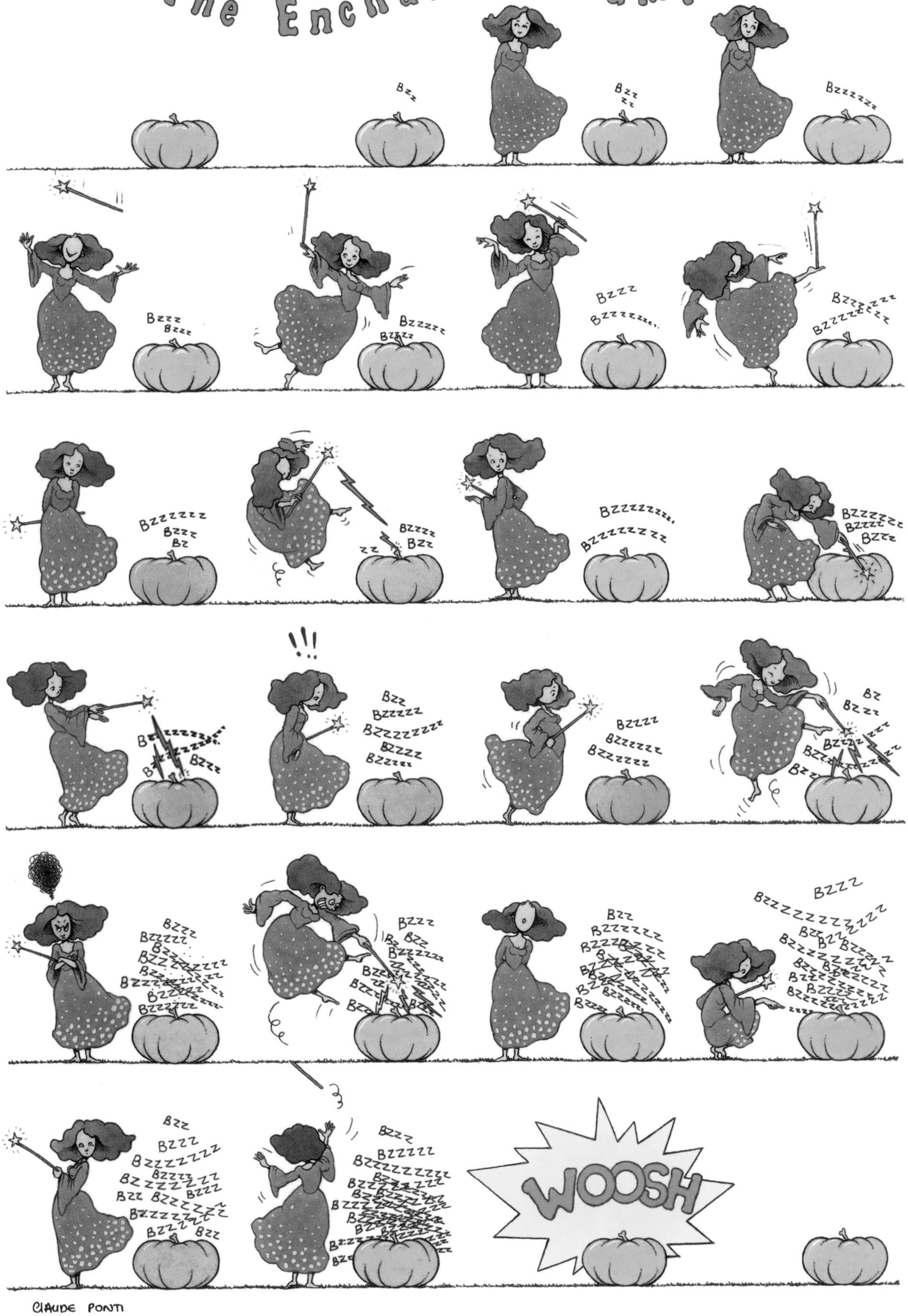
Bzz
Bzzz
Bzzzzzz
Bzzz
Bzzz
Bzzzzz
!!!
WOOSH
CLAUDE PONTI

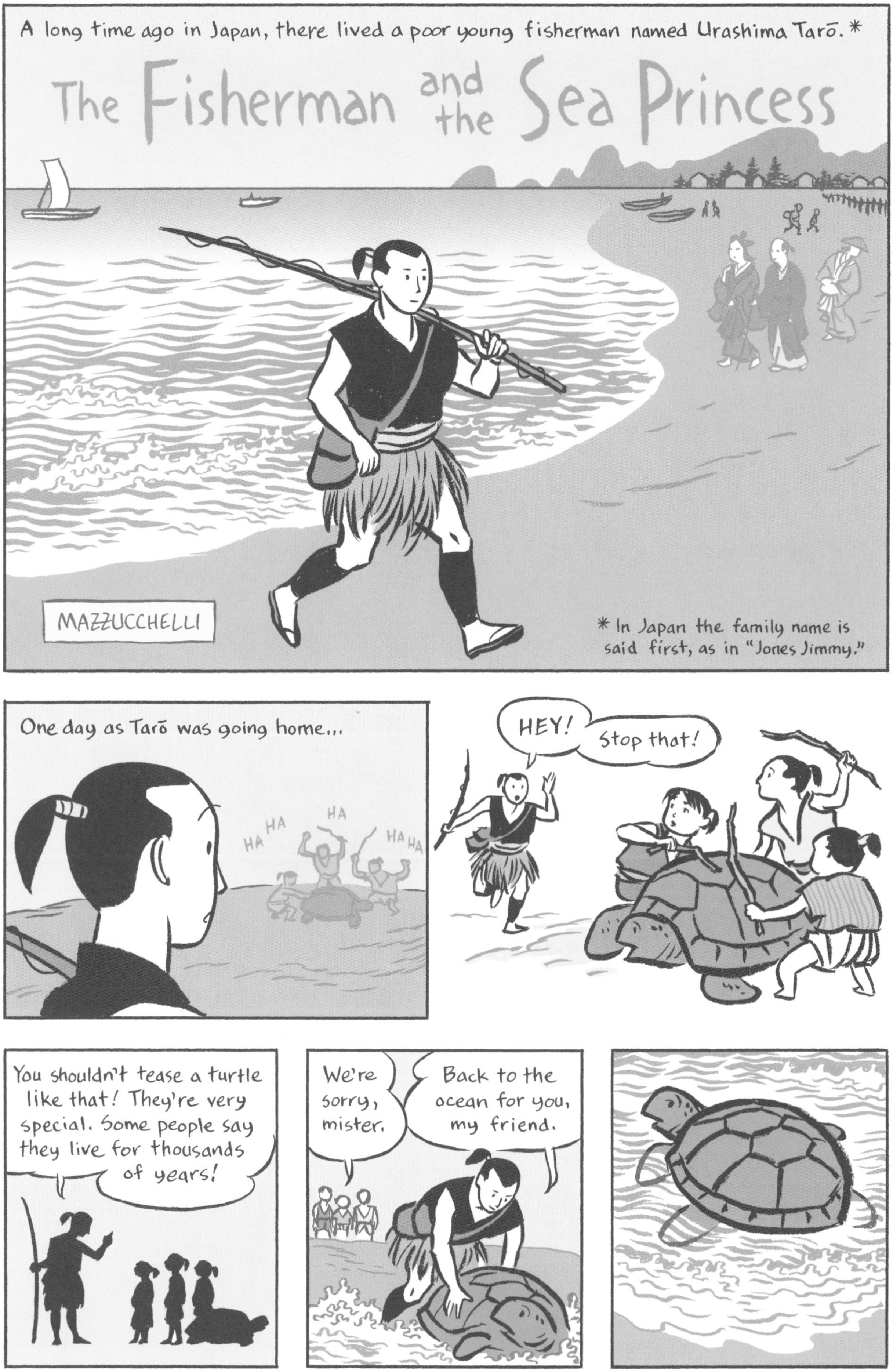
A long time ago in Japan, there lived a poor young fisherman named Urashima Tarō. *
The Fisherman and the Sea Princess
MAZZUCCHELLI
* In Japan the family name is said first, as in "Jones Jimmy."
One day as Tarō was going home...
HA HA
HA
HA HA
HEY!
Stop that!
You shouldn't tease a turtle like that! They're very special. Some people say they live for thousands of years!
We're sorry, mister.
Back to the ocean for you, my friend.

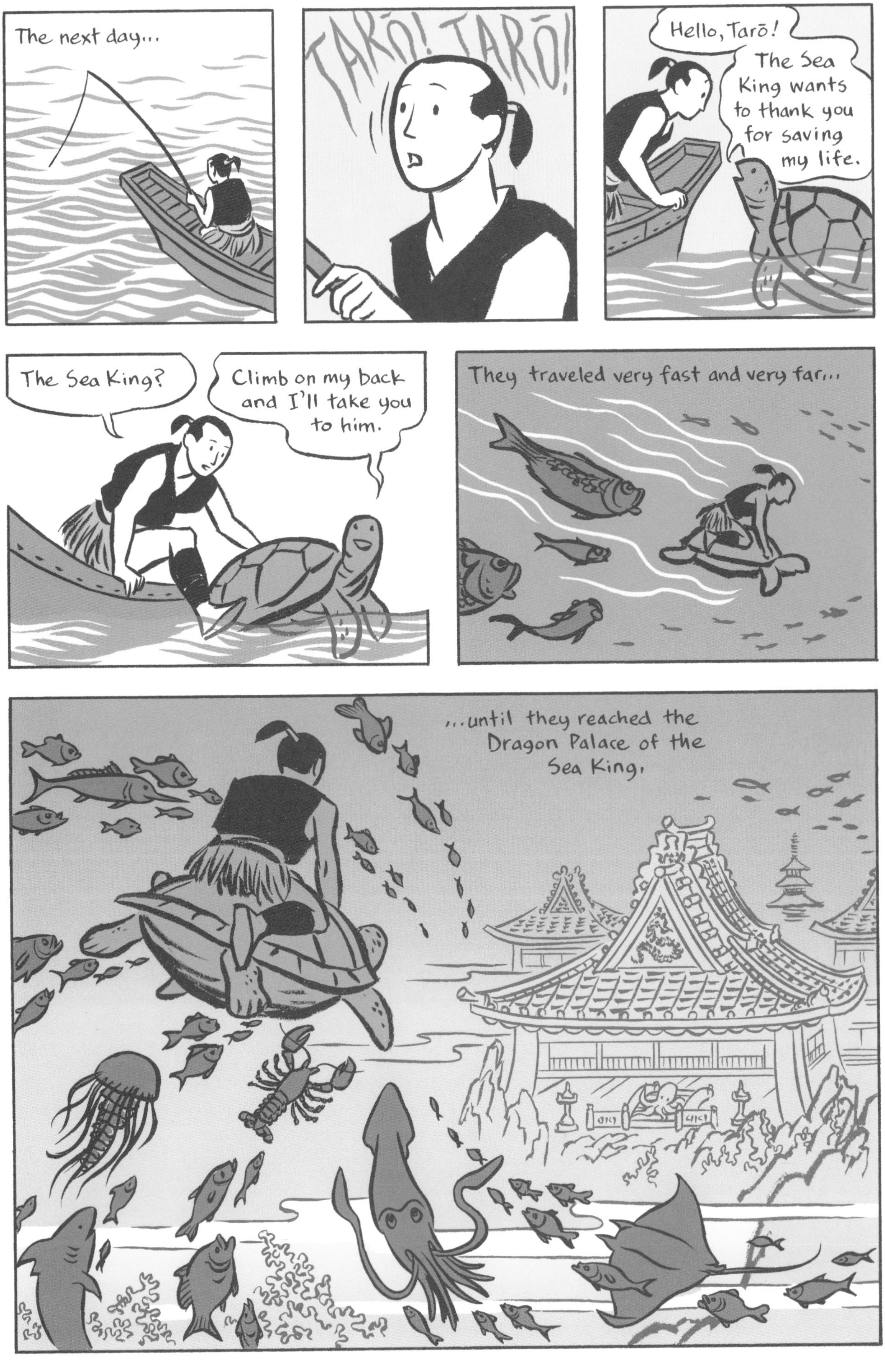
The next day...
TARŌ! TARŌ!
Hello, Tarō!
The Sea King wants to thank you for saving my life.
The Sea King?
Climb on my back and I'll take you to him.
They traveled very fast and very far...
...until they reached the Dragon Palace of the Sea King.

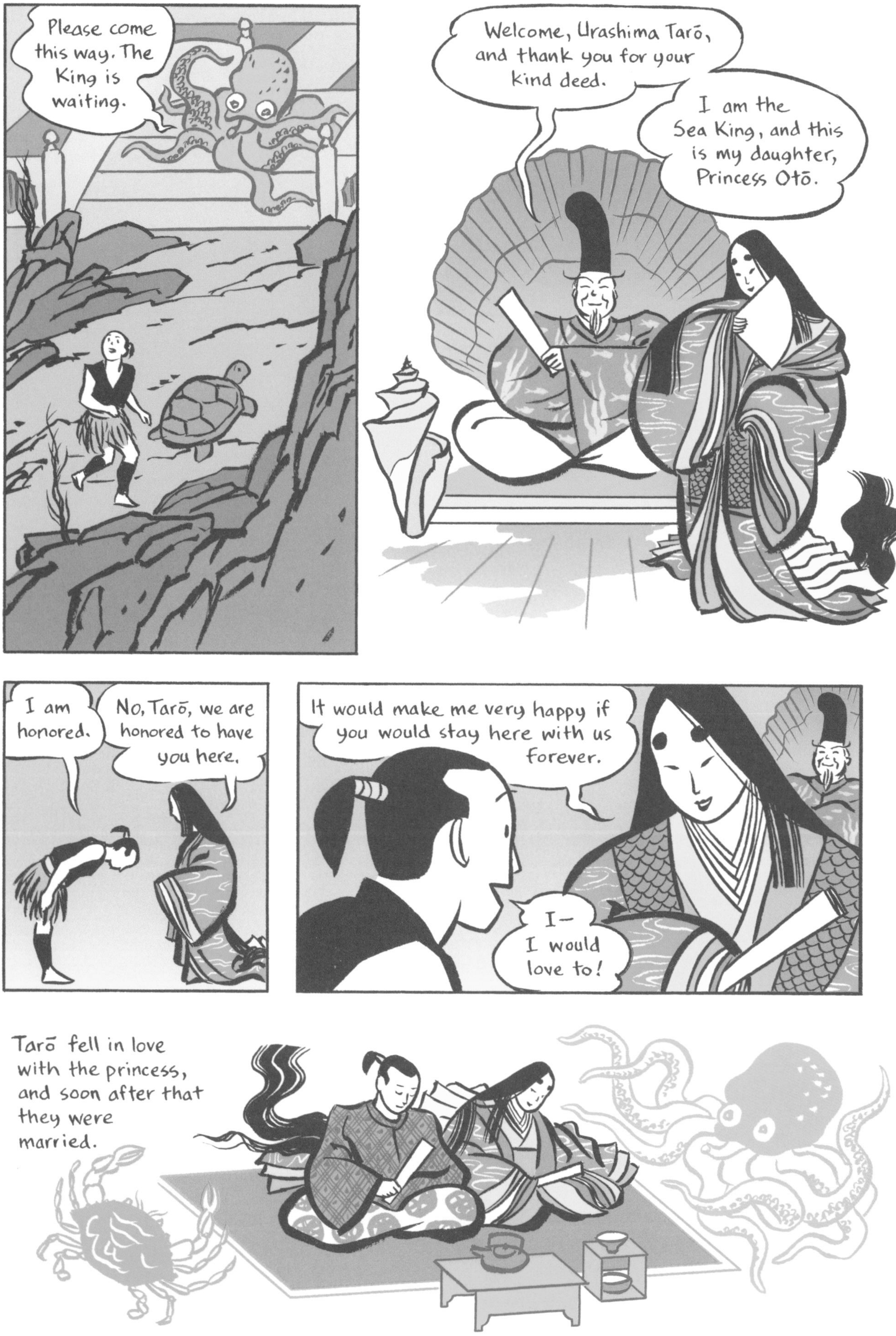
Please come this way. The King is waiting.
Welcome, Urashima Tarō, and thank you for your kind deed.
I am the Sea King, and this is my daughter, Princess Otō.
I am honored.
No, Tarō, we are honored to have you here.
It would make me very happy if you would stay here with us forever.
I— I would love to!
Tarō fell in love with the princess, and soon after that they were married.

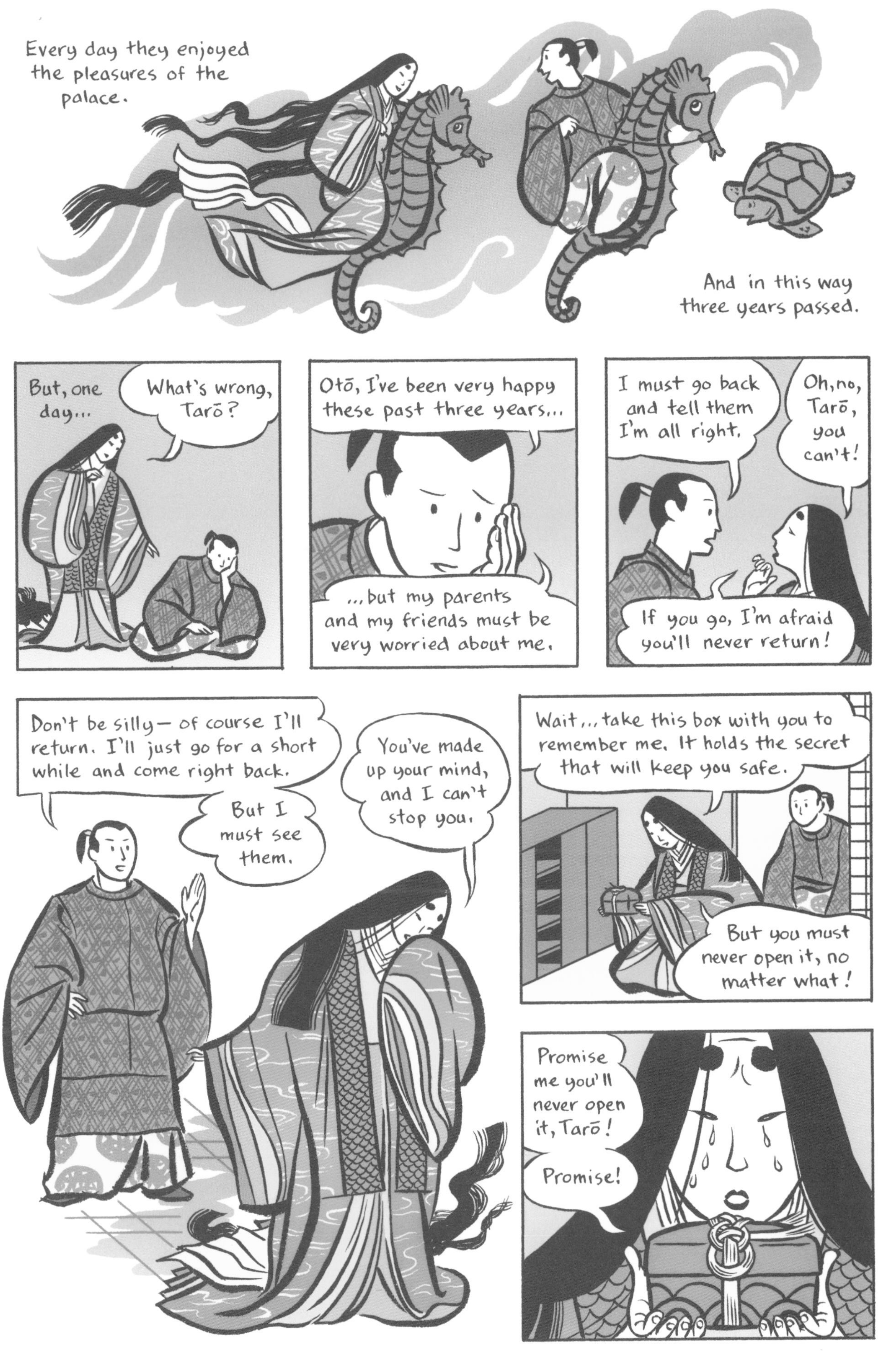

Every day they enjoyed the pleasures of the palace.
And in this way three years passed.
But, one day...
What's wrong, Tarō?
Otō, I've been very happy these past three years...
...but my parents and my friends must be very worried about me.
I must go back and tell them I'm all right.
Oh, no, Tarō, you can't!
If you go, I'm afraid you'll never return!
Don't be silly— of course I'll return. I'll just go for a short while and come right back.
But I must see them.
You've made up your mind, and I can't stop you.
Wait... take this box with you to remember me. It holds the secret that will keep you safe.
But you must never open it, no matter what!
Promise me you'll never open it, Tarō!
Promise!

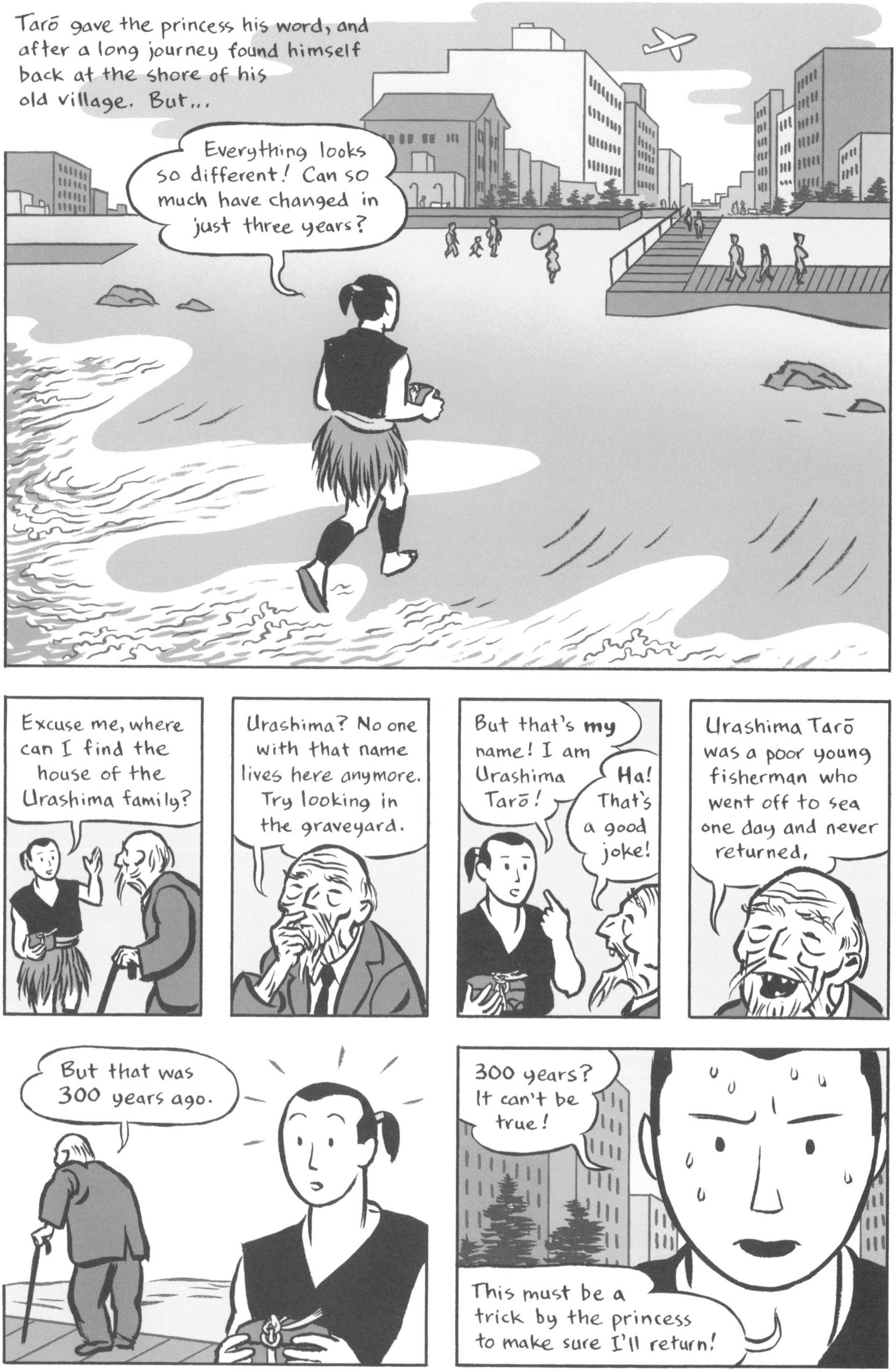
Tarō gave the princess his word, and after a long journey found himself back at the shore of his old village. But...
Everything looks so different! Can so much have changed in just three years?
Excuse me, where can I find the house of the Urashima family?
Urashima? No one with that name lives here anymore. Try looking in the graveyard.
But that's **my** name! I am Urashima Tarō!
Ha! That's a good joke!
Urashima Tarō was a poor young fisherman who went off to sea one day and never returned,
But that was 300 years ago.
300 years? It can't be true!
This must be a trick by the princess to make sure I'll return!

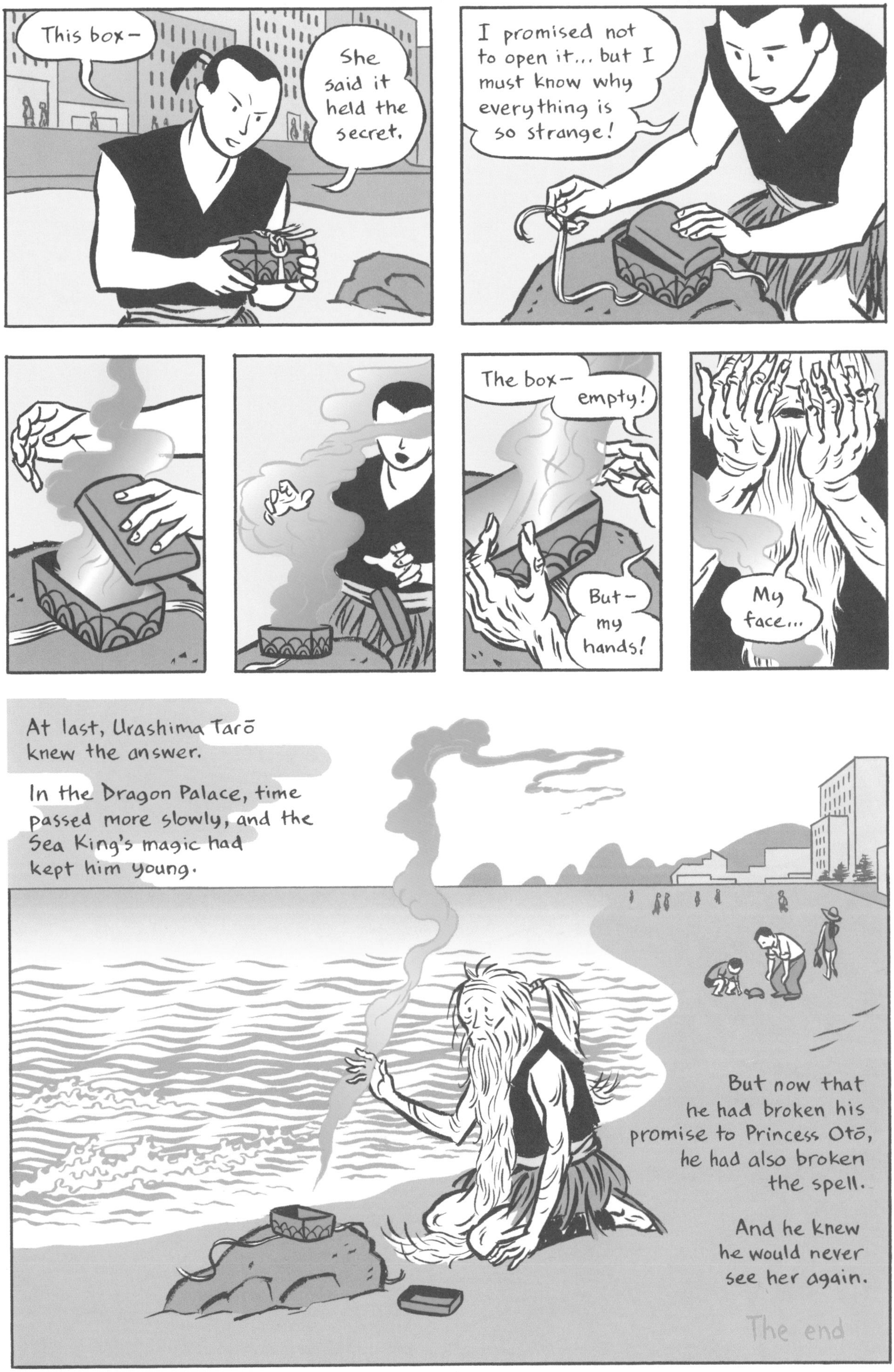

This box—
She said it held the secret.
I promised not to open it... but I must know why everything is so strange!
The box—
empty!
But—my hands!
My face...
At last, Urashima Tarō knew the answer.
In the Dragon Palace, time passed more slowly, and the Sea King's magic had kept him young.
But now that he had broken his promise to Princess Otō, he had also broken the spell.
And he knew he would never see her again.
The end

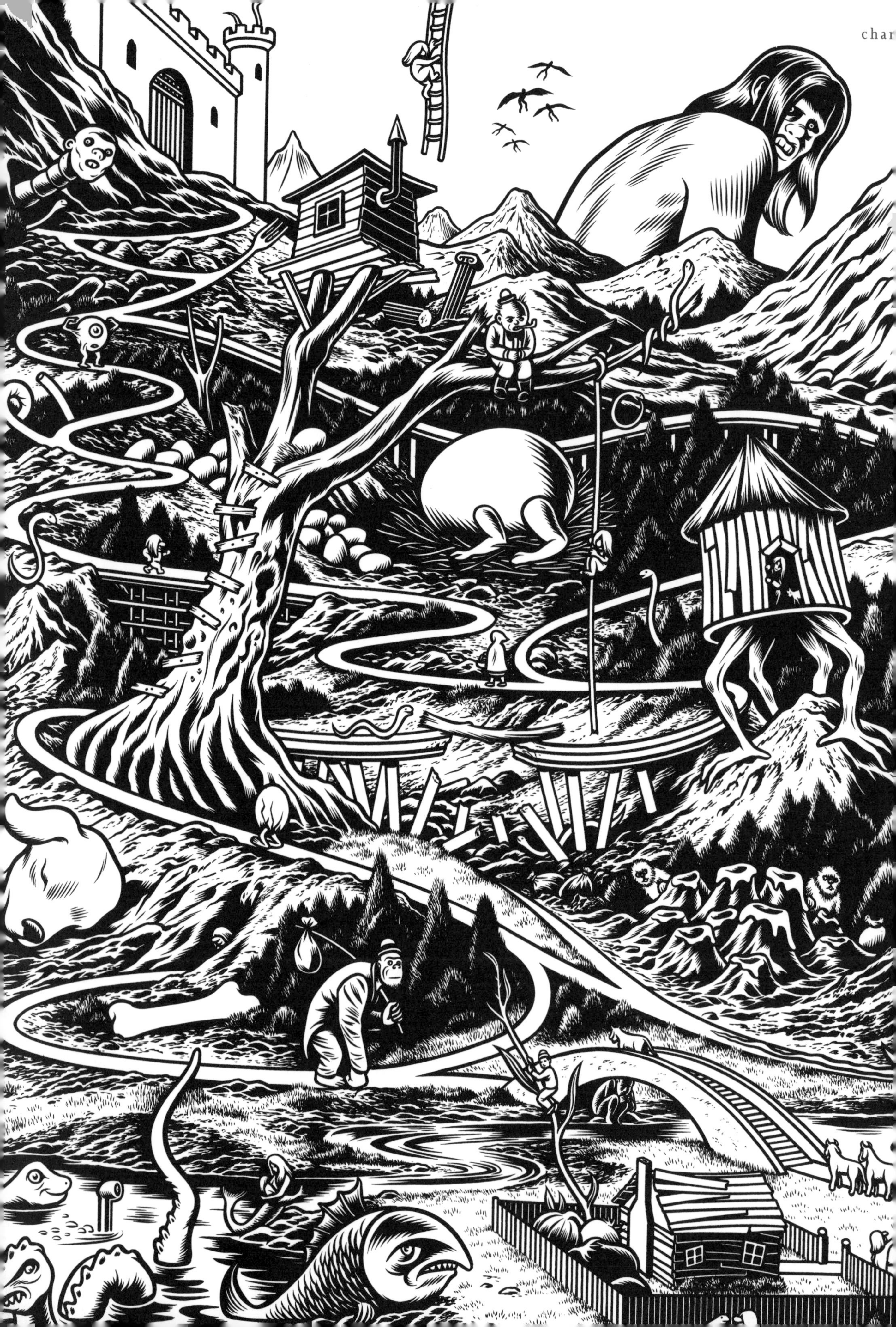

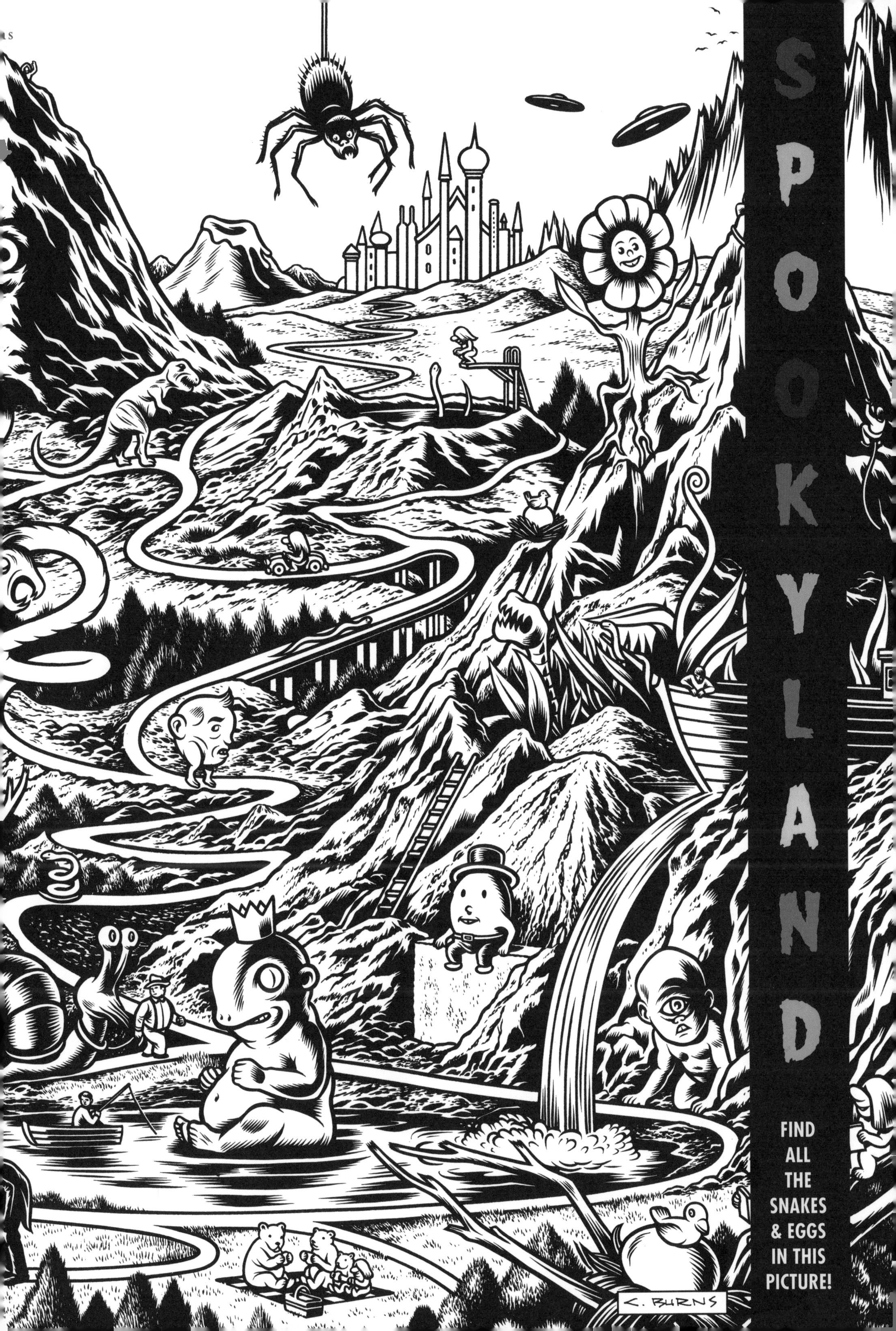
SPOOKYLAND
FIND ALL THE SNAKES & EGGS IN THIS PICTURE!
C. BURNS

IT WAS A DARK AND SILLY NIGHT...

...AND AFTER A LONG DAY'S SLEEP, THE OWL GOT INTO HIS CAR AND WENT SHOPPING. THIS IS A COMIC STRIP ABOUT HIS SHOPPING TRIP, BUT SOMEHOW THE CARTOONIST MIXED UP THE PANELS! CAN YOU REARRANGE THEM SO THAT THE STORY MAKES SENSE?

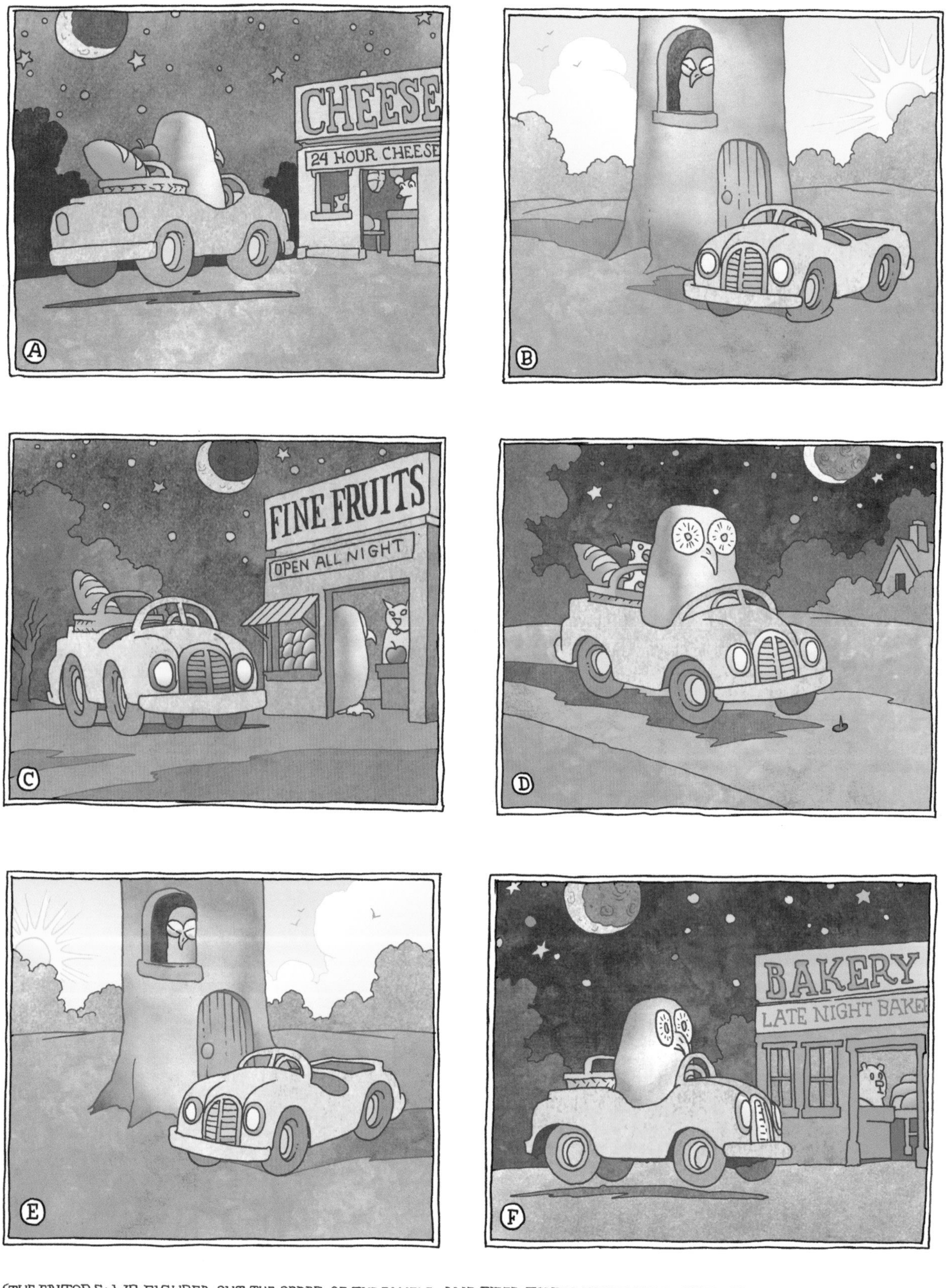
CHEESE
24 HOUR CHEESE
A
B
FINE FRUITS
OPEN ALL NIGHT
C
D
E
BAKERY
LATE NIGHT BAKE
F

(THE EDITORS: WE FIGURED OUT THE ORDER OF THE PANELS, AND FIRED TONY MILLIONAIRE. HERE IS THE ANSWER: (E,F,C,A,D,B)

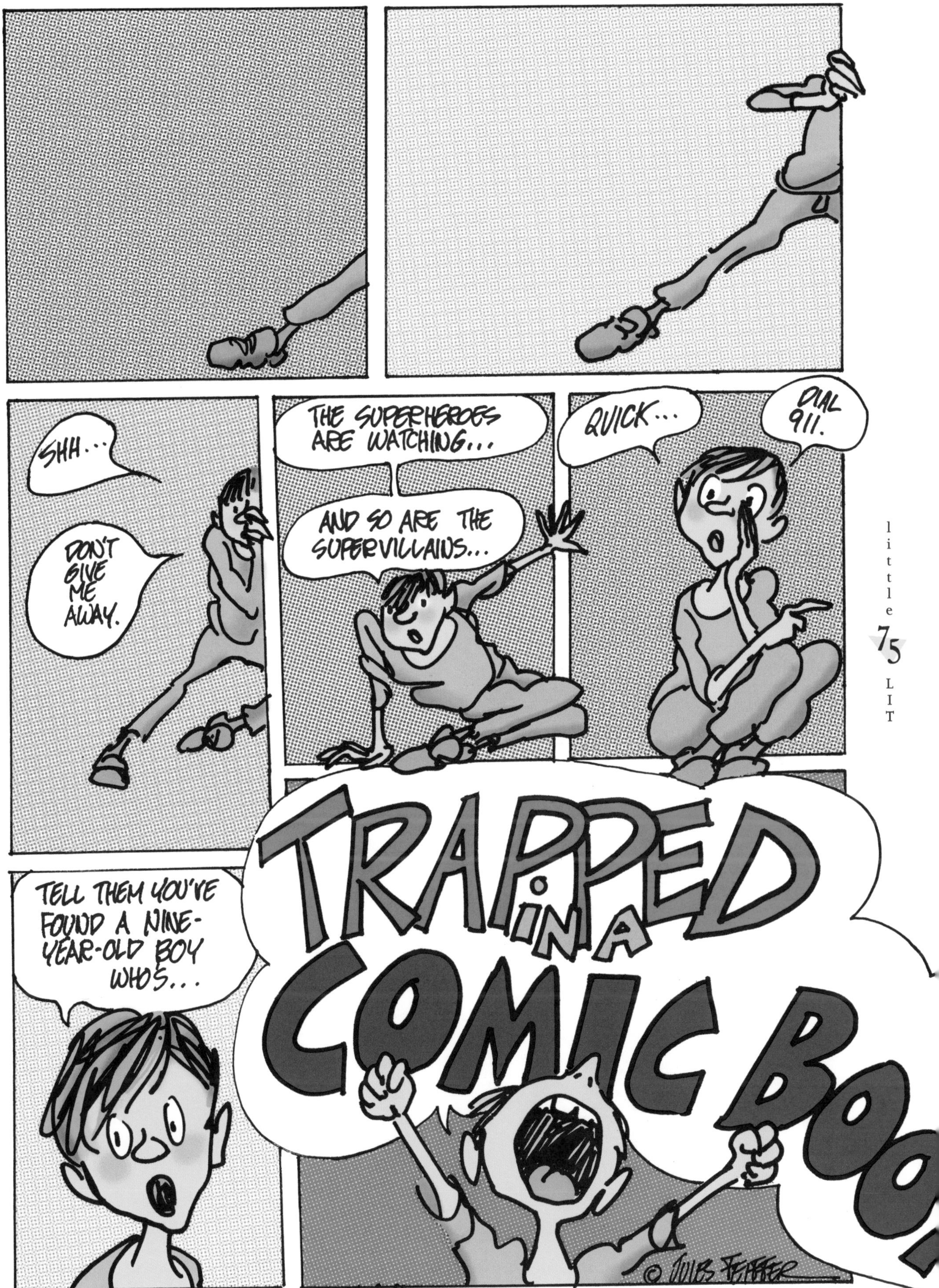
SHH...
DON'T GIVE ME AWAY.
THE SUPERHEROES ARE WATCHING...
AND SO ARE THE SUPERVILLAINS...
QUICK...
DIAL 911.
TELL THEM YOU'VE FOUND A NINE-YEAR-OLD BOY WHO'S...
TRAPPED IN A COMIC BOO
© JULES FEIFFER
www.julesfeiffer.com

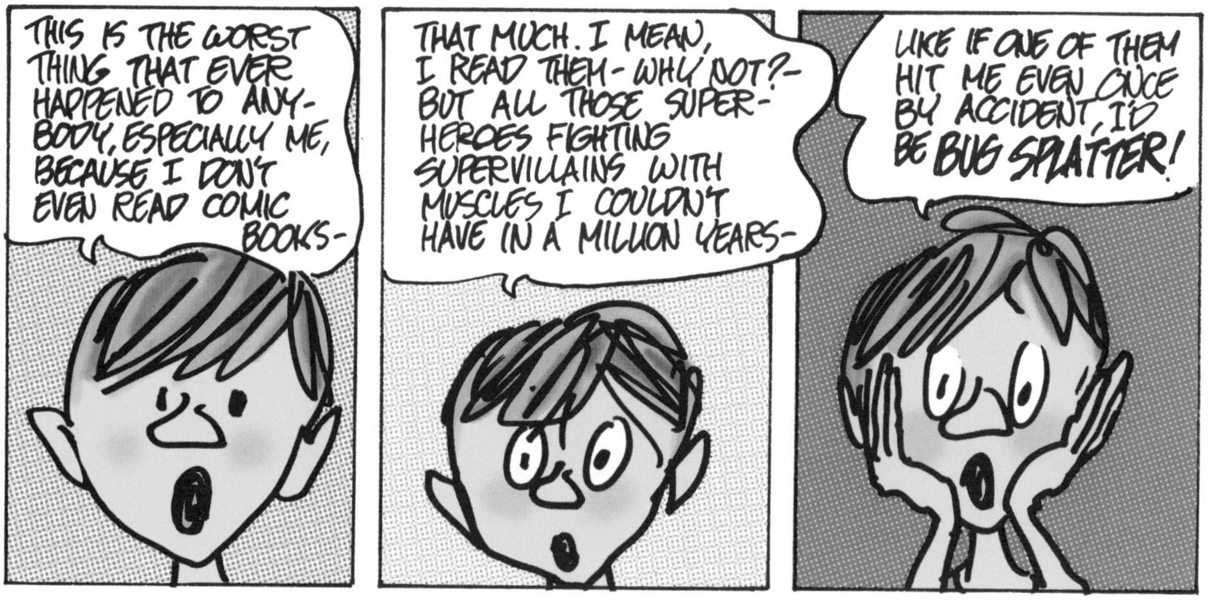
THIS IS THE WORST THING THAT EVER HAPPENED TO ANYBODY, ESPECIALLY ME, BECAUSE I DON'T EVEN READ COMIC BOOKS-
THAT MUCH. I MEAN, I READ THEM - WHY NOT? - BUT ALL THOSE SUPER-HEROES FIGHTING SUPERVILLAINS WITH MUSCLES I COULDN'T HAVE IN A MILLION YEARS-
LIKE IF ONE OF THEM HIT ME EVEN ONCE BY ACCIDENT, I'D BE **BUG SPLATTER**!

AND THIS IS WHAT I'M EXPLAINING TO THIS CARTOONIST IN HIS STUDIO WHERE I'M ON A SCHOOL VISIT WITH MY CLASS:

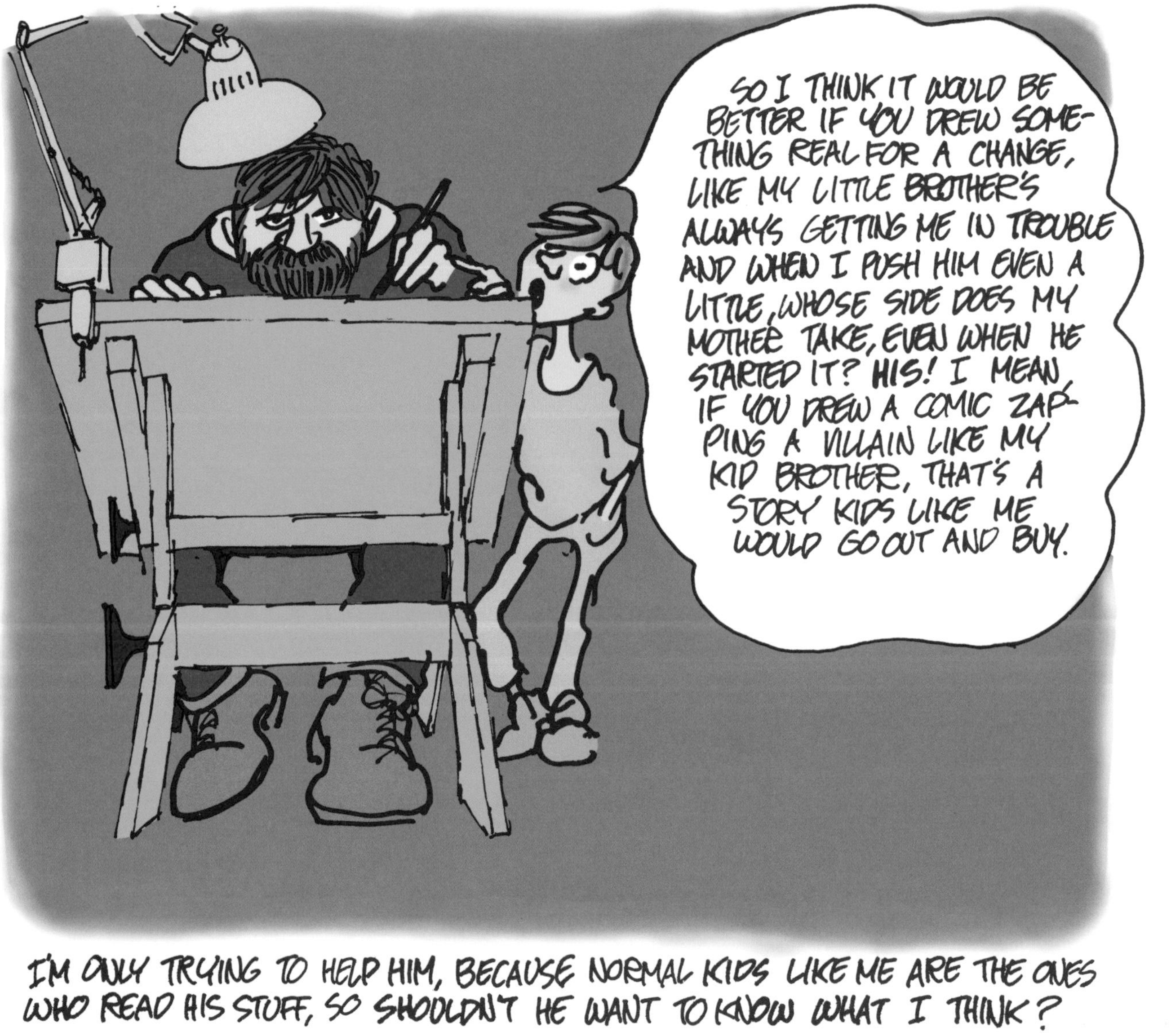
SO I THINK IT WOULD BE BETTER IF YOU DREW SOMETHING REAL FOR A CHANGE, LIKE MY LITTLE BROTHER'S ALWAYS GETTING ME IN TROUBLE AND WHEN I PUSH HIM EVEN A LITTLE, WHOSE SIDE DOES MY MOTHER TAKE, EVEN WHEN HE STARTED IT? **HIS**! I MEAN, IF YOU DREW A COMIC ZAPPING A VILLAIN LIKE MY KID BROTHER, THAT'S A STORY KIDS LIKE ME WOULD GO OUT AND BUY.

I'M ONLY TRYING TO HELP HIM, BECAUSE NORMAL KIDS LIKE ME ARE THE ONES WHO READ HIS STUFF, SO SHOULDN'T HE WANT TO KNOW WHAT I THINK?

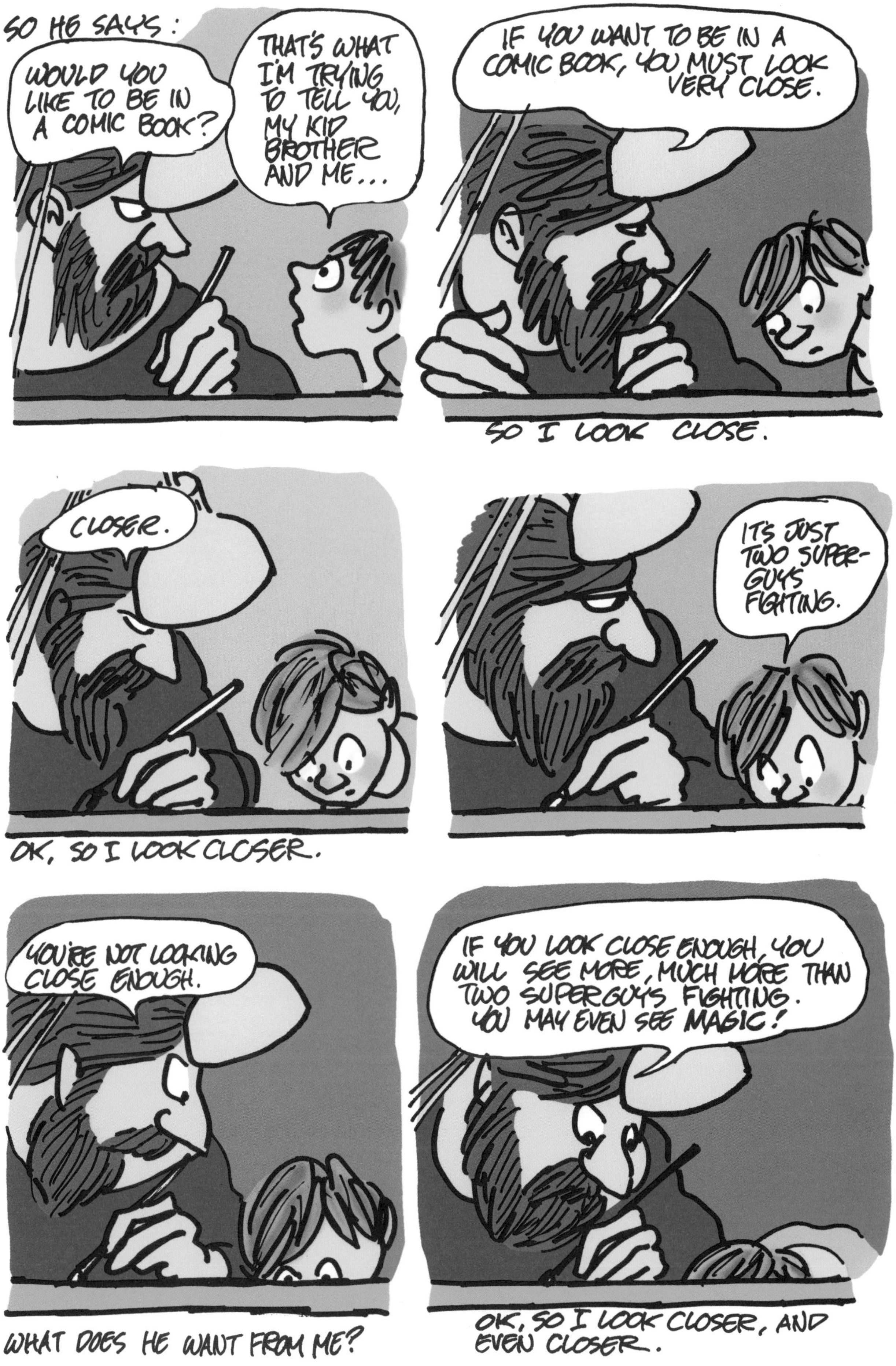
SO HE SAYS:
WOULD YOU LIKE TO BE IN A COMIC BOOK?
THAT'S WHAT I'M TRYING TO TELL YOU, MY KID BROTHER AND ME...
IF YOU WANT TO BE IN A COMIC BOOK, YOU MUST LOOK VERY CLOSE.
SO I LOOK CLOSE.
CLOSER.
OK, SO I LOOK CLOSER.
IT'S JUST TWO SUPER-GUYS FIGHTING.
YOU'RE NOT LOOKING CLOSE ENOUGH.
WHAT DOES HE WANT FROM ME?
IF YOU LOOK CLOSE ENOUGH, YOU WILL SEE MORE, MUCH MORE THAN TWO SUPERGUYS FIGHTING. YOU MAY EVEN SEE MAGIC!
OK, SO I LOOK CLOSER, AND EVEN CLOSER.

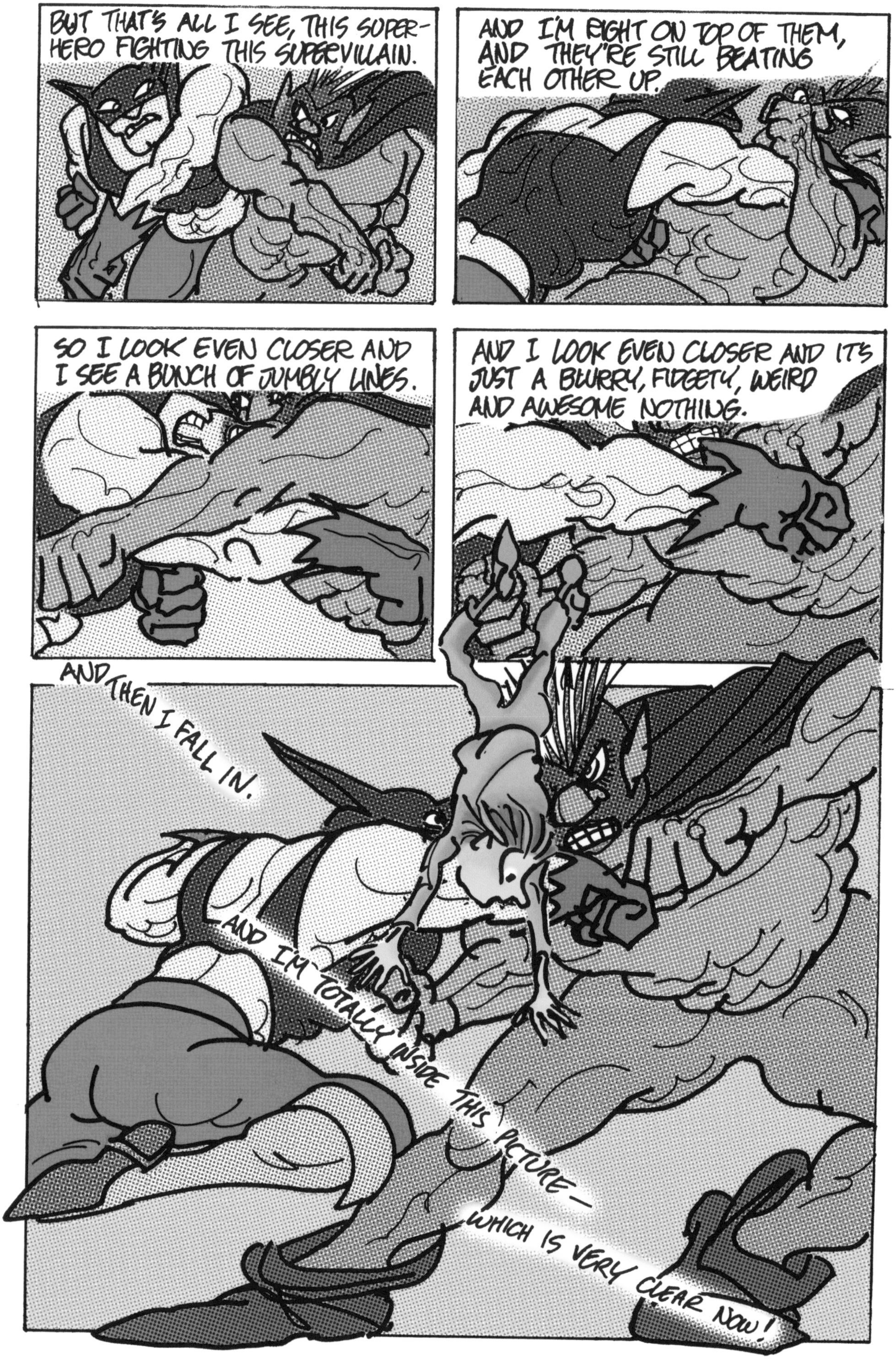
BUT THAT'S ALL I SEE, THIS SUPER-HERO FIGHTING THIS SUPERVILLAIN.
AND I'M RIGHT ON TOP OF THEM, AND THEY'RE STILL BEATING EACH OTHER UP.
SO I LOOK EVEN CLOSER AND I SEE A BUNCH OF JUMBLY LINES.
AND I LOOK EVEN CLOSER AND IT'S JUST A BLURRY, FIDGETY, WEIRD AND AWESOME NOTHING.
AND THEN I FALL IN.
AND I'M TOTALLY INSIDE THIS PICTURE—
WHICH IS VERY CLEAR NOW!

BUT WHEN YOU'RE STANDING ONLY A FOOT AWAY FROM FIGHTING SUPERGUYS IT'S NOT WHAT YOU THINK.

THWACK POW

IT'S LIKE "THIS IS IT? DON'T YOU DO ANYTHING ELSE?"

THUDR SMASH WHOMP

AND THE SOUND EFFECTS CAN DRIVE YOU CRAZY!

PLUNG EDOP SOKK

SO I JUMP PANELS.

BUT THESE TWO NOISY SUPER-JERKS FOLLOW ME EVERYWHERE!

KCHUK

I KNOW IF I WAS READING THIS I'D LOVE IT!

BUT I'M **NOT** READING IT, I'M TOTALLY IN IT—AND IT'S EVIL, STUPID, BORING PUKE!

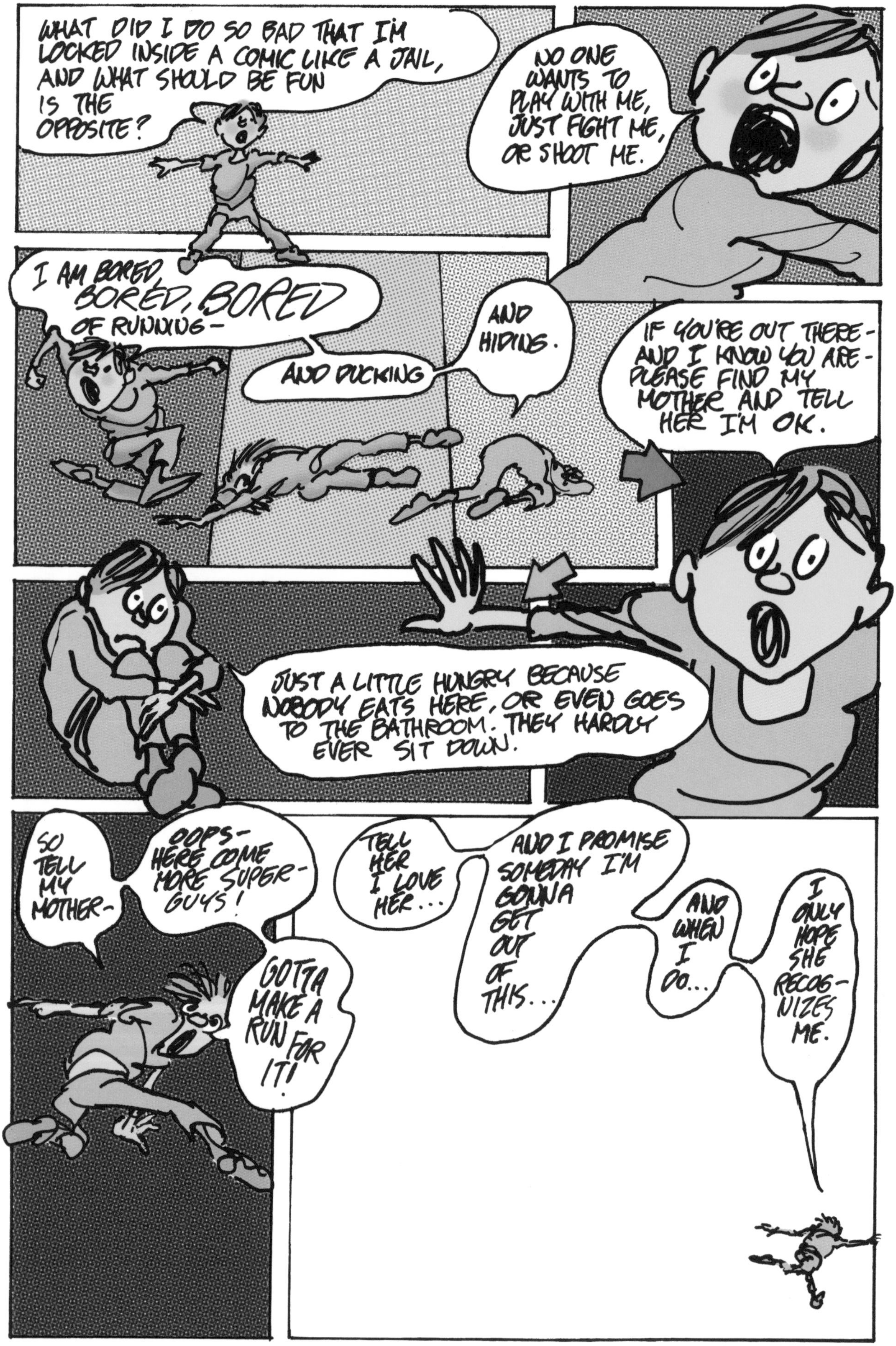
WHAT DID I DO SO BAD THAT I'M LOCKED INSIDE A COMIC LIKE A JAIL, AND WHAT SHOULD BE FUN IS THE OPPOSITE?
NO ONE WANTS TO PLAY WITH ME, JUST FIGHT ME, OR SHOOT ME.
I AM BORED, BORED, BORED OF RUNNING-
AND DUCKING
AND HIDING.
IF YOU'RE OUT THERE- AND I KNOW YOU ARE- PLEASE FIND MY MOTHER AND TELL HER I'M OK.
JUST A LITTLE HUNGRY BECAUSE NOBODY EATS HERE, OR EVEN GOES TO THE BATHROOM. THEY HARDLY EVER SIT DOWN.
SO TELL MY MOTHER-
OOPS- HERE COME MORE SUPER-GUYS!
GOTTA MAKE A RUN FOR IT!
TELL HER I LOVE HER...
AND I PROMISE SOMEDAY I'M GONNA GET OUT OF THIS...
AND WHEN I DO...
I ONLY HOPE SHE RECOGNIZES ME.

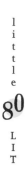

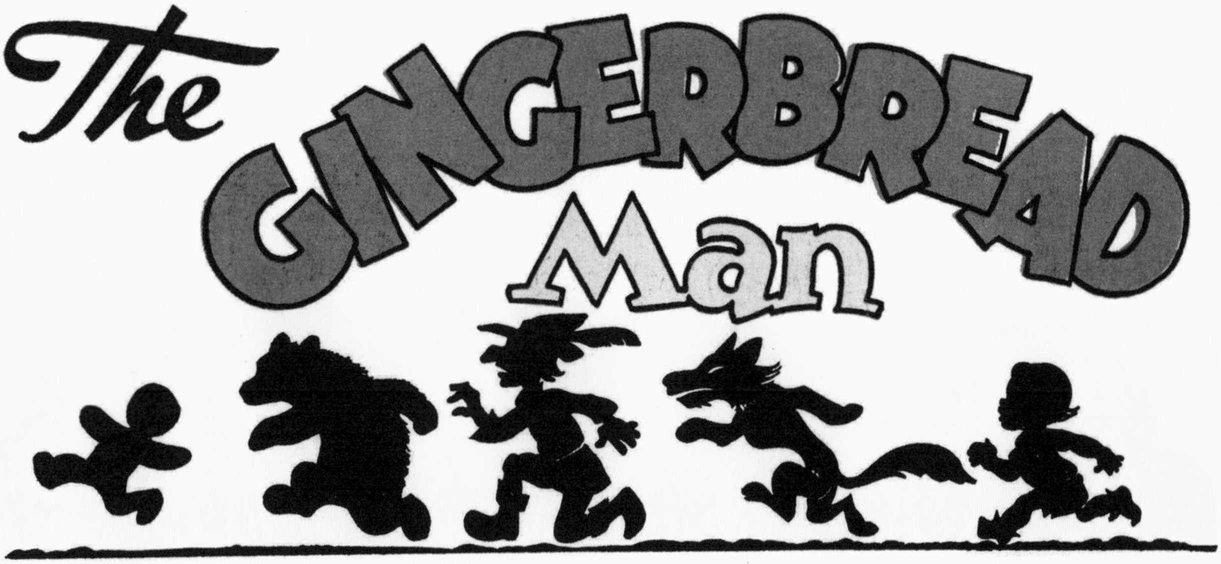
The GINGERBREAD Man

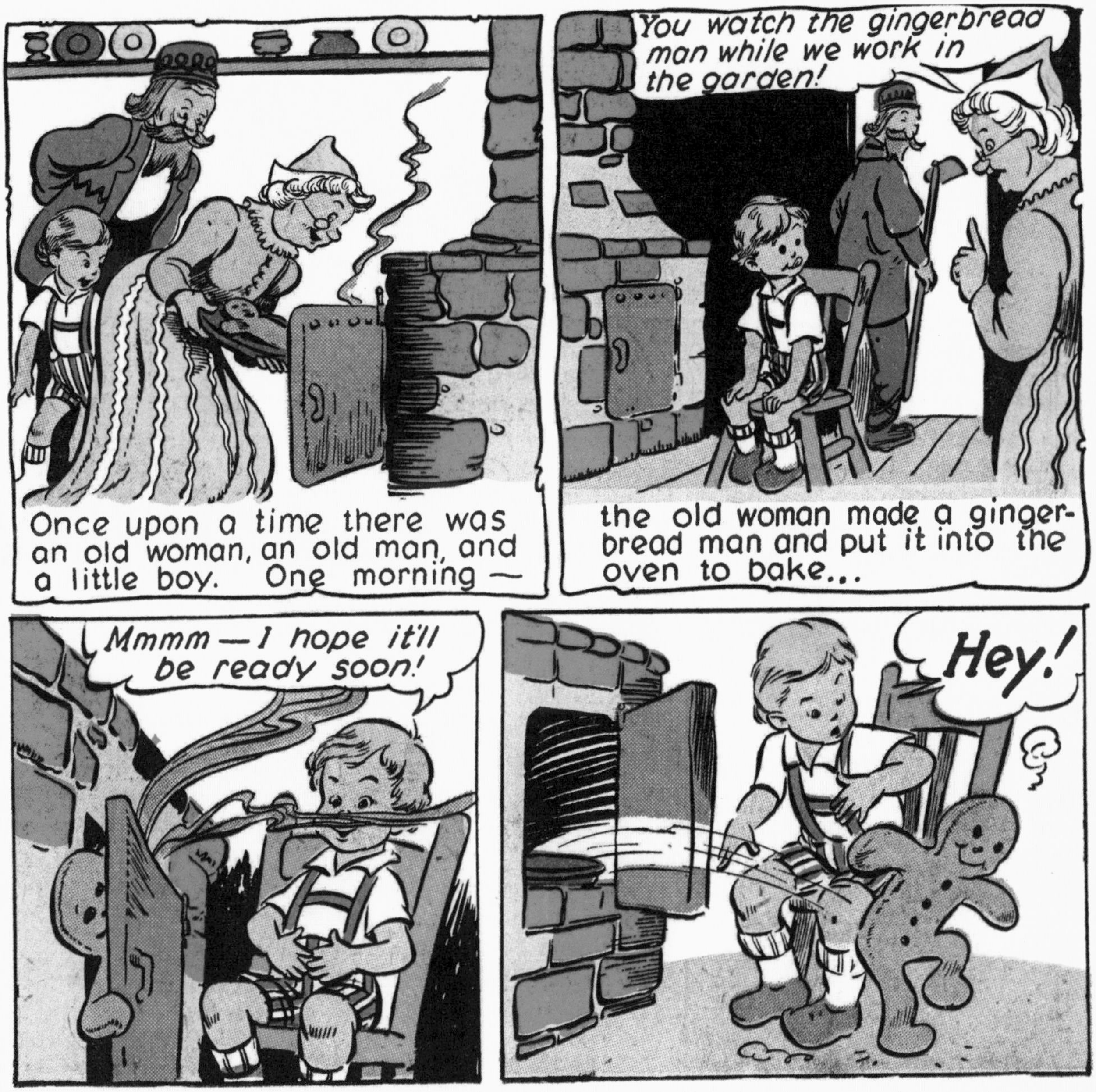
Once upon a time there was an old woman, an old man, and a little boy. One morning —
You watch the gingerbread man while we work in the garden!
the old woman made a gingerbread man and put it into the oven to bake...
Mmmm — I hope it'll be ready soon!
Hey!

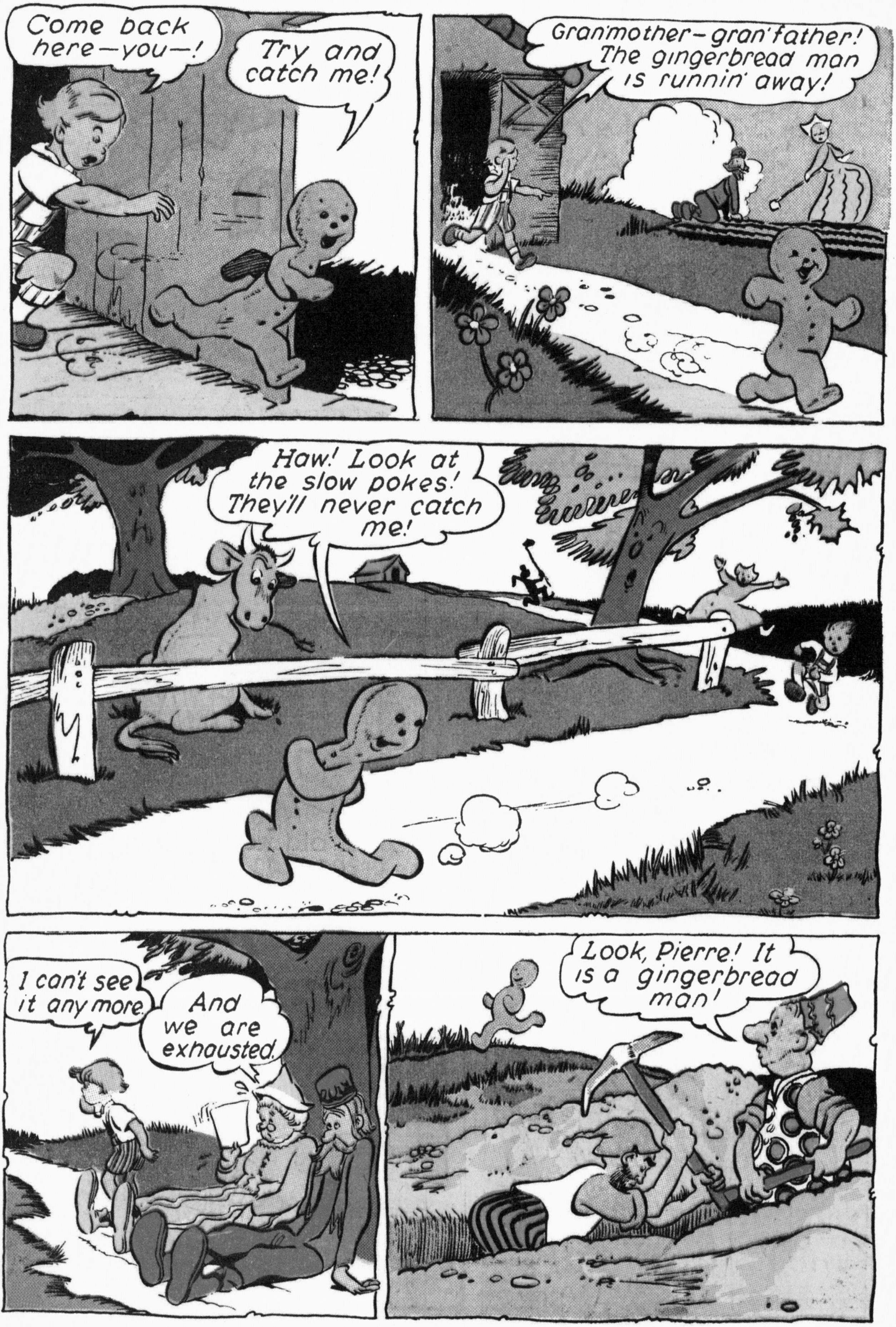
Come back here—you—!
Try and catch me!
Granmother—gran'father! The gingerbread man is runnin' away!
Haw! Look at the slow pokes! They'll never catch me!
I can't see it any more.
And we are exhausted.
Look, Pierre! It is a gingerbread man!

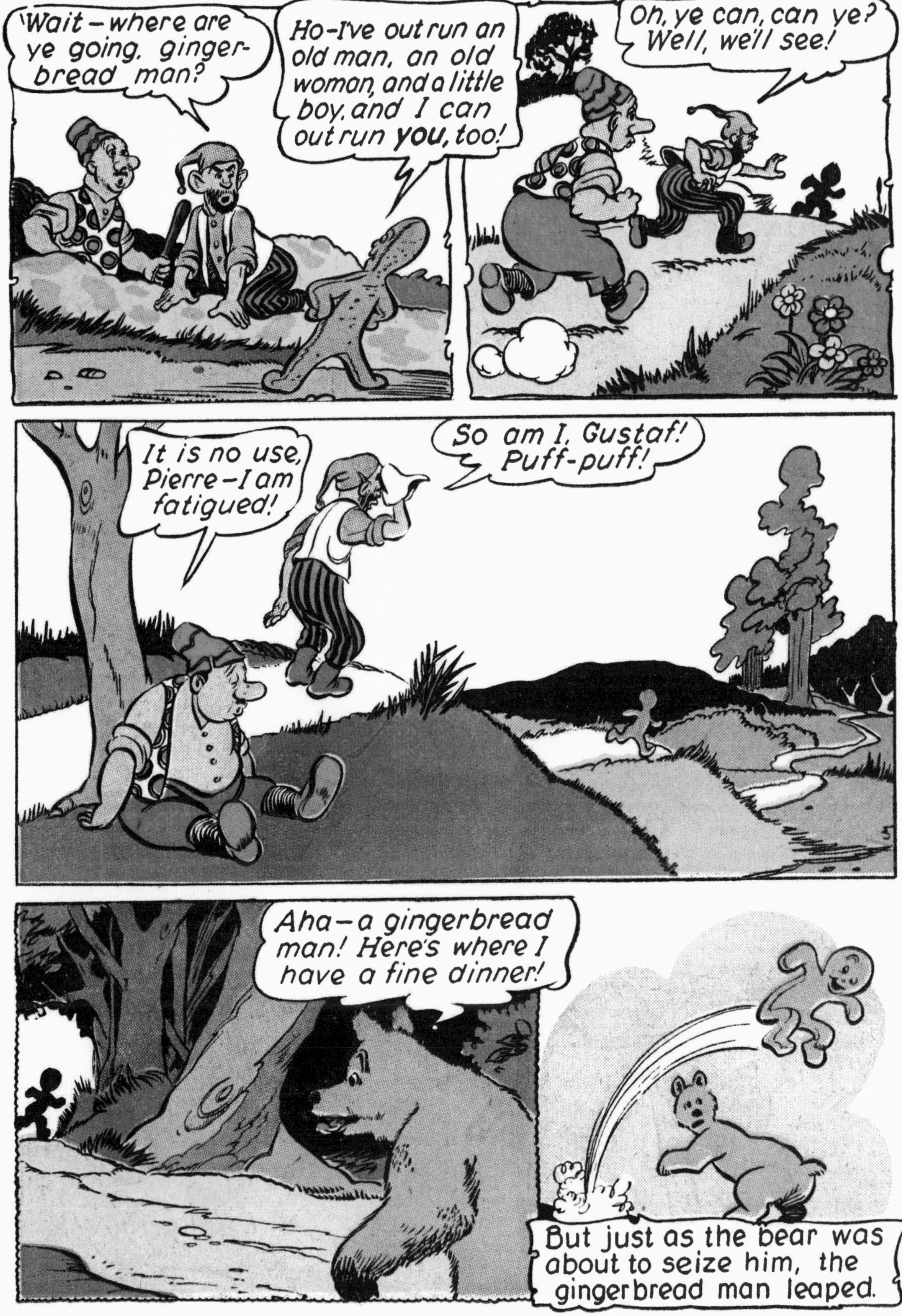
'Wait – where are ye going, gingerbread man?
Ho–I've outrun an old man, an old woman, and a little boy, and I can outrun **YOU**, too!
Oh, ye can, can ye? Well, we'll see!
It is no use, Pierre–I am fatigued!
So am I, Gustaf! Puff-puff!
Aha–a gingerbread man! Here's where I have a fine dinner!
But just as the bear was about to seize him, the gingerbread man leaped.

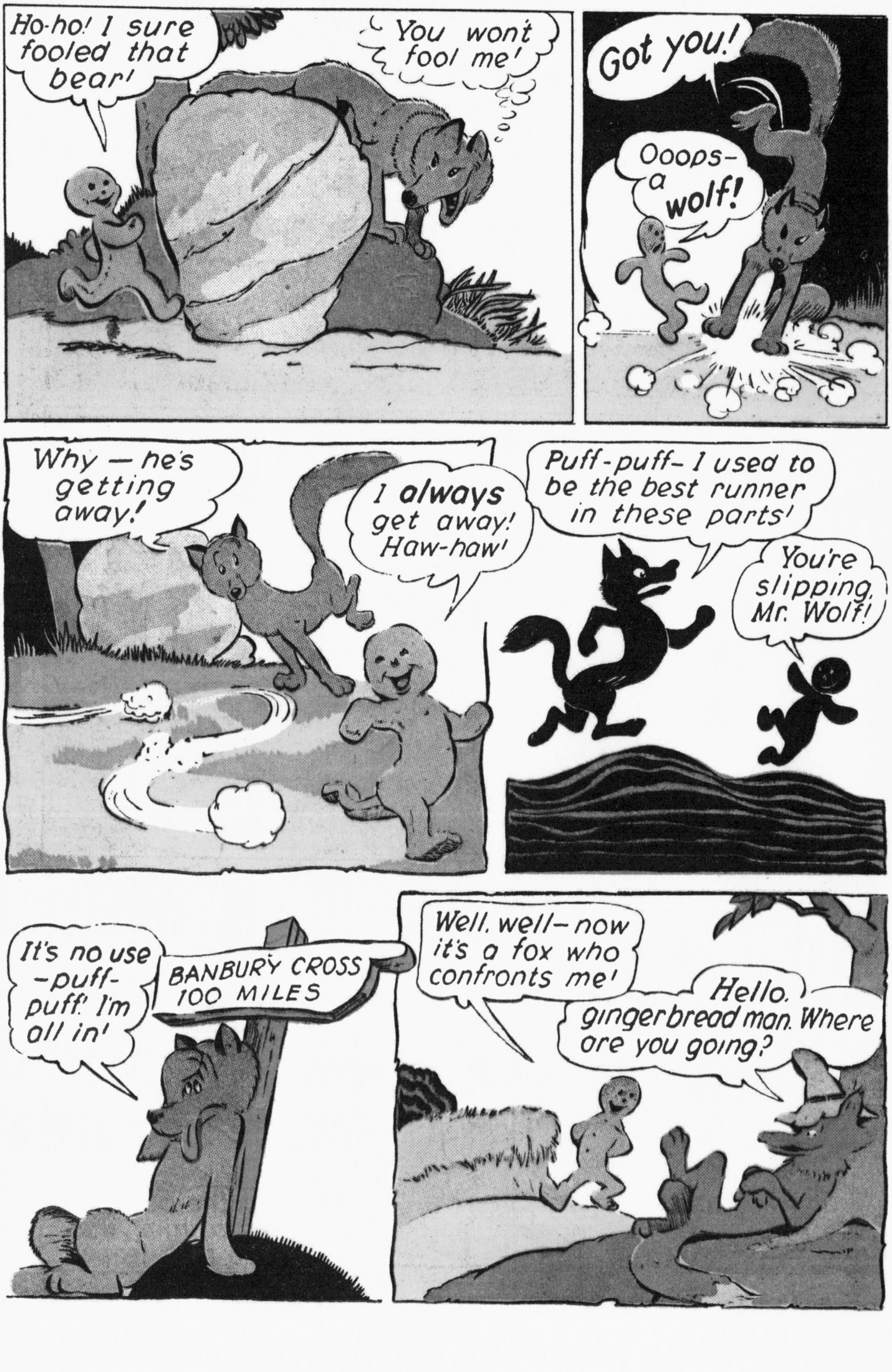
Ho-ho! I sure fooled that bear!
You won't fool me!
Got you!
Ooops-a wolf!
Why — he's getting away!
I always get away! Haw-haw!
Puff-puff- I used to be the best runner in these parts!
You're slipping, Mr. Wolf!
It's no use -puff-puff! I'm all in!
BANBURY CROSS 100 MILES
Well, well- now it's a fox who confronts me!
Hello, gingerbread man. Where are you going?

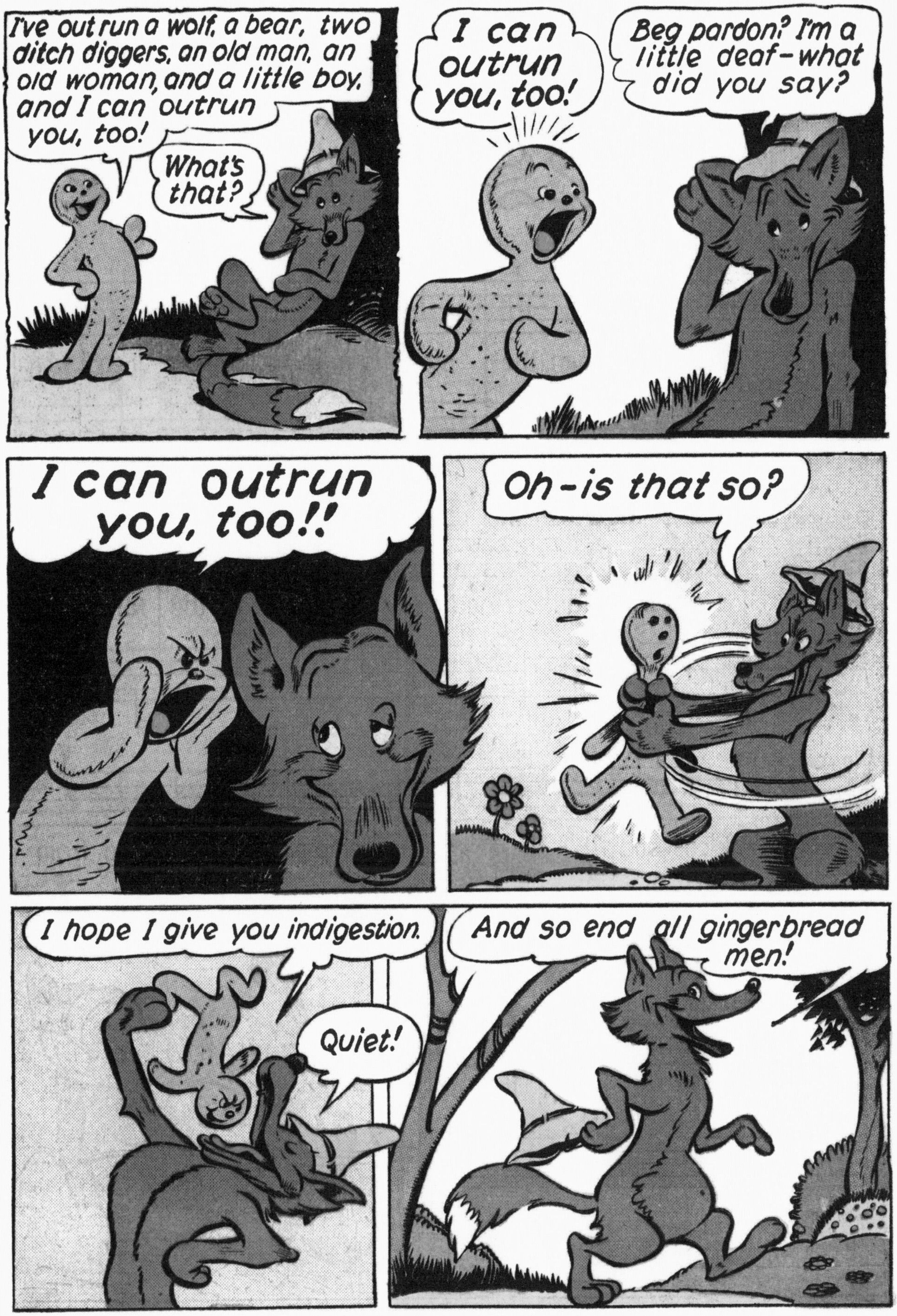
I've outrun a wolf, a bear, two ditch diggers, an old man, an old woman, and a little boy, and I can outrun you, too!
What's that?
I can outrun you, too!
Beg pardon? I'm a little deaf—what did you say?
I can outrun you, too!!
Oh—is that so?
I hope I give you indigestion.
Quiet!
And so end all gingerbread men!

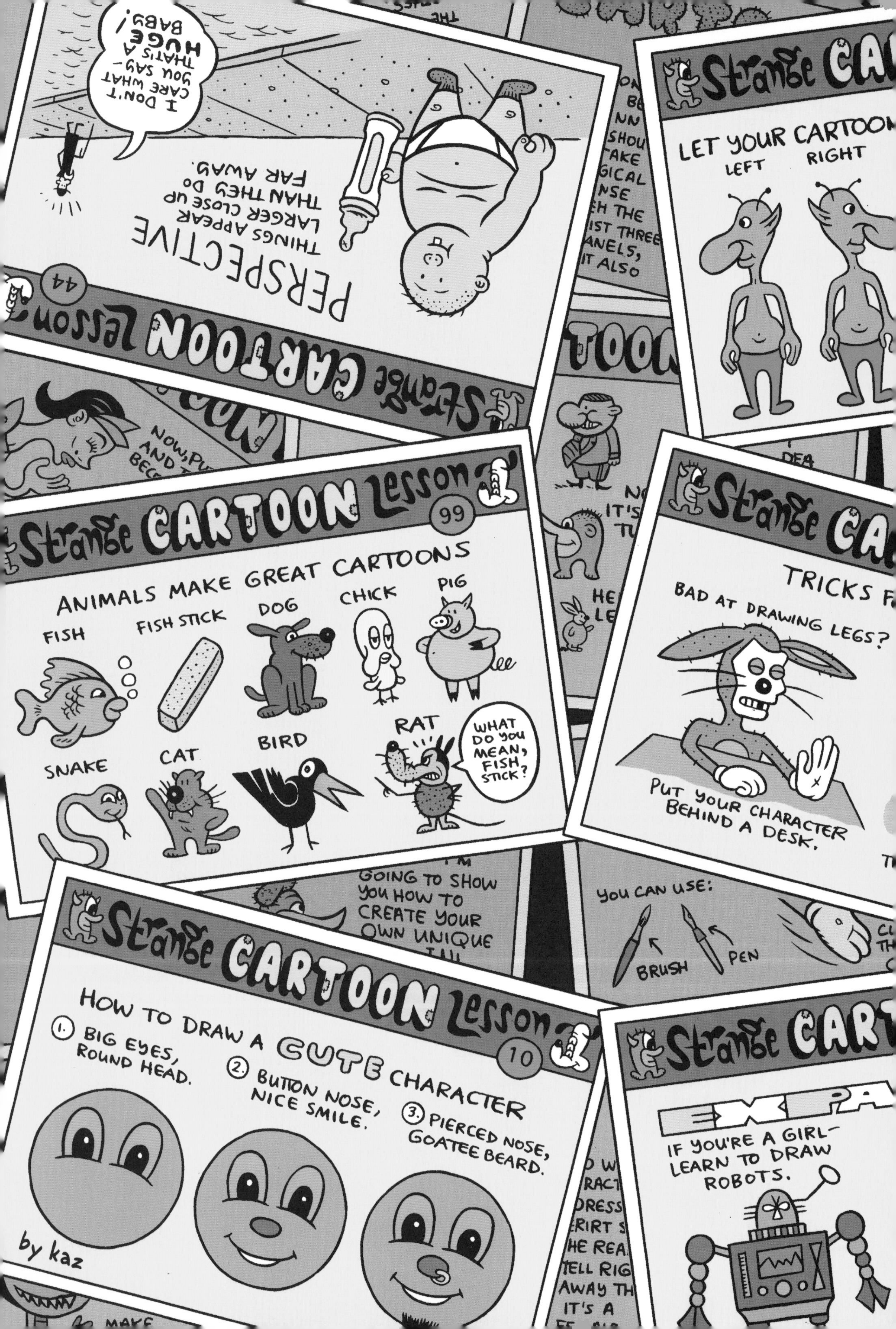

Strange CARTOON Lesson
44
PERSPECTIVE
THINGS APPEAR LARGER CLOSE UP THAN THEY DO FAR AWAY.
I DON'T CARE WHAT YOU SAY- THAT'S A HUGE BABY!
Strange CARTOON Lesson
99
ANIMALS MAKE GREAT CARTOONS
FISH
FISH STICK
DOG
CHICK
PIG
SNAKE
CAT
BIRD
RAT
WHAT DO YOU MEAN, FISH STICK?
Strange CA
LET YOUR CARTOON
LEFT
RIGHT
Strange CA
TRICKS F
BAD AT DRAWING LEGS?
PUT YOUR CHARACTER BEHIND A DESK.
GOING TO SHOW YOU HOW TO CREATE YOUR OWN UNIQUE
YOU CAN USE:
BRUSH
PEN
Strange CARTOON Lesson
10
HOW TO DRAW A CUTE CHARACTER
1. BIG EYES, ROUND HEAD.
2. BUTTON NOSE, NICE SMILE.
3. PIERCED NOSE, GOATEE BEARD.
by kaz
Strange CART
IF YOU'RE A GIRL- LEARN TO DRAW ROBOTS.

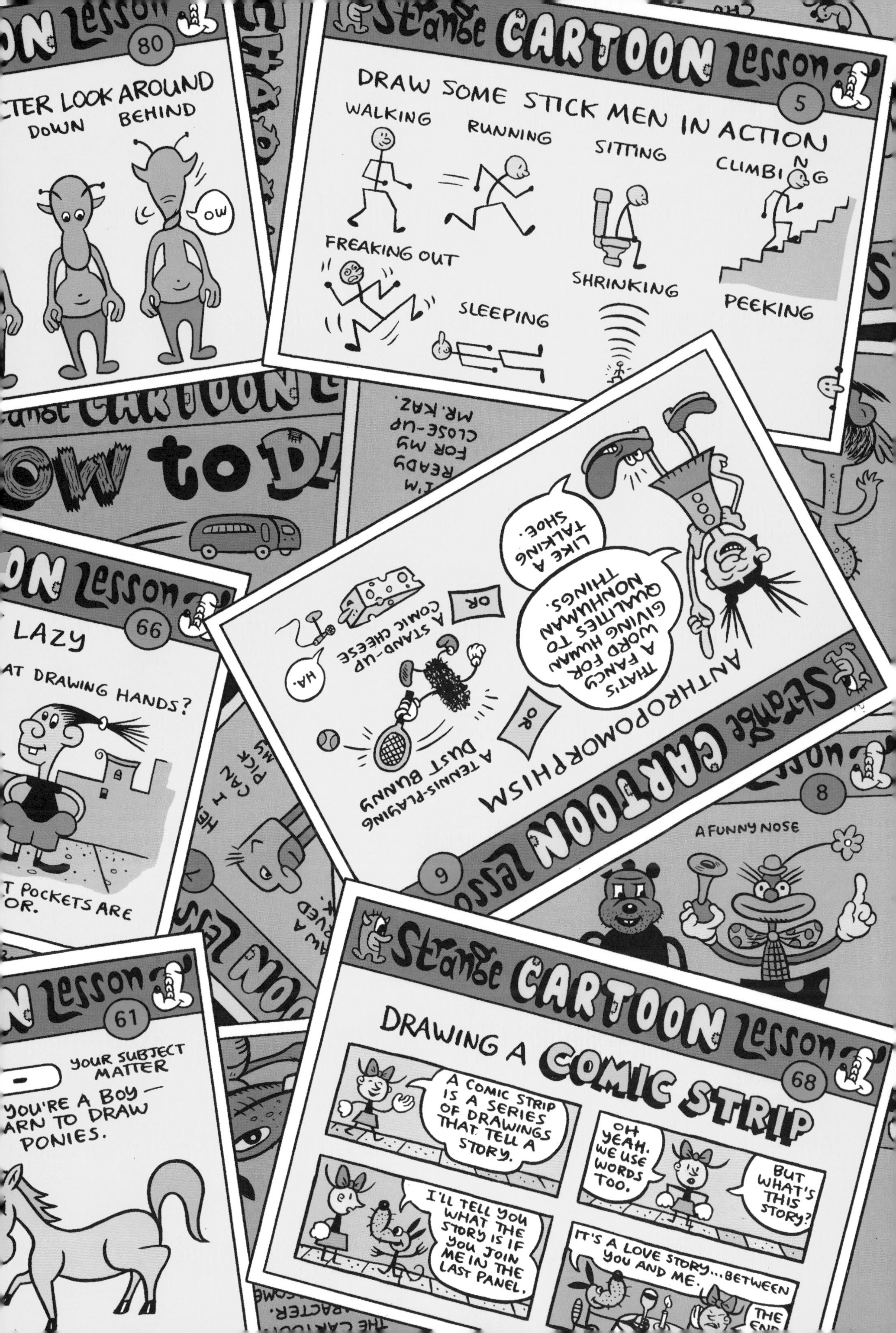

Strange CARTOON Lesson 5
DRAW SOME STICK MEN IN ACTION
WALKING
RUNNING
SITTING
CLIMBING
FREAKING OUT
SHRINKING
PEEKING
SLEEPING
80
DOWN
BEHIND
OW
I'M READY FOR MY CLOSE-UP MR. KAZ.
Strange CARTOON Lesson 9
ANTHROPOMORPHISM
THAT'S A FANCY WORD FOR GIVING HUMAN QUALITIES TO NONHUMAN THINGS.
LIKE A TALKING SHOE.
A TENNIS-PLAYING DUST BUNNY
OR
A STAND-UP COMIC CHEESE
OR
HA.
66
LAZY
AT DRAWING HANDS?
8
A FUNNY NOSE
61
YOUR SUBJECT MATTER
PONIES.
Strange CARTOON Lesson 68
DRAWING A COMIC STRIP
A COMIC STRIP IS A SERIES OF DRAWINGS THAT TELL A STORY.
OH YEAH. WE USE WORDS TOO.
BUT WHAT'S THIS STORY?
I'LL TELL YOU WHAT THE STORY IS IF YOU JOIN ME IN THE LAST PANEL.
IT'S A LOVE STORY...BETWEEN YOU AND ME.

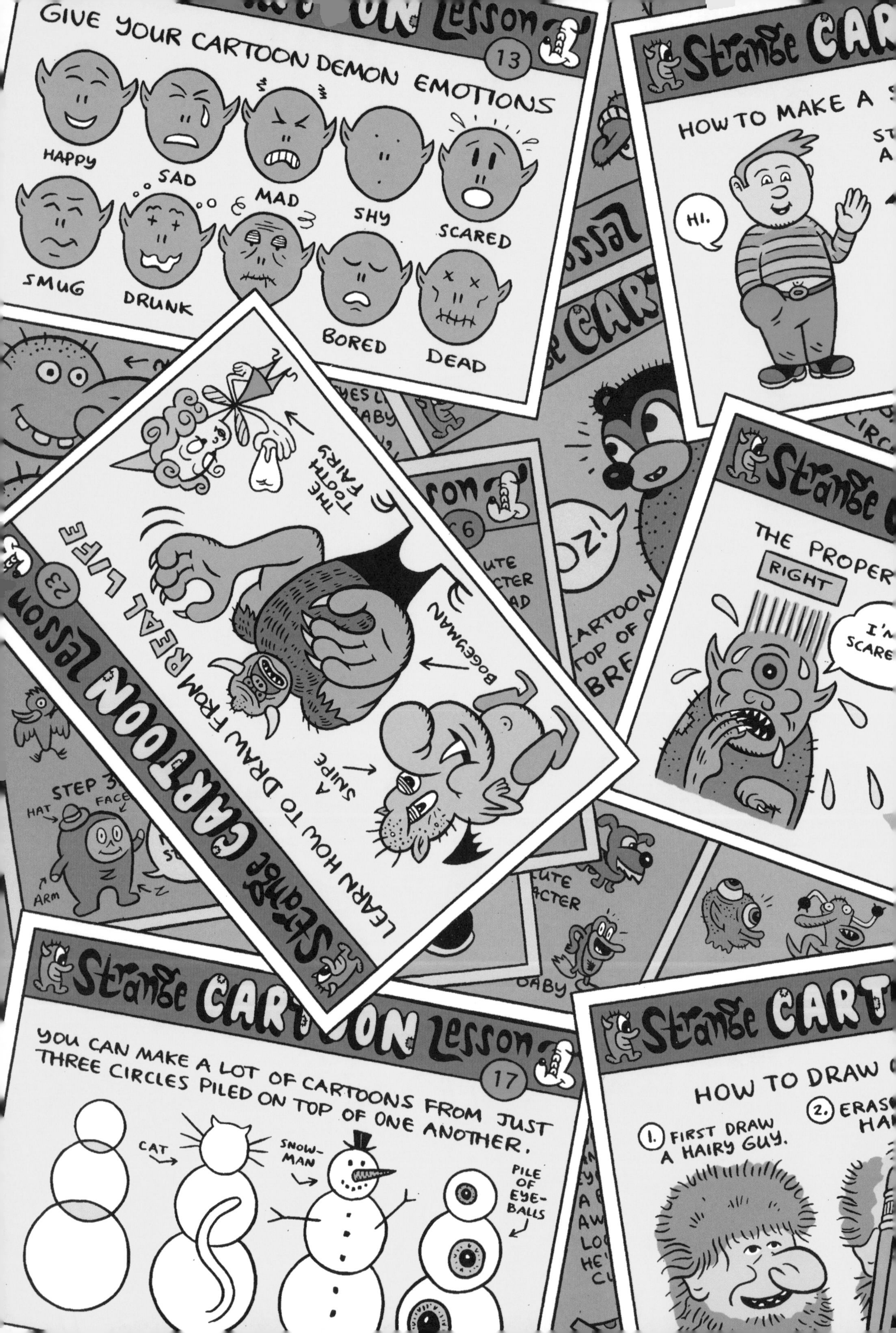

CARTOON Lesson
13
GIVE YOUR CARTOON DEMON EMOTIONS
HAPPY
SAD
MAD
SHY
SCARED
SMUG
DRUNK
BORED
DEAD
Strange CAR
HOW TO MAKE A
HI.
Strange CARTOON Lesson
23
LEARN HOW TO DRAW FROM REAL LIFE
THE TOOTH FAIRY
BOGEYMAN
A SNIPE
Strange
THE PROPER
RIGHT
STEP 3
HAT
FACE
ARM
6
Strange CARTOON Lesson
17
YOU CAN MAKE A LOT OF CARTOONS FROM JUST THREE CIRCLES PILED ON TOP OF ONE ANOTHER.
CAT
SNOW-MAN
PILE OF EYE-BALLS
Strange CART
HOW TO DRAW
1. FIRST DRAW A HAIRY GUY.
2. ERAS

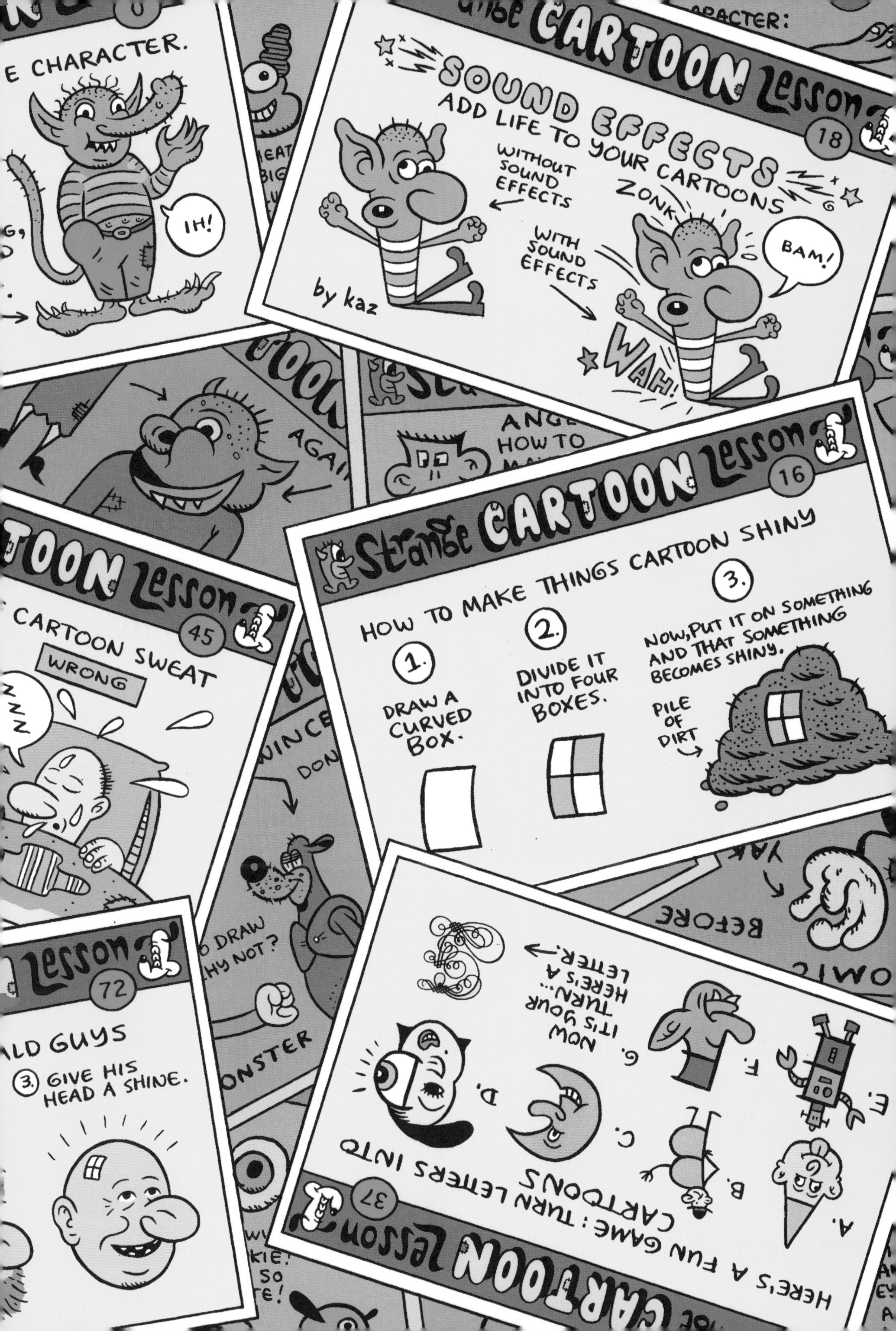

E CHARACTER.
IH!
CARTOON Lesson
SOUND EFFECTS
ADD LIFE TO YOUR CARTOONS
18
WITHOUT SOUND EFFECTS
WITH SOUND EFFECTS
ZONK
BAM!
WAH!
by kaz
ANGE
HOW TO
AGAI
Strange CARTOON Lesson
16
HOW TO MAKE THINGS CARTOON SHINY
1. DRAW A CURVED BOX.
2. DIVIDE IT INTO FOUR BOXES.
3. NOW, PUT IT ON SOMETHING AND THAT SOMETHING BECOMES SHINY.
PILE OF DIRT
TOON Lesson
45
CARTOON SWEAT
WRONG
ZZZ
WINCE
DON
O DRAW
HY NOT?
ONSTER
Lesson
72
LD GUYS
3. GIVE HIS HEAD A SHINE.
KIE!
SO
E!
YAK
BEFORE
CARTOON Lesson
37
HERE'S A FUN GAME: TURN LETTERS INTO CARTOONS
A.
B.
C.
D.
E.
F.
6. NOW IT'S YOUR TURN... HERE'S A LETTER.

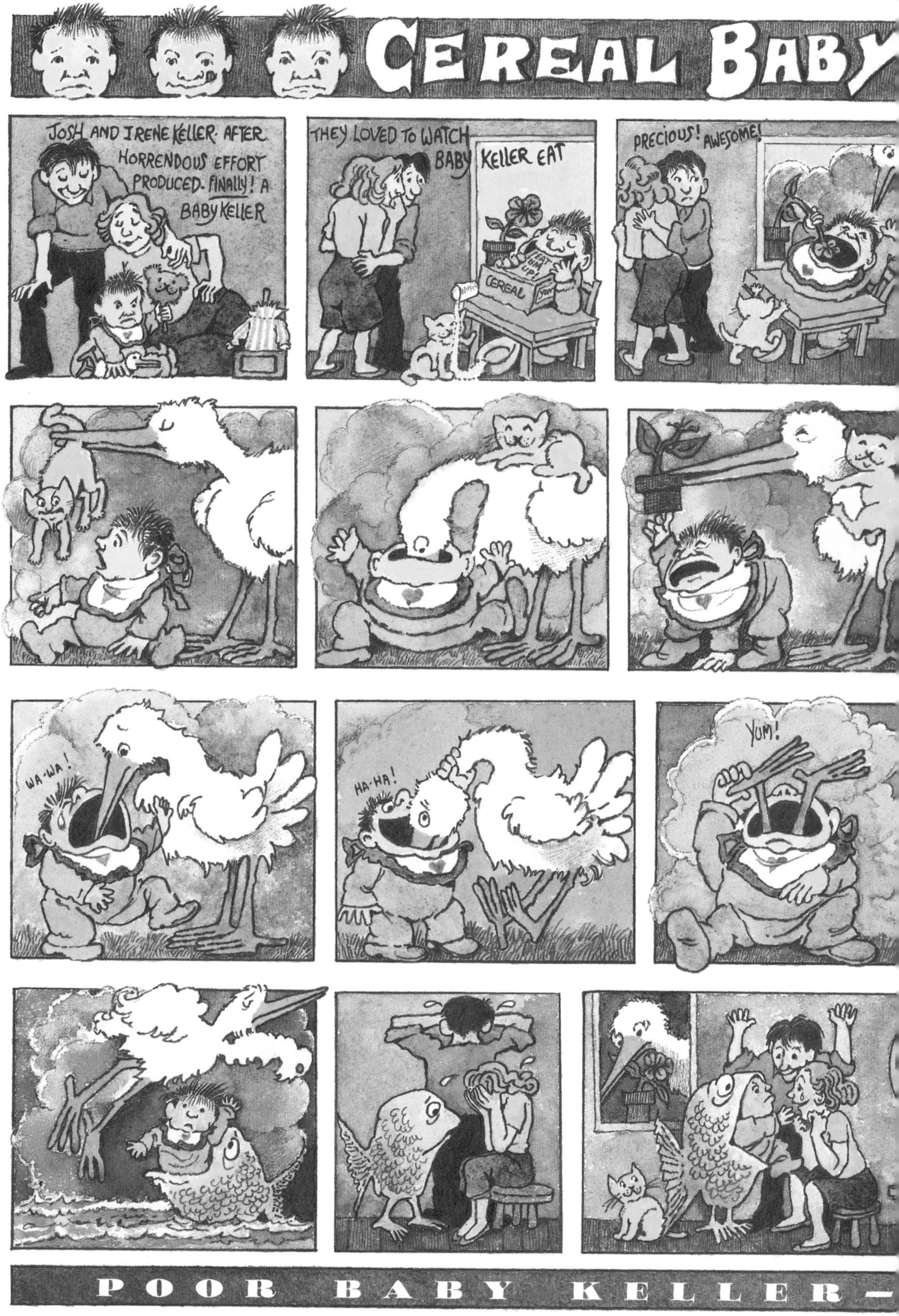
CEREAL BABY
JOSH AND IRENE KELLER. AFTER HORRENDOUS EFFORT PRODUCED. FINALLY! A BABY KELLER
THEY LOVED TO WATCH BABY KELLER EAT
CEREAL
PRECIOUS!
AWESOME!
WA-WA!
HA-HA!
YUM!
POOR BABY KELLER—

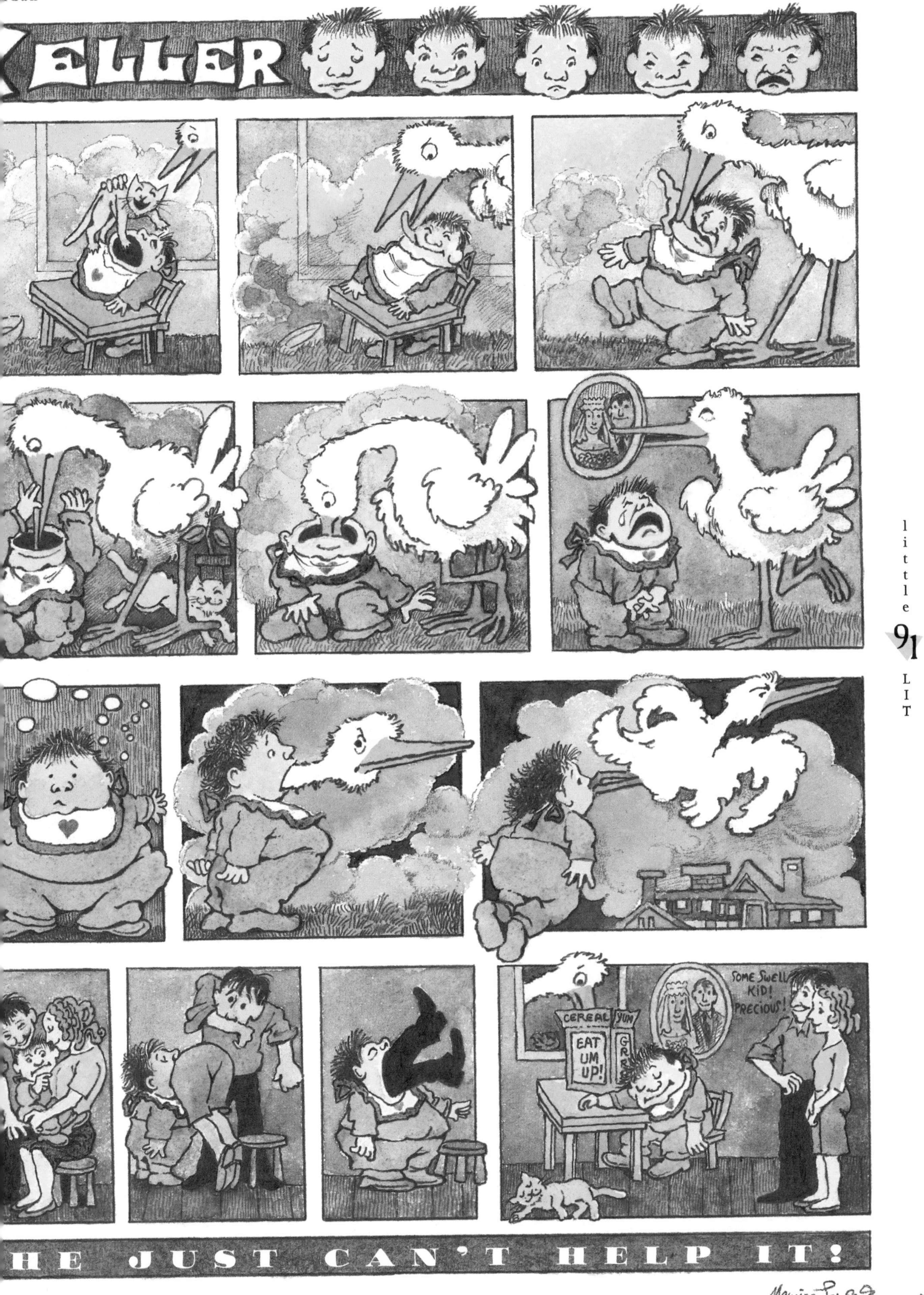
ELLER
CEREAL
YUM
EAT UM UP!
GRR
SOME SWELL KID! PRECIOUS!
HE JUST CAN'T HELP IT!
Maurice Sendak

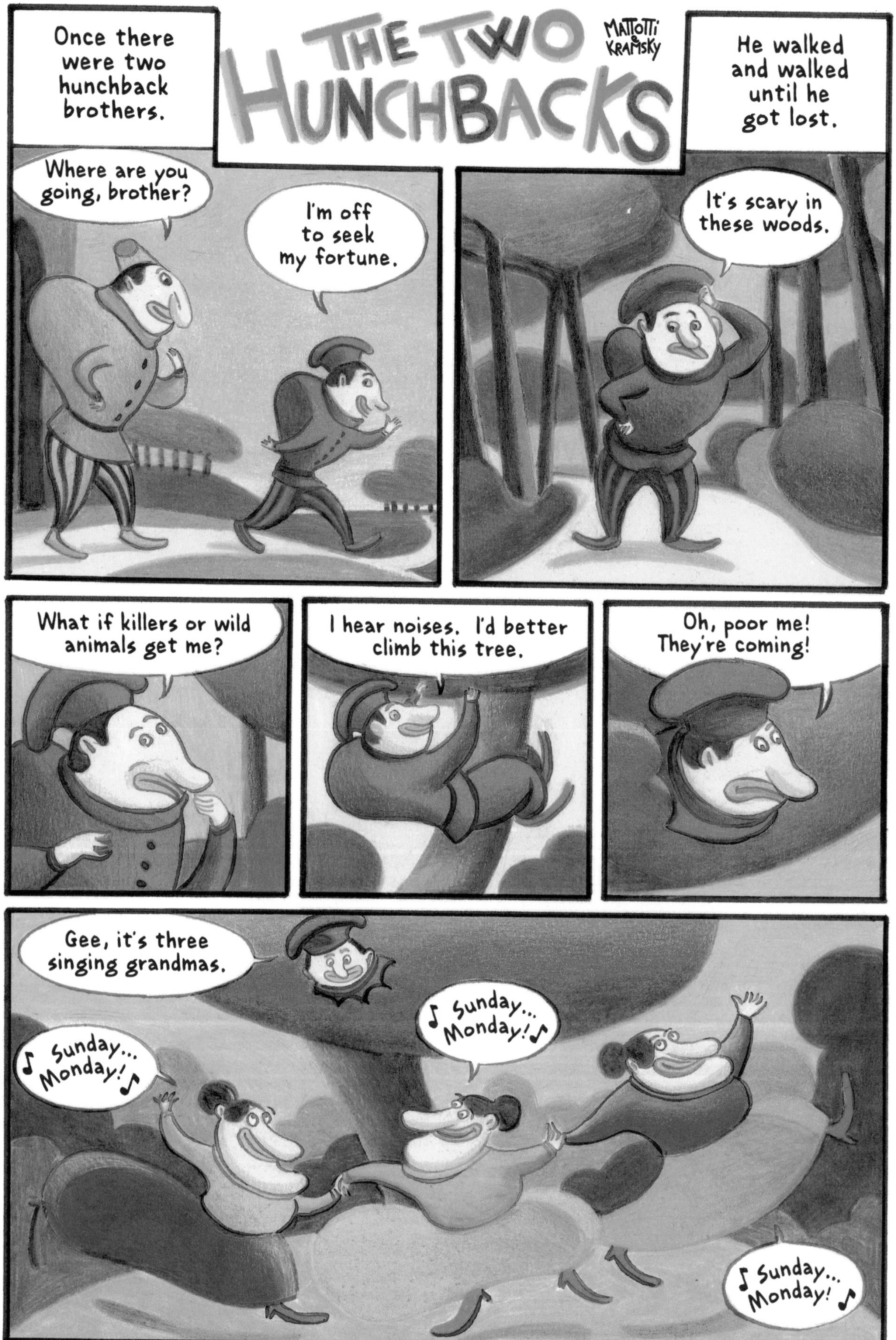
Once there were two hunchback brothers.
THE TWO HUNCHBACKS
MATTOTTI & KRAMSKY
He walked and walked until he got lost.
Where are you going, brother?
I'm off to seek my fortune.
It's scary in these woods.
What if killers or wild animals get me?
I hear noises. I'd better climb this tree.
Oh, poor me! They're coming!
Gee, it's three singing grandmas.
♪ Sunday... Monday! ♪
♪ Sunday... Monday! ♪
♪ Sunday... Monday! ♪

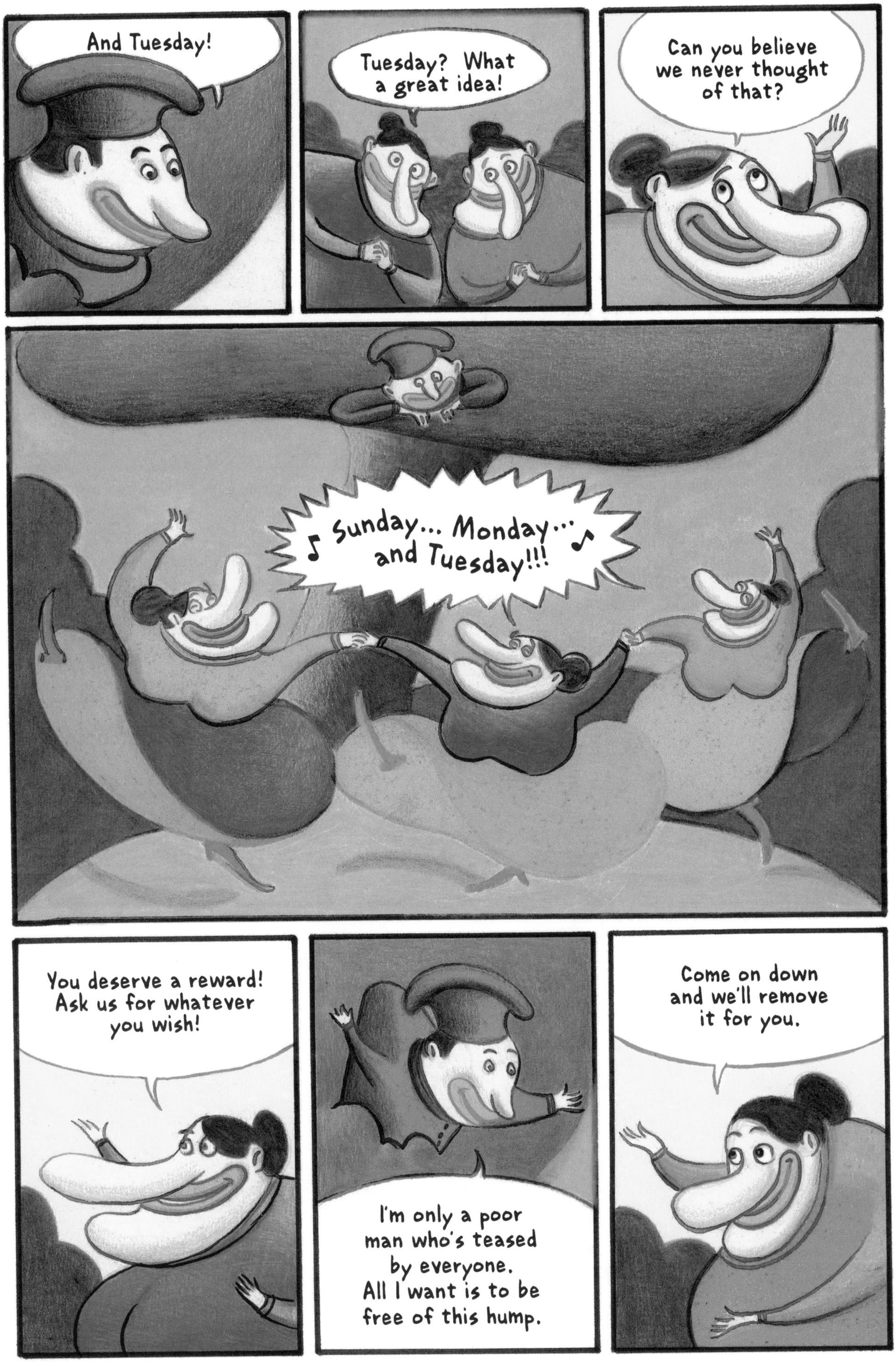

And Tuesday!
Tuesday? What a great idea!
Can you believe we never thought of that?
♪ Sunday... Monday... and Tuesday!!! ♪
You deserve a reward! Ask us for whatever you wish!
I'm only a poor man who's teased by everyone. All I want is to be free of this hump.
Come on down and we'll remove it for you.

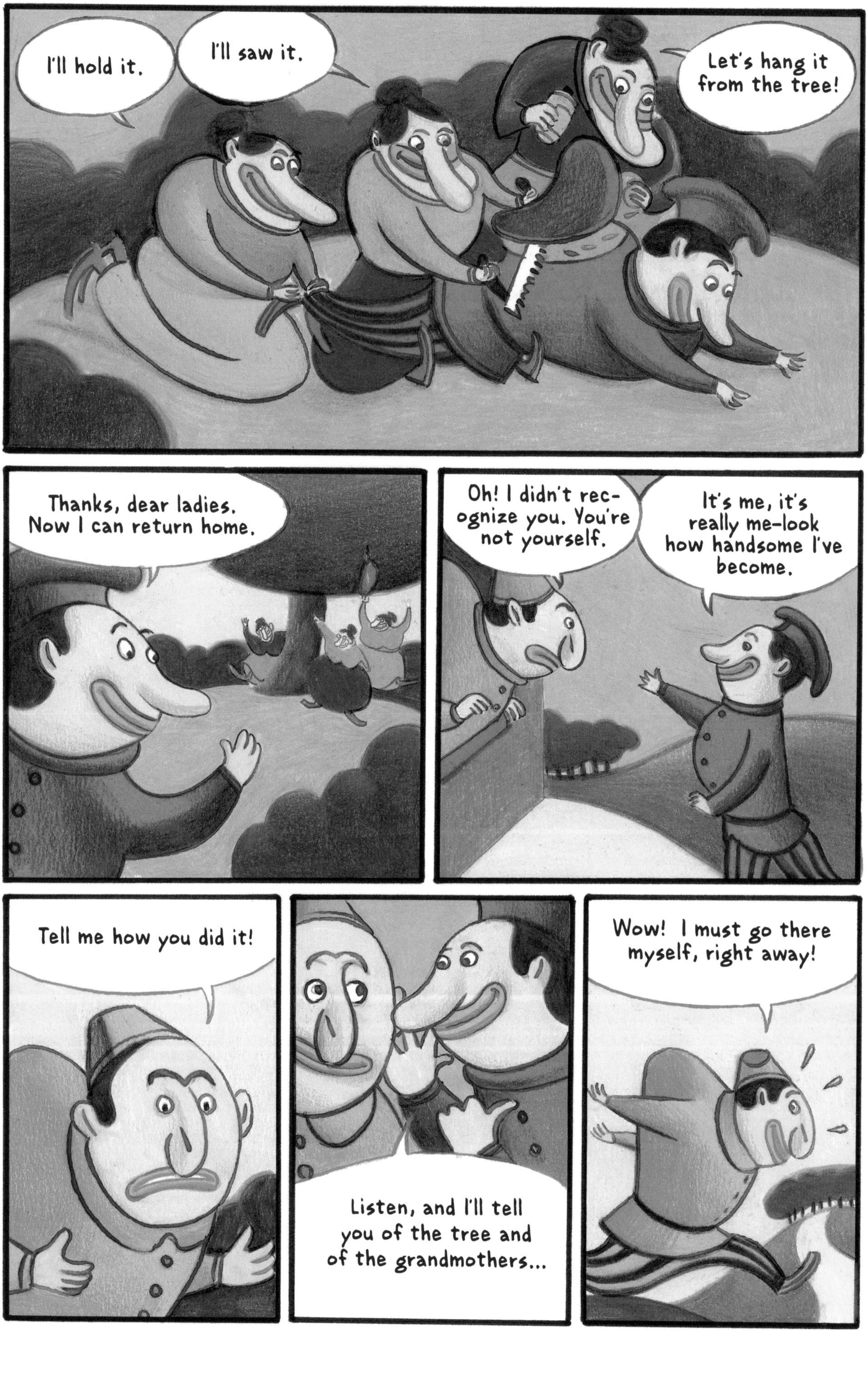
I'll hold it.
I'll saw it.
Let's hang it from the tree!
Thanks, dear ladies. Now I can return home.
Oh! I didn't rec-ognize you. You're not yourself.
It's me, it's really me-look how handsome I've become.
Tell me how you did it!
Listen, and I'll tell you of the tree and of the grandmothers...
Wow! I must go there myself, right away!

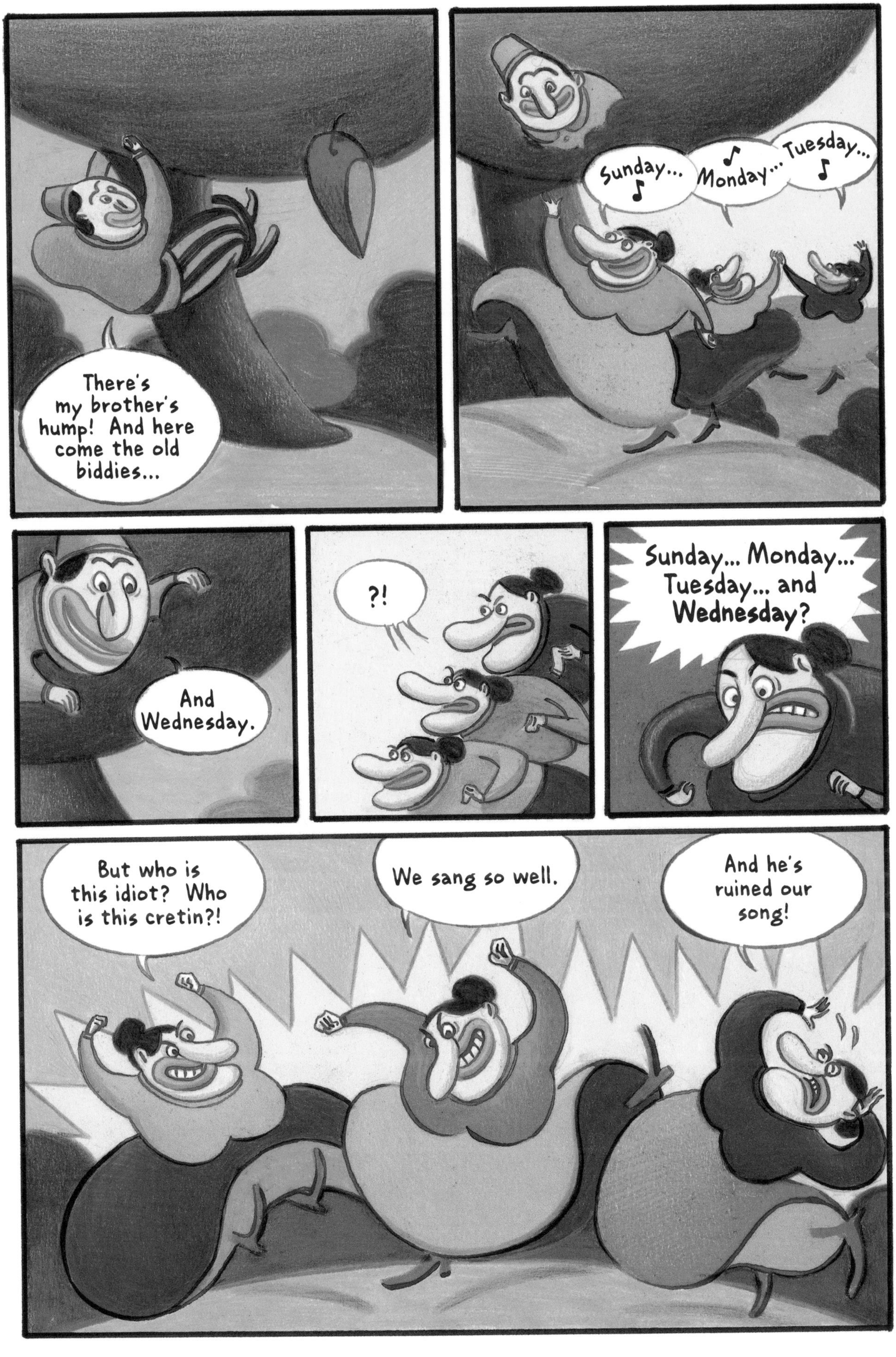
There's my brother's hump! And here come the old biddies...
Sunday... ♪
♪ Monday...
Tuesday... ♪
And Wednesday.
?!
Sunday... Monday... Tuesday... and Wednesday?
But who is this idiot? Who is this cretin?!
We sang so well.
And he's ruined our song!

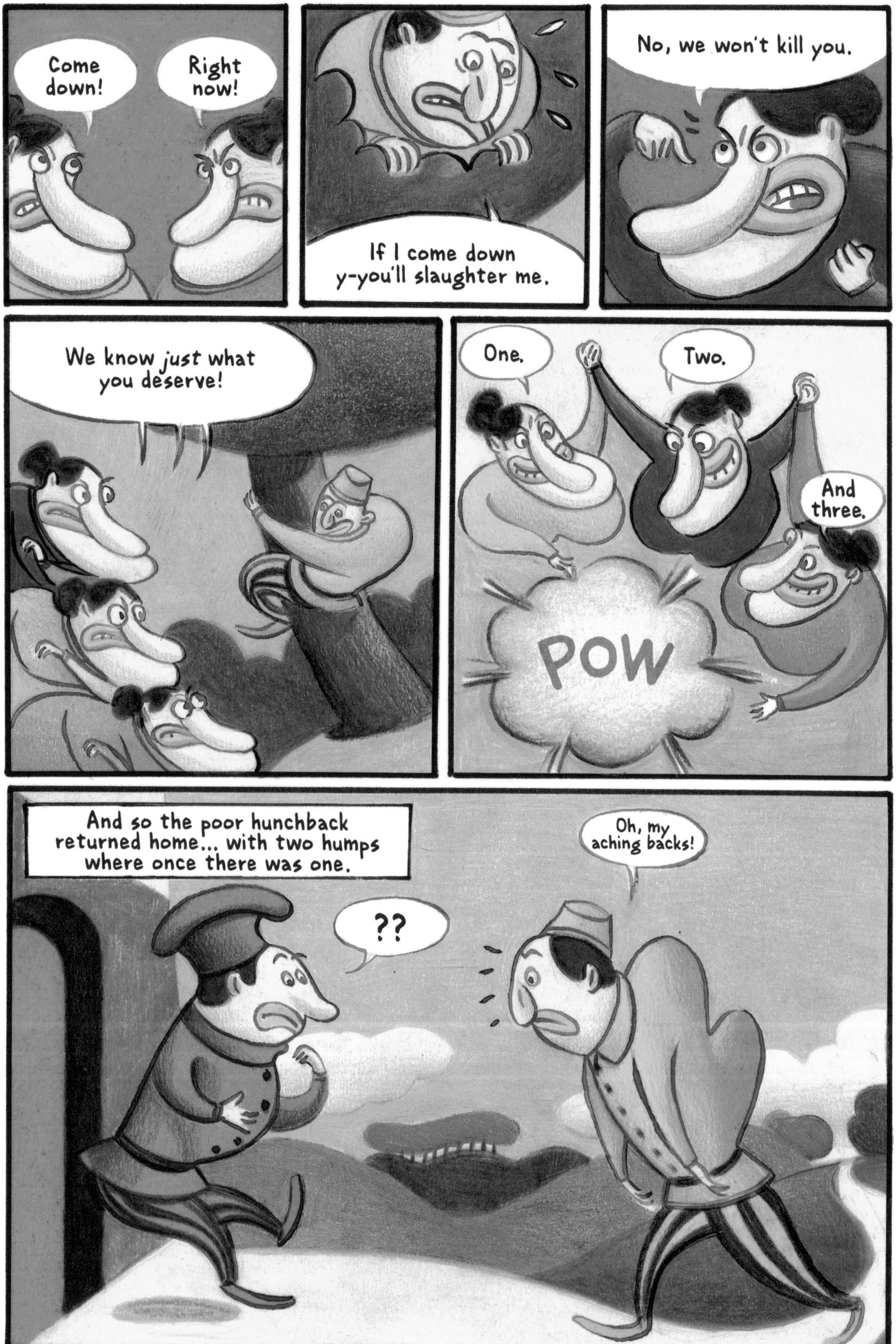
Come down!
Right now!
If I come down y-you'll slaughter me.
No, we won't kill you.
We know *just* what you deserve!
One.
Two.
And three.
POW
And so the poor hunchback returned home... with two humps where once there was one.
Oh, my aching backs!
??

kim deitch

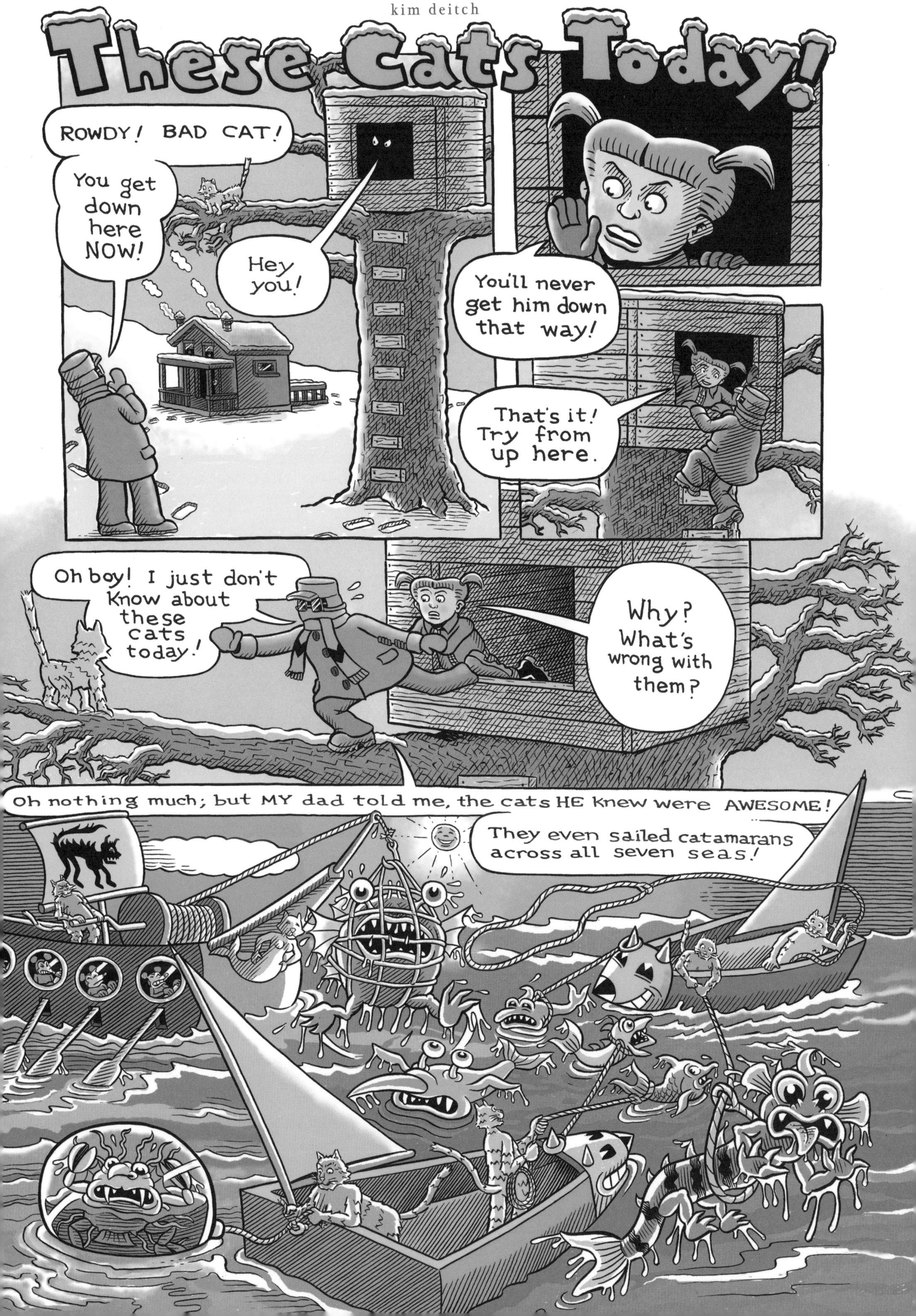

These Cats Today!
ROWDY! BAD CAT!
You get down here NOW!
Hey you!
You'll never get him down that way!
That's it! Try from up here.
Oh boy! I just don't know about these cats today!
Why? What's wrong with them?
Oh nothing much; but MY dad told me, the cats HE knew were AWESOME!
They even sailed catamarans across all seven seas!

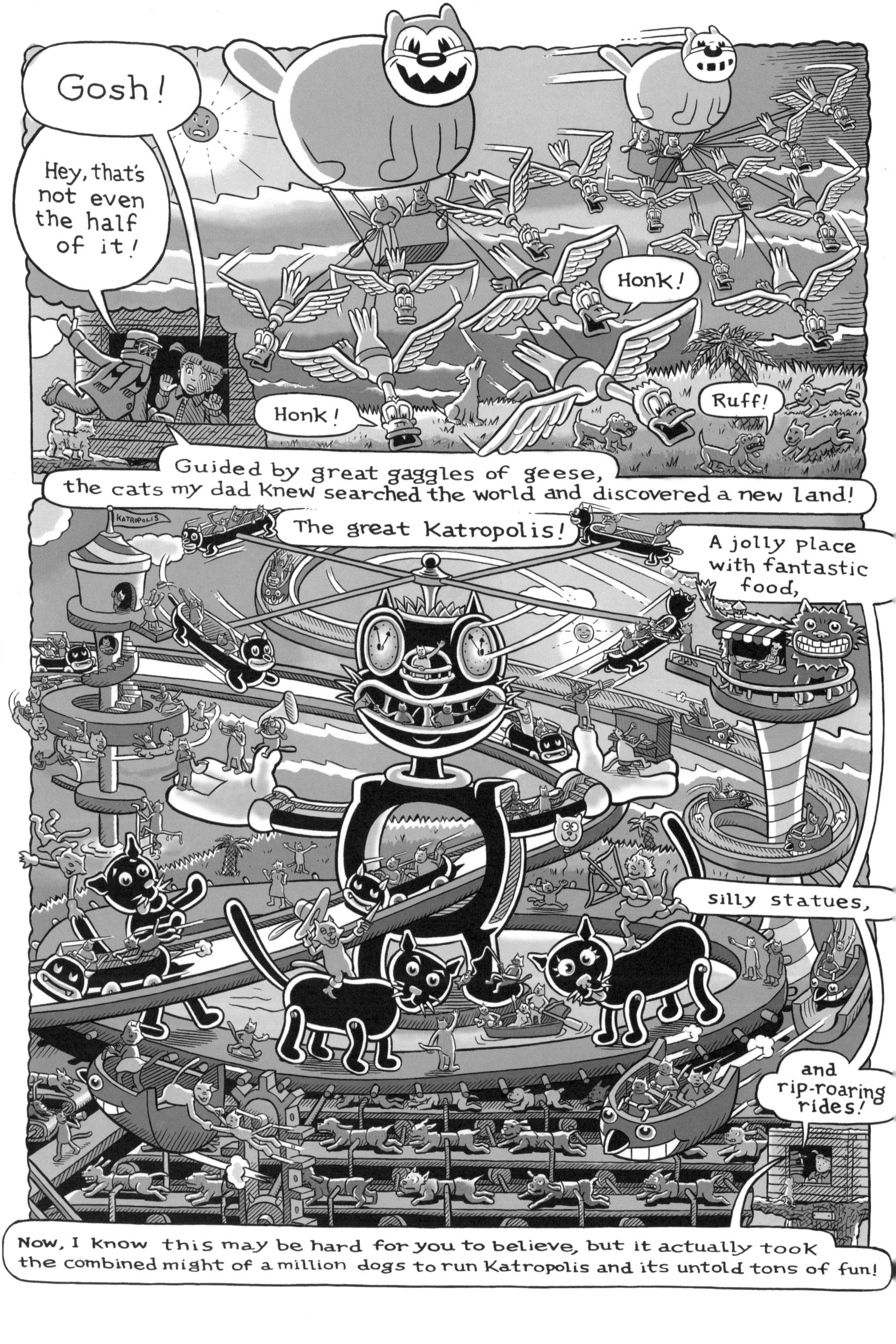
Gosh!
Hey, that's not even the half of it!
Honk!
Honk!
Ruff!
Guided by great gaggles of geese, the cats my dad knew searched the world and discovered a new land!
KATROPOLIS
The great Katropolis!
A jolly place with fantastic food,
silly statues,
and rip-roaring rides!
Now, I know this may be hard for you to believe, but it actually took the combined might of a million dogs to run Katropolis and its untold tons of fun!

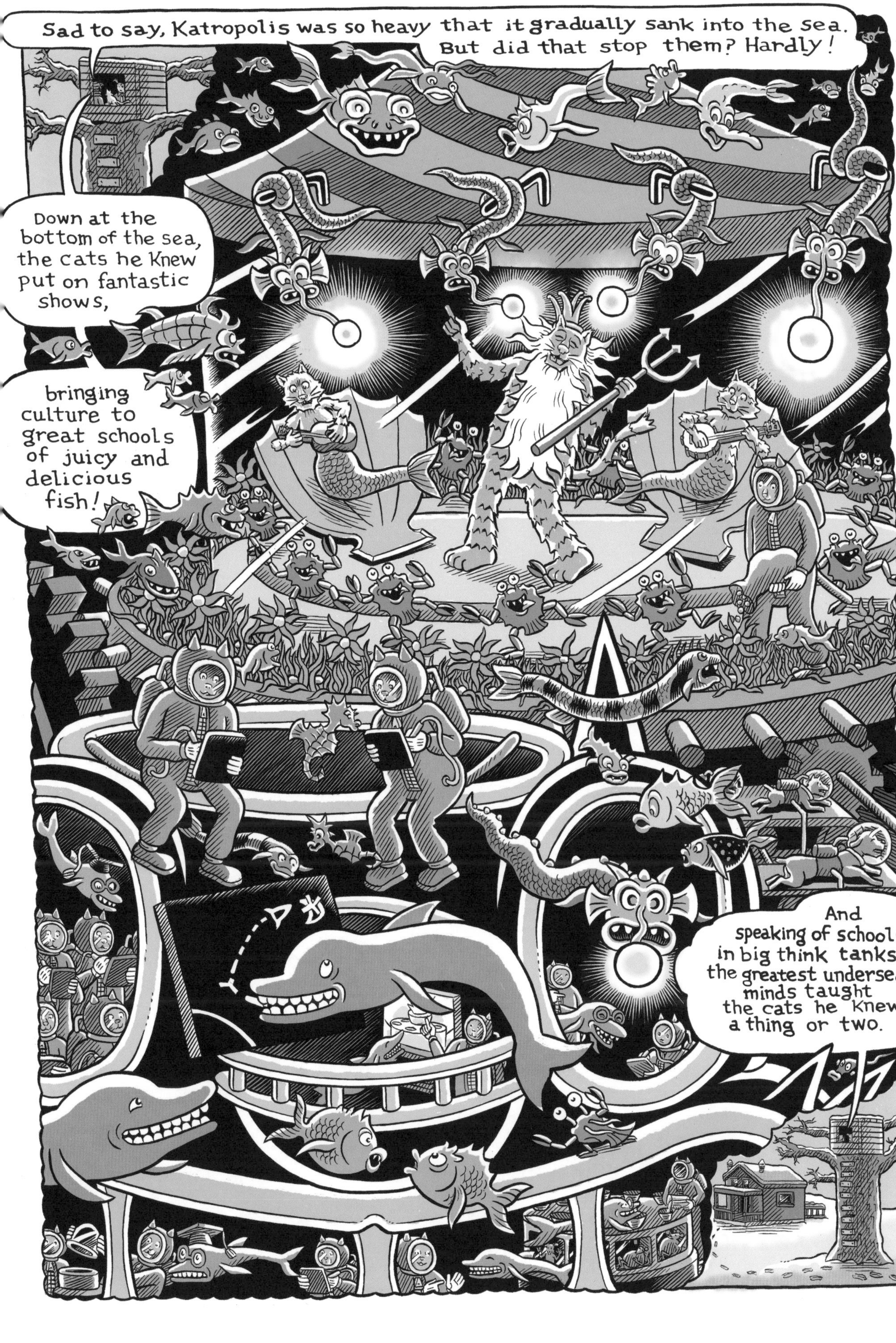
Sad to say, Katropolis was so heavy that it gradually sank into the sea. But did that stop them? Hardly!
Down at the bottom of the sea, the cats he Knew put on fantastic shows,
bringing culture to great schools of juicy and delicious fish!
And speaking of schools, in big think tanks, the greatest undersea minds taught the cats he Knew a thing or two.

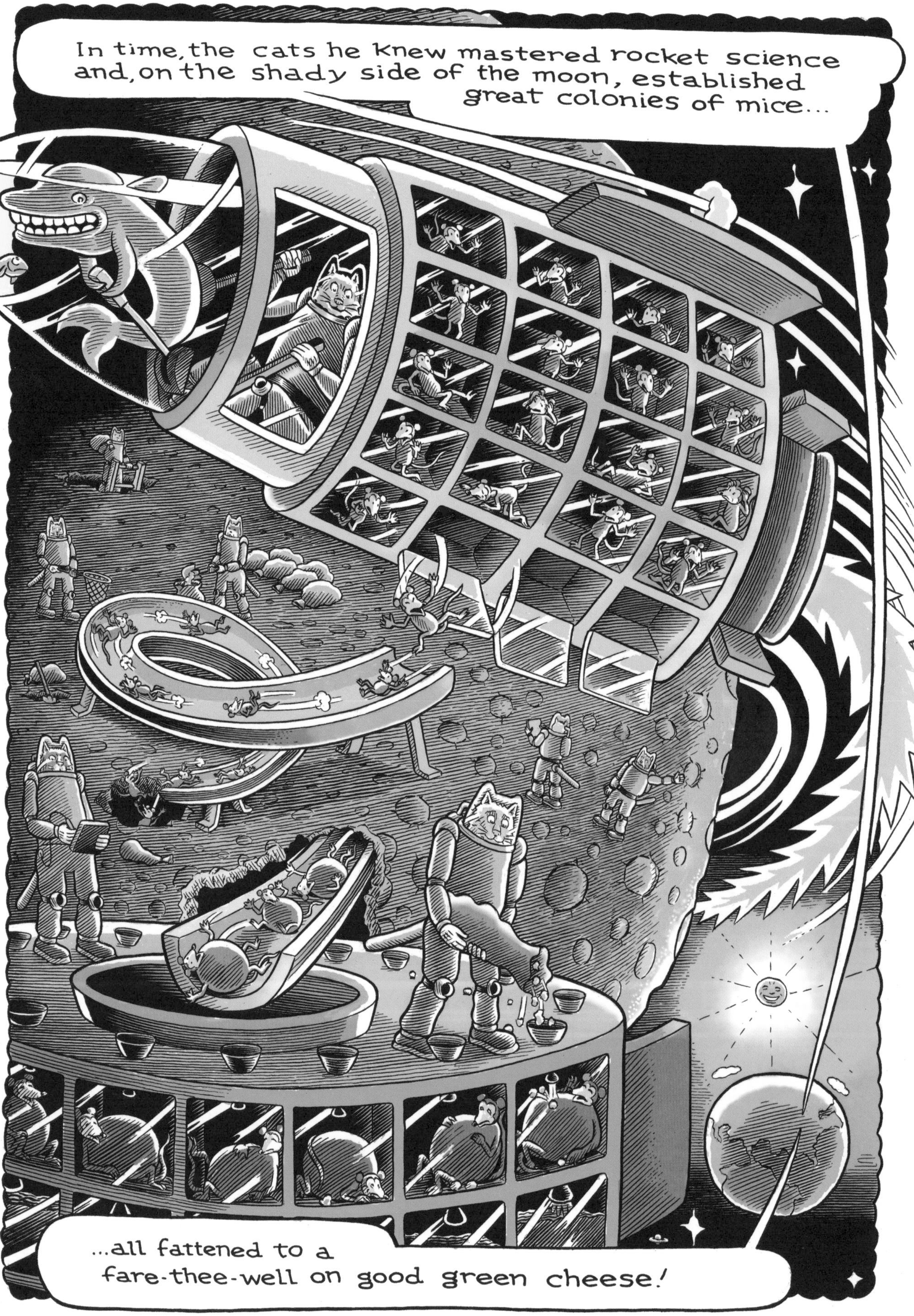
In time, the cats he knew mastered rocket science and, on the shady side of the moon, established great colonies of mice...
...all fattened to a fare-thee-well on good green cheese!

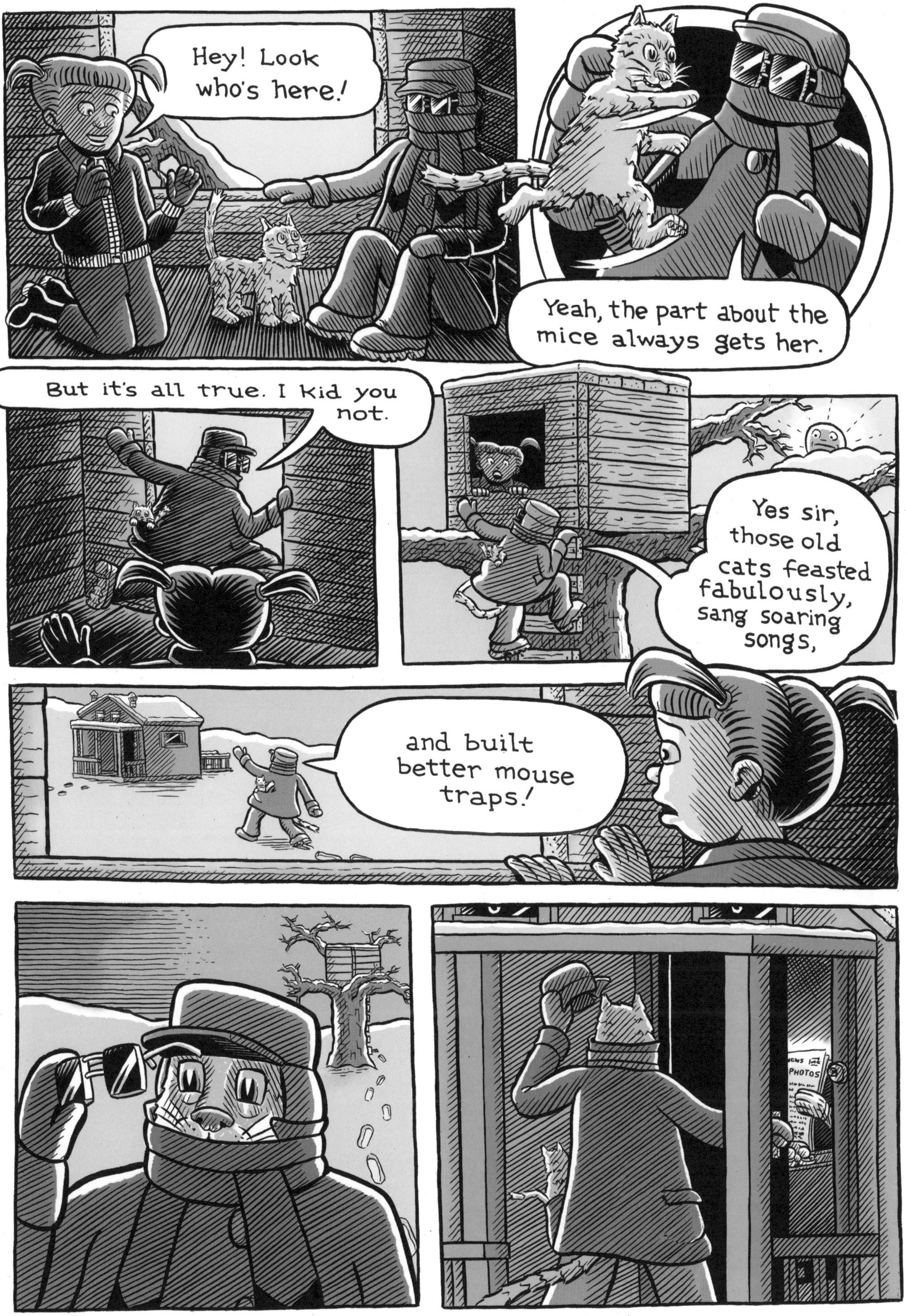
Hey! Look who's here!
Yeah, the part about the mice always gets her.
But it's all true. I kid you not.
Yes sir, those old cats feasted fabulously, sang soaring songs,
and built better mouse traps!

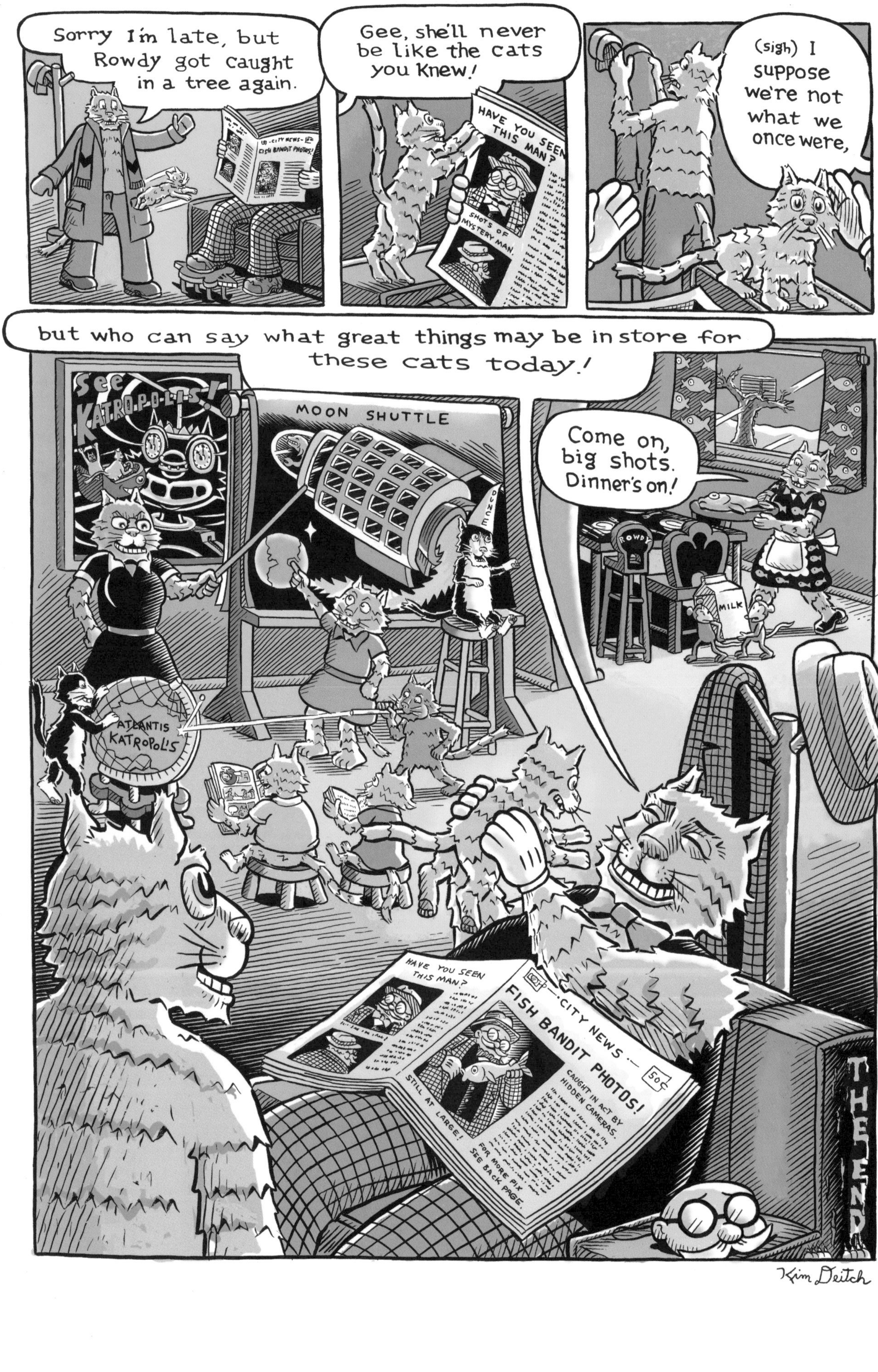
Sorry I'm late, but Rowdy got caught in a tree again.
CITY NEWS
FISH BANDIT PHOTOS!
Gee, she'll never be like the cats you knew!
HAVE YOU SEEN THIS MAN?
SHOTS OF MYSTERY MAN
(sigh) I suppose we're not what we once were,
but who can say what great things may be in store for these cats today!
See KATROPOLIS!
MOON SHUTTLE
DUNCE
Come on, big shots. Dinner's on!
ROWDY
MILK
ATLANTIS
KATROPOLIS
HAVE YOU SEEN THIS MAN?
CITY NEWS
50¢
FISH BANDIT PHOTOS!
CAUGHT IN ACT BY HIDDEN CAMERAS.
STILL AT LARGE!
FOR MORE PIX SEE BACK PAGE.
THE END
Kim Deitch

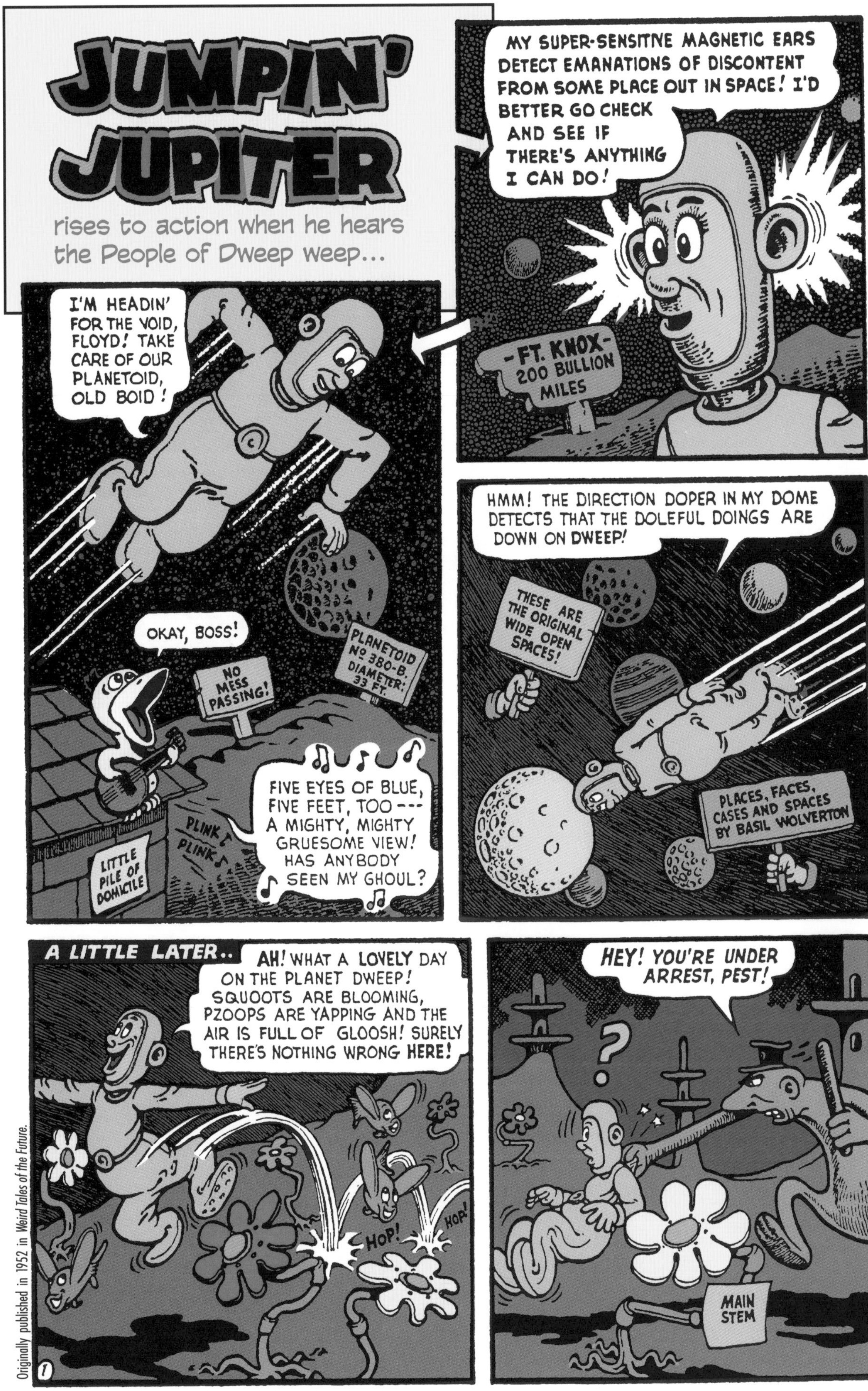
JUMPIN' JUPITER
rises to action when he hears the People of Dweep weep...
MY SUPER-SENSITIVE MAGNETIC EARS DETECT EMANATIONS OF DISCONTENT FROM SOME PLACE OUT IN SPACE! I'D BETTER GO CHECK AND SEE IF THERE'S ANYTHING I CAN DO!
-FT. KNOX- 200 BULLION MILES
I'M HEADIN' FOR THE VOID, FLOYD! TAKE CARE OF OUR PLANETOID, OLD BOID!
OKAY, BOSS!
NO MESS PASSING!
PLANETOID № 380-B. DIAMETER: 33 FT.
FIVE EYES OF BLUE, FIVE FEET, TOO--- A MIGHTY, MIGHTY GRUESOME VIEW! HAS ANYBODY SEEN MY GHOUL?
PLINK PLINK
LITTLE PILE OF DOMICILE
HMM! THE DIRECTION DOPER IN MY DOME DETECTS THAT THE DOLEFUL DOINGS ARE DOWN ON DWEEP!
THESE ARE THE ORIGINAL WIDE OPEN SPACES!
PLACES, FACES, CASES AND SPACES BY BASIL WOLVERTON
A LITTLE LATER..
AH! WHAT A LOVELY DAY ON THE PLANET DWEEP! SQUOOTS ARE BLOOMING, PZOOPS ARE YAPPING AND THE AIR IS FULL OF GLOOSH! SURELY THERE'S NOTHING WRONG HERE!
HOP! HOP!
1
HEY! YOU'RE UNDER ARREST, PEST!
?
MAIN STEM

Originally published in 1952 in *Weird Tales of the Future.*

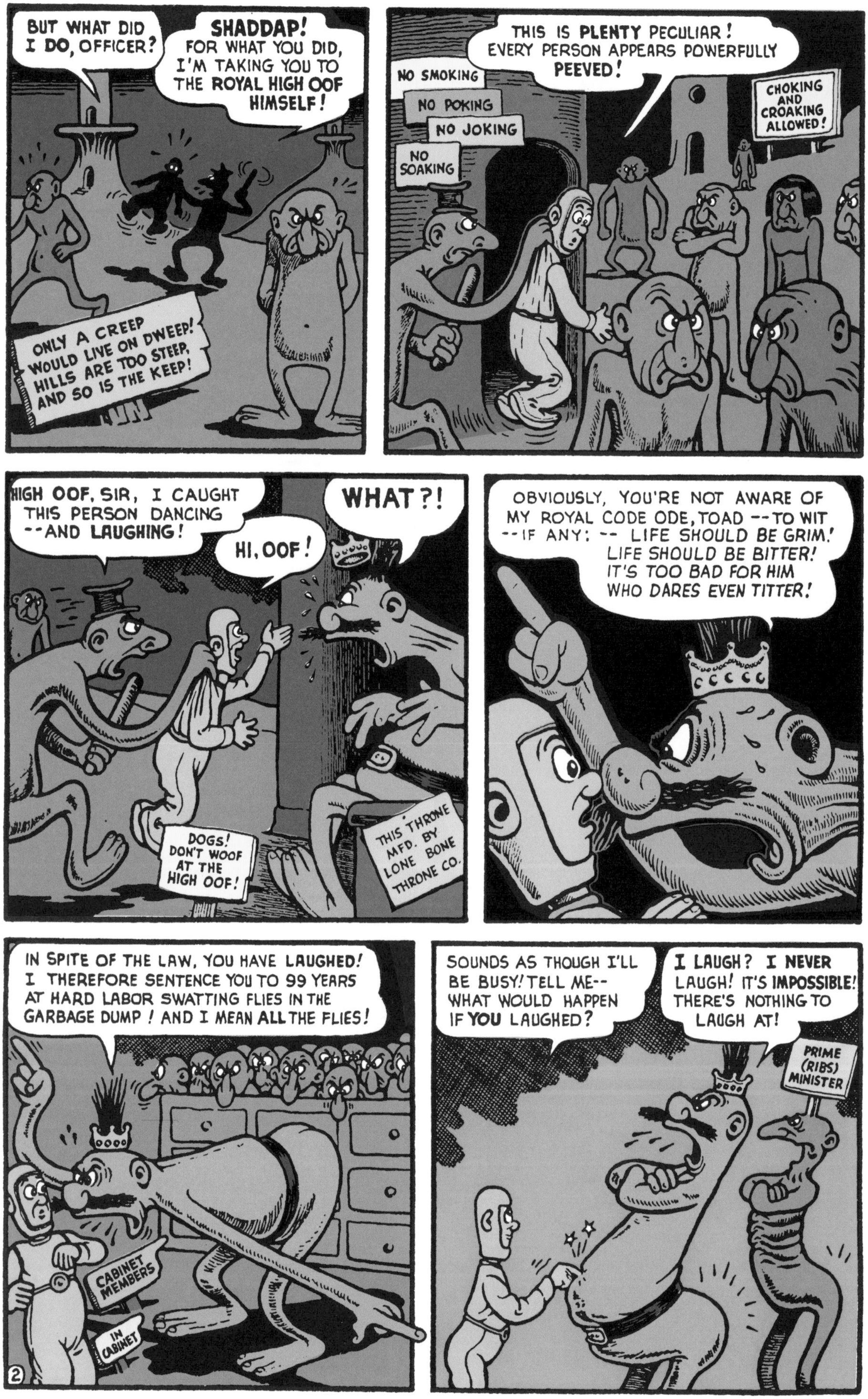
BUT WHAT DID I DO, OFFICER?
SHADDAP! FOR WHAT YOU DID, I'M TAKING YOU TO THE ROYAL HIGH OOF HIMSELF!
ONLY A CREEP WOULD LIVE ON DWEEP! HILLS ARE TOO STEEP, AND SO IS THE KEEP!
THIS IS PLENTY PECULIAR! EVERY PERSON APPEARS POWERFULLY PEEVED!
NO SMOKING
NO POKING
NO JOKING
NO SOAKING
CHOKING AND CROAKING ALLOWED!
HIGH OOF, SIR, I CAUGHT THIS PERSON DANCING --AND LAUGHING!
HI, OOF!
WHAT?!
DOGS! DON'T WOOF AT THE HIGH OOF!
THIS THRONE MFD. BY LONE BONE THRONE CO.
OBVIOUSLY, YOU'RE NOT AWARE OF MY ROYAL CODE ODE, TOAD --TO WIT --IF ANY: -- LIFE SHOULD BE GRIM! LIFE SHOULD BE BITTER! IT'S TOO BAD FOR HIM WHO DARES EVEN TITTER!
IN SPITE OF THE LAW, YOU HAVE LAUGHED! I THEREFORE SENTENCE YOU TO 99 YEARS AT HARD LABOR SWATTING FLIES IN THE GARBAGE DUMP! AND I MEAN ALL THE FLIES!
CABINET MEMBERS
IN CABINET
2
SOUNDS AS THOUGH I'LL BE BUSY! TELL ME-- WHAT WOULD HAPPEN IF YOU LAUGHED?
I LAUGH? I NEVER LAUGH! IT'S IMPOSSIBLE! THERE'S NOTHING TO LAUGH AT!
PRIME (RIBS) MINISTER

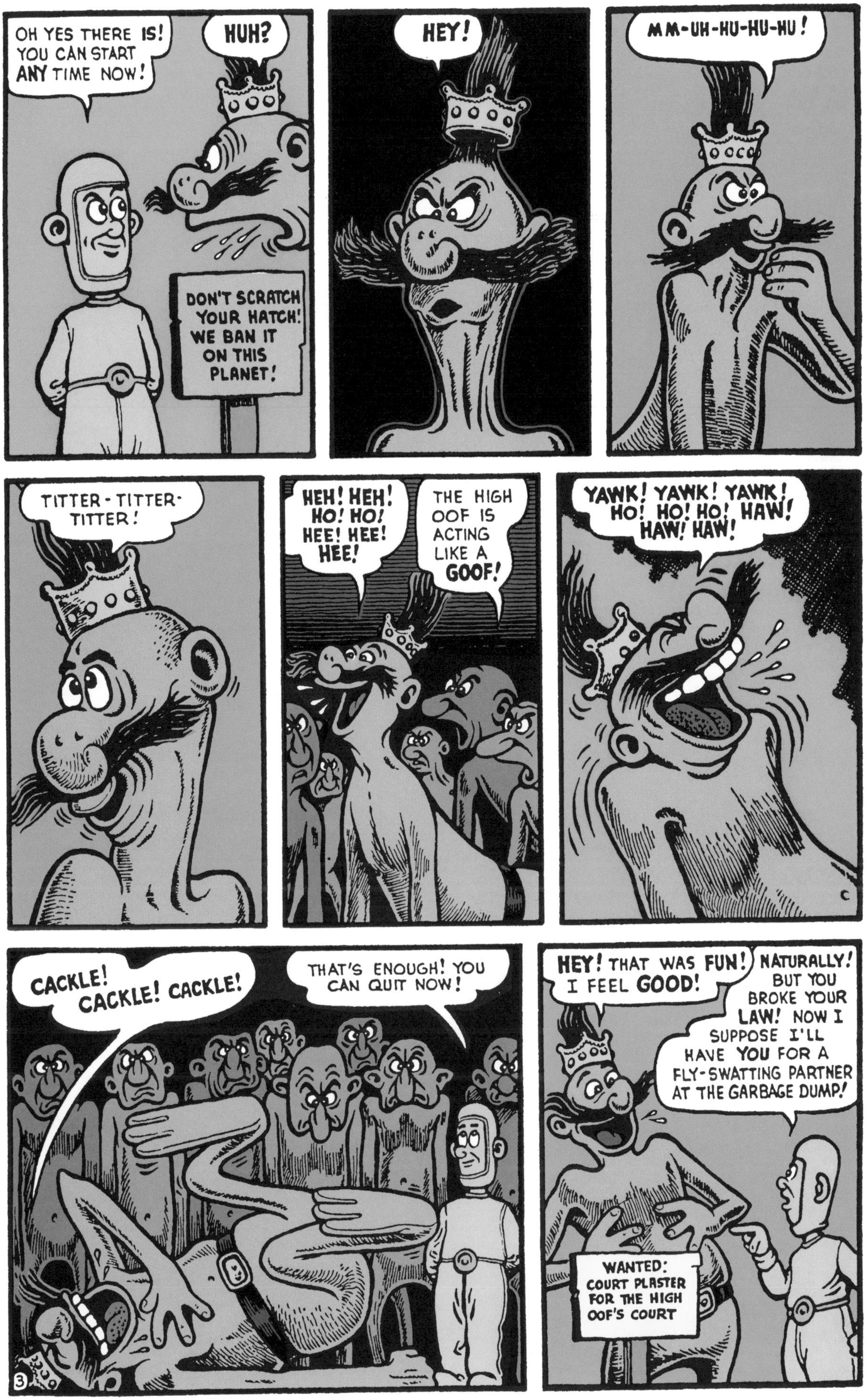
OH YES THERE IS! YOU CAN START ANY TIME NOW!
HUH?
DON'T SCRATCH YOUR HATCH! WE BAN IT ON THIS PLANET!
HEY!
MM-UH-HU-HU-HU!
TITTER-TITTER-TITTER!
HEH! HEH! HO! HO! HEE! HEE! HEE!
THE HIGH OOF IS ACTING LIKE A GOOF!
YAWK! YAWK! YAWK! HO! HO! HO! HAW! HAW! HAW!
CACKLE! CACKLE! CACKLE!
THAT'S ENOUGH! YOU CAN QUIT NOW!
3
HEY! THAT WAS FUN! I FEEL GOOD!
NATURALLY! BUT YOU BROKE YOUR LAW! NOW I SUPPOSE I'LL HAVE YOU FOR A FLY-SWATTING PARTNER AT THE GARBAGE DUMP!
WANTED: COURT PLASTER FOR THE HIGH OOF'S COURT

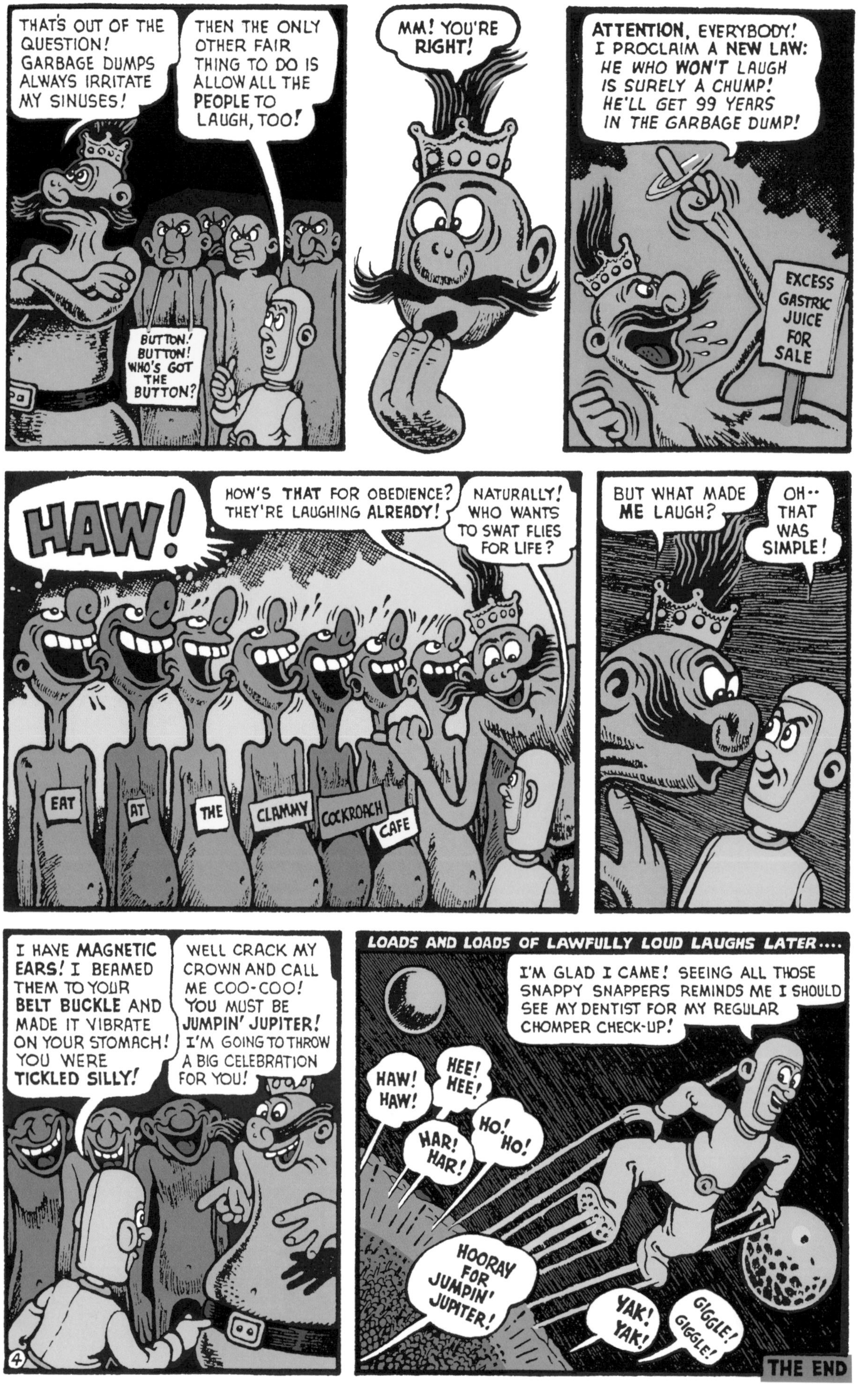
THAT'S OUT OF THE QUESTION! GARBAGE DUMPS ALWAYS IRRITATE MY SINUSES!
THEN THE ONLY OTHER FAIR THING TO DO IS ALLOW ALL THE PEOPLE TO LAUGH, TOO!
BUTTON! BUTTON! WHO'S GOT THE BUTTON?
MM! YOU'RE RIGHT!
ATTENTION, EVERYBODY! I PROCLAIM A NEW LAW: HE WHO WON'T LAUGH IS SURELY A CHUMP! HE'LL GET 99 YEARS IN THE GARBAGE DUMP!
EXCESS GASTRIC JUICE FOR SALE
HAW!
HOW'S THAT FOR OBEDIENCE? THEY'RE LAUGHING ALREADY!
NATURALLY! WHO WANTS TO SWAT FLIES FOR LIFE?
EAT AT THE CLAMMY COCKROACH CAFE
BUT WHAT MADE ME LAUGH?
OH.. THAT WAS SIMPLE!
I HAVE MAGNETIC EARS! I BEAMED THEM TO YOUR BELT BUCKLE AND MADE IT VIBRATE ON YOUR STOMACH! YOU WERE TICKLED SILLY!
WELL CRACK MY CROWN AND CALL ME COO-COO! YOU MUST BE JUMPIN' JUPITER! I'M GOING TO THROW A BIG CELEBRATION FOR YOU!
4
LOADS AND LOADS OF LAWFULLY LOUD LAUGHS LATER....
I'M GLAD I CAME! SEEING ALL THOSE SNAPPY SNAPPERS REMINDS ME I SHOULD SEE MY DENTIST FOR MY REGULAR CHOMPER CHECK-UP!
HAW! HAW!
HEE! HEE!
HO! HO!
HAR! HAR!
HOORAY FOR JUMPIN' JUPITER!
YAK! YAK!
GIGGLE! GIGGLE!
THE END

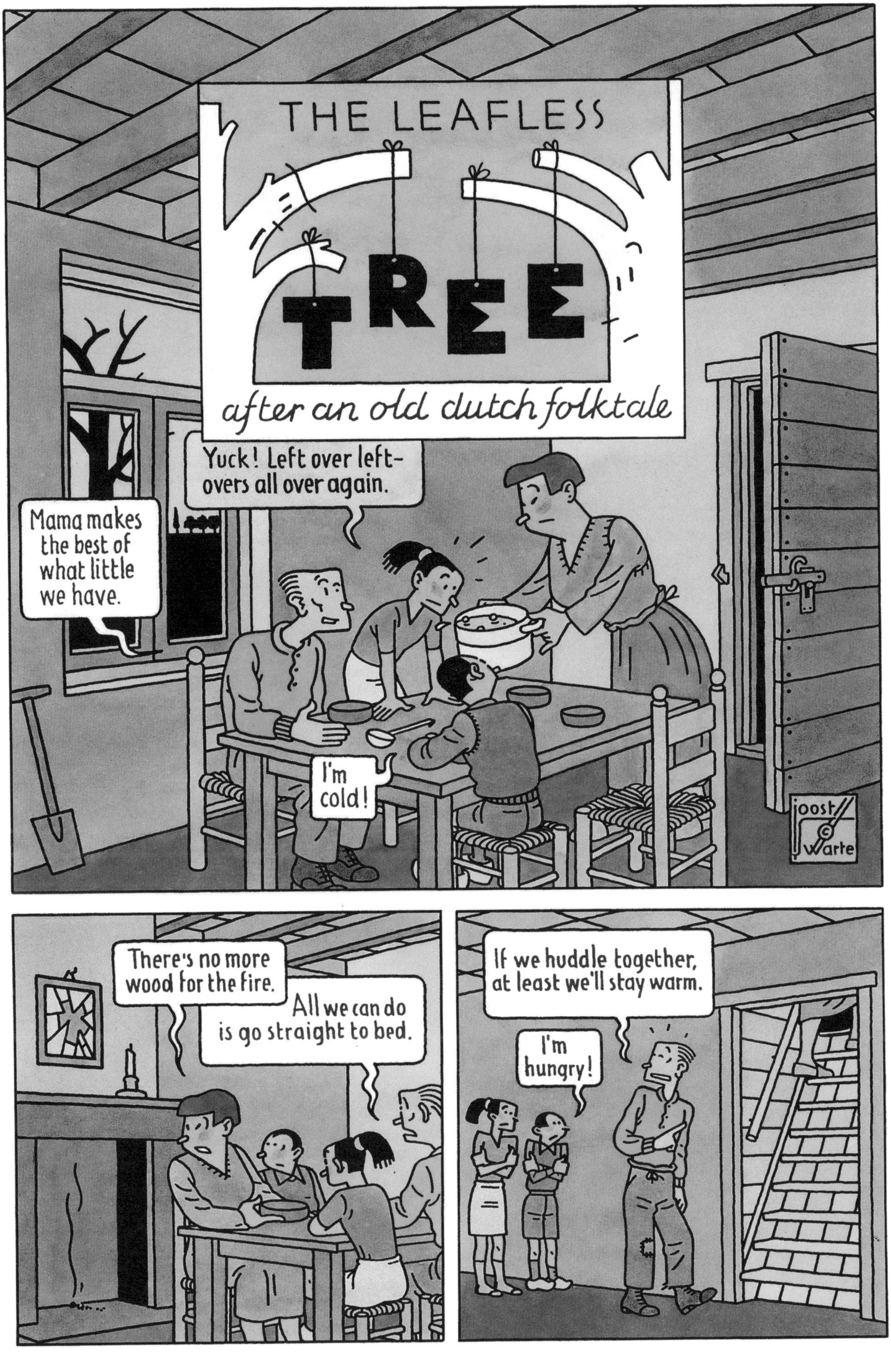
THE LEAFLESS
TREE
after an old dutch folktale
Yuck! Left over left-overs all over again.
Mama makes the best of what little we have.
I'm cold!
joost swarte
There's no more wood for the fire.
All we can do is go straight to bed.
If we huddle together, at least we'll stay warm.
I'm hungry!

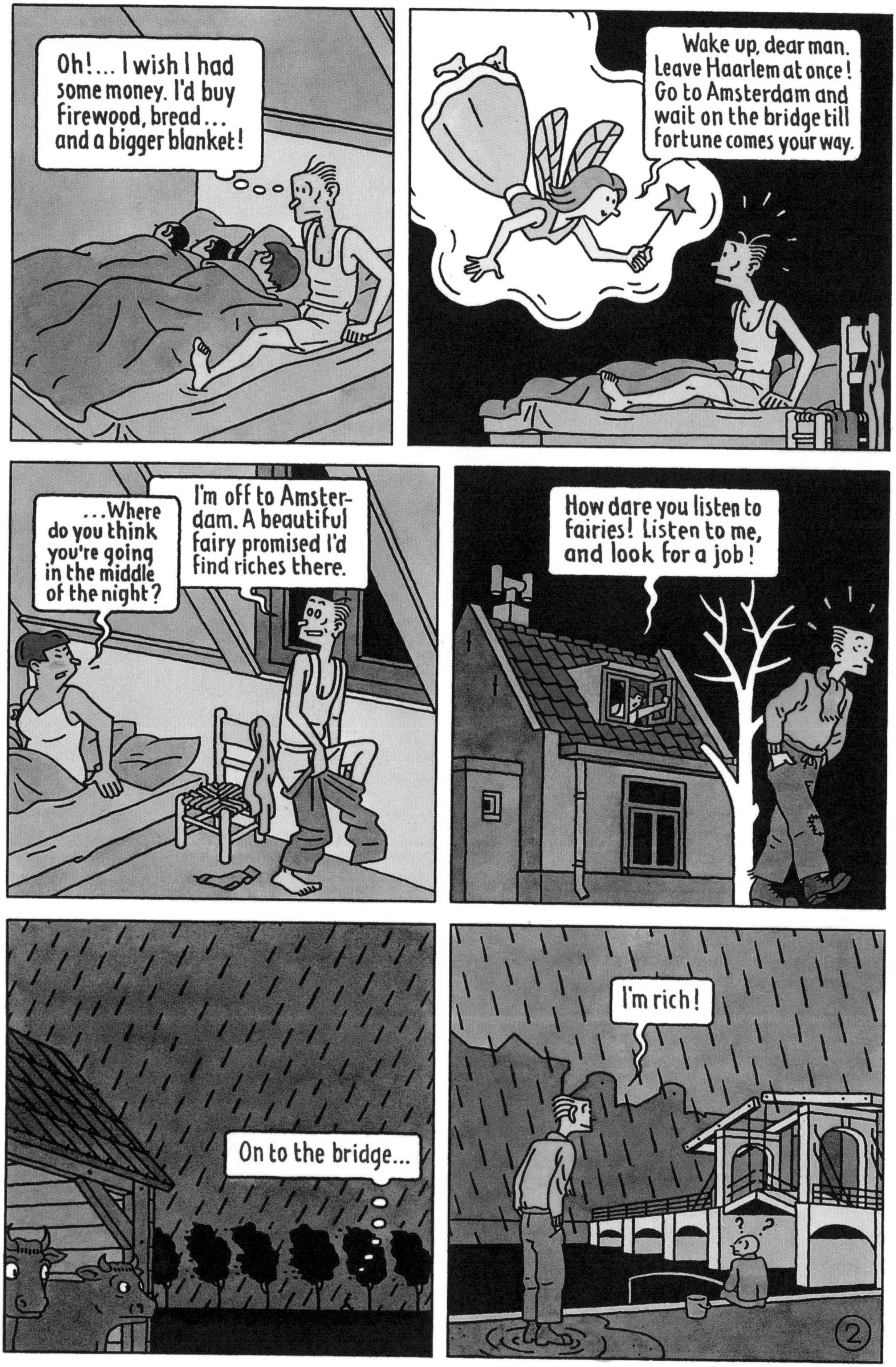
Oh!... I wish I had some money. I'd buy firewood, bread... and a bigger blanket!
Wake up, dear man. Leave Haarlem at once! Go to Amsterdam and wait on the bridge till fortune comes your way.
...Where do you think you're going in the middle of the night?
I'm off to Amster-dam. A beautiful fairy promised I'd find riches there.
How dare you listen to fairies! Listen to me, and look for a job!
On to the bridge...
I'm rich!
2

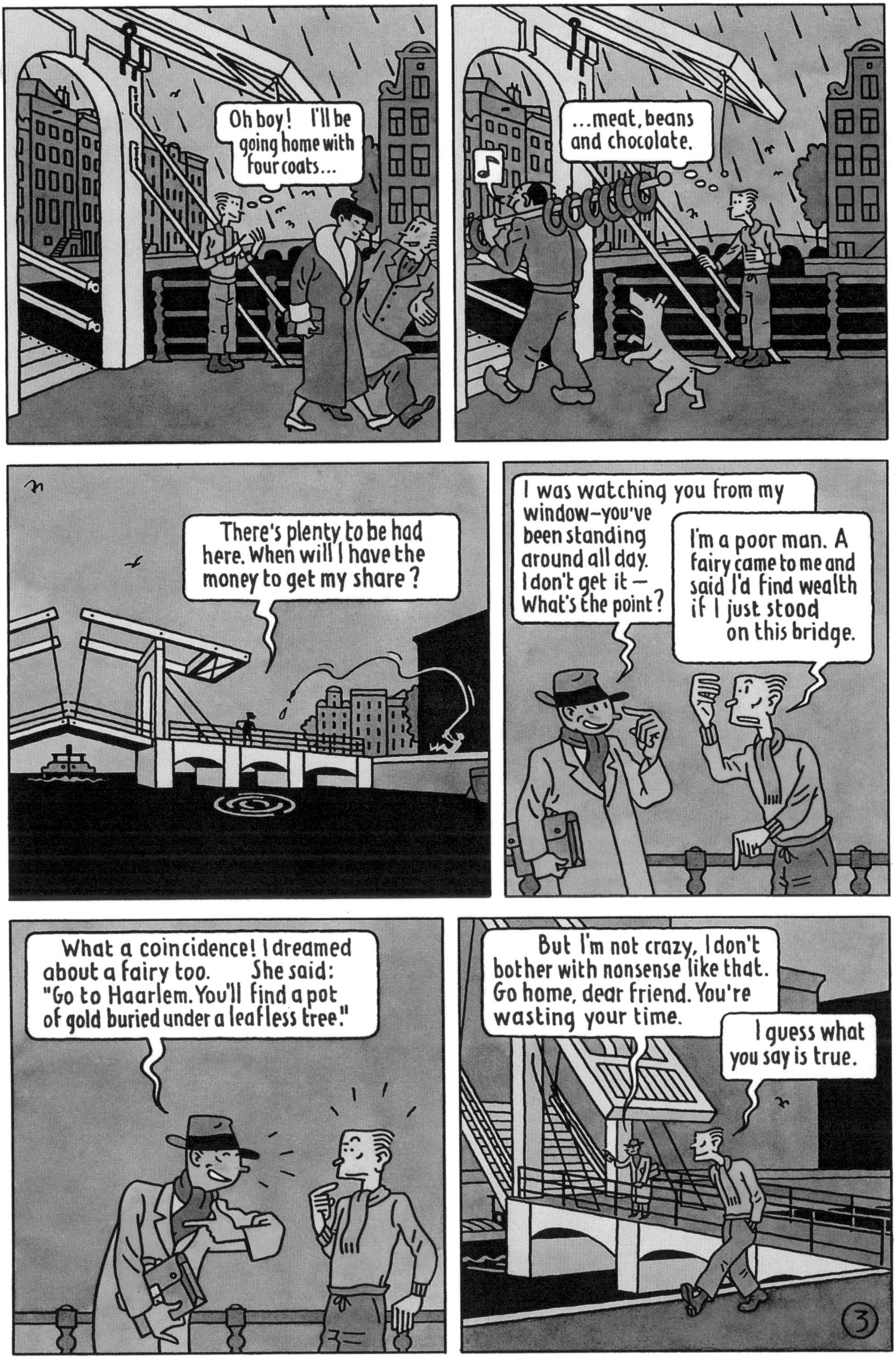
Oh boy! I'll be going home with four coats...
...meat, beans and chocolate.
There's plenty to be had here. When will I have the money to get my share?
I was watching you from my window—you've been standing around all day. I don't get it — What's the point?
I'm a poor man. A fairy came to me and said I'd find wealth if I just stood on this bridge.
What a coincidence! I dreamed about a fairy too. She said: "Go to Haarlem. You'll find a pot of gold buried under a leafless tree."
But I'm not crazy, I don't bother with nonsense like that. Go home, dear friend. You're wasting your time.
I guess what you say is true.
3

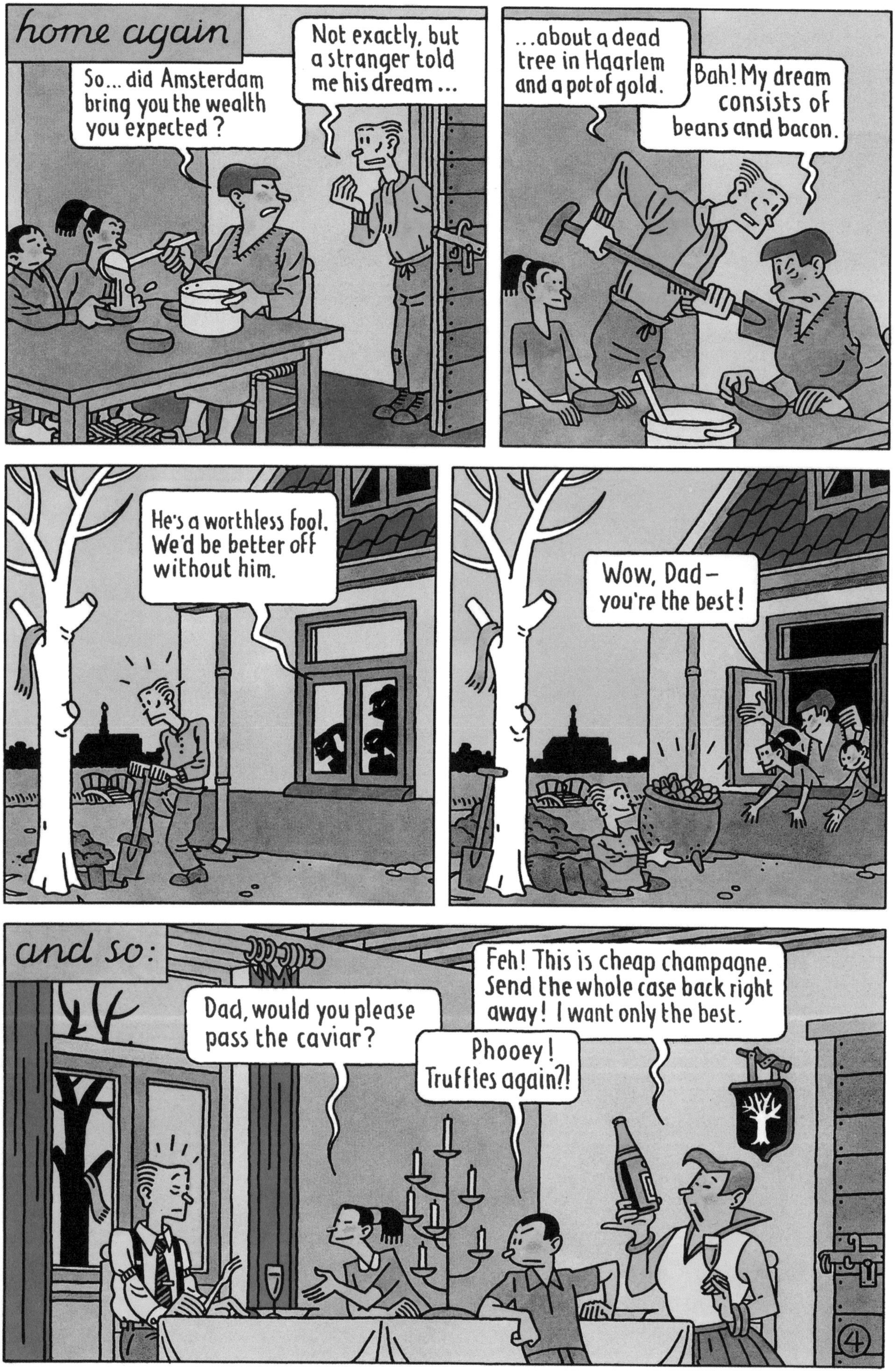

home again
So... did Amsterdam bring you the wealth you expected?
Not exactly, but a stranger told me his dream...
...about a dead tree in Haarlem and a pot of gold.
Bah! My dream consists of beans and bacon.
He's a worthless fool. We'd be better off without him.
Wow, Dad – you're the best!
and so:
Dad, would you please pass the caviar?
Feh! This is cheap champagne. Send the whole case back right away! I want only the best.
Phooey! Truffles again?!
4

WAKE UP KIDS! COMIC SUPPLEMENT of the NEW YORK DAILY AMERICAN APRIL 1, 1909 YIPEE! OH BOY!

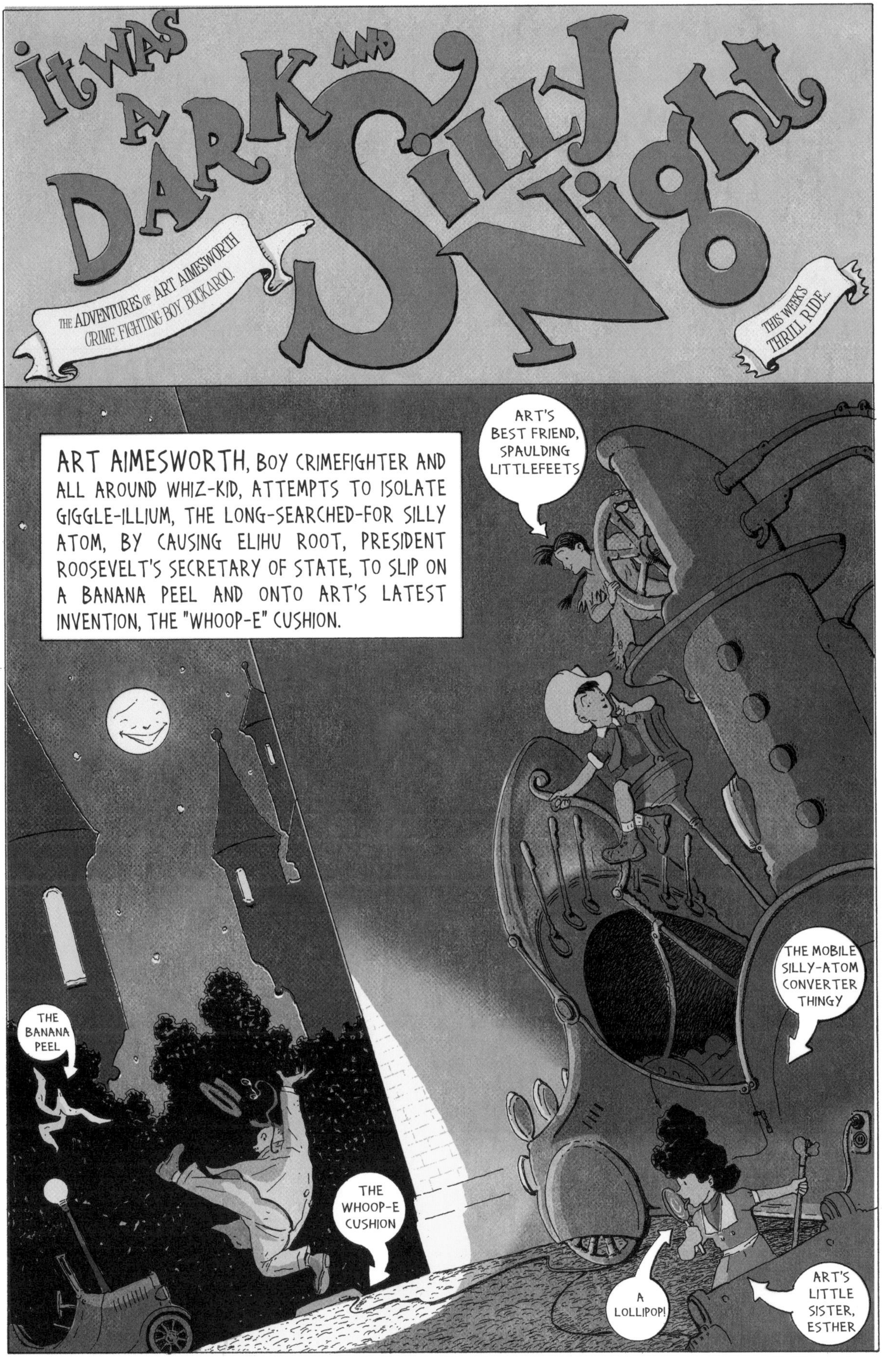
It was a Dark and Silly Night
THE ADVENTURES OF ART AIMESWORTH CRIME FIGHTING BOY BUCKAROO.
THIS WEEKS THRILL RIDE...
ART AIMESWORTH, BOY CRIMEFIGHTER AND ALL AROUND WHIZ-KID, ATTEMPTS TO ISOLATE GIGGLE-ILLIUM, THE LONG-SEARCHED-FOR SILLY ATOM, BY CAUSING ELIHU ROOT, PRESIDENT ROOSEVELT'S SECRETARY OF STATE, TO SLIP ON A BANANA PEEL AND ONTO ART'S LATEST INVENTION, THE "WHOOP-E" CUSHION.
ART'S BEST FRIEND, SPAULDING LITTLEFEETS
THE MOBILE SILLY-ATOM CONVERTER THINGY
THE BANANA PEEL
THE WHOOP-E CUSHION
A LOLLIPOP!
ART'S LITTLE SISTER, ESTHER

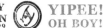

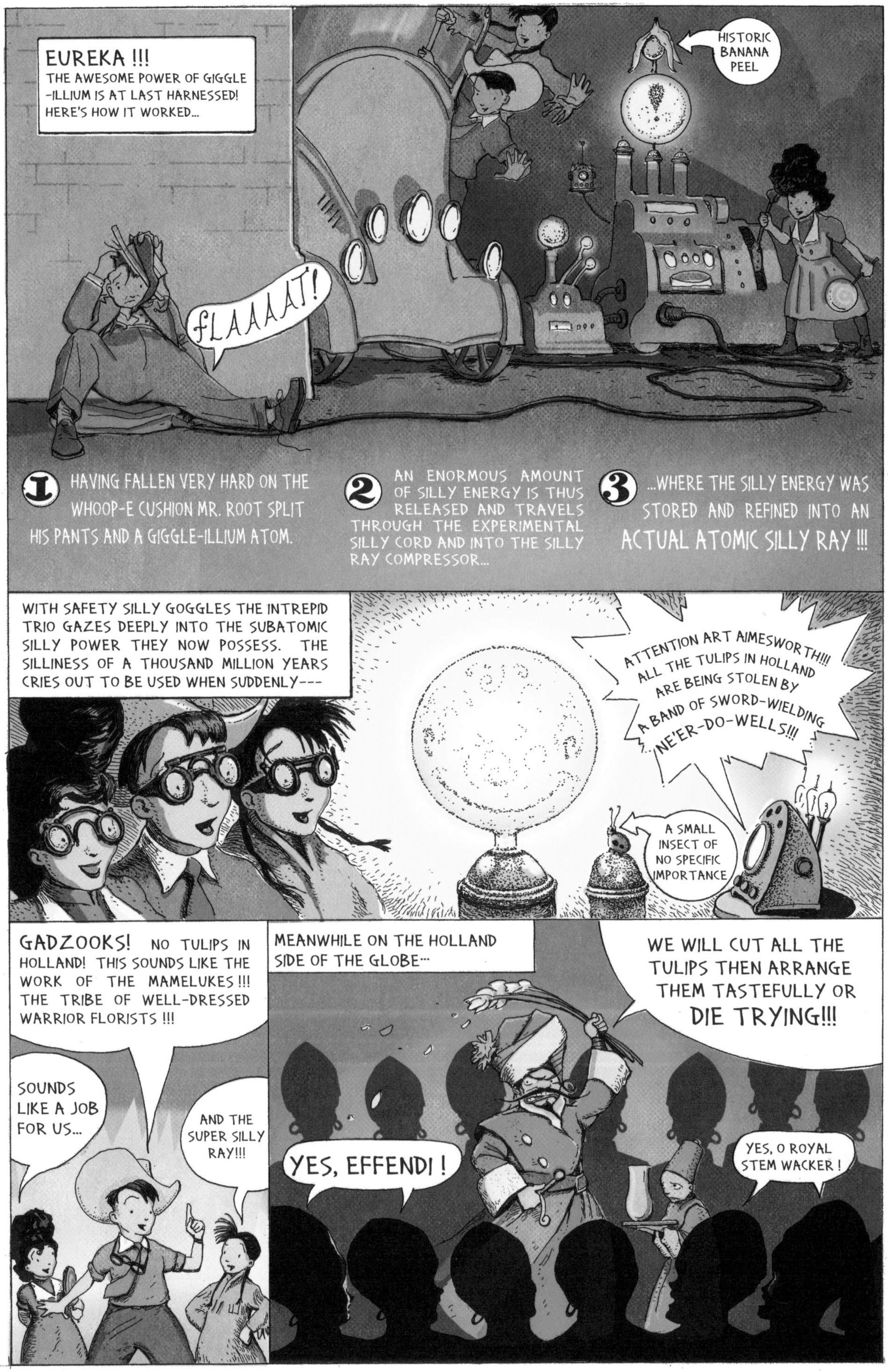
EUREKA !!!
THE AWESOME POWER OF GIGGLE-ILLIUM IS AT LAST HARNESSED! HERE'S HOW IT WORKED...
HISTORIC BANANA PEEL
FLAAAAT!
1 HAVING FALLEN VERY HARD ON THE WHOOP-E CUSHION MR. ROOT SPLIT HIS PANTS AND A GIGGLE-ILLIUM ATOM.
2 AN ENORMOUS AMOUNT OF SILLY ENERGY IS THUS RELEASED AND TRAVELS THROUGH THE EXPERIMENTAL SILLY CORD AND INTO THE SILLY RAY COMPRESSOR...
3 ...WHERE THE SILLY ENERGY WAS STORED AND REFINED INTO AN ACTUAL ATOMIC SILLY RAY !!!
WITH SAFETY SILLY GOGGLES THE INTREPID TRIO GAZES DEEPLY INTO THE SUBATOMIC SILLY POWER THEY NOW POSSESS. THE SILLINESS OF A THOUSAND MILLION YEARS CRIES OUT TO BE USED WHEN SUDDENLY---
ATTENTION ART AIMESWORTH!!! ALL THE TULIPS IN HOLLAND ARE BEING STOLEN BY A BAND OF SWORD-WIELDING NE'ER-DO-WELLS!!!
A SMALL INSECT OF NO SPECIFIC IMPORTANCE
GADZOOKS! NO TULIPS IN HOLLAND! THIS SOUNDS LIKE THE WORK OF THE MAMELUKES!!! THE TRIBE OF WELL-DRESSED WARRIOR FLORISTS !!!
SOUNDS LIKE A JOB FOR US...
AND THE SUPER SILLY RAY!!!
MEANWHILE ON THE HOLLAND SIDE OF THE GLOBE...
WE WILL CUT ALL THE TULIPS THEN ARRANGE THEM TASTEFULLY OR DIE TRYING!!!
YES, EFFENDI !
YES, O ROYAL STEM WACKER !

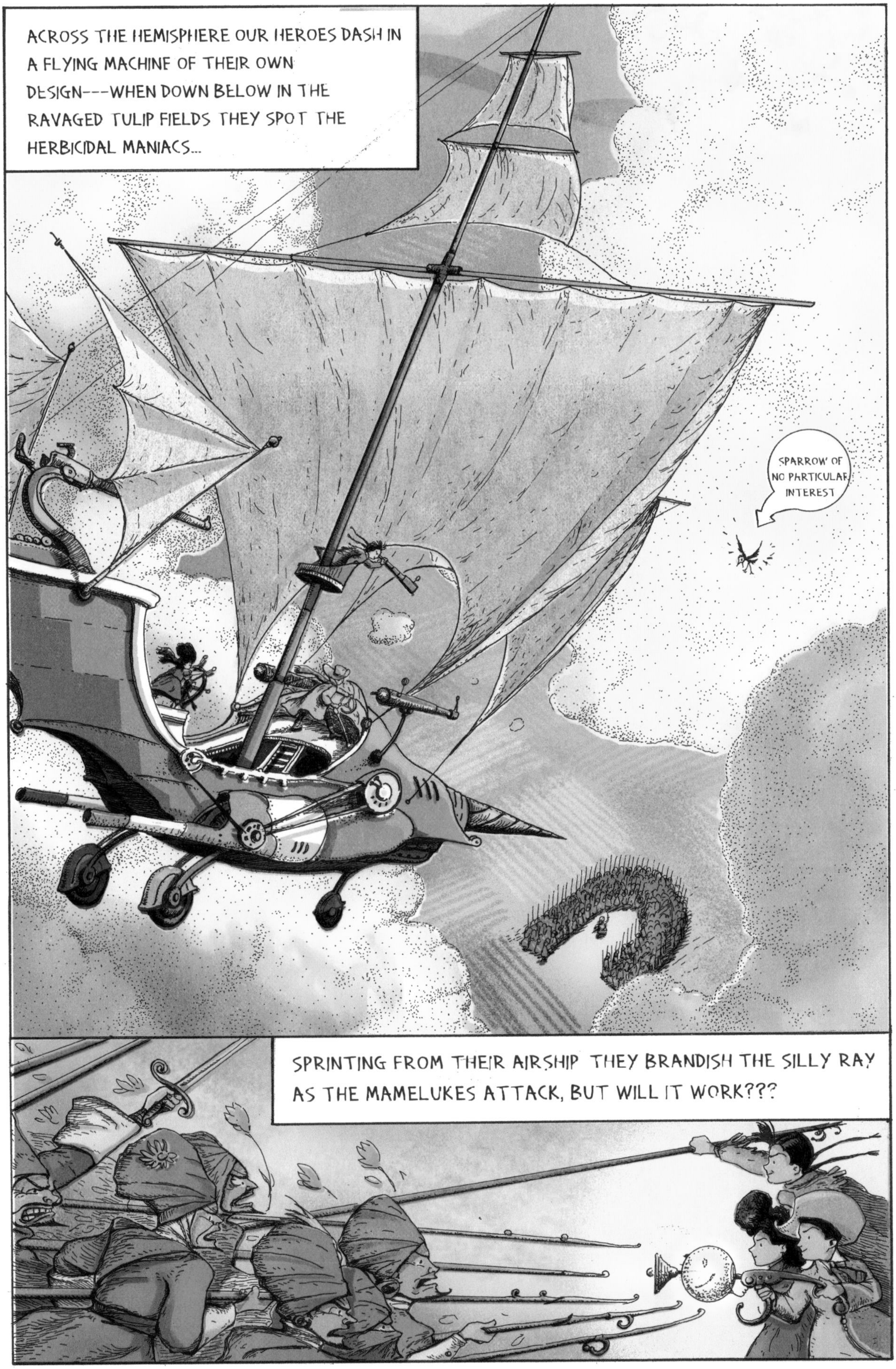
ACROSS THE HEMISPHERE OUR HEROES DASH IN A FLYING MACHINE OF THEIR OWN DESIGN---WHEN DOWN BELOW IN THE RAVAGED TULIP FIELDS THEY SPOT THE HERBICIDAL MANIACS...
SPARROW OF NO PARTICULAR INTEREST
SPRINTING FROM THEIR AIRSHIP THEY BRANDISH THE SILLY RAY AS THE MAMELUKES ATTACK, BUT WILL IT WORK???

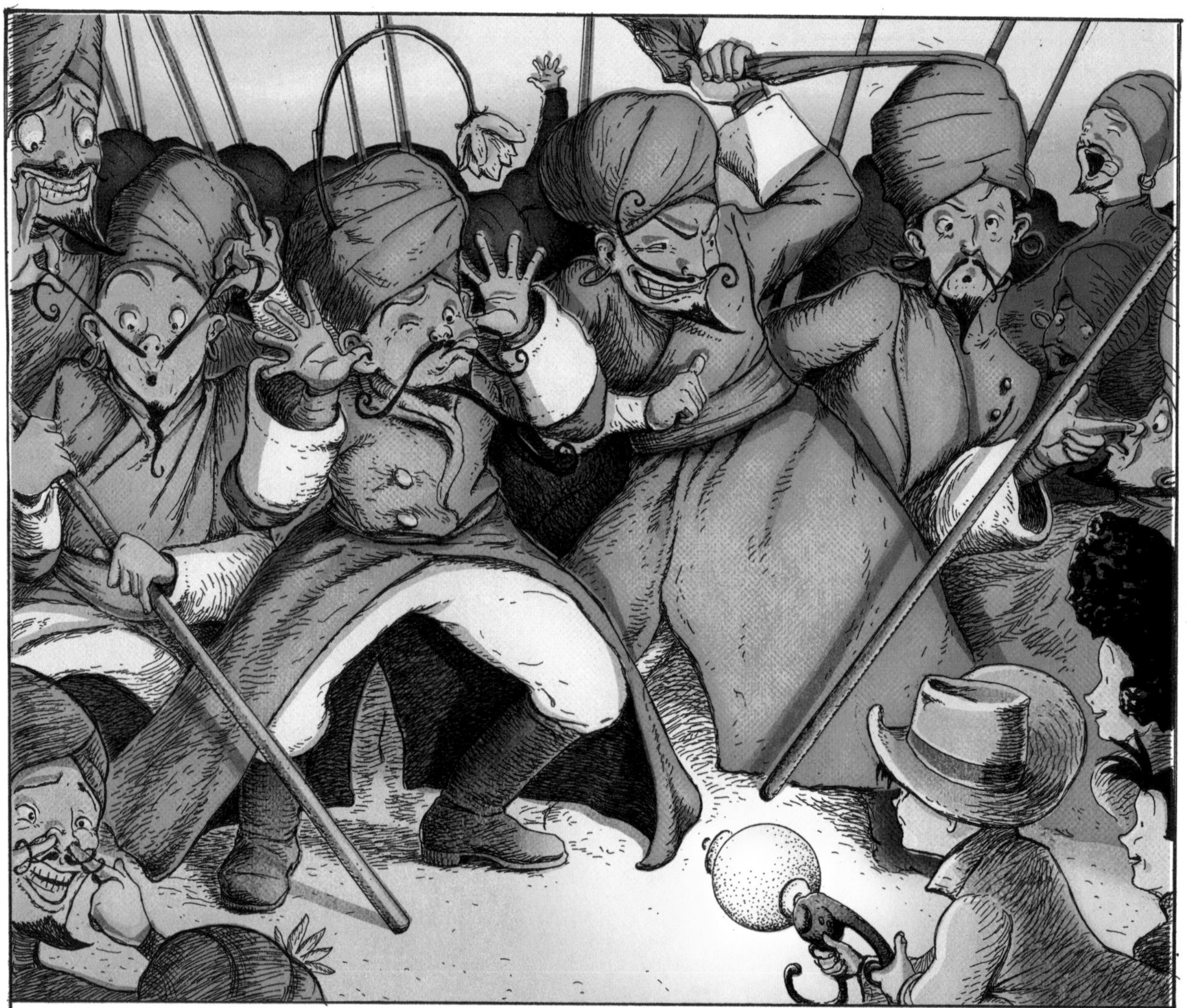

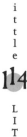

ZAPP! WITH A SINGLE BLAST THE MAMELUKES FORGET THEIR WARLIKE WAYS AND BEGIN ACTING **EXTREMELY SILLY**, EVEN **RIDICULOUS. THE SILLY RAY WORKS!!!** FENDUND KLOOKALOOKADOOK III, KING OF ALL HOLLAND, IS OVERJOYED AND AWARDS ART, ESTHER, AND SPAULDING "THE ORDER OF THE GOLDEN WOODEN SHOE" OR "THE WOODEN GOLDEN SHOE" OR WHATEVER THAT THING IS CALLED.

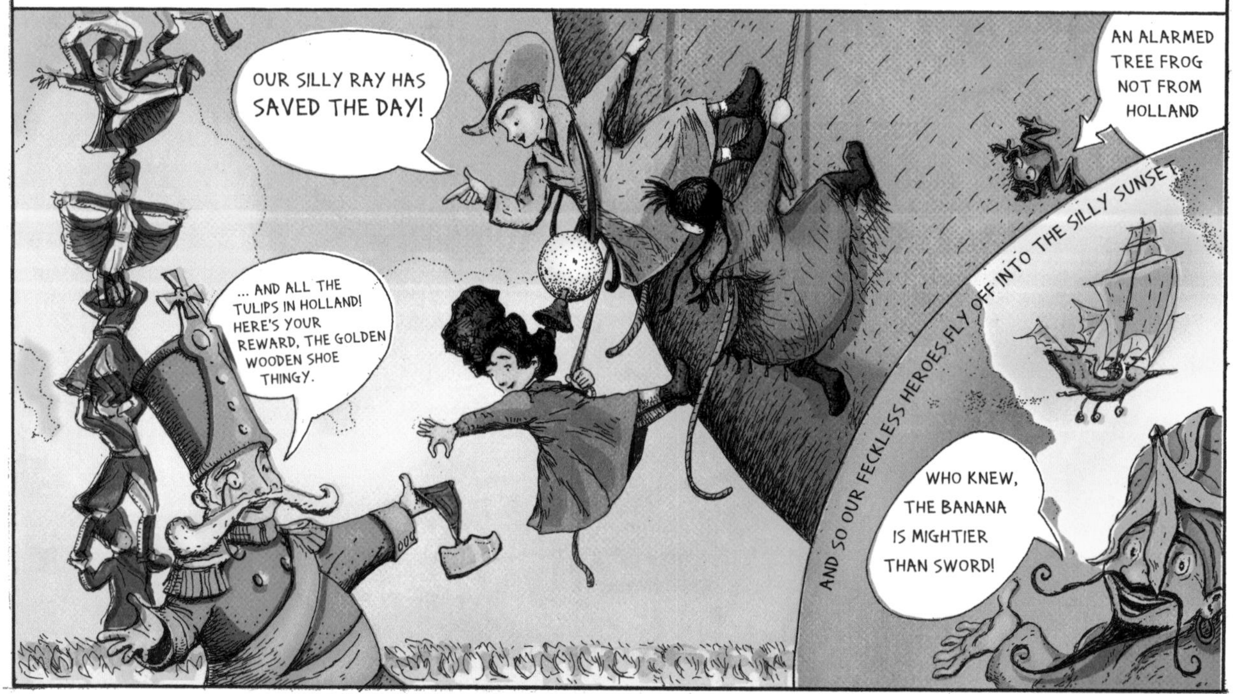
OUR SILLY RAY HAS SAVED THE DAY!
... AND ALL THE TULIPS IN HOLLAND! HERE'S YOUR REWARD, THE GOLDEN WOODEN SHOE THINGY.
AN ALARMED TREE FROG NOT FROM HOLLAND
AND SO OUR FECKLESS HEROES FLY OFF INTO THE SILLY SUNSET
WHO KNEW, THE BANANA IS MIGHTIER THAN SWORD!

WATCH FOR NEXT WEEK'S EXCITING ADVENTURE... **SHINE ON HARVEST LOON!**

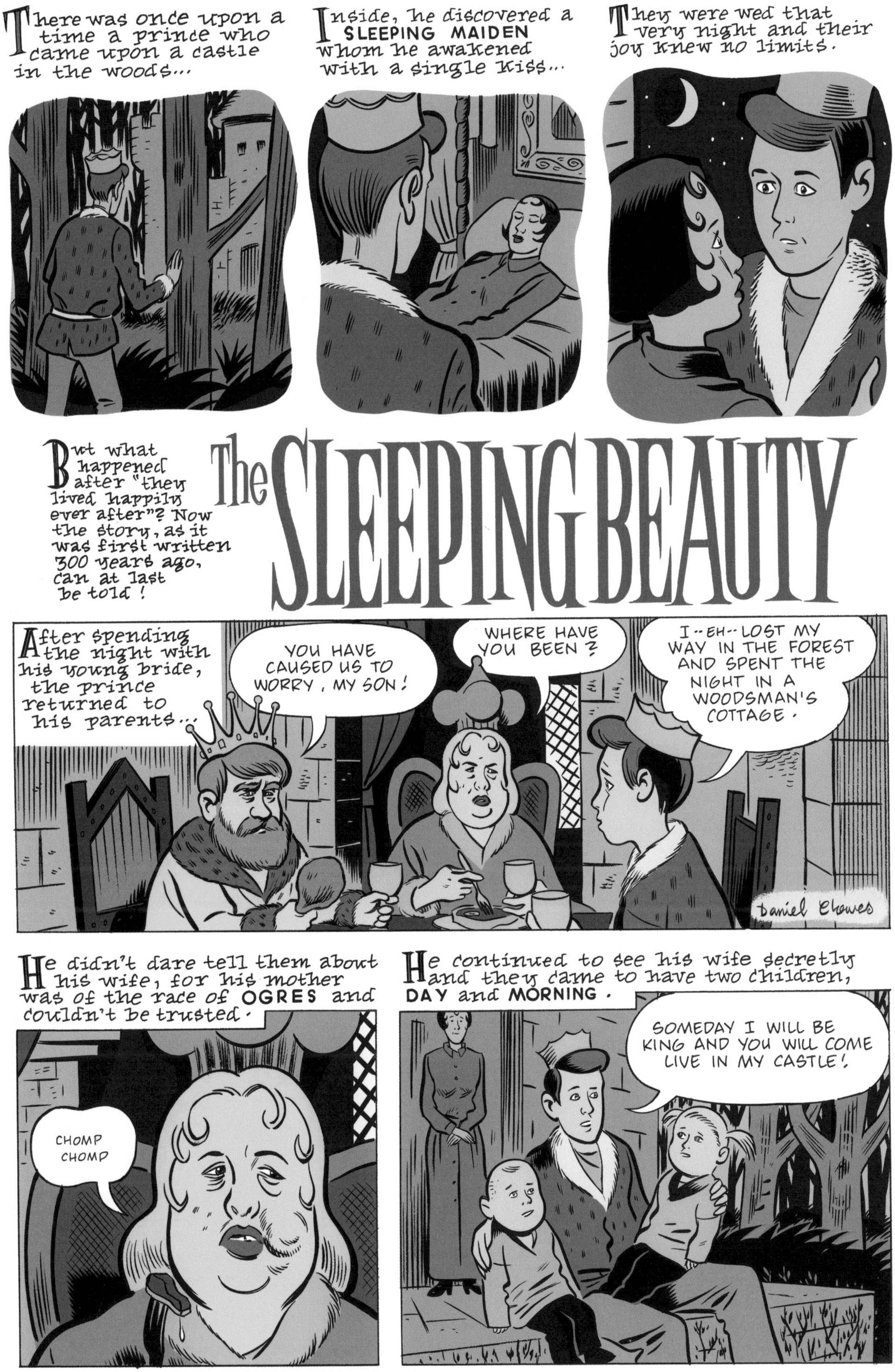
There was once upon a time a prince who came upon a castle in the woods...
Inside, he discovered a SLEEPING MAIDEN whom he awakened with a single kiss...
They were wed that very night and their joy knew no limits.
But what happened after "they lived happily ever after"? Now the story, as it was first written 300 years ago, can at last be told!
The SLEEPING BEAUTY
After spending the night with his young bride, the prince returned to his parents...
YOU HAVE CAUSED US TO WORRY, MY SON!
WHERE HAVE YOU BEEN?
I--EH--LOST MY WAY IN THE FOREST AND SPENT THE NIGHT IN A WOODSMAN'S COTTAGE.
Daniel Clowes
He didn't dare tell them about his wife, for his mother was of the race of OGRES and couldn't be trusted.
CHOMP CHOMP
He continued to see his wife secretly and they came to have two children, DAY and MORNING.
SOMEDAY I WILL BE KING AND YOU WILL COME LIVE IN MY CASTLE!

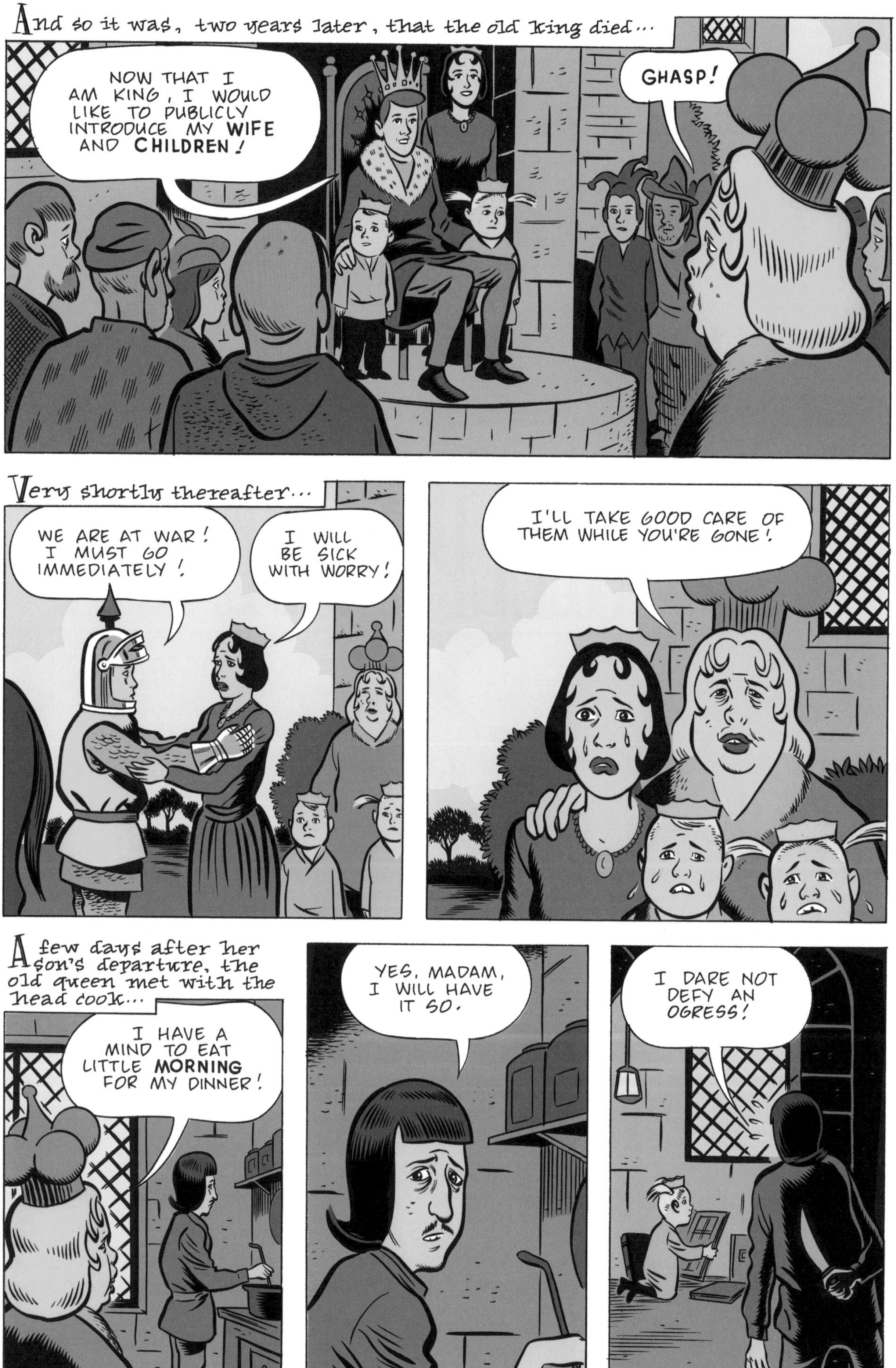
And so it was, two years later, that the old king died...
NOW THAT I AM KING, I WOULD LIKE TO PUBLICLY INTRODUCE MY WIFE AND CHILDREN!
GHASP!
Very shortly thereafter...
WE ARE AT WAR! I MUST GO IMMEDIATELY!
I WILL BE SICK WITH WORRY!
I'LL TAKE GOOD CARE OF THEM WHILE YOU'RE GONE!
A few days after her son's departure, the old queen met with the head cook...
I HAVE A MIND TO EAT LITTLE MORNING FOR MY DINNER!
YES, MADAM, I WILL HAVE IT SO.
I DARE NOT DEFY AN OGRESS!

Little Morning knew not what the cook intended for her...

OH SIR! I AM SO HAPPY TO SEE YOU! HAVE YOU BROUGHT ME SOME SUGAR CANDY?

The poor cook could do no harm to such a child. He took her to his own home and left her in the care of his wife.

In her stead, a tender lamb was covered with a delicious sauce...

I HOPE IT IS TO YOUR LIKING, YOUR MAJESTY.

I HAVE NEVER TASTED ANYTHING SO WONDERFUL!

A week later, she came once again to him...

NOW I BELIEVE I'LL SUP ON THE LITTLE BOY!

The cook agreed and proceeded to deceive her as before.

But this was not the end of his troubles...

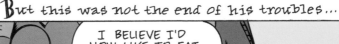

I BELIEVE I'D NOW LIKE TO EAT THE YOUNG QUEEN!

≈SIGH≈ IT SHALL BE DONE.

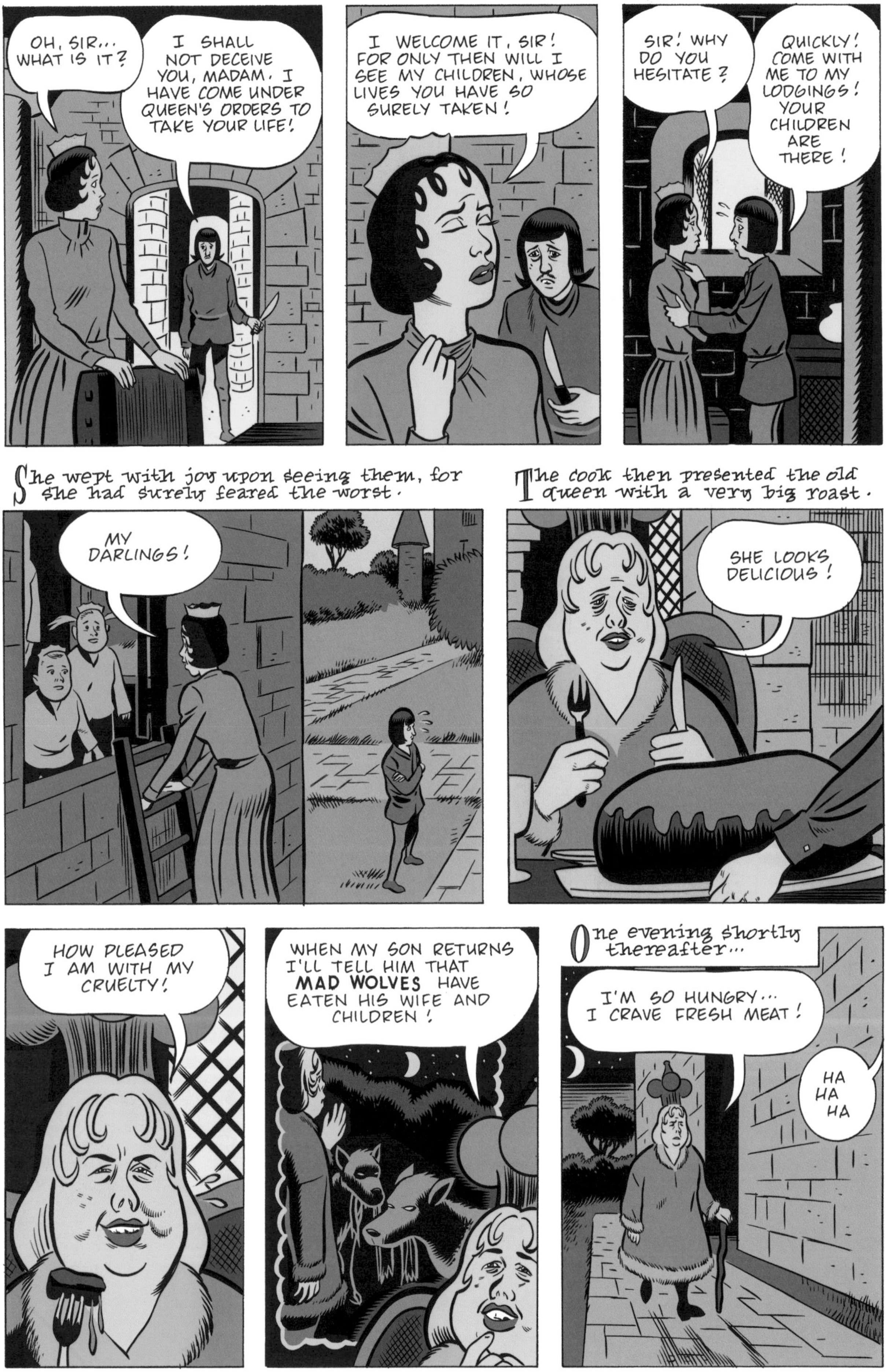
OH, SIR... WHAT IS IT?
I SHALL NOT DECEIVE YOU, MADAM. I HAVE COME UNDER QUEEN'S ORDERS TO TAKE YOUR LIFE!
I WELCOME IT, SIR! FOR ONLY THEN WILL I SEE MY CHILDREN, WHOSE LIVES YOU HAVE SO SURELY TAKEN!
SIR! WHY DO YOU HESITATE?
QUICKLY! COME WITH ME TO MY LODGINGS! YOUR CHILDREN ARE THERE!
She wept with joy upon seeing them, for she had surely feared the worst.
MY DARLINGS!
The cook then presented the old queen with a very big roast.
SHE LOOKS DELICIOUS!
HOW PLEASED I AM WITH MY CRUELTY!
WHEN MY SON RETURNS I'LL TELL HIM THAT MAD WOLVES HAVE EATEN HIS WIFE AND CHILDREN!
One evening shortly thereafter...
I'M SO HUNGRY... I CRAVE FRESH MEAT!
HA HA HA

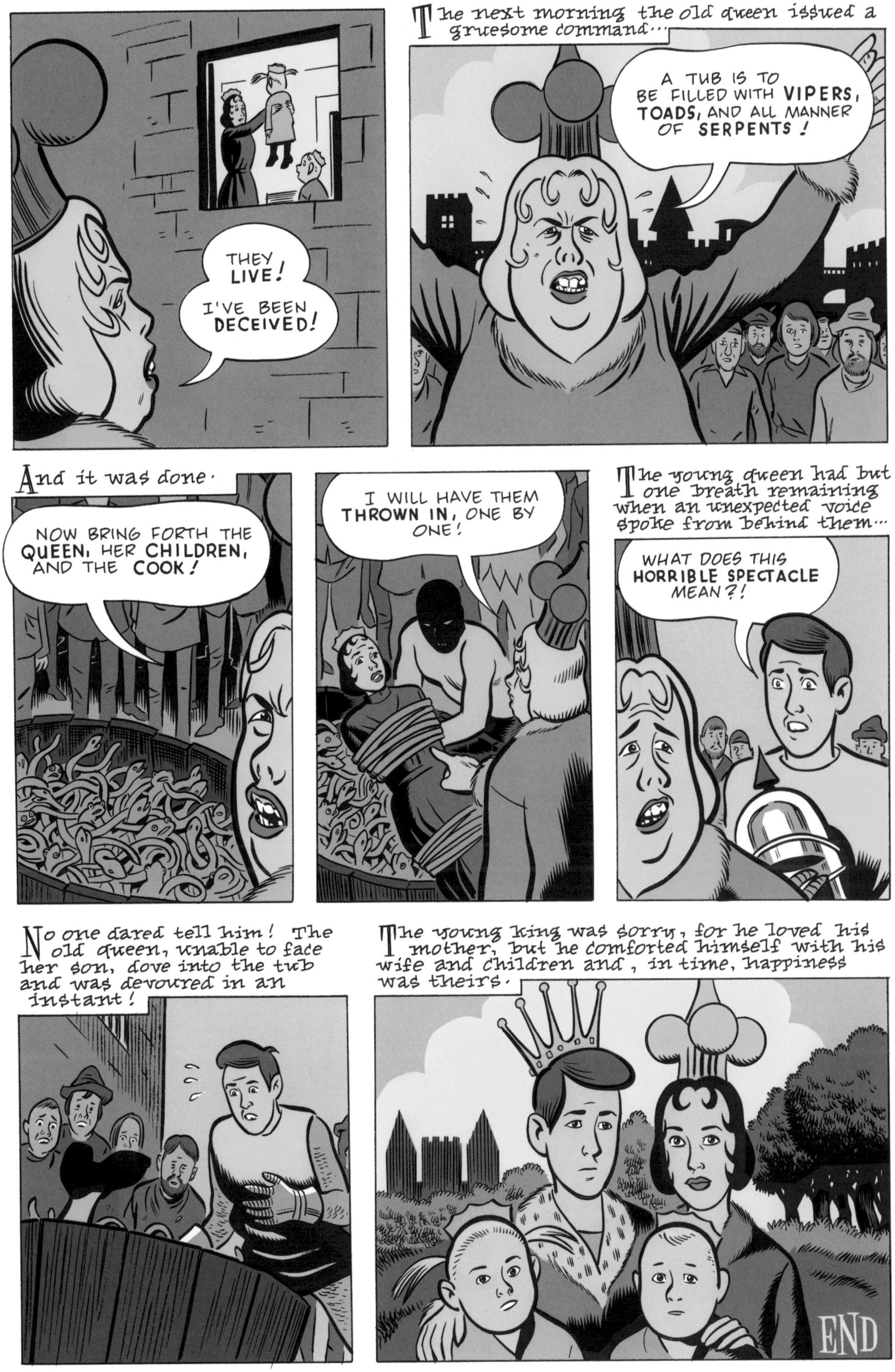
THEY LIVE!
I'VE BEEN DECEIVED!
The next morning the old queen issued a gruesome command...
A TUB IS TO BE FILLED WITH VIPERS, TOADS, AND ALL MANNER OF SERPENTS!
And it was done.
NOW BRING FORTH THE QUEEN, HER CHILDREN, AND THE COOK!
I WILL HAVE THEM THROWN IN, ONE BY ONE!
The young queen had but one breath remaining when an unexpected voice spoke from behind them...
WHAT DOES THIS HORRIBLE SPECTACLE MEAN?!
No one dared tell him! The old queen, unable to face her son, dove into the tub and was devoured in an instant!
The young king was sorry, for he loved his mother, but he comforted himself with his wife and children and, in time, happiness was theirs.
END

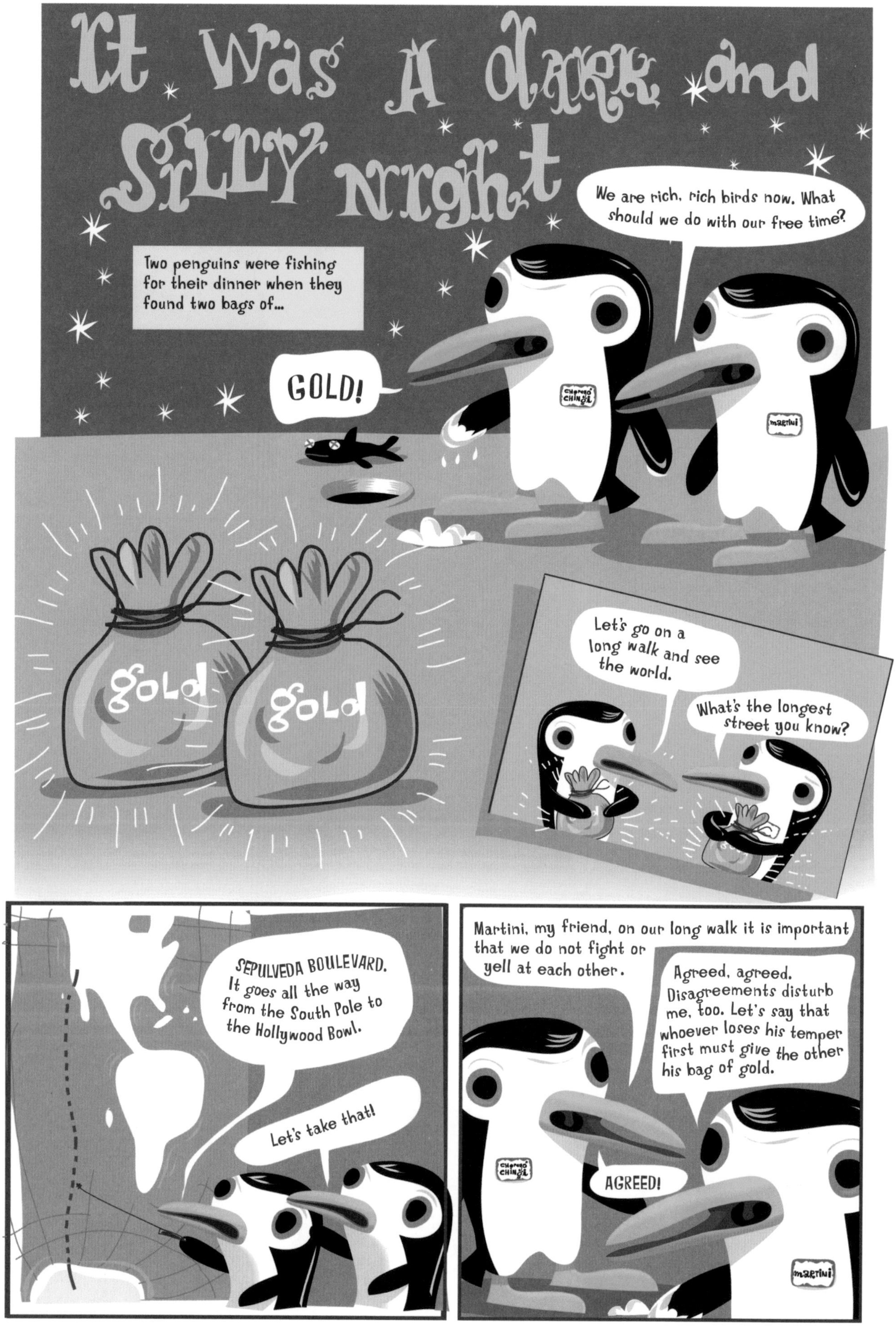
It Was A Dark and Silly Night
Two penguins were fishing for their dinner when they found two bags of...
GOLD!
We are rich, rich birds now. What should we do with our free time?
gold
gold
Let's go on a long walk and see the world.
What's the longest street you know?
SEPULVEDA BOULEVARD. It goes all the way from the South Pole to the Hollywood Bowl.
Let's take that!
Martini, my friend, on our long walk it is important that we do not fight or yell at each other.
Agreed, agreed. Disagreements disturb me, too. Let's say that whoever loses his temper first must give the other his bag of gold.
AGREED!

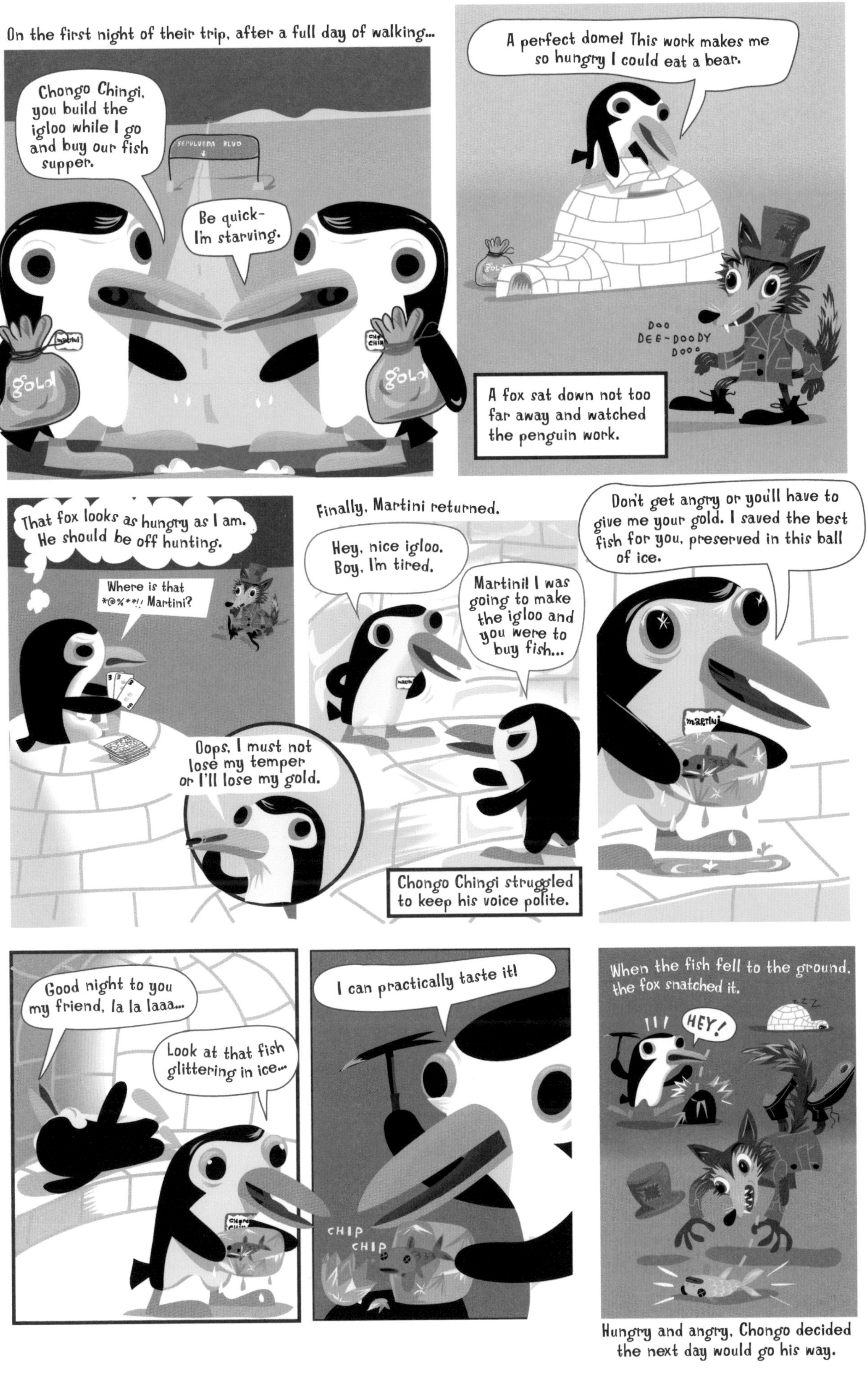
On the first night of their trip, after a full day of walking...
Chongo Chingi, you build the igloo while I go and buy our fish supper.
SEPULVEDA BLVD
Be quick- I'm starving.
gold
gold
A perfect dome! This work makes me so hungry I could eat a bear.
DOO DEE-DOODY DOOO
A fox sat down not too far away and watched the penguin work.
That fox looks as hungry as I am. He should be off hunting.
Where is that *@%**!! Martini?
Oops, I must not lose my temper or I'll lose my gold.
Finally, Martini returned.
Hey, nice igloo. Boy, I'm tired.
Martini! I was going to make the igloo and you were to buy fish...
Chongo Chingi struggled to keep his voice polite.
Don't get angry or you'll have to give me your gold. I saved the best fish for you, preserved in this ball of ice.
martini
Good night to you my friend, la la laaa...
Look at that fish glittering in ice...
I can practically taste it!
CHIP CHIP
When the fish fell to the ground, the fox snatched it.
HEY!
Hungry and angry, Chongo decided the next day would go his way.

The next afternoon, the two penguins strolled into Hollywood.

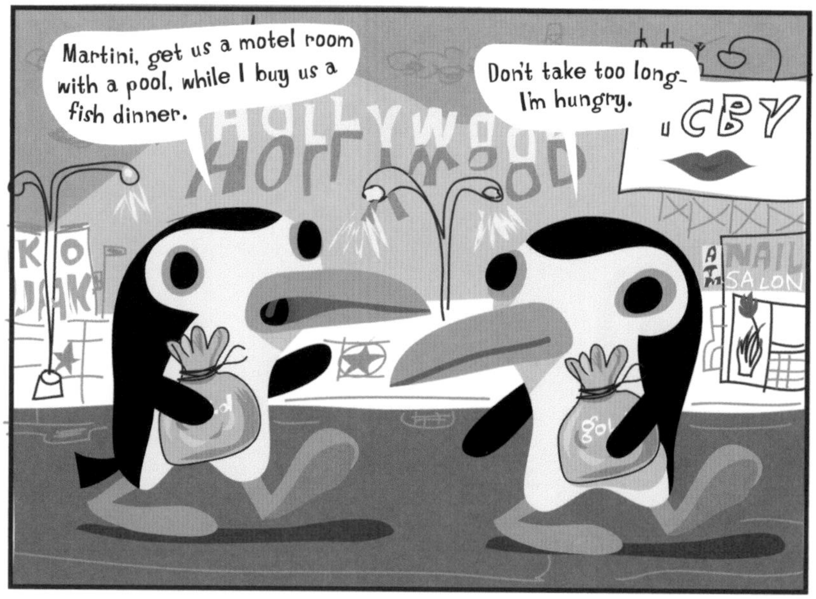
Martini, get us a motel room with a pool, while I buy us a fish dinner.
Don't take too long- I'm hungry.
HOLLYWOOD
NAIL SALON

Martini found a nice motel and started waiting...

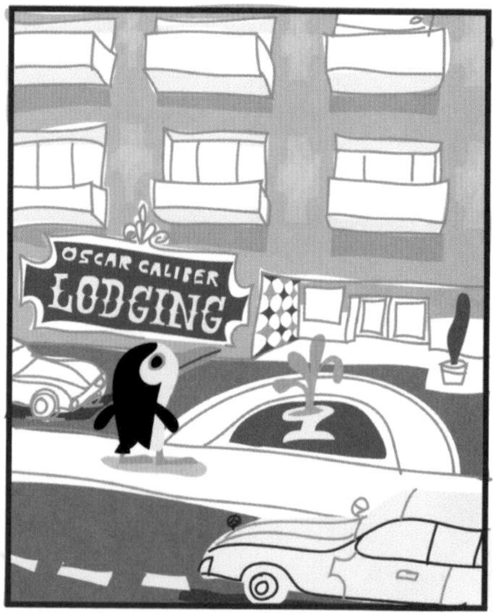
OSCAR CALIBER LODGING

...and waiting.

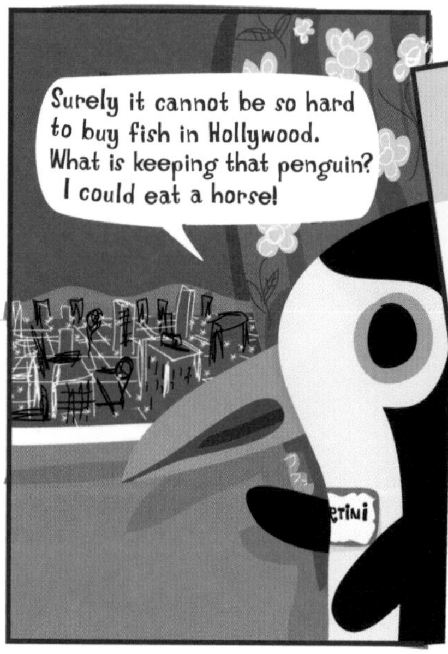
Surely it cannot be so hard to buy fish in Hollywood. What is keeping that penguin? I could eat a horse!

When suddenly...

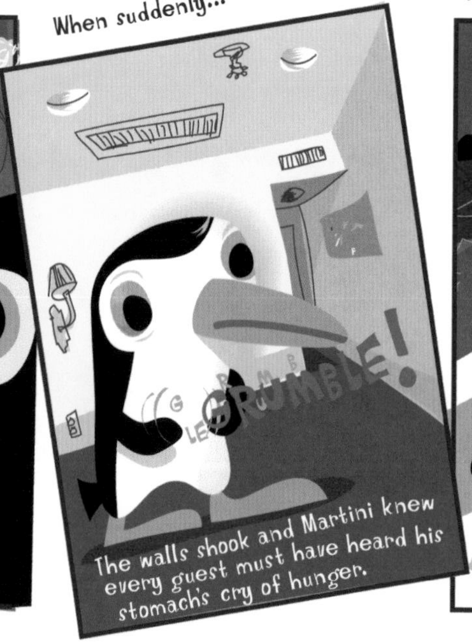
GRUMBLE!
The walls shook and Martini knew every guest must have heard his stomach's cry of hunger.

Sure enough, on the balcony facing Martini's, a fox appeared.

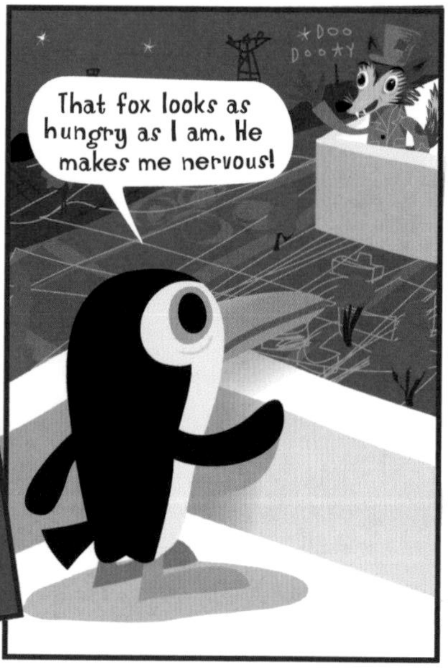
That fox looks as hungry as I am. He makes me nervous!

He pulled the curtains to escape the fox's watchful eyes.

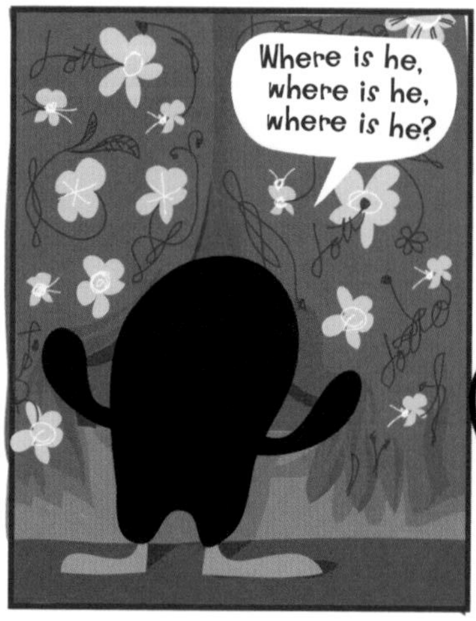
Where is he, where is he, where is he?

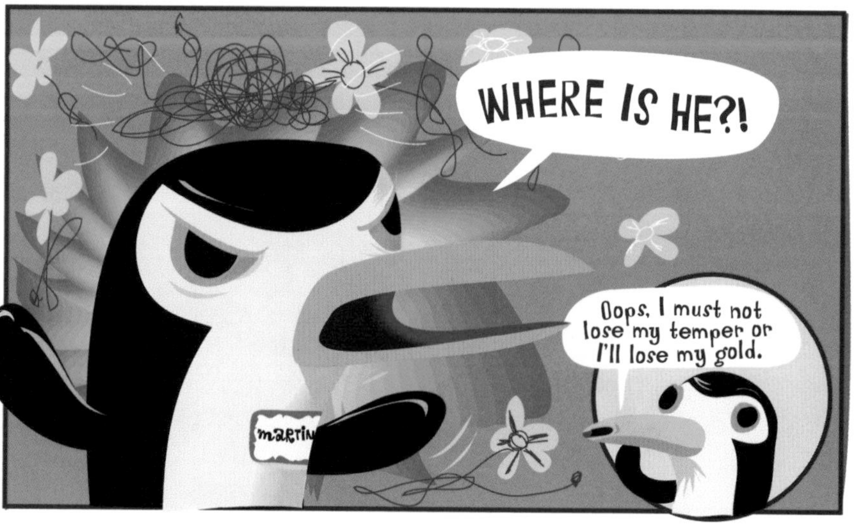
WHERE IS HE?!
Oops, I must not lose my temper or I'll lose my gold.

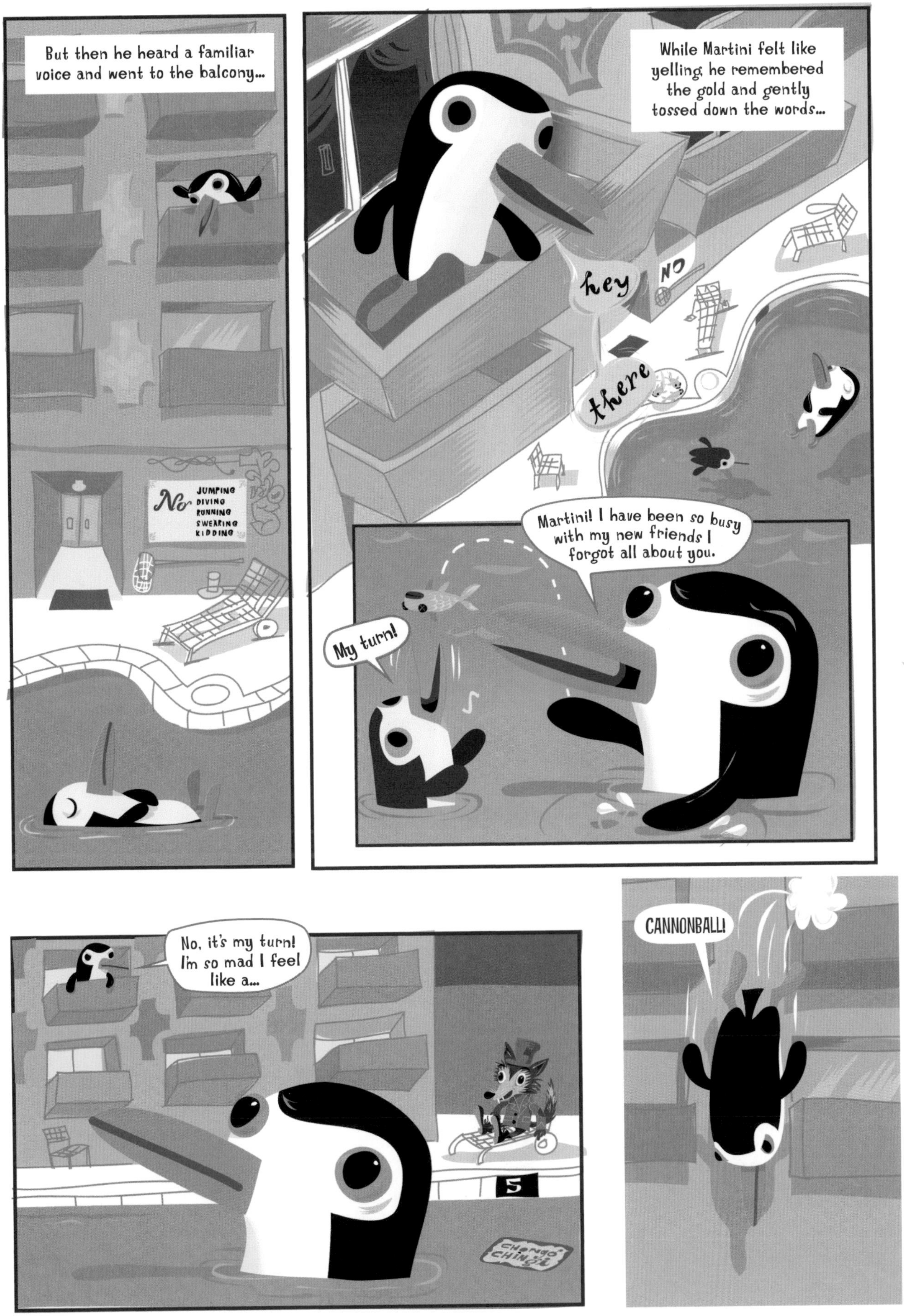
But then he heard a familiar voice and went to the balcony...
No JUMPING DIVING RUNNING SWEARING KIDDING
While Martini felt like yelling, he remembered the gold and gently tossed down the words...
hey
there
NO
Martini! I have been so busy with my new friends I forgot all about you.
My turn!
No, it's my turn! I'm so mad I feel like a...
5
CANNONBALL!

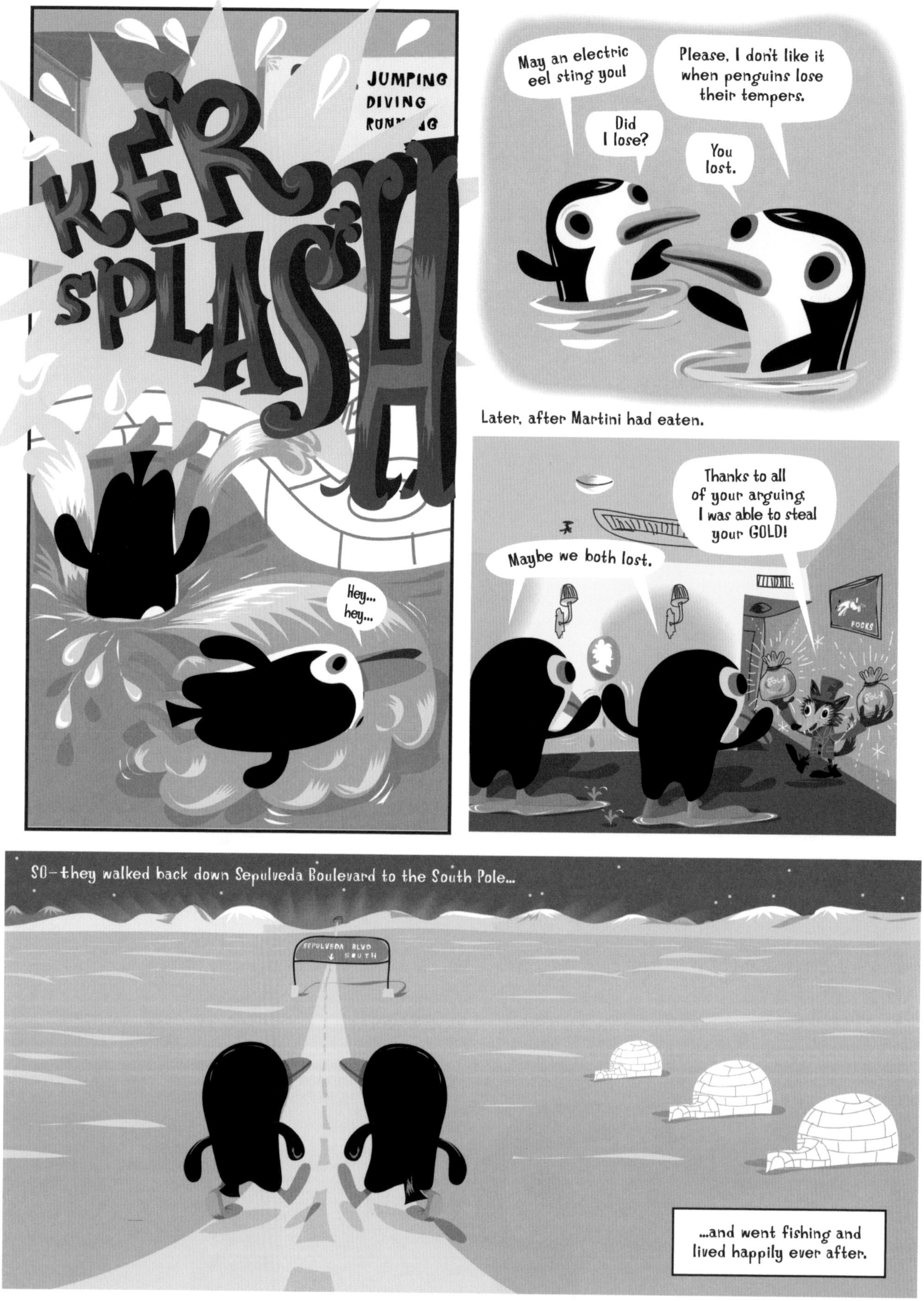

JUMPING
DIVING
KER
SPLASH
Hey... hey...
May an electric eel sting you!
Did I lose?
Please, I don't like it when penguins lose their tempers.
You lost.
Later, after Martini had eaten.
Maybe we both lost.
Thanks to all of your arguing, I was able to steal your GOLD!
SO—they walked back down Sepulveda Boulevard to the South Pole...
SEPULVEDA BLVD
SOUTH
...and went fishing and lived happily ever after.

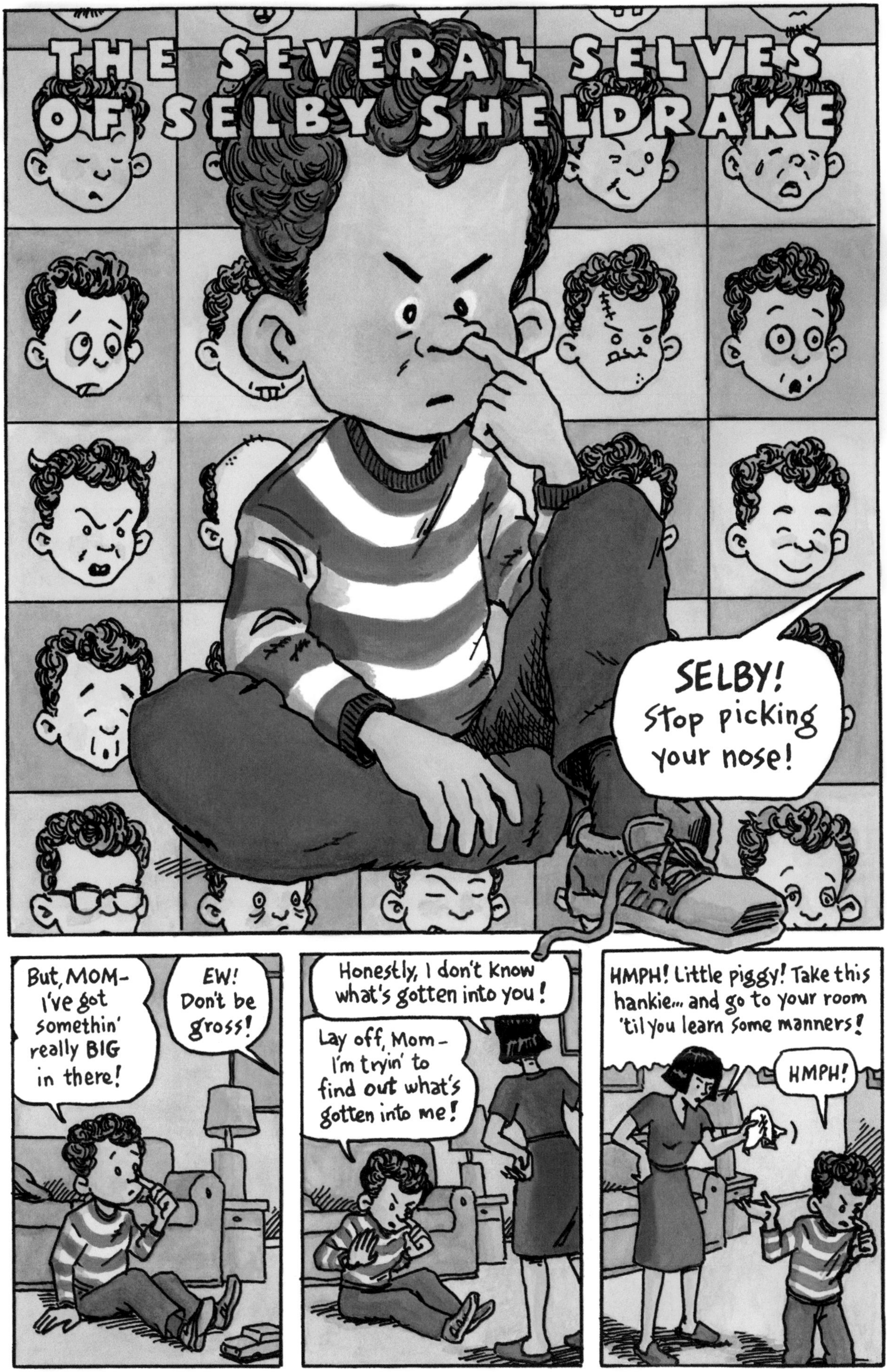
THE SEVERAL SELVES OF SELBY SHELDRAKE
SELBY! Stop picking your nose!
But, MOM- I've got somethin' really BIG in there!
EW! Don't be gross!
Honestly, I don't know what's gotten into you!
Lay off, Mom - I'm tryin' to find out what's gotten into me!
HMPH! Little piggy! Take this hankie... and go to your room 'til you learn some manners!
HMPH!

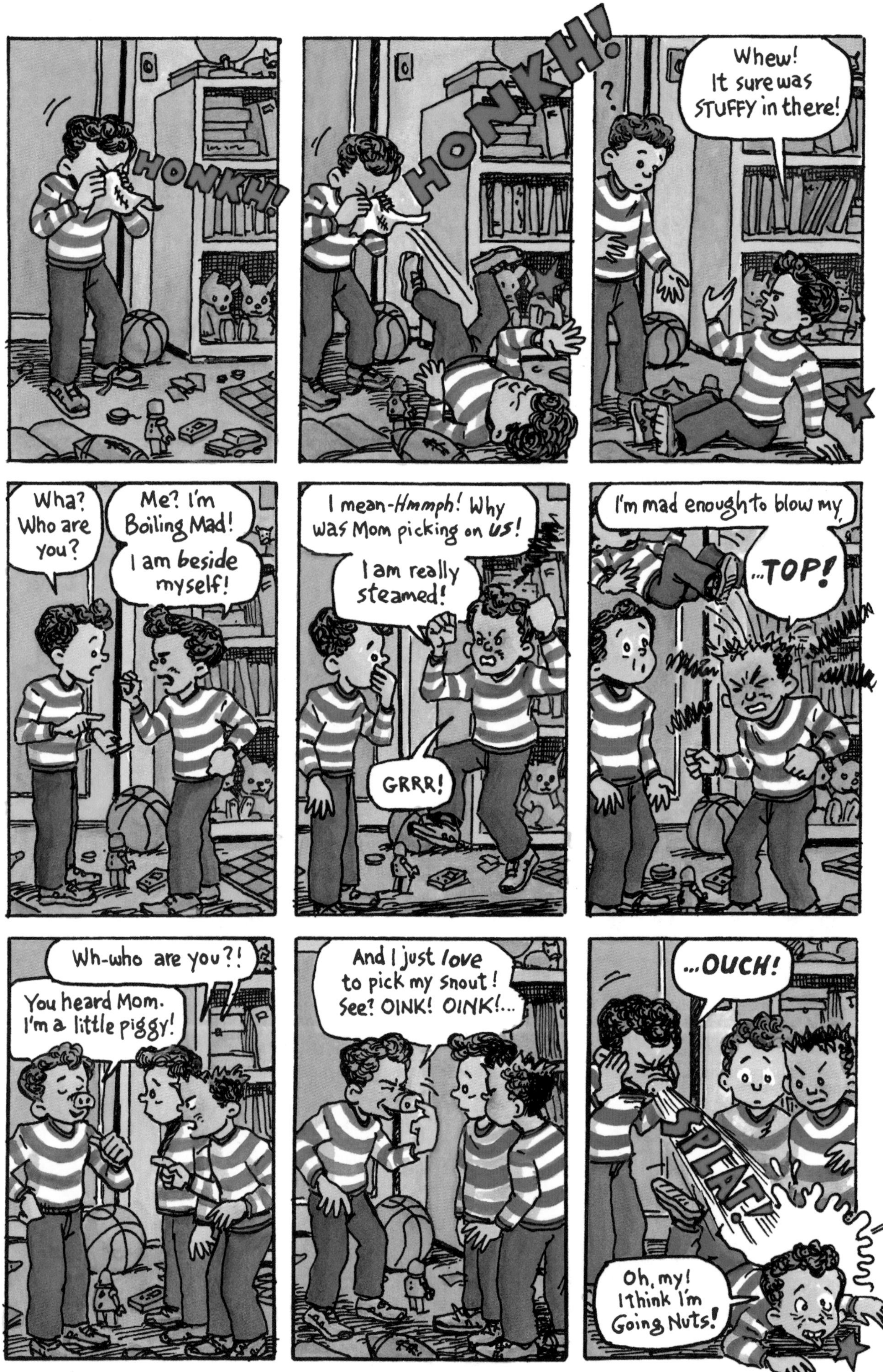
HONKH!
HONKH!
?
Whew! It sure was STUFFY in there!
Wha? Who are you?
Me? I'm Boiling Mad!
I am beside myself!
I mean-Hmmph! Why was Mom picking on US!
I am really steamed!
GRRR!
I'm mad enough to blow my
...TOP!
Wh-who are you?!
You heard Mom. I'm a little piggy!
And I just love to pick my snout! See? OINK! OINK!...
...OUCH!
SPLAT!
Oh, my! I think I'm Going Nuts!

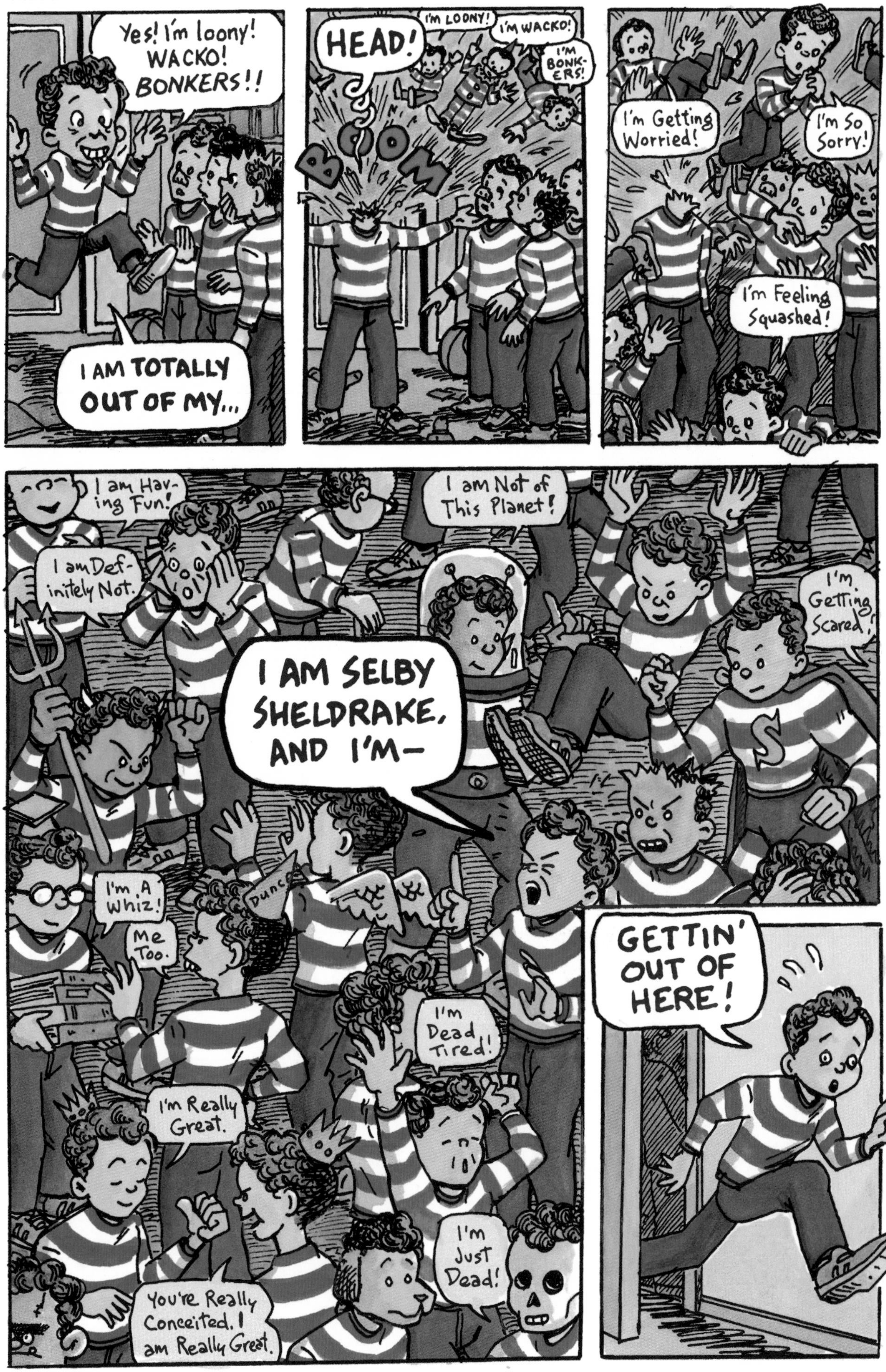
Yes! I'm loony! WACKO! BONKERS!!
I AM TOTALLY OUT OF MY...
HEAD!
BOOM
I'M LOONY!
I'M WACKO!
I'M BONK-ERS!
I'm Getting Worried!
I'm So Sorry!
I'm Feeling Squashed!
I am Hav-ing Fun!
I am Def-initely Not.
I am Not of This Planet!
I'm Getting Scared!
I AM SELBY SHELDRAKE, AND I'M—
I'm A Whiz!
Me Too.
DUNC
I'm Dead Tired!
I'm Really Great.
You're Really Conceited. I am Really Great.
I'm Just Dead!
GETTIN' OUT OF HERE!

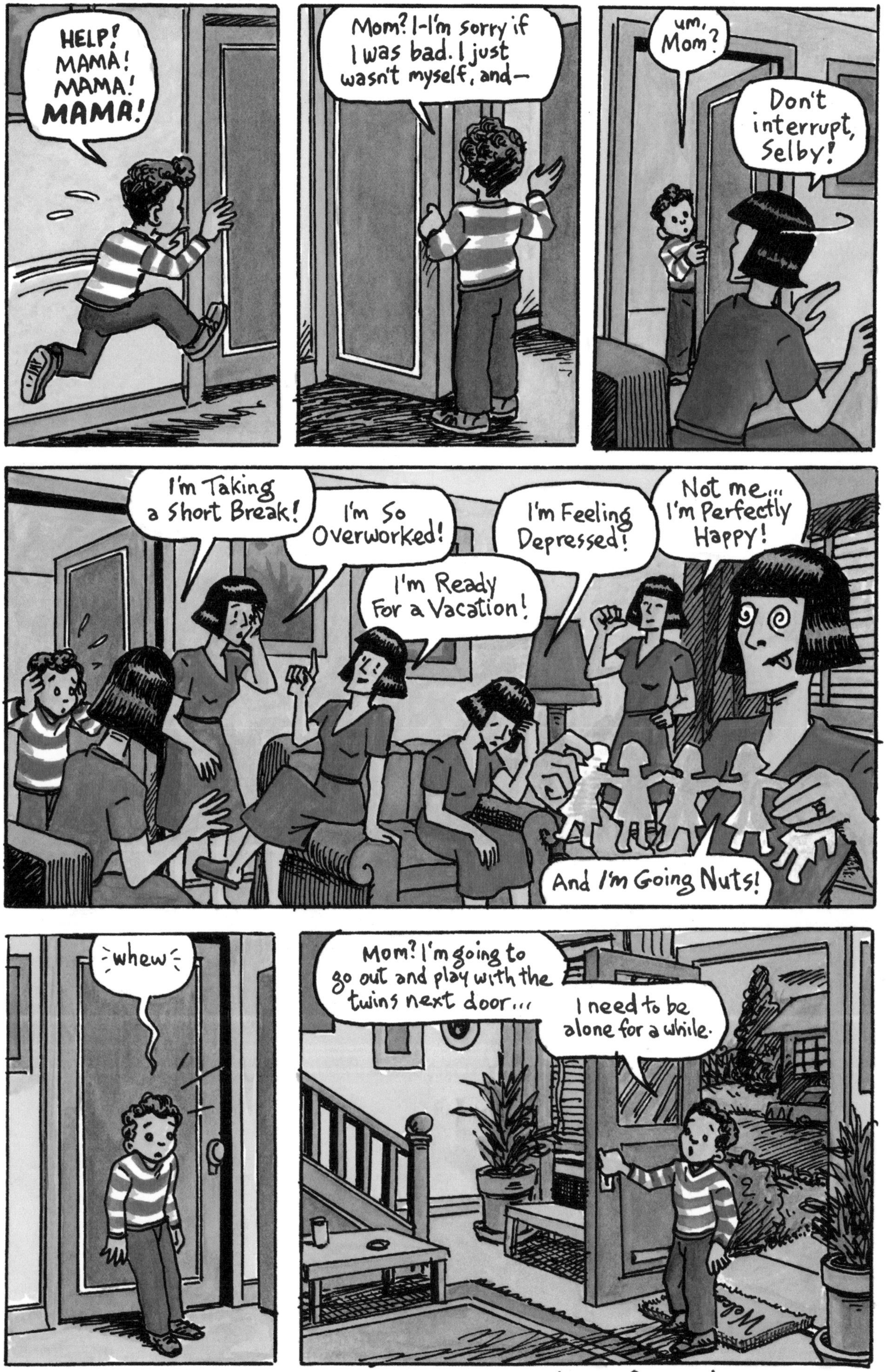
HELP! MAMA! MAMA! MAMA!
Mom? I-I'm sorry if I was bad. I just wasn't myself, and—
um, Mom?
Don't interrupt, Selby!
I'm Taking a Short Break!
I'm So Overworked!
I'm Ready For a Vacation!
I'm Feeling Depressed!
Not me... I'm Perfectly Happy!
And I'm Going Nuts!
whew
Mom? I'm going to go out and play with the twins next door...
I need to be alone for a while.
art spiegelman 01

CAN YOU FIND...?

1. Igloo with a Shoe
2. Endless Noodle
3. Floating Sombrero
4. Invisible Egg
5. Rubber Gorilla
6. Snowball with a Nose
7. Runaway Sock & Mitten
8. Frog Disguised as a Rock
9. Big Idea Stuck in a Tree
10. Whispering Ear
11. Asteroid with a Passenger
12. Cloud with a Beard
13. Propeller Head
14. Hiccupping Ghost
15. Shadow of a Donut
16. Unknown Bump

RICHARD MCGUIRE

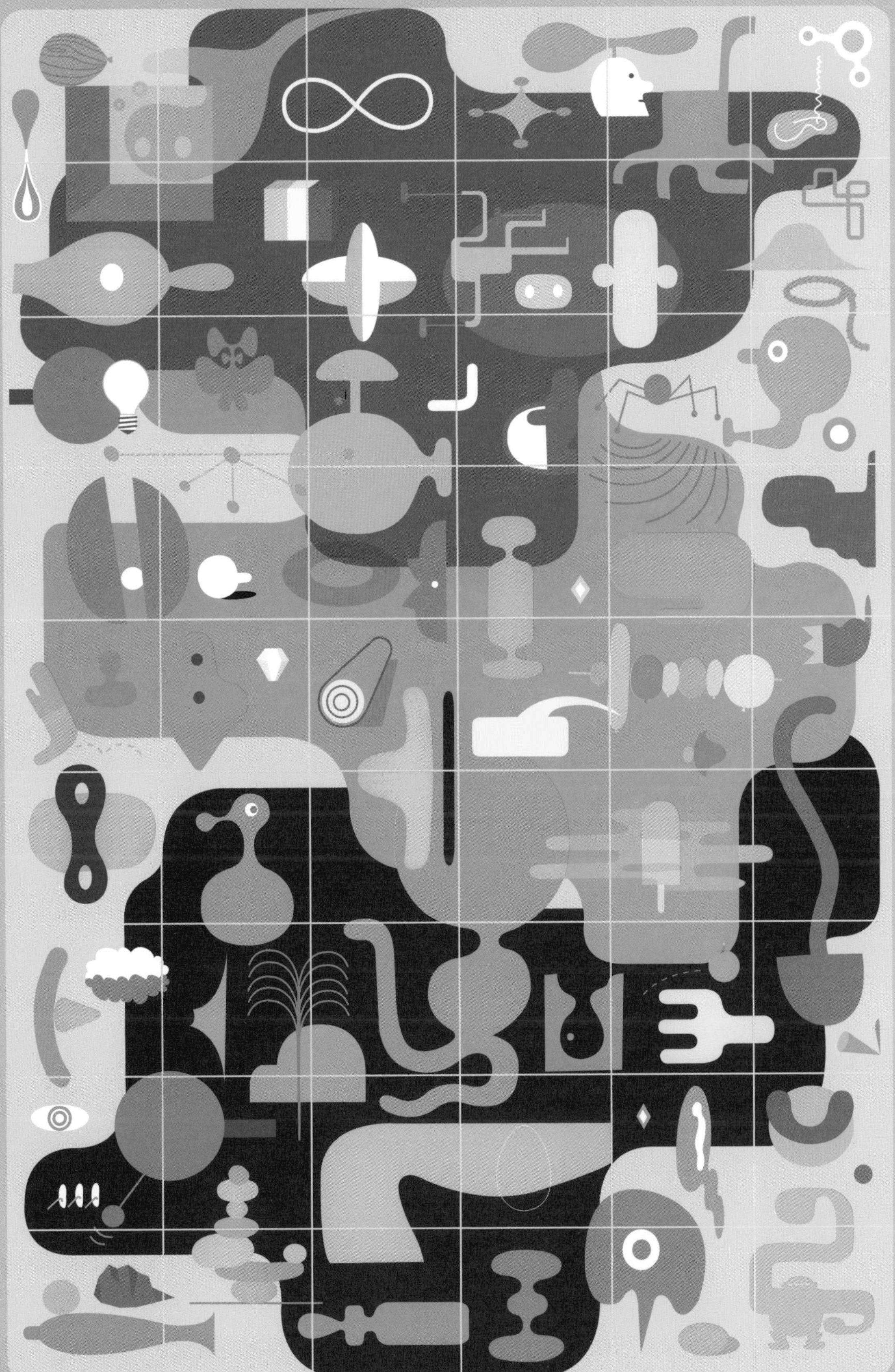

A
B
C
D
E
F
G
H
I
1
2
3
4
5
6

answers

1.C4 \ 2.A3 \ 3.E3+F3 \ 4.H4 \ 5.I6 \ 6.D2 \ 7.E1 \ 8.I1 \ 9.C1 \ 10.A6 \ 11.G5 \ 12.G1 \ 13.A4+A5 \ 14.1A+2A+3A \ 15.D3 \ 16.B6

Jack and his Mom and the Beanstalk

Jack and his mother were very poor. They had been forced to sell all their possessions, except for the cow. Then the cow dried up...

Mature cow for sale.

COW FOR SALE

I'll give you five magic beans for her.

WOW! What a deal!

Don't forget to plant them.

Oh boy! LOOK, MOM!

LOOK! I got five magic beans for our cow!

YOU DID WHAT?

You fool! What will we eat?

Uh... Did I mention they're MAGIC?

All night long the beans grew

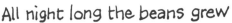

and by morning:

WOW! What a beanstalk!

There goes the view.

Jack climbed all the way up...

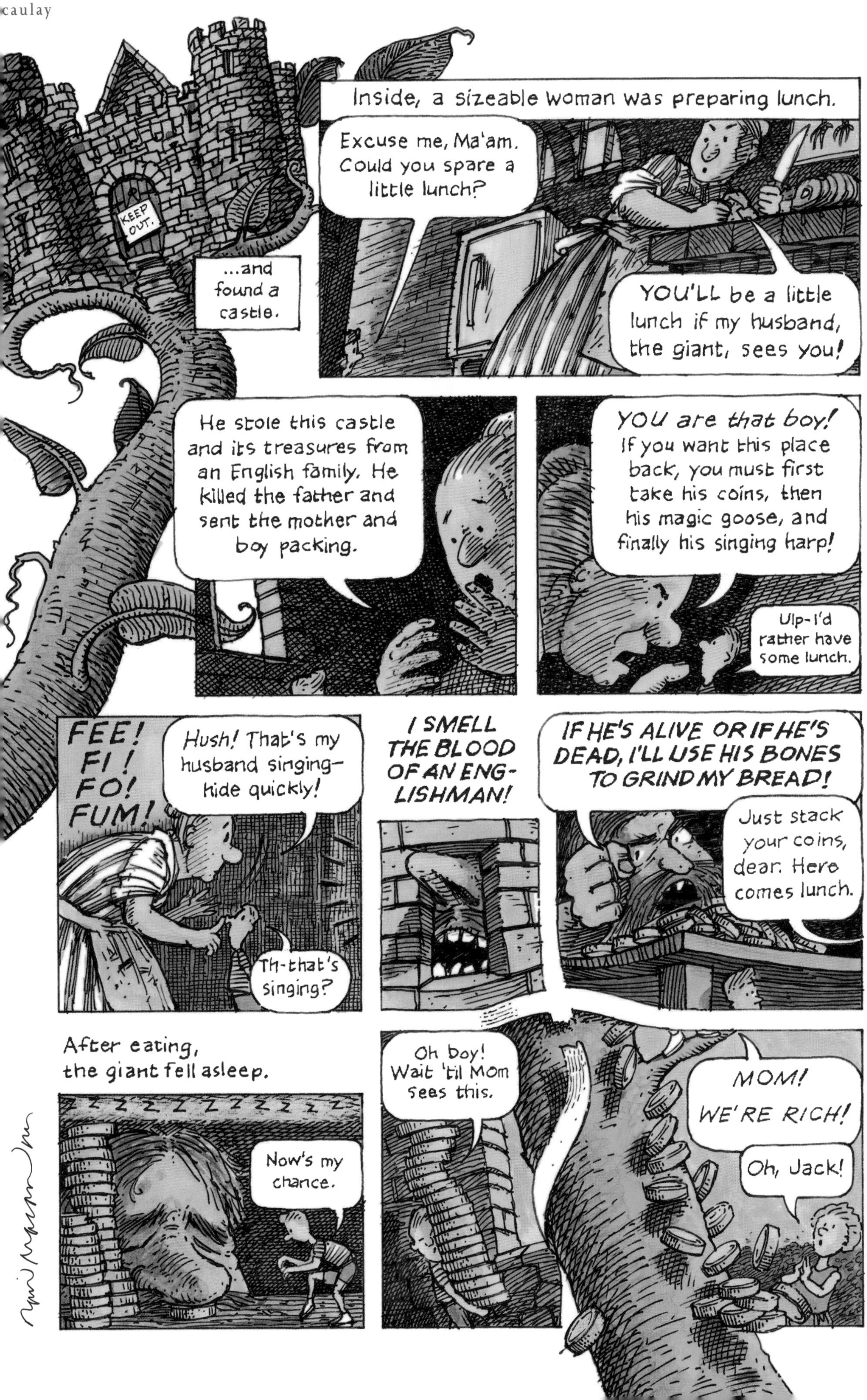
KEEP OUT.
...and found a castle.
Inside, a sizeable woman was preparing lunch.
Excuse me, Ma'am. Could you spare a little lunch?
YOU'LL be a little lunch if my husband, the giant, sees you!
He stole this castle and its treasures from an English family. He killed the father and sent the mother and boy packing.
YOU are that boy! If you want this place back, you must first take his coins, then his magic goose, and finally his singing harp!
Ulp-I'd rather have some lunch.
FEE! FI! FO! FUM!
Hush! That's my husband singing-hide quickly!
Th-that's singing?
I SMELL THE BLOOD OF AN ENG-LISHMAN!
IF HE'S ALIVE OR IF HE'S DEAD, I'LL USE HIS BONES TO GRIND MY BREAD!
Just stack your coins, dear. Here comes lunch.
After eating, the giant fell asleep.
Z Z Z Z Z Z Z Z Z Z Z Z Z Z
Now's my chance.
Oh boy! Wait 'til Mom sees this.
MOM! WE'RE RICH!
Oh, Jack!

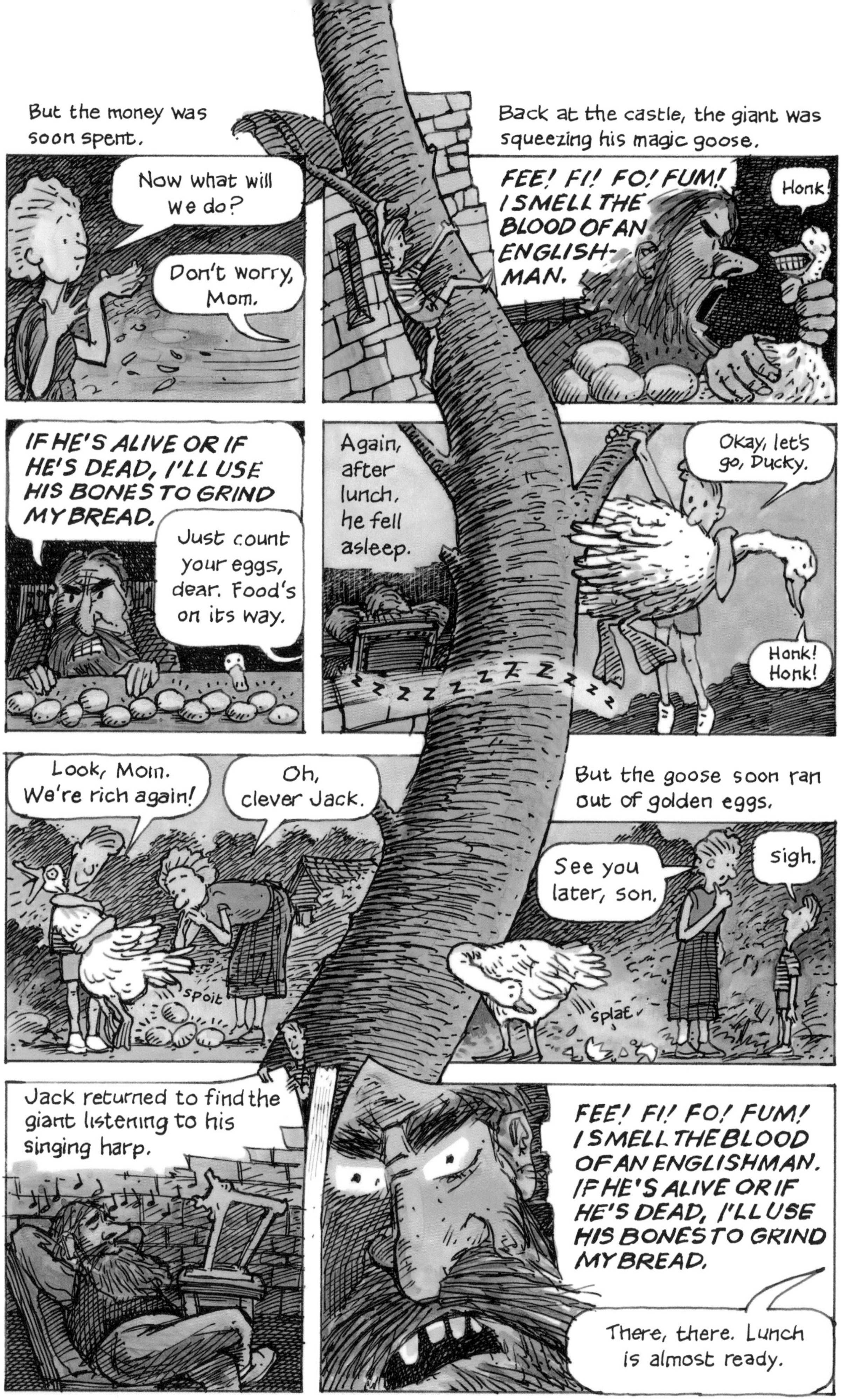

But the money was soon spent.
Now what will we do?
Don't worry, Mom.
Back at the castle, the giant was squeezing his magic goose.
FEE! FI! FO! FUM! I SMELL THE BLOOD OF AN ENGLISH-MAN.
Honk!
IF HE'S ALIVE OR IF HE'S DEAD, I'LL USE HIS BONES TO GRIND MY BREAD.
Just count your eggs, dear. Food's on its way.
Again, after lunch, he fell asleep.
Okay, let's go, Ducky.
Honk! Honk!
ZZZZZZZZZZZZZ
Look, Mom. We're rich again!
Oh, clever Jack.
spoit
But the goose soon ran out of golden eggs.
See you later, son.
sigh.
splat
Jack returned to find the giant listening to his singing harp.
FEE! FI! FO! FUM! I SMELL THE BLOOD OF AN ENGLISHMAN. IF HE'S ALIVE OR IF HE'S DEAD, I'LL USE HIS BONES TO GRIND MY BREAD.
There, there. Lunch is almost ready.

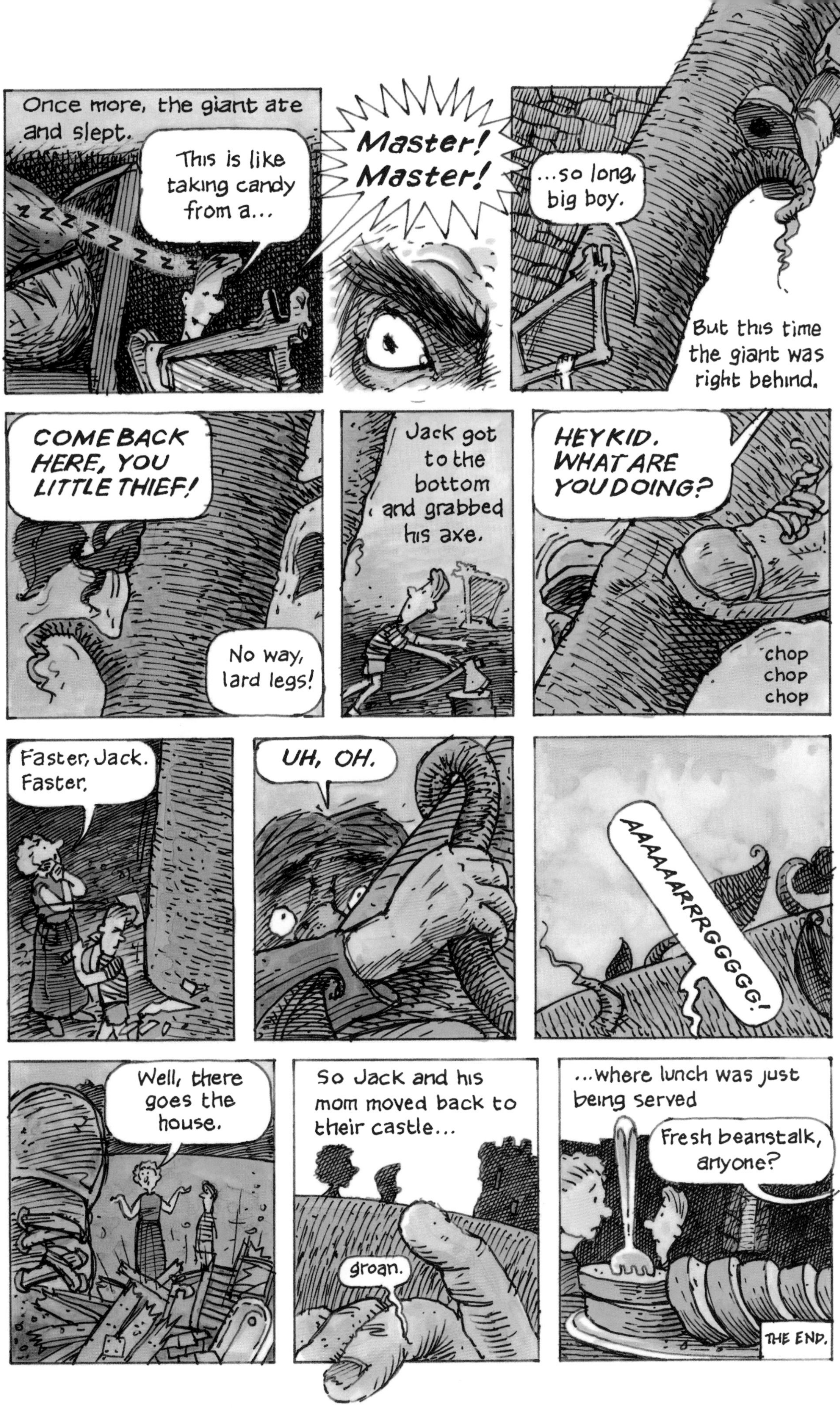

Once more, the giant ate and slept.
This is like taking candy from a...
Master! Master!
...so long, big boy.
But this time the giant was right behind.
COME BACK HERE, YOU LITTLE THIEF!
No way, lard legs!
Jack got to the bottom and grabbed his axe.
HEY KID. WHAT ARE YOU DOING?
chop chop chop
Faster, Jack. Faster.
UH, OH.
AAAAAARRRGGGGG!
Well, there goes the house.
So Jack and his mom moved back to their castle...
groan.
...where lunch was just being served
Fresh beanstalk, anyone?
THE END.

START HERE

There are many ways to travel through Lewis Trondheim's

A-MAZE-INC

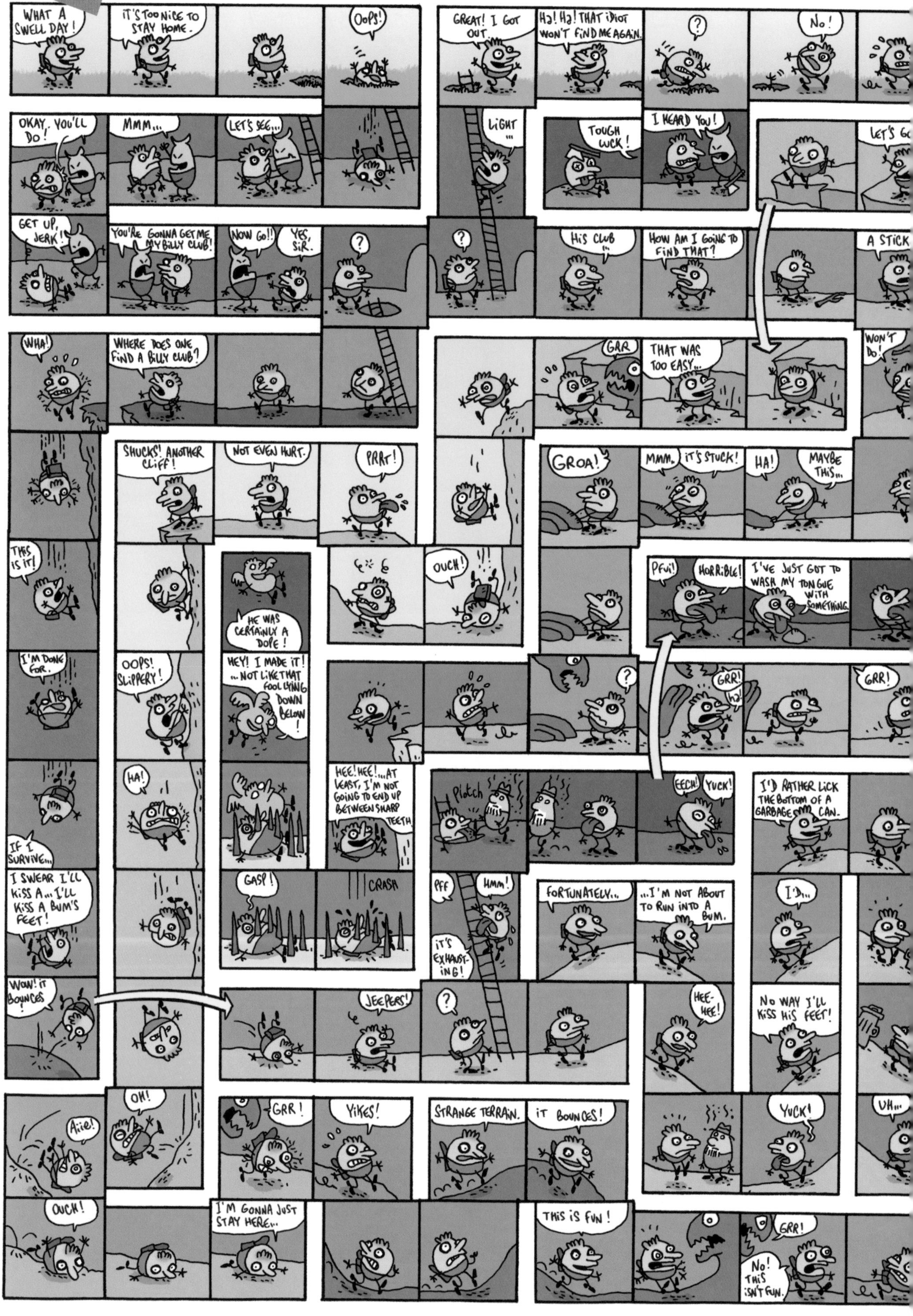
WHAT A SWELL DAY!
IT'S TOO NICE TO STAY HOME.
OOPS!
GREAT! I GOT OUT.
HA! HA! THAT IDIOT WON'T FIND ME AGAIN.
?
NO!
OKAY, YOU'LL DO!
MMM...
LET'S SEE...
LIGHT...
TOUGH LUCK!
I HEARD YOU!
LET'S G
GET UP, JERK!
YOU'RE GONNA GET ME MY BILLY CLUB!
NOW GO!!
YES, SIR.
?
?
HIS CLUB...
HOW AM I GOING TO FIND THAT?
A STICK
WHA!
WHERE DOES ONE FIND A BILLY CLUB?
GRR
THAT WAS TOO EASY...
WON'T DO!
SHUCKS! ANOTHER CLIFF!
NOT EVEN HURT.
PRRT!
GROA!
MMM.
IT'S STUCK!
HA!
MAYBE THIS...
THIS IS IT!
HE WAS CERTAINLY A DOPE!
OUCH!
PFUI!
HORRIBLE!
I'VE JUST GOT TO WASH MY TONGUE WITH SOMETHING.
I'M DONE FOR.
OOPS! SLIPPERY!
HEY! I MADE IT! ...NOT LIKE THAT FOOL LYING DOWN BELOW!
?
GRR!
HA!
GRR!
HA!
IF I SURVIVE...
HEE! HEE! ...AT LEAST, I'M NOT GOING TO END UP BETWEEN SHARP TEETH
PLOTCH
EECH!
YUCK!
I'D RATHER LICK THE BOTTOM OF A GARBAGE CAN.
I SWEAR I'LL KISS A... I'LL KISS A BUM'S FEET!
GASP!
CRASH
PFF
HMM!
IT'S EXHAUSTING!
FORTUNATELY...
...I'M NOT ABOUT TO RUN INTO A BUM.
I'D...
WOW! IT BOUNCES!
JEEPERS!
?
HEE-HEE!
NO WAY I'LL KISS HIS FEET!
AIIE!
OH!
GRR!
YIKES!
STRANGE TERRAIN.
IT BOUNCES!
YUCK!
UH...
OUCH!
I'M GONNA JUST STAY HERE...
THIS IS FUN!
GRR!
NO! THIS ISN'T FUN.

ADVENTURE

but there's only one way to reach the end and not be in the monster's clutches forever.

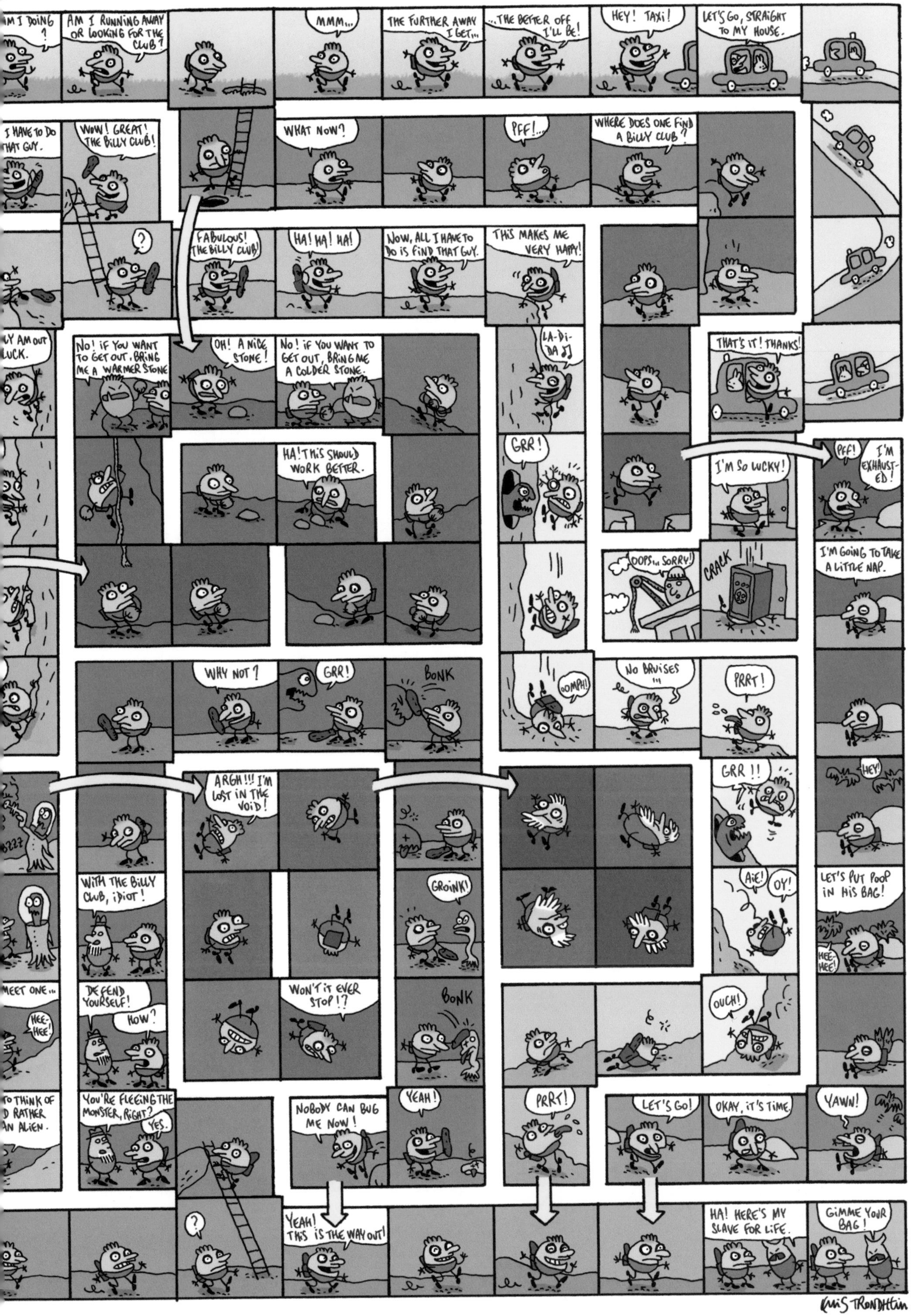
M I DOING ?
AM I RUNNING AWAY OR LOOKING FOR THE CLUB?
MMM...
THE FURTHER AWAY I GET...
...THE BETTER OFF I'LL BE!
HEY! TAXI!
LET'S GO, STRAIGHT TO MY HOUSE.
I HAVE TO DO THAT GUY.
WOW! GREAT! THE BILLY CLUB!
WHAT NOW?
PFF!...
WHERE DOES ONE FIND A BILLY CLUB?
?
FABULOUS! THE BILLY CLUB!
HA! HA! HA!
NOW, ALL I HAVE TO DO IS FIND THAT GUY.
THIS MAKES ME VERY HAPPY!
Y AM OUT LUCK.
NO! IF YOU WANT TO GET OUT, BRING ME A WARMER STONE
OH! A NICE STONE!
NO! IF YOU WANT TO GET OUT, BRING ME A COLDER STONE.
LA-DI-DA
THAT'S IT! THANKS!
HA! THIS SHOULD WORK BETTER.
GRR!
I'M SO LUCKY!
PFF!
I'M EXHAUSTED!
OOPS... SORRY!
CRACK
I'M GOING TO TAKE A LITTLE NAP.
WHY NOT?
GRR!
BONK
OOMPH!
NO BRUISES
PRRT!
GRR!!
HEY!
ARGH!!! I'M LOST IN THE VOID!
ZZZZ
WITH THE BILLY CLUB, IDIOT!
GROINK!
AIE!
OY!
LET'S PUT POOP IN HIS BAG!
HEE-HEE!
MEET ONE...
HEE-HEE!
DEFEND YOURSELF!
HOW?
WON'T IT EVER STOP!?
BONK
OUCH!
TO THINK OF D RATHER AN ALIEN.
YOU'RE FLEEING THE MONSTER, RIGHT?
YES.
NOBODY CAN BUG ME NOW!
YEAH!
PRRT!
LET'S GO!
OKAY, IT'S TIME.
YAWN!
?
YEAH! THIS IS THE WAY OUT!
HA! HERE'S MY SLAVE FOR LIFE.
GIMME YOUR BAG!
KRIS TRONDHEIM

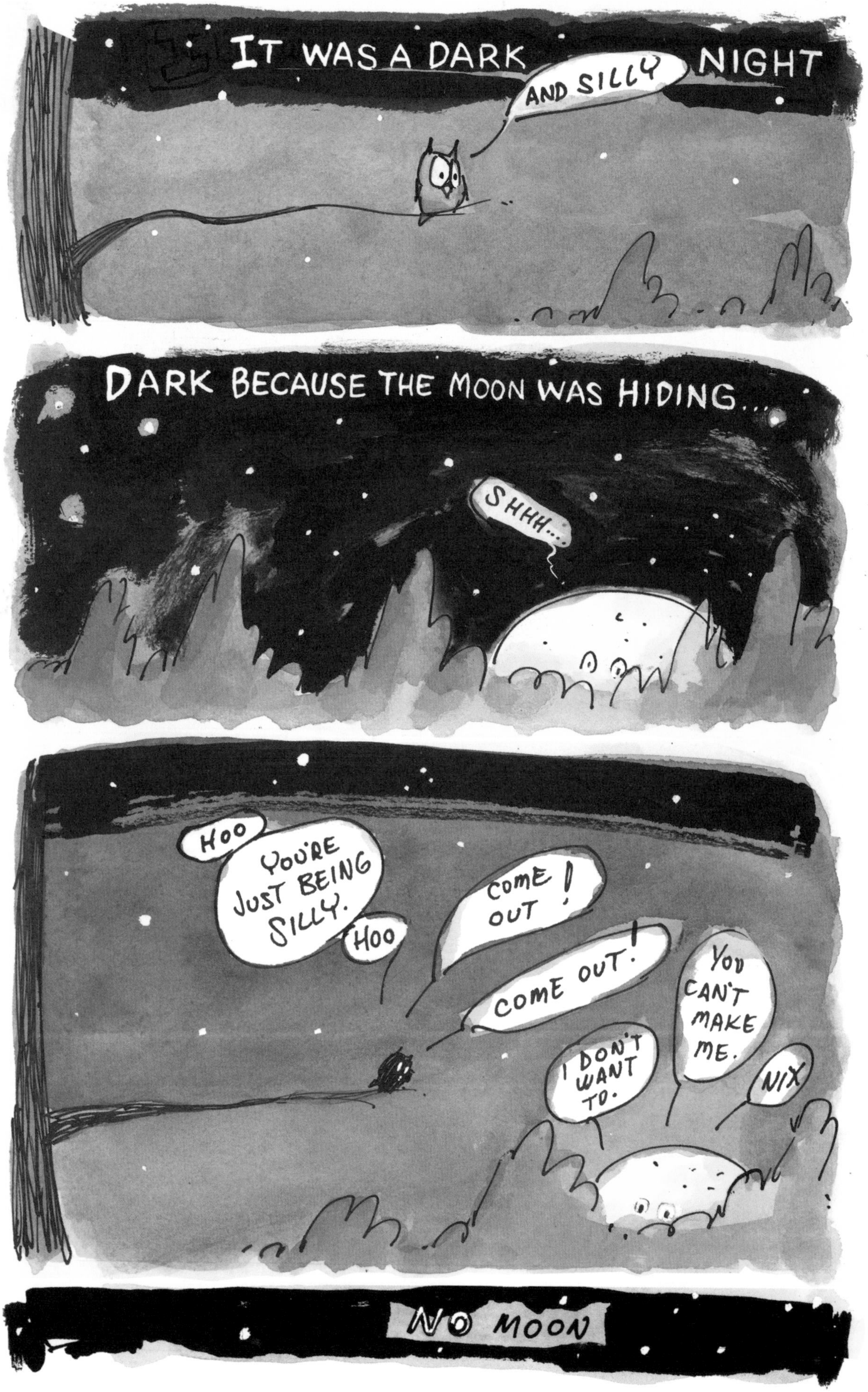
IT WAS A DARK
AND SILLY
NIGHT
DARK BECAUSE THE MOON WAS HIDING...
SHHH...
HOO
YOU'RE JUST BEING SILLY.
HOO
COME OUT!
COME OUT!
I DON'T WANT TO.
YOU CAN'T MAKE ME.
NIX
NO MOON

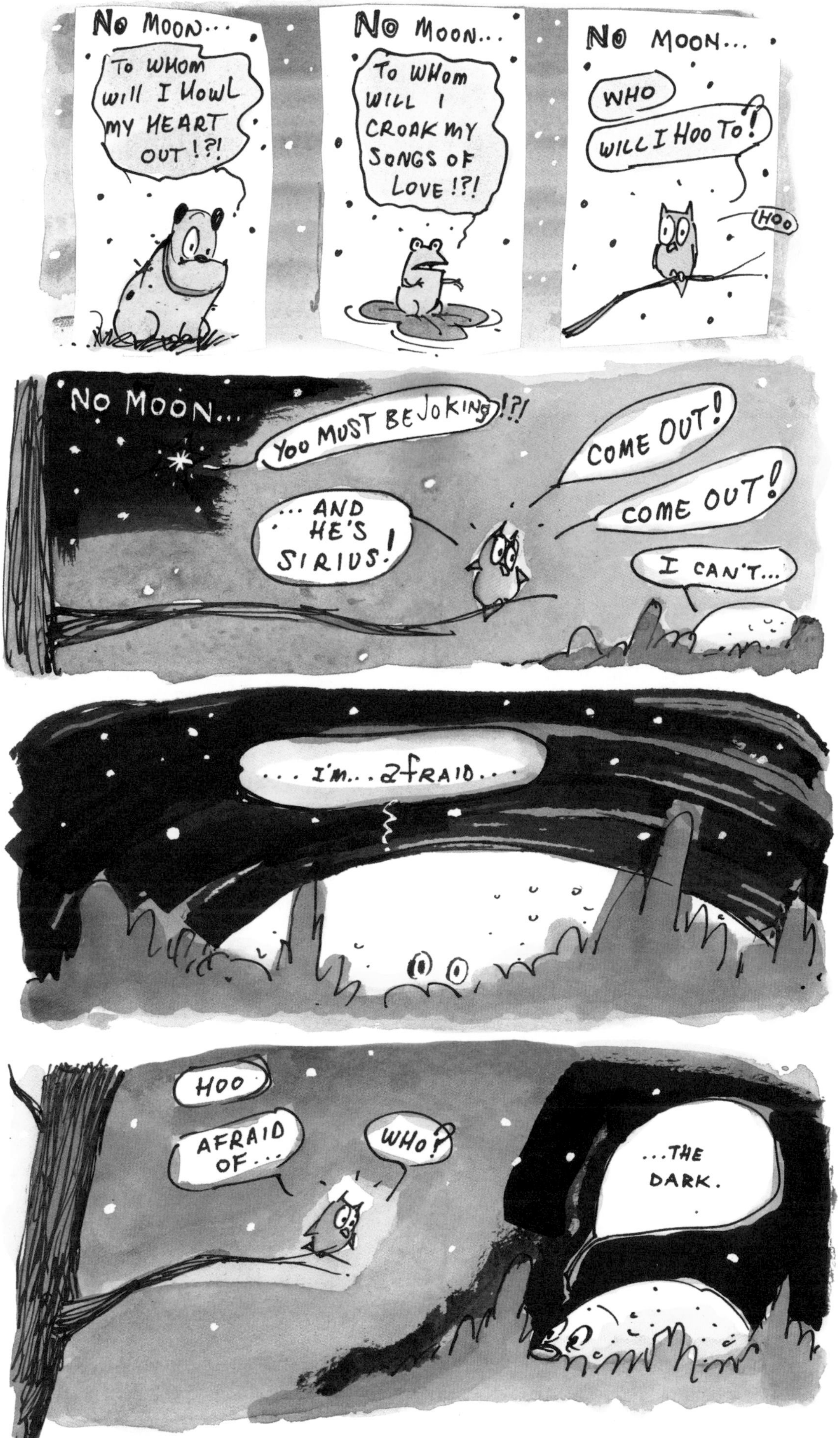
NO MOON...
TO WHOM WILL I HOWL MY HEART OUT!?!
NO MOON...
TO WHOM WILL I CROAK MY SONGS OF LOVE!?!
NO MOON...
WHO WILL I HOO TO!
HOO
NO MOON...
YOU MUST BE JOKING!?!
...AND HE'S SIRIUS!
COME OUT!
COME OUT!
I CAN'T...
...I'M...AFRAID...
HOO
AFRAID OF...
WHO?
...THE DARK.

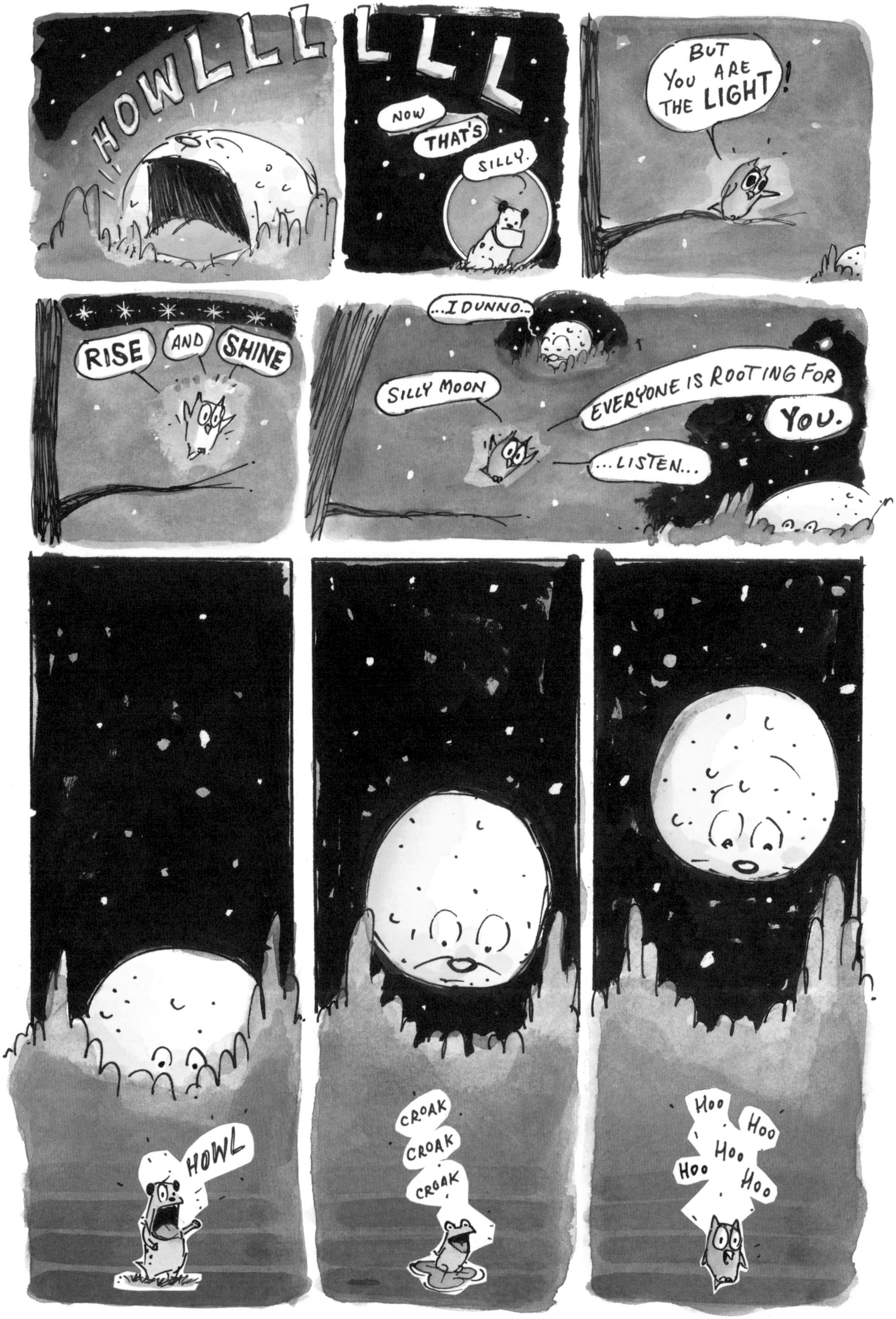
HOWLLL
LLL
NOW
THAT'S
SILLY.
BUT YOU ARE THE LIGHT!
RISE
AND
SHINE
...I DUNNO...
SILLY MOON
EVERYONE IS ROOTING FOR
YOU.
...LISTEN...
HOWL
CROAK
CROAK
CROAK
HOO
HOO
HOO
HOO
HOO

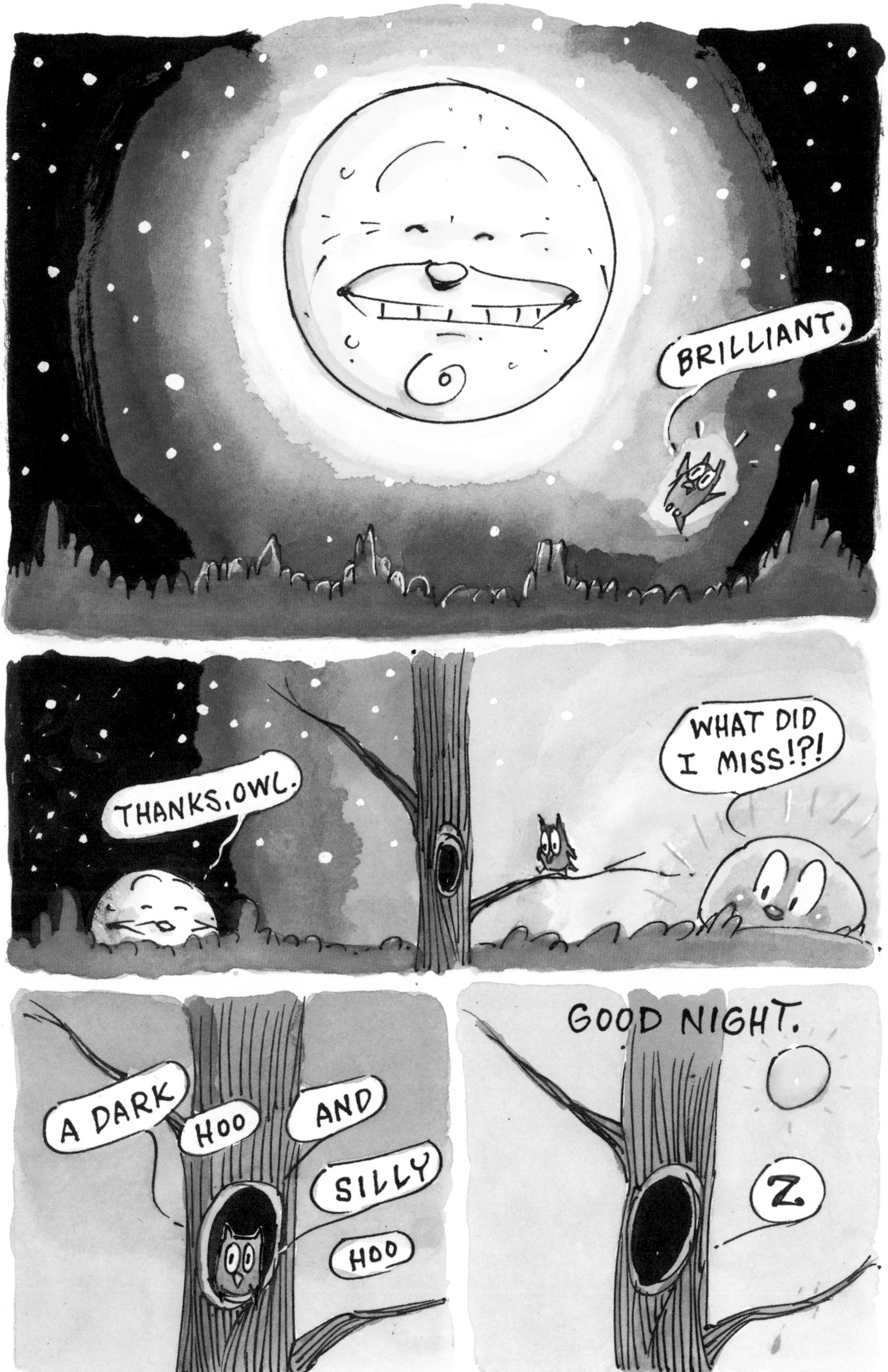
BRILLIANT.
THANKS, OWL.
WHAT DID I MISS!?!
A DARK
HOO
AND
SILLY
HOO
GOOD NIGHT.
Z

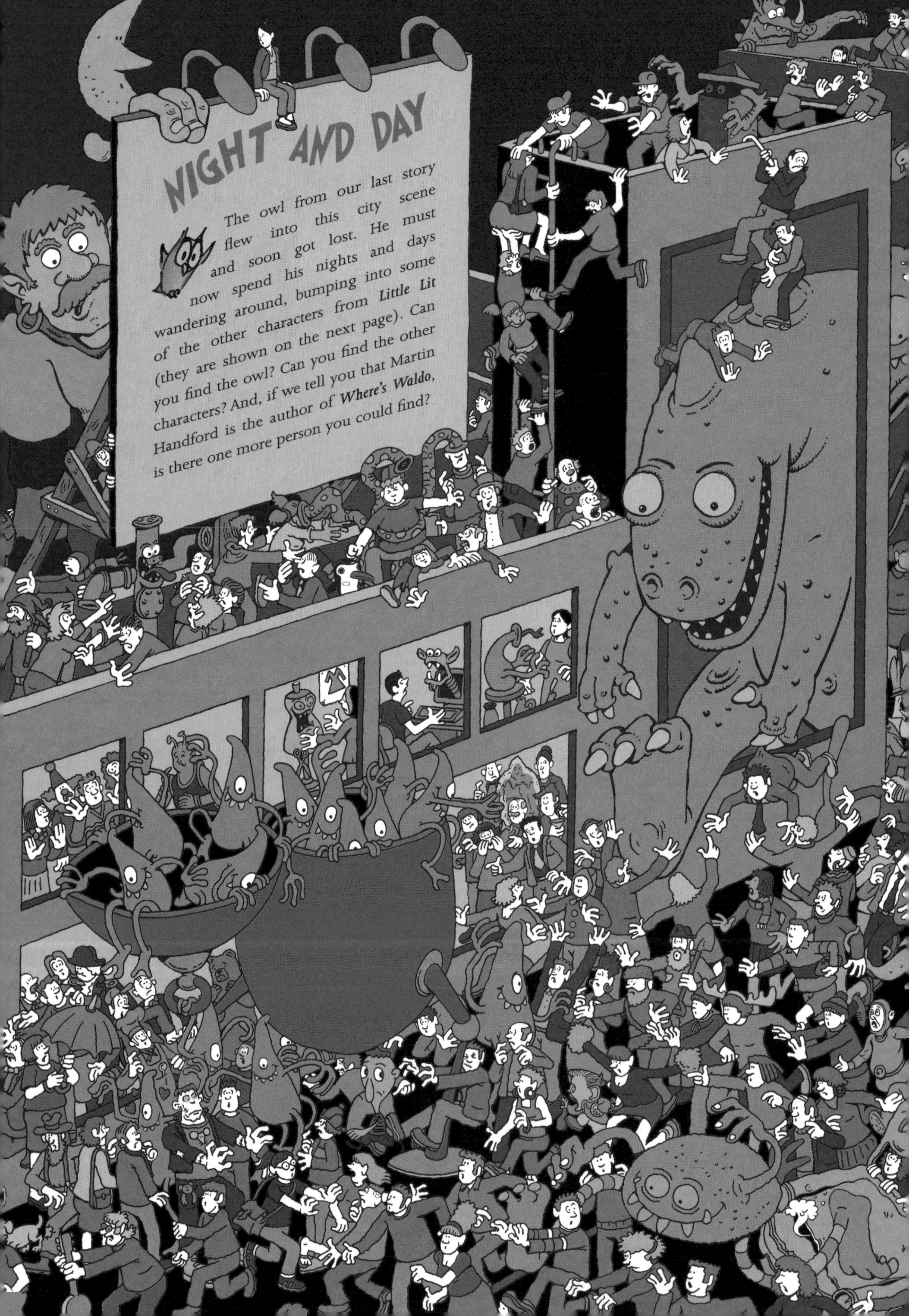
NIGHT AND DAY
The owl from our last story flew into this city scene and soon got lost. He must now spend his nights and days wandering around, bumping into some of the other characters from *Little Lit* (they are shown on the next page). Can you find the owl? Can you find the other characters? And, if we tell you that Martin Handford is the author of ***Where's Waldo***, is there one more person you could find?

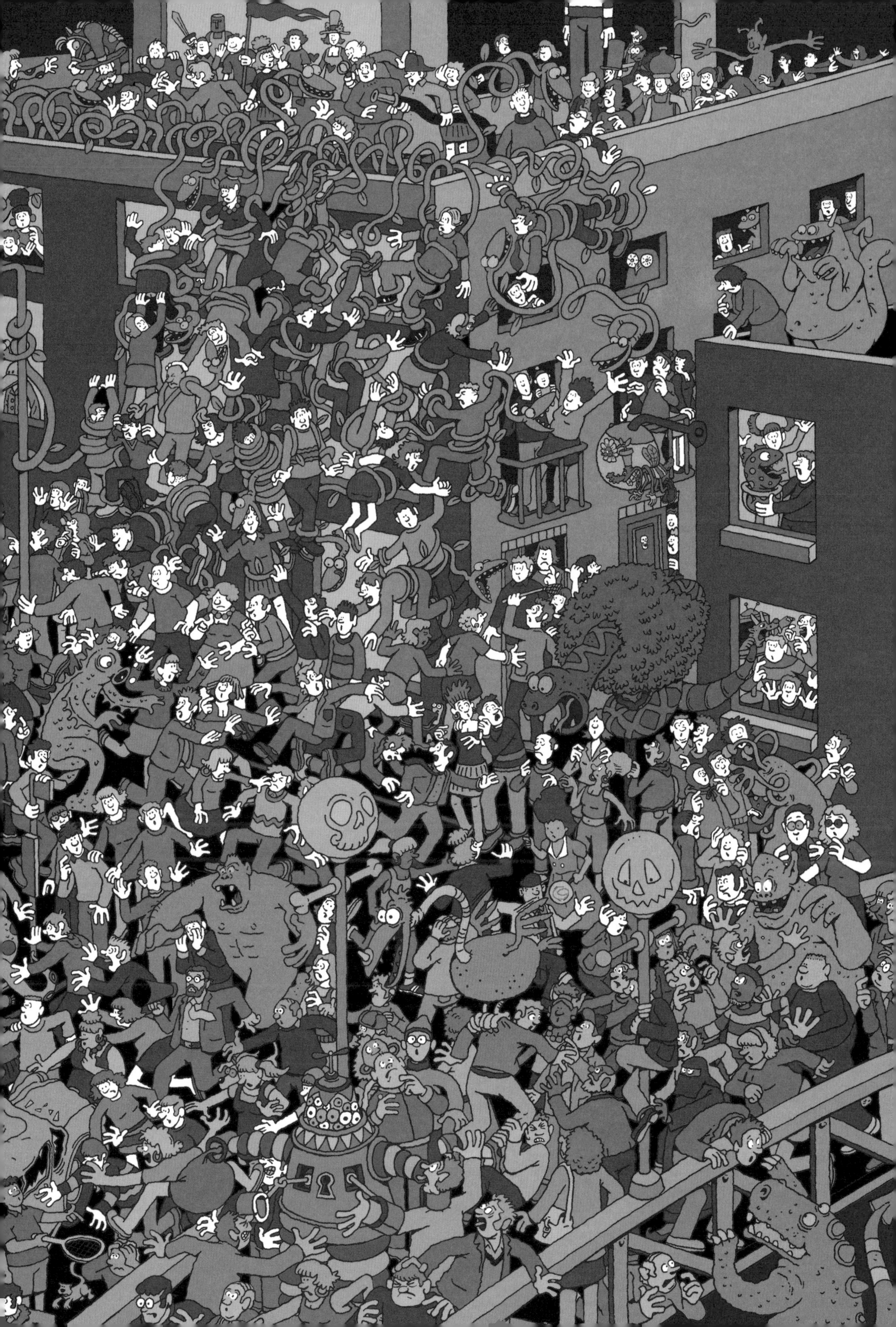

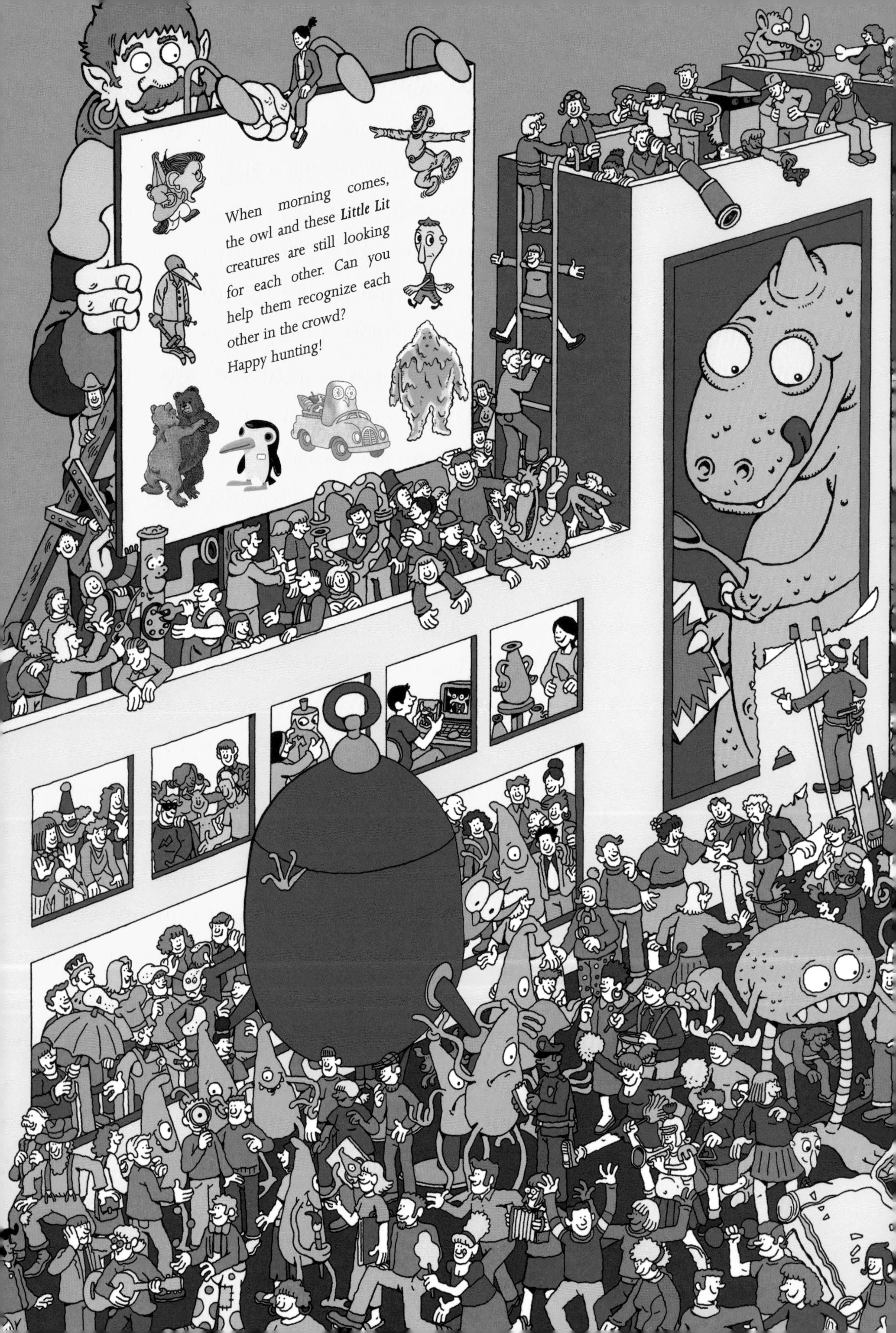
When morning comes, the owl and these *Little Lit* creatures are still looking for each other. Can you help them recognize each other in the crowd? Happy hunting!

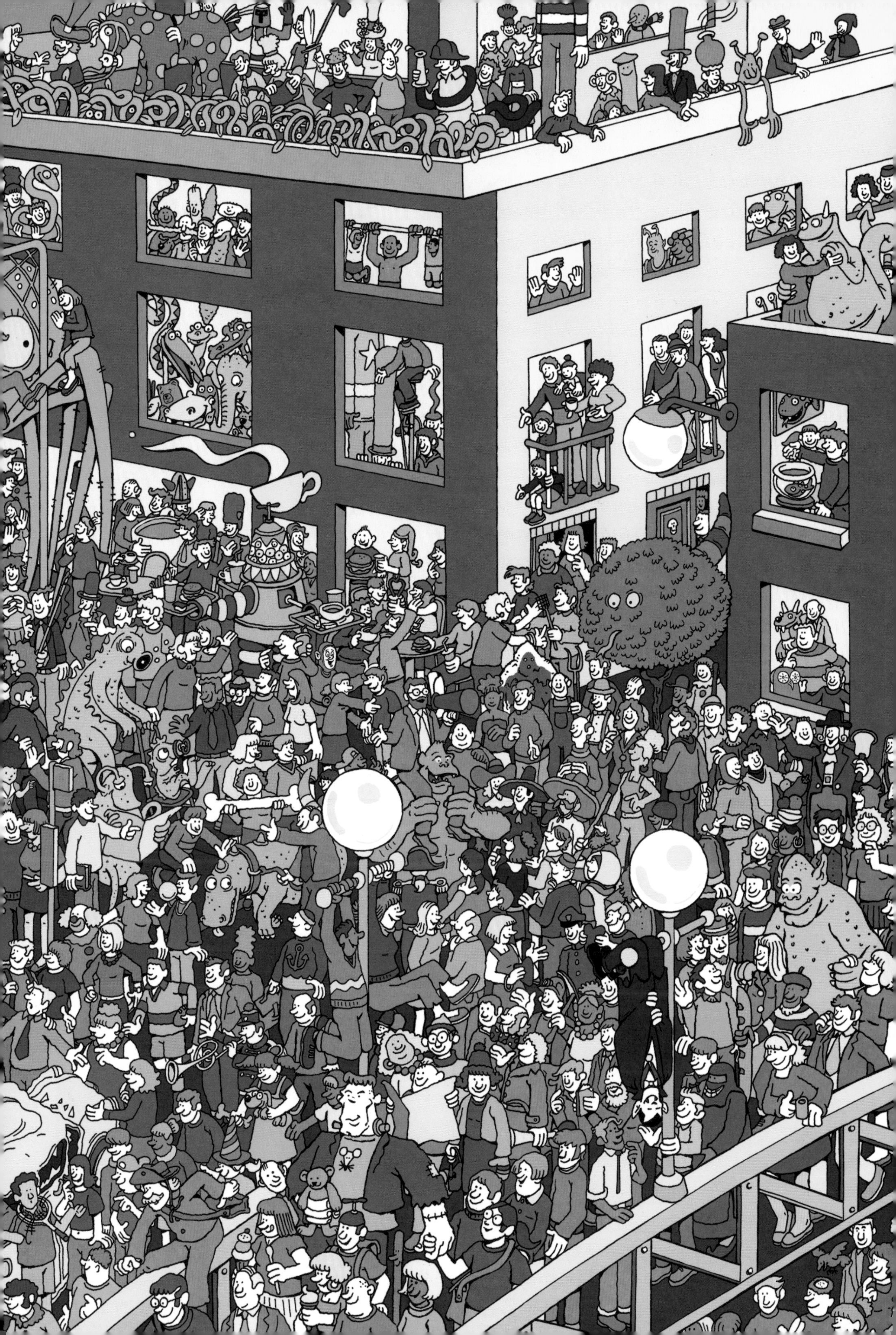

marc rosenthal

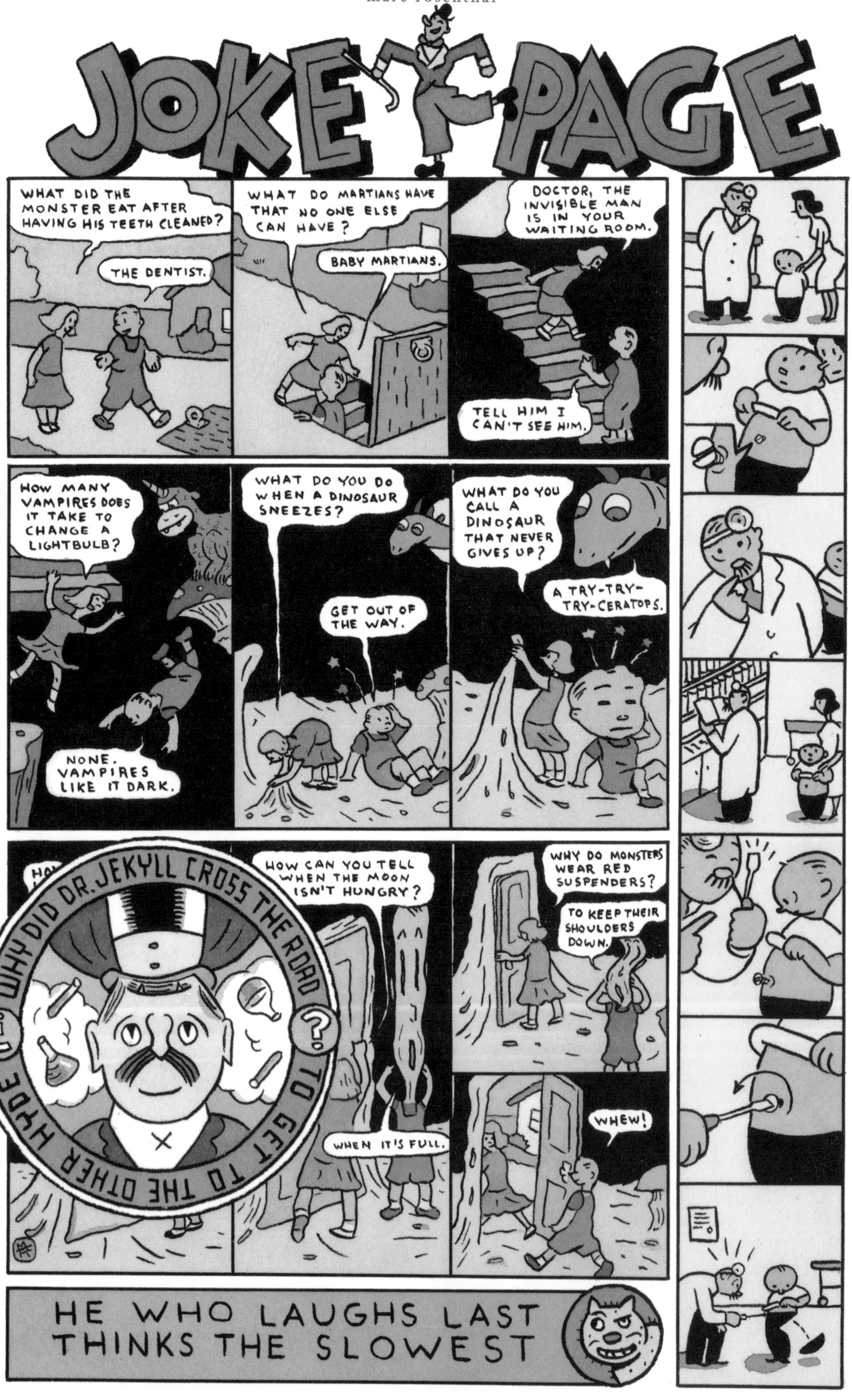
JOKE PAGE
WHAT DID THE MONSTER EAT AFTER HAVING HIS TEETH CLEANED?
THE DENTIST.
WHAT DO MARTIANS HAVE THAT NO ONE ELSE CAN HAVE?
BABY MARTIANS.
DOCTOR, THE INVISIBLE MAN IS IN YOUR WAITING ROOM.
TELL HIM I CAN'T SEE HIM.
HOW MANY VAMPIRES DOES IT TAKE TO CHANGE A LIGHTBULB?
NONE. VAMPIRES LIKE IT DARK.
WHAT DO YOU DO WHEN A DINOSAUR SNEEZES?
GET OUT OF THE WAY.
WHAT DO YOU CALL A DINOSAUR THAT NEVER GIVES UP?
A TRY-TRY-TRY-CERATOPS.
WHY DID DR. JEKYLL CROSS THE ROAD TO GET TO THE OTHER HYDE
HOW CAN YOU TELL WHEN THE MOON ISN'T HUNGRY?
WHEN IT'S FULL.
WHY DO MONSTERS WEAR RED SUSPENDERS?
TO KEEP THEIR SHOULDERS DOWN.
WHEW!
HE WHO LAUGHS LAST THINKS THE SLOWEST